Special Agent John Puller, combat veteran and the army's most tenacious investigator, is back in this action-packed thriller from worldwide #1 bestselling author David Baldacci.

NO MAN'S LAND

Two men. Thirty years.

John Puller's mother, Jackie, vanished thirty years ago from Fort Monroe, Virginia, when Puller was just a boy. Paul Rogers has been in prison for ten years. But twenty years before that, he was at Fort Monroe. One night three decades ago, Puller's and Rogers's worlds collided with devastating results, and the truth has been buried ever since.

Until now.

Military investigators, armed with a letter from a friend of Jackie's, arrive in the hospital room of Puller's father—a legendary three-star general now sinking into dementia—and reveal that Puller Sr. has been accused of murdering Jackie. Aided by his brother Robert Puller, an Air Force major, and Veronica Knox, who works for a shadowy U.S. intelligence organization, Puller begins a journey that will take him into his own past, to find the truth about his mother.

Paul Rogers's time is running out. With the clock ticking, he begins his own journey, one that will take him across the country to the place where all his troubles began: a mysterious building on the grounds of Fort Monroe. There, thirty years ago, the man Rogers had once been vanished too and was replaced with a monster. Now the monster wants revenge. And the only person standing in his way is John Puller.

ACCLAIM FOR DAVID BALDACCI'S THRILLERS

NO MAN'S LAND

"Be prepared for an action-packed ride...Baldacci once again partners [John Puller] with Veronica Knox, making for a lethal and legendary combination. Anticipation intensifies on each page."

—*RT Book Reviews*

"This thriller, featuring U.S. Army criminal investigator John Puller, has a very plausible theme with a compelling and action-packed plot....[A] riveting and heart-wrenching story...NO MAN'S LAND is an edge-of-your-seat thriller. Readers will be hooked from page one."

—*Military Press*

"David Baldacci is one of America's favorite mystery writers, and he has earned that adulation fair and square. He is constantly turning out one readable and enjoyable adventure after another. His latest novel, NO MAN'S LAND, is his fourth John Puller story and it is a good one. It is fast reading from the start as the pages grab the readers' interest and off they go."

—*Huffington Post*

"[A novel of] dramatic depth and intensity...an unforgettable read...Action-packed and thought-provoking."

—Associated Press

"Bestseller Baldacci makes the implausible plausible in his riveting fourth thriller featuring U.S. Army criminal investigator John Puller...Baldacci maintains tension throughout and imbues his characters with enough humanity to make readers care what happens to them."

—*Publishers Weekly*

THE LAST MILE

"Entertaining and enlightening, *The Last Mile* is a rich novel that has much to offer...In the best Baldacci tradition, the action is fast and furious. But *The Last Mile* is more than a good action thriller. It sheds light on racism, a father-son relationship and capital punishment. Both Mars and Decker are substantive, solid characters....Utterly absorbing."

—Associated Press

"[Amos Decker is] one of the most unique protagonists seen in thriller fiction....David Baldacci has always been a top-notch thriller writer...[his] fertile imagination and intricate plotting abilities make each of his books a treat for thriller readers. *The Last Mile* is no exception."

—BookReporter.com

"The intricate details in Baldacci's explosive new novel engage until the final word. He's hit the pinnacle traveling the Deep South and exploring its traditions. Decker and his compatriots are characters to remember long after reading this impressive undertaking."

—*RT Book Reviews* (4 1/2 stars, Top Pick!)

"A compelling mystery with emotional resonance. Just when the story line heads to what seems an obvious conclusion, Baldacci veers off course with a surprising twist. The end result is another exciting read from a thriller master."

—*Library Journal* (Starred Review)

"Baldacci excels at developing interesting, three-dimensional protagonists...Baldacci fans will not be disappointed, and *The Last Mile* gives good reason to look forward to the next Amos Decker thriller."

—*New York Journal of Books*

THE GUILTY

"The story sings...Baldacci is a gifted storyteller, and he knows how to keep the pages turning."
—Associated Press

"Baldacci fans will not be disappointed. The action is slam-bang with his trademarked twist. Once past the climax, you'll find yourself flipping back and rereading to find the clues the author has sprinkled throughout."
—*Florida Times-Union*

"A fast-moving thriller that will force readers into that 'zone,' where you don't want to put the book down...Whether you are a diehard fan or a newcomer to his work, you will not be disappointed in *The Guilty*."
—*BookReporter*

"A first-class thriller...David Baldacci's four best-selling novels about government assassin Will Robie have straddled that line of edgy, high-concept suspense, augmented with a bit of the political thriller, and deep character studies. In *The Guilty*, Baldacci takes a different tack with a more personal, but just as thrilling tale about Will's past, giving compelling insight about how he became a man so willing to kill for his country."
—*Sun-Sentinel* (FL)

"David Baldacci has never been better than in *The Guilty*. His latest to feature conflicted assassin extraordinaire Will Robie takes the character—and series—to new heights...A stunning success from one of America's great literary talents."

—*Providence Sunday Journal*

"It's indisputable that Baldacci's handling of action just gets better and better...the action in small-town Texas will end up rivaling anything Robie has encountered in his long years of serving his government."

—NJ.com

"Another tremendous entry in the best-selling thriller-master's increasingly impressive resume...A multi-layered conspiracy tale that, despite the Grisham-esque backdrop of a legal mystery set in small-town Mississippi, quickly explodes into full-Baldacci thriller territory...It is the relationships that truly stand out. Among the most noteworthy is the rapport between Robie and Reel, with the professional and personal trust and respect that the two share for one another—having risked it all for each other several times before—feeling believable and compelling, not to mention being the source of a fair amount of witty banter. The tense dynamic between Robie and his father is palpable as well, and their shifting relationship—and how they both deal with the wounds of the past—is one of the book's highlights...A labyrinthine journey full of dead ends and surprising turns, with new reveals doled out at regular intervals as the story builds to its shocking conclusion, a spectacular double-twist climax that will leave even the most jaded thriller readers impressed."

—*The Strand Magazine*

MEMORY MAN

"It's big, bold and almost impossible to put down...Decker is one of the most unusual detectives any novelist has dreamed up...I called this novel a master class on the bestseller because of its fast-moving narrative, the originality of its hero and its irresistible plot....Highly entertaining."

—*Washington Post*

"David Baldacci has written another thriller that will have readers engaged from the first page....Baldacci is a master storyteller...*Memory Man* works because Amos Decker is an amazing character. Reading how Decker journeys from hitting rock bottom to finding ultimate redemption is nothing short of rewarding."

—Associated Press

"Perennial bestseller Baldacci unveils an offbeat hero with an unusual skill set and tragic past who takes on the evil mastermind behind a devastating school shooting.[Decker] proves a quirky, original antihero with a definite method to his madness...Readers will want to see Decker back on the printed page again and again."

—*Kirkus Reviews*

"[A] strong first in a new thriller series from bestseller Baldacci....Baldacci supplies a multitude of clever touches as his wounded bear of a detective takes on a most ingenious enemy."

—*Publishers Weekly*

"Compelling...David Baldacci has definitely hit a home run with *Memory Man*."

—*Crimespree Magazine*

"Baldacci makes it feel fresh."

—Booklist

"Baldacci weaves a suspenseful story right up to the climactic face-off between these complex and compelling characters. Highly recommended for all thriller fans who love elusive, taunting criminals and the slightly bent but always determined detectives who pursue them."

—*Library Journal* (Starred Review)

THE ESCAPE

"One of the most compelling characters in David Baldacci's thrillers is John Puller, a crackerjack investigator of military crimes...Twists and turns come fast and furious in the best Baldacci tradition. *The Escape* is much more than a thriller. It's a moving tale of two military brothers and their father, a retired Army general and fighting legend now suffering from dementia. Emotionally intense, *The Escape* is Baldacci's best to date."

—Associated Press

"A heck of an opening chapter, guaranteed to jettison readers into hours of addictive reading...Baldacci's last few books have been among the best in his long, busy career, and *The Escape* stands near the top for sheer adrenalin-fueled entertainment. It's alarmingly topical, too, taking us into the intelligence community and raising questions about privacy rights in the age of government surveillance and other buzz-worthy issues (no spoilers here). Indeed, the crime at the center of *The Escape* could have been pulled from recent newspaper headlines. Who says thrillers have to be the stuff of escapist fantasies?"

—*Richmond Times-Dispatch*

"Highly entertaining...*The Escape* is a terrific read."
—*CT News*

"A phenomenal read, as usual, from David Baldacci—don't miss it!"

—BookLoons.com

THE TARGET

"Brilliant use of language...vivid supporting characters, and numerous sudden and unexpected plot twists...[Baldacci] doesn't let the action sag at any point...In [Chung-Cha], Mr. Baldacci has created one of his most memorable characters."

—*Pittsburgh Post-Gazette*

"[A] no-holds-barred tale of perfidy and murder at the highest level...Baldacci's prose crackles with urgency...Robie and Reel fans will thrill to see their favorite spies back in action."

—*Kirkus Reviews*

"Robie and Reel are complex characters, and anything they do is a pleasure to follow...Baldacci knows how to get readers to turn the pages, and he's in top form here."

—Associated Press

"A heck of a ride...Baldacci has been on a hot streak for the past few years, and *The Target* continues the trend. This isn't a garden-variety thriller or even a garden-variety Baldacci. It's among his most exhilarating books yet."

—*Richmond Times-Dispatch*

"Baldacci deftly plots *The Target* so that readers can never get a firm grasp on what is going to happen next."

—BookReporter.com

"*The Target* is as much a tale of base humanity as a thriller...With the drama and action unfolding at the author's usual breakneck speed and with simmering plot lines just waiting to explode, this is a sure-fire winner for all Baldacci fans."

—*Blackpool Gazette* (UK)

"As ever Baldacci keeps things moving at express-train speed...This one will whet appetites for the next appearance of his agent hero."

—*Daily Express* (UK)

THE HIT

"A winner...nonstop action and twists...The best Baldacci novel in years."

—Associated Press

"What makes *The Hit* live up to its title is the payoff at the novel's end. By then, Baldacci has planted an emotional hook that remains long after readers have turned the last page."

—Washington Post

"Engrossing, action-packed...another winner from this master of the thriller genre."

—Examiner.com

"Entertaining...Will Robie is a riveting character... With a lightning pace, captivating characters, and astonishing twists throughout, *The Hit* is guaranteed to keep your attention from the first page to the last."

—Burlington Times-News (NC)

"Warning: If you plan to crack this thriller at poolside or on the beach, apply sunscreen before opening. Baldacci's a master at creating tense espionage and confrontations with lots of fire power, and you'll lose yourself in *The Hit*."

—Newark Star-Ledger

"For the past seventeen years, Baldacci has produced at least one bestselling thriller a year. It has been an exemplary performance. His recent work stands out, though...Its pace is relentless, and Baldacci's reworking of his perennial theme—absolute power corrupts absolutely—gives the book a sense of urgency and cultural relevance that many thrillers lack...Forget waiting until your beach vacation to read it."

—*Richmond Times-Dispatch*

"Page-turning, pulse-racing action, with surprises and thrills galore. Or as a one-word review: Mesmerizing."

—*Deseret News* (UT)

NO MAN'S
LAND

ALSO BY DAVID BALDACCI

DAVID BALDACCI

NO MAN'S LAND

GRAND CENTRAL
PUBLISHING

NEW YORK   BOSTON

Grand Central Publishing
Hachette Book Group
1290 Avenue of the Americas, New York, NY 10104
grandcentralpublishing.com
twitter.com/grandcentralpub

First published in hardcover and ebook in November 2016

First US trade and international mass market editions: March 2017

Grand Central Publishing is a division of Hachette Book Group, Inc. The Grand Central Publishing name and logo is a trademark of Hachette Book Group, Inc.

The publisher is not responsible for websites (or their content) that are not owned by the publisher.

The Hachette Speakers Bureau provides a wide range of authors for speaking events. To find out more, go to www.hachettespeakersbureau.com or call (866) 376-6591.

Library of Congress Cataloging-in-Publication Data has been applied for.

ISBNs: 978-1-4555-8650-9 (US trade), 978-1-478-92057-1 (international mass market), 978-1-4555-8649-3 (ebook)

Printed in the United States of America

RRD-C (US trade), OPM (international mass market)

10 9 8 7 6 5 4 3 2 1

To the memory of Lynette Collin,
an angel to us all

NO MAN'S LAND

CHAPTER

I

PAUL ROGERS WAS waiting for them to come and kill him.

For ten years he had done this.

Now he had twenty-four more hours to go.

Or to live.

Rogers was six feet one inches tall and tipped the scale at one hundred and eighty pounds; hardly any of it was fat. Most people looking only at his chiseled body would be surprised to learn that he was over fifty years old. From the neck down he looked like an anatomical chart, each muscle hardened and defined as it melded into its neighbor.

However, from the neck up the years were clearly imprinted on his features, and a guess of fifty would actually have been kind. The hair was thick but mostly gray, and the face, though it had been behind bars and out of the sun for a decade, was roughly weathered, with deep crevices around the eyes and mouth and furrows whittled across the broad brow.

He had an unruly beard that matched the color of his hair. Facial hair wasn't really permitted in here, but he knew that no one had the guts to make him shave it off.

He was like a timber rattler without the benefit of a warning sound, likely to bite if you drew too close.

The eyes lurking under the tufted eyebrows were perhaps his most distinctive feature: a pale, liquid blue that carried a sense of being both depthless and also empty of life.

He sat up straighter when he heard them coming.

Still twenty-four hours to go. This was not a good sign.

There were two sets of heels walking in unison.

The door slid open and the pair of guards stood there.

"Okay, Rogers," said the older guard. "Let's go."

Rogers stood and looked at the men, confusion on his features.

The guard said, "I know it was supposed to be tomorrow, but apparently the court clerk put the wrong date on the order and it was too much trouble to try to change it. So voilà, today is your big day."

Rogers moved forward and held out his hands so they could shackle him.

The older guard shook his head. "Your parole was granted, Rogers. You get to walk out as a free man. No more chains." But as he said this, he clutched the handle of his baton a little more tightly and a vein throbbed at his temple.

The two guards led Rogers down a long hallway. On each side were barred cell doors. The men behind them had been talking, but when Rogers came into view they abruptly stopped. The prisoners watched mutely as he passed, then the whispers started up once more.

Upon entering a small room he was given a set of new clothes, shiny lace-up shoes, his ring, his watch, and three hundred dollars in cash. Thirty bucks for every year he'd been inside; that was the state's magnanimous policy.

And, maybe most important, a bus ticket that would take him to the nearest town.

He took off his prison jumpsuit and put on new skivvies and the fresh clothes. He had to cinch the belt extra tight around his lean waist to keep the pants up, but the jacket was tight against his wide shoulders. He put on the new shoes. They were a size too small and pinched his long feet. He next put on the watch, set the correct time using the clock on the wall, slipped the cash into his jacket, and forced the ring over a knotty knuckle.

He was led to the front entrance of the prison and handed a packet of materials outlining his duties and responsibilities as a parolee. These included regular meetings with his parole officer and tight restrictions on his movements and associations with other people for the duration of his parole. He couldn't leave the area and couldn't knowingly go within a hundred feet of someone with a criminal record. He couldn't do drugs and he couldn't own or carry a weapon.

The hydraulic rams came to life and the metal door opened, revealing the outside world to Rogers for the first time in a decade.

He stepped across the threshold as the older guard said, "Good luck, and don't let me see you back here."

Then the rams were engaged once more and the massive door shut behind him with the whisper of fluid-charged machinery coming to rest.

The older guard shook his head while the younger one stared at the back of the door.

"If I had to bet, he'll be back in prison before long," said the older guard.

"Why's that?"

"Paul Rogers has spoken maybe five words since he's been in this place. But the look on his face sometimes." The guard shivered. "We've got some unholy badasses in here, as you know. But nobody gave me the creeps like Rogers. It was as though there was nothing behind the eyes. He was up for parole twice before and didn't get it. I heard he scared the crap out of the parole board just by looking at them. The third time was the charm, I suppose."

"What did he do to get sent to prison?"

"Killed somebody."

"And he only got ten years?"

"Extenuating circumstances, I guess."

"Did the other inmates ever try to bully him?" asked the younger guard.

"Bully him! Did you ever see that guy work out in the rec yard? He's older than me and he's stronger than the biggest SOB we have in here. And I think the guy slept like an hour a night. I'd make my rounds at two in the morning and there he'd be in his cell just staring off or talking to himself and rubbing the back of his head. Really weird." He paused. "But when he first came here a couple of the toughest inmates *did* try to go alpha on him."

"What happened?"

"Let's just say they're not alphas anymore. One ended up paralyzed, and the other sits in a wheelchair dribbling water down his front, because Rogers permanently damaged his brain. One blow cracked the guy's skull. I saw it with my own eyes."

"How'd he get hold of a weapon in here?"

"Weapon? He used his bare hands."

"Holy shit!"

The older guard nodded thoughtfully. "That made his cred in here. Nobody bothered him after that. Prisoners respect the alpha. You saw how they all went quiet when he passed by just now. He was a legend in here getting bigger and badder without lifting a finger. But to his credit, Rogers was an alpha like I've never seen before. And more."

"How do you mean?"

The guard thought about this for a few moments. "When

they first brought him here we did the standard strip search, no orifice overlooked."

"Right."

"Well, Rogers had scars on him."

"Hell, lots of cons have scars. And tats!"

"Not like this. They were up and down both arms and both legs and on his head and around his torso. *And* along his fingers. Ugly shit. And we couldn't take prints off the guy. I mean, he didn't have any! Never seen anything like it before. Hope I never see anything like it again."

"How'd he get the scars?"

"Like I said, dude only said five words since he came here. And it wasn't like we could force him to tell us how he got them. I always assumed Rogers belonged to some sort of freak cult or had been tortured. Hell, it would've taken an Army battalion to do that to him. But the fact is I really didn't want to know. Rogers is a freak. An out-and-out freak that I'm really glad to see the back of."

"Surprised they let him out, then."

As the guards walked back to the cellblocks the older one muttered, "God help anybody who runs into that son of a bitch."

CHAPTER

2

OUTSIDE, ROGERS DREW a slow breath and then let it go, watching the chilly vapor materialize momentarily and then vanish just as quickly. He stood there for a few seconds getting his bearings. In some ways it was like being born and slipping out of the womb and seeing a world you didn't know existed a moment before.

His gaze went from left to right and right to left. Then to the sky. Choppers were not out of the question, he thought. Not for this.

Not for *him*.

But there was no one waiting for him.

It could be the passage of time. Three decades. People died, memories faded.

Or it could be that they really thought he was dead.

Their mistake.

Then he settled on the screwed-up release date.

If they were coming, it would be tomorrow.

Thank God for stupid court clerks.

Following the directions given on his discharge papers, he walked to the bus stop. It was four rusted posts with a shingled roof and a wooden seat worn down by decades of people waiting for a ride to somewhere else. While he was waiting he took the packet of parole materials from his jacket and dumped them in a trash can standing next to the enclosure. He had no intention of attending any parole hearings. He had places to go that were far away from here.

He touched the spot on the left side of his head, halfway between the occipital bone and the lambdoid suture. He then traced his finger over the sutural bones to the parietal bones and finally to the sagittal suture. They were important parts of the skull protecting significant elements of the brain.

He had once thought that what had been added there was a ticking time bomb.

Now he simply thought of it as *him*.

He let his hand drop to his side as he watched the bus pull up to the curb. The doors opened and he climbed on, gave his ticket to the driver, and walked to the back.

A cascade of smells enveloped him, mostly of the fried-food and unwashed-bodies variety. Everyone on the bus watched him as he passed. Women's fingers curled more tightly around their purses. Men watched him with defensive looks and fists ready. Children simply stared wide-eyed.

He just had that effect on people, he supposed.

He sat in the very rear, where the stench from the lone restroom might have overwhelmed someone who had not smelled far worse.

Rogers had smelled far worse.

In seats catty-corner across the aisle from him were a man in his twenties and a girl of the same age. The girl was in the aisle seat. Her boyfriend was huge, about six-six and all muscle. They had not watched Rogers walk back here, mainly because they had been too busy exploring each other's mouths with their tongues.

When the bus pulled off, they separated lips and the man glanced over the seat at Rogers with hostile eyes. Rogers looked back until the man glanced away. The woman gazed back too and smiled.

"Did you just get out?" she asked.

Rogers looked down at his clothes. It occurred to him that this must be standard-issue garb for those leaving prison. Perhaps the correctional system ordered the items in bulk, including shoes that were too small so the ex-cons couldn't outrun anybody. And maybe the bus stop was known to folks around here as the "prisoners' stop." That would explain the looks he'd been given.

Rogers never thought to return her smile, but he did nod in answer to her query.

"How long were you in for?"

In answer, Rogers held up all ten fingers.

She gave him a sympathetic look. "That's a long time." She crossed her legs so that one long slender and bare limb was thrust out into the aisle, giving him an admirable view of pale skin.

They rode for nearly an hour, the distance from the prison to the closest town. All that time the high-heeled shoe dangled enticingly off the woman's foot.

Rogers never once looked away.

When they pulled into the bus depot it was dark. Nearly everyone got off. Rogers was last because he liked it that way.

His feet hit the pavement and he looked around. Some of the passengers were greeted by friends or family. Others pulled their luggage from the storage compartment at the rear of the bus. Rogers simply stood there and looked around as he had done outside the prison. He had no friends or family to greet him, and no luggage to retrieve.

But he was waiting for something to happen.

The young man who had glared at him went to collect

his and the woman's bags. While he did so she came over to Rogers.

"You look like you could use some fun."

He didn't answer.

She glanced in the direction of her boyfriend. "We go our separate ways in a little bit. After that, why don't we go have a good time, just you and me? I know a place."

When the boyfriend came around the side of the bus carrying a long duffel and a smaller suitcase, she gripped his arm and they walked off. But she looked back at Rogers and winked.

His gaze tracked the young couple as they headed down the street, turned left, and disappeared from sight.

Rogers started to walk. He turned down the same alley and saw the couple up ahead. They were nearly out of sight. But not quite.

Rogers touched his head again at the same spot and then ran his finger back, as he had before, as though tracing the route of a meandering river.

They kept walking for a long time, block after block the couple just in sight. Always just in sight.

It was quite dark now. The couple turned a corner and disappeared from view.

Rogers picked up his pace and turned the same corner.

His arm caught the blow from the bat. The wood shattered and the top half of the bat flew off and hit the wall.

"Shit!" roared the young man holding it. The duffel lay open on the ground. The woman was a few feet behind her boyfriend. She had ducked when the bat had broken in half and sailed in her direction, causing her to drop her purse.

The man let go of the other half of the bat, pulled a switchblade from his pocket, and opened it.

"Give up the three hundred bucks, Mr. Ex-Con, and the ring and the watch, and you don't get gutted."

Three hundred bucks? So they knew the amount based on his decade in prison.

Rogers twisted his neck to the right and felt the pop.

He looked around. The walls were brick, high, and had no windows, meaning no witnesses. The alley was dark. There was no one else around. He had noted all this while he was walking.

"Did you hear me?" said the young man as he towered over Rogers.

Rogers nodded, for he had indeed heard the man.

"Well then, give me the cash and the other stuff. You simple or what?"

Rogers shook his head. For he was not simple. And he was also not going to give up anything.

"Suit yourself," barked the man. He lunged at Rogers and slashed with the blade.

Rogers partially blocked the thrust of the knife, but the blade still bit into his arm. This slowed him down not even a little because he felt nothing. As the blood soaked into his clothing he gripped the hand holding the knife and squeezed.

The man dropped the knife. "Shit, shit!" he screamed. "Let go, let the fuck go!"

Rogers did not let go. The man fell to his knees, futilely trying to pry Rogers's fingers off him.

The woman watched all of this in stunned disbelief.

With his free hand Rogers slowly reached down, gripped the handle of the broken bat, and held it up.

The young man looked up at him. "Please, man, don't."

Rogers swung the bat. The force of the blow crushed the side of the man's skull. Bits of bone mixed with gray meninges pooled down the side of his head.

Rogers let go of the dead man's hand and he slumped sideways to the pavement.

The woman was screaming and backing away now. She eyed her purse but made no move toward it.

"Help me! Help me!"

Rogers dropped the bat and looked at her.

This part of town was deserted at this hour, which was why they had picked it as their ambush spot.

There was no one available to help anybody. They had thought that would work in their favor. When Rogers had stepped into the alley he knew it would work in *his* favor.

He had realized this was a setup from the moment the woman had looked at him on the bus. Her dead boyfriend was her age and good-looking. Rogers was neither of those. The only things he had that she would want rested in his pocket, on his wrist, and on his finger.

They must prey on the men getting out.

Well, tonight they had picked the wrong target.

She backed up against a brick wall. Tears sliding down her face, she moaned, "Please, please don't hurt me. I swear I won't tell nobody what you done. I swear to God. Please."

Rogers bent down and picked up the switchblade.

She started to sob. "Please, don't. Please . . . He made me do it. He said he'd hurt me."

Rogers walked over to the woman and studied her quaking features. None of it had an effect on him, just like the knife biting into his arm.

Nothing because he was nothing.

Felt nothing.

She obviously wanted him to feel pity for her. He knew that. He understood that. But there was a difference between understanding and actually *feeling* something.

In some ways, it was the greatest difference there was.

He felt nothing. Not for her. Not for him. He rubbed his head, probing the same spot, as though his fingers could reach through bone and tissue and brain matter and rip out what was there. It burned, but then it always burned when he did what he did.

Rogers had not always been this way. Sometimes, when he thought long and hard about it, he could dimly remember a different person.

He looked down at the knife, now a stainless steel extension of his limb. He loosened his grip.

"Will you let me go?" she gasped. "I . . . I really do like you."

He took a step back.

She forced a smile. "I promise I won't tell."

Rogers took another step back. He could just leave, he thought.

She looked over his shoulder. "I think he just moved," she said breathlessly. "Are you sure he's dead?"

Rogers turned to look.

The flash of movement caught his attention. She had snagged her purse and pulled a gun from it. He saw the muzzle of the nickel-plated revolver sweeping upward to take aim at his chest.

He struck with astonishing swiftness and then stepped to the side as the arterial spray from her slashed neck erupted outward, narrowly missing him.

She toppled forward and smacked the pavement face first, ruining her pretty features, not that it mattered now. The revolver she had pulled from her handbag struck the hard surface and clattered away.

Rogers, pressed for time, cleaned out the cash from the young man's wallet and the woman's purse. He neatly folded the bills into his pocket.

He positioned the shattered bat in the hand of the young woman and put the gun back in her purse. He replaced the switchblade in the hand of the dead man.

He would let the local police try to figure out what had happened.

He field-dressed his arm as best he could and the blood stopped flowing.

He took a few moments to count the folded money. His cash had just been doubled.

He had a long, difficult journey ahead of him

And after all these years, it was time to get started.

CHAPTER

3

JOHN PULLER STARED across at his father, who was sleeping in his bed in the room that had become his home.

He wondered for how much longer.

Puller Sr. had been going through a transition of late. And it wasn't all to do with the deteriorating state of his personal health.

His older son, Robert Puller, once incarcerated in a military prison in Leavenworth, Kansas, had been formally cleared of all charges of treason and his record expunged. Then he had been reinstated as an officer in the United States Air Force. Puller Sr. and his older son had experienced a reunion that had brought rare tears to John Puller.

But the exuberance of his son's being free had been followed by a period of rapid decline, at least mentally. Physically, the former three-star general was far fitter than men his age. But it was a strong body paired with a fading mind. And maybe the old man had been holding out until his son's freedom was granted. That goal accomplished, perhaps his father had simply given up, his energy and along with it his will to live gone.

So Puller sat and watched his father, wondering what he would find behind the chiseled granite features when the old man woke. His father had been born to lead men into battle. And he had done so with considerable success over several decades, earning virtually every medal, ribbon, commendation, and rank promotion the service offered. Yet once his fighting days were over, it was like a switch had been turned off and his father had swiftly devolved into...this.

The doctors described it as dementia transitioning to something else. And worse.

Puller described it as losing his father.

His brother was overseas on a new assignment that would keep him away for several months. John Puller had just come off an investigation in Germany, and once the plane's wheels hit tarmac he had driven here to see his father.

It was late, but he hadn't seen his dad in a while.

And so he sat, and wondered which version of his father would awake and greet him.

Puller Sr. the screaming hardass?

Puller Sr. the stoic?

Puller Sr. with nothing behind the eyes?

He would take either of the first two over the last one.

There was a knock on the door. Puller rose and opened it.

Two men stared back at him. One was in the uniform of a full colonel. One was in plain clothes.

"Yes?" said Puller.

"John Puller Jr.?" said the plainclothes.

"That's right. And who are you?"

"Ted Hull." He took out his ID pack and displayed it. "CID. Out of the Twelfth MPs, Fort Lee."

"And I'm Colonel David Shorr," said the uniformed man.

Puller didn't know him. But there were lots of colonels in the Army.

Puller stepped out and closed the door behind him. "My father is sleeping. What can I do for you? Is this about another assignment? I was supposed to be on leave for the next two days. You can talk to my CO, Don White."

Shorr added, "We've already spoken with your CO. He told us where you were."

"So what's the issue?"

"It's about your father, actually, Chief. And I guess you as well."

Since Puller was technically a chief warrant officer in the CID, or Criminal Investigation Command, of the United States Army, those in uniform referred to him as "Chief." He was not a commissioned officer like those who had graduated from West Point. He had started his Army career as an enlisted man, and thus was lower in rank than Shorr.

"I don't understand, sir," he said.

At nearly six feet four he towered over the two men. His height came from his father. His calm demeanor came from his mother. His father had two emotional settings: loud and DEFCON One.

"There's a visitors' room down the hall," said Shorr. "Let's talk there."

He led the way to the room, found it empty, and shut the door behind them. They all sat, Puller facing the other two men.

Shorr looked at Hull and nodded. Hull took an envelope from his pocket and tapped it against his palm.

"Fort Eustis received this communication. They forwarded it to my office. We've been doing some digging on it. Then we found out you were scheduled to come back today, so we rode up to see you."

Shorr added, "I'm stationed at JBLE. That's the connection."

Puller nodded. He knew that was in the Tidewater area, which included Norfolk, Hampton, and Newport News, Virginia. In 2010 the Army's Fort Eustis in Newport News and Langley Air Force Base in nearby Hampton had come together to form the new base configuration known in the service as JBLE.

"Transport and logistics," noted Puller.

"Right."

"And while the Twelfth MPs are headquartered at Fort Lee, we also operate out of both JBLE and Fort Lee and constitute the CID office for JBLE," said Hull. "I toggle back and forth. Prince George's County isn't that far from Tidewater."

Puller nodded. He knew all this. "So what's in the letter?"

He said this warily because his father had gotten a letter once before, from his sister in Florida. That had led Puller on a journey to the Sunshine State that had very nearly cost him his life.

"It was addressed to the CID Office at JBLE. The woman who wrote it is Lynda Demirjian?" Hull said this in an inquiring way, as though the name would mean something to Puller. "Do you remember her?"

"Yes. From Fort Monroe. When I was a kid."

"She lived near you when your father was stationed there before it was closed and its operations transferred over to Fort Eustis. She was a friend of the family. More particularly, she was friends with your *mother*."

Puller thought back around thirty years and his memory finally arrived at a short, plump, pretty-faced woman who was always smiling and who baked the best cakes Puller could ever remember eating.

"Why is she writing to CID?"

"She's very ill, unfortunately. Final-stage pancreatic cancer."

"I'm really sorry to hear that." Puller glanced at the letter.

Hull said, "She wrote to the CID because she was dying and she wanted to air something that she had been feeling for a long time. Almost like a deathbed statement."

"Okay," said Puller, who was now growing impatient. "But what does it have to do with me? I was just a kid back then."

"As was your brother," said Shorr.

"You're not with the MPs," said Puller.

Shorr shook his head. "But it was decided that some officer heft was required for this, um, meeting."

"And why was that?" asked Puller.

"Mrs. Demirjian's husband, Stan, served at Fort Monroe with your father. He was a sergeant first class back then. He's retired now, of course. Do you remember him?"

"Yes. He served with my father over in Vietnam. They went way back. But can you tell me what's in that letter?"

Hull said, "I think it best if you read it for yourself, Chief."

He handed it over. It was three pages in length and it seemed to be in a man's hand.

"She didn't write this herself?" said Puller.

"No, she's too weak. Her husband wrote it, to her dictation."

Puller spread out the pages on the small table next to his chair and began to read. The two men watched him anxiously as he did so.

The sentences were long and rambling and Puller could imagine the terminally ill woman trying to sufficiently collect her thoughts to communicate them to her husband. Yet it was still more a stream-of-consciousness outpouring than anything else. She was probably medicated when she had dictated it. Puller had to admire her determination to accomplish this when so near death.

And then, with the introductory preambles out of the way, he got into the substance of the letter.

And his mouth gaped.

And his hand shook.

And his stomach felt like someone had sucker-punched him there.

He kept reading, faster and faster, his pace probably neatly matching the breathless dictation of the dying woman.

When he had finished he looked up to find the two men staring at him.

"She's accusing my father of murdering my mother."

"That's right," said Hull. "That's exactly right."

CHAPTER

4

"THIS IS RIDICULOUS," said Puller. "When my mother went missing my father wasn't even in the country."

Ted Hull glanced at Colonel Shorr, cleared his throat, and said, "As I said, we've done some preliminary digging."

Puller said, "Wait a minute, when did you receive this letter?"

"A week ago."

"And you're only *now* telling me about it?"

Shorr interjected, "Chief Puller, I know how upsetting this must be for you."

"You're damn right." Puller caught himself, remembering that the man he was talking to was well above him in rank. "It is upsetting, sir," he said more calmly.

"And because of the seriousness of the allegation we wanted to do some investigation before bringing the matter to your attention."

"And what did your investigation show?" Puller said curtly.

"That while your father *was* out of the country, he arrived back a day earlier than planned. He was in Virginia and in the vicinity of Fort Monroe five or six hours before your mother disappeared."

Puller felt his heart skip a beat. "That doesn't prove he was involved."

"Not at all. But we checked the earlier investigation record. Your father said he was out of the country, and preliminary travel records backed that up. That's why when the investigation was done back then it cleared him of any possible involvement."

"So why do you say otherwise now?"

"Because we uncovered additional travel records and vouchers that show your father, who was scheduled to travel back stateside via military transport, actually flew back on a private jet."

"A private jet? Whose?"

"We're not certain of that yet. Keep in mind this was thirty years ago."

Puller rubbed his eyes, truly disbelieving that this was actually happening. "I know how long ago it was. I lived through it. My brother and I. And my father. It was a living hell for us all. It tore our family apart."

"I can understand that," said Hull. "But the point is that if your father said he was out of the country and the records indicate otherwise?" He left the obvious implications of that contradiction unspoken.

Puller decided to simply say it. "So you're saying he lied? Well, the records you uncovered could be wrong. If his name was on a flight manifest it doesn't alone prove he was on the plane."

"We need to dig deeper, certainly."

Puller eyed both men. "But if that was all you had you wouldn't be sitting here with me."

Shorr said, "I nearly forgot what you do for a living. You're well versed in how investigations operate."

"So what *else* do you have, Colonel?"

Hull spoke up. "We can't get into that, Chief. It's an ongoing investigation."

"So you've opened an investigation based on a letter from a terminally ill woman about events thirty years ago?"

"And the fact that your father was not out of the country as he said he was," replied Hull defensively. "Look, if we hadn't turned that up I don't think we'd be having this conversation. It's not like I woke up one morning looking to tear down an Army legend, Chief. But it's a different time too. Back then maybe things got buried that shouldn't have been. The Army's taken some knocks over the years for not being transparent." He stopped and looked at Shorr.

Shorr said, "An investigation file has been opened, Chief Puller, so it has to be followed through. But if no new evidence is turned up, I don't see this going anywhere. The Army is not looking to destroy your father's reputation based on a single letter from a dying woman."

"What sort of new evidence?" asked Puller.

Shorr said firmly, "This was a courtesy meeting, Chief Puller. That's all. CID will carry on now, but we wanted you to know how things stood and certainly about the letter. Your father being what he is, we thought it only proper to let you know of the status of things."

Puller didn't know what to say to this.

Hull said, "We will want to formally interview you later, Chief. And your brother. And your father, of course."

"My father has dementia."

"We understand that. And we also understand that he sometimes is coherent."

"And who do you understand that from?"

Shorr rose and so did Hull. Shorr said, "Thank you for your time, Chief. Agent Hull will be in touch."

"Have you spoken to Lynda Demirjian?" asked Puller. "And her husband?"

"Again, CID will be in touch," Hull said. "Thanks for your time. And I'm sorry to have been the one to communicate something this upsetting."

The two men left, while Puller sat there staring at the floor.

He pulled out his phone a few moments later and punched in the number.

Two rings later his brother answered.

"Hey, little bro, I'm tied up right now. And if you're back in Virginia I'm eight hours ahead of you. So can I call—"

"Bobby, we have a big problem. It's about Dad."

Robert Puller instantly said, "What's wrong?"

Puller told his older brother everything that had just occurred.

Robert Puller didn't say anything for about thirty seconds. All Puller could hear was the other man's breathing.

"What do you remember about that day?" Robert finally asked.

Puller leaned back in his seat and ran a hand over his forehead. "I was playing outside. I turned to the window and saw Mom there. She was in a robe with a towel around her hair. She had evidently just gotten out of the shower."

"No, I mean later."

"Later? That was the last time I saw her."

"No it wasn't. We had dinner that night and then she left and went out. The next-door neighbor's daughter came over to stay with us."

Puller sat up. "I don't remember that."

"Well, we never really talked about it, John."

"Where did she go that night?"

"I don't know. To a friend's, I guess."

"And she never came back?"

"Obviously not," Robert said curtly. "And so Dad was back in the country. He told the police he wasn't."

"How do you know he told them he wasn't?"

"CID agents came to the house, John. The next day. Dad was there. They talked to him. We were upstairs, but I could still hear."

"Why don't I remember any of this, Bobby?"

"You were eight years old. You didn't understand any of it."

"You weren't even ten yet."

"I was never much of a kid, John, you know that." He added, "And it was a traumatic time for all of us. You've probably blocked a lot of it from your memories. A defense mechanism."

"They're going to want to interview us. And Dad too."

"Well, they can interview us. But I don't see them making much headway with the old man."

"But he may understand what they're saying. That they think he killed Mom."

"I don't see how we can prevent that, John. It's an investigation. You know how that works better than most. You can't get in the way of it."

"I think I need to get Dad a lawyer."

"Know anybody good?"

"Shireen Kirk. She just left JAG to go into private practice."

"Then you should give her a call."

"Do you remember Lynda Demirjian?"

"Yes. Nice lady. Baked cakes. She and Mom were close."

"Could she have been visiting her that night?" asked Puller.

"I don't know. She didn't tell me where she was going."

"Demirjian is convinced that Dad killed Mom."

"I wonder why that is. I mean, CID may have found out he was back in the country when he said he wasn't, but that was only *after* they got her letter and looked into it. She must have other reasons."

"And I'm going to find out what they are."

"You think they're going to let you investigate this case? It's Dad. Hell, they wouldn't let you near my case, remember?"

"And you'll remember that I did get near your case. Very near."

"And it almost cost you your career. So my advice is to stay the hell away from this."

"We can't just walk away, Bobby."

"Let me check some things out on my end and I'll get back to you."

"You...you don't think he..." Puller couldn't actually say the words.

"The truth is I don't know for sure, and neither do you."

CHAPTER

5

IT WAS PAUL Rogers's third day of freedom. And no grass
had grown under his feet. He had already put a thousand
miles between him and the prison.

He had looked for and found news of the double homicide back in the alley. The paper said the police were leaning
toward it being a fatal fight between a young couple. There
had obviously been a falling-out, because they had been seen
earlier on a bus together kissing.

Yep, thought Rogers, there had been a really big falling-
out.

On the second day of freedom he had stolen a beat-to-shit
Chevy from an automotive repair place, swapping out plates
he had taken from an impoundment lot. He'd driven six hundred miles that day, followed by over three hundred so far
today.

He had spent a chunk of his cash on gas and about the
same on food. He had slept in the car, finding a place to park
and bed down for the night. He had purchased shoes that
fit and an extra pair of pants, a shirt, a new jacket, underwear, socks, and a baseball cap. He'd also purchased some
bandages and other medical supplies for his arm. And he'd
bought a pair of off-the-rack reading glasses even though his

eyesight was perfect and nearly catlike in his ability to see in the dark.

He'd also bought some hair clippers and a razor. The beard was now gone and so was all his hair. He'd even taken off the peach fuzz on his scalp and his eyebrows.

When he looked at himself in the mirror Rogers could barely recognize the image. He hoped the effect on others, in particular law enforcement, would be even more pronounced.

The scar on the back left side of his head was now visible. It was easier to feel now every time he rubbed it.

He had a couple hundred dollars left and still quite a ways to go. He stopped for supper at a diner and ate at the counter, keeping all the goings-on behind him in full view by virtue of the large mirror hanging on the wall in front of him.

Two police officers came in and sat at a booth not that far from him. He tugged down his cap and focused on his meal and the newspaper in front of him.

The world had changed some in ten years. But in many ways it hadn't changed at all.

Countries were at war.

Terrorists were slaughtering innocent people.

American politics was at a standstill.

The rich were richer, the poor poorer.

The middle class was rapidly fading away.

Everyone seemed angry and vocal and generally pissed off at everything and everybody.

Beginning of the end, surmised Rogers, who did not care a whit that the country and apparently the rest of the world were in sharp decline. He just needed to get to where he was headed. He needed to figure some things out along the way, but once he got there his plan was pretty well set.

His only problem was it had been so long. Not just ten

years. That was manageable. But in total it had been three decades. People moved. People died. Companies folded. Time marched on, things changed, conditions on the ground could be totally different. But he also told himself he would not, could not waver. There was no reason on earth that he could not accomplish what he had told himself for the last ten years he was going to do.

No reason at all.

He finished his meal, laid down his cash, and walked past the cops without looking at them. He closed the door behind him and reached his car. He drove off, the night beginning to fill in all around him.

His wounded arm was healing nicely. There had been minimal infection. His new jacket covered the bandage.

He drove east.

He did not need much sleep. He only stopped and rested now because he wanted to get into the habit of doing so, like other people did. Rogers did not want to stick out. He did not want to do anything that would make others notice him. And he could do lots of things to make other people notice. But if people with badges and guns took note, he was screwed. And he did not intend to be screwed.

Not ever again.

His hand reached up and rubbed the spot. He could still remember when it was done. Over thirty years ago. Lots of things had been done to him at that time.

What he couldn't stand were the thoughts that he had, and also the thoughts that he no longer had. Like back in the alley when the woman had been pleading for her life, Rogers had remembered something. It was just a fragment of a fragment and he couldn't delve into it too deeply, because there was a mental wall preventing him from doing so. He could scale many walls, yet not that one. But there was something there. Something he would have done differently if he was still who he had once been.

But he no longer was that man. Not even close. And the fragment would never be more than that. They hadn't told him that part, of course. Why would they? He apparently had no reason to know in a strict "need to know" world.

He removed his hand and with it any hope that things one day could be different for him.

He slept in his car on a side street of a town he was passing through.

Two days later he was eight hundred miles closer to his destination. By now a bench warrant had certainly been issued for his arrest for his failure to show up for his parole meeting. Perhaps they had found the tossed materials in the trash can by the bus stop. That evidenced his clear intent to never, ever perform any of the duties imposed on him in return for his having been released from prison ahead of time.

He actually felt that ten years of his life locked up in a cage was payment enough.

He was down to fifty dollars.

The next morning he stopped at a construction site and offered his services for a hundred dollars for ten solid hours of labor.

His task was to haul bags of cement from a truck to a construction elevator stuck back in a corner where the big trucks couldn't reach. There were three other men assigned to this job as well. They were all in their twenties. Rogers carried more fifty-pound bags than the three of them combined. He never spoke, never looked at the other men. He just hefted bags, hauled them a hundred feet to the elevator, dumped them, and walked back for more. Ten hours with a twenty-minute break for a food truck sandwich and a cup of coffee.

"Thanks for making us look good, Gramps," said one of them sarcastically when the day's work was done.

Rogers had turned to look at him. He eyed the man's neck where his jugular wobbled underneath the fat. Rogers could have crushed the vein between his fingers and watched the man bleed out in less than a minute. But what would have been the point?

"You're welcome," he said.

When the young punk snorted at him, Rogers fixed his gaze on him. He wasn't looking at him so much as *through* him to a destination on the other side of his skull.

The punk blinked, his sneer vanished, he glanced at his companions, and then they all turned and hustled off.

It was then that Rogers did something he almost never did.

He smiled. And it wasn't because he had intimidated the punk. He had intimidated many men. And he had never smiled any of those times.

He walked back to his car, climbed in, tucked his money away, and looked at the map he'd bought.

The Virginia border was still two hundred miles from here. And the place within Virginia he was heading to would tack on about another three hundred or so miles.

He should be tired, exhausted really, but he wasn't. He should be a lot of things. But he wasn't.

Now he was only what he was.

He drove to a diner, parked at the curb, and went inside. He ordered food, drank his coffee and two glasses of water, and let his mind wander back to the point where it had all started.

He made a fist and looked down at it. The skin on top was real but not his. The bone underneath was real *and* his. The other things, the add-ons, he had come to call them, were not real and were definitely not his. But he could not remove them. So, he supposed, they were real and they *were* his.

Or rather I am him. Paul Rogers. The thing.

The scars had faded over the years, particularly the ones on his fingers, but he would always see them as though they had just been done.

Sitting up in that bed, wrapped in bloody bandages, feeling… different.

His old self, his *real* self, gone forever.

He next rubbed the ring. It was a platinum band that had been given to him by someone who had once been special in his life.

There was an inscription engraved on the inside of the band. Rogers had no need to look at it. The words were burned into his brain.

For the good of all.

He had once believed in those words more than anything else in his life. But that was then, this was now.

Now he believed in nothing.

He ate with his face pointed down. He was hungry, but he could survive without eating for a long time. He could survive without liquids for a long time too although the average person would become dehydrated and die fairly quickly. The same with lack of sleep. You don't sleep for two weeks, you hallucinate and then you die, your brain and other organs all going wacky on you before they shut down and the lights go out forever.

Yet it was all physiological. It was all about slowing things down, lessening the internal burn. Like animals hibernating, everything went from flat-out to glacial. Humans could learn a lot from animals about survival, because animals could do it far better than humans.

And I'm not a human anymore. I'm a fucking wild animal. Maybe the most dangerous of all, because I've got a human brain to go along with the "wild" part.

He finished his meal, sat back, and rubbed the spot on his head.

He took a sip of coffee and then his face screwed up. The pain came and went without warning.

He let out a tortured breath. It was the one pain that he could not ignore. The wound on his arm didn't bother him. He had never even felt the bite of the knife.

But the pain in his head was different. It was special, apparently. They had never fully explained that one. It was his brain after all. The most important organ he had. It was what made him him. Or *not* him, in Rogers's case.

He paid the bill and walked back to his car. He drove to another part of the small town, parked, and settled down for the night.

As the hours passed and the darkness deepened, Rogers lay there and stared at the ceiling of the car. It was stained and faded and generally worn out.

He was stained, faded, and should have been worn out. But his energy level had never been higher.

It was only during his last year in prison that certain parts of his mind had become fully accessible to him. And that was why he had marshaled all of his strength and determination and sat in front of the parole board and said all the right things. His remorse. His learning from his mistakes. His wanting to lead a good, productive life going forward. He was being sincere—well, mostly. He *had* learned from his mistakes. He *did* want to be productive going forward. He had even forced some tears.

But he felt no remorse, because he was incapable of the emotion.

He had only one goal now. And it lay, he hoped, about five hundred miles from here.

He was going back to the beginning to get to the end.

But the remnants in his head? That previously inaccessible spot? He focused on that.

The man was young, not yet twenty. Good-natured. Trusting.

That had been his mistake. The *trusting* part.

It was the same old story: a strange man in a strange land. No friends, no allies, no one to turn to for help.

He had come to this place for a better life, as had millions of others.

He had not found a better life. He had found a very different man at the end of the day living inside his body. He knew this and yet could not fully control it. To change himself back to what he was. He had tried. Over the last year when he had finally punched through that wall, he had desperately tried to uncurl the fist. To banish from his mind the desire to maim, wound, or more often kill.

But he had made a little progress.

The punk back at the construction site was fortunate that Rogers had somehow managed to walk away with sarcastic words instead of a lethal jab.

It had been a little thing, certainly.

But it had felt empowering nonetheless.

That was why he had smiled.

I can exercise some control. I don't have to strike every time. I can walk away.

In prison, after his encounter with the men who wanted to force their will on him, Rogers had been placed in a cell by himself. Better that he be completely alone, for none of the guards wanted to have to intervene in another fight involving Paul Rogers.

Thus there was no one to antagonize him. No one to bring out the monster that lurked just under his skin.

But as Rogers closed his eyes for the night, his thoughts held on that young man just recently arrived in this country with another name and a far different ambition for his life. A nice young man. A young man with a future, one would say.

Now that man was long gone.

The monster was all that was left.

And the monster had one more thing to do.

CHAPTER

6

PULLER SAT IN the chair and stared over at his father, who was still sleeping.

Colonel Shorr and Agent Hull had been gone for a while.

The VA hospital they were in was quiet, all activity ratcheting down as everyone tucked in for the night. Puller had come back here and sat down and stared at his father because he couldn't think of what else to do.

When his father had first come here his moments of lucidity had been fairly frequent. Not enough to allow him to live by himself. He might have burned his house down by putting a metal can of soup in the microwave or using the gas stove to heat his kitchen.

Puller had acted out a game with his father in those earlier days. He'd been his father's XO, or second in command. He would report in for duty and let his father order him around. He'd felt like an idiot for doing so, but the doctors here thought, other things being equal, that the charade might allow his father an easier transition to his next stage in the disease.

So Puller had played along. Now it wasn't necessary to do that. His father *had* reached the next stage in his disease. The doctors said there was no going back.

It was a humble future for a three-star who should have

been awarded one more star, along with the Medal of Honor. But politics, which existed in the military as it did in the civilian corridors of power, had prevented the additional star and the nation's highest military honor from being bestowed.

Still, Puller Sr. was a legend in the military. "Fighting John Puller," captain of the basketball team at West Point, where the term "Pullered" had come into vogue. They had never won a championship while his father played, but every team that beat them went home probably feeling as though they had actually lost the battle. That was what every conflict was to Puller Sr., whether it occurred on a battlefield or on a basketball court. You would know you'd been in a war when you went up against the man.

He had gone to West Point after the end of the Korean War and lamented that it was over before he could go fight in it.

As a combat leader in Vietnam he had almost never lost an engagement.

His division, the 101st Airborne, known as the Screaming Eagles, consisted of ten battalions of airmobile light infantry, plus a half dozen battalions of artillery supported by three aviation battalions of gunships and transports. It had fully arrived in Vietnam in 1967 and had fought its way across the Central Highlands. One of its most famous engagements was the battle for Hill 937, more famously known as Hamburger Hill. Puller Sr. had been right in the middle of the fight commanding his regiment in some of the most difficult terrain imaginable against an entrenched foe. He had been wounded twice, but had never once left the field of battle. Later, as they were stitching him up, he was barking orders over the radio detailing how the next engagement should be fought.

Throughout his tours in Vietnam, Puller Sr. had accomplished whatever had been demanded of him by his commanders and more. Once he gained ground he did not give it up. He had been nearly overrun multiple times by an enemy that valued dying in battle as a great honor. He had killed and nearly been killed—sometimes by his own side as errant bombs exploded dangerously close to his positions. He gave no quarter, asked for none, and expected his men to perform at ever higher levels.

The 101st was the last division to leave Vietnam and did so with over twenty thousand men killed and wounded during the course of the war. This was more than twice the division's losses in World War II.

Seventeen members of the 101st won the Medal of Honor in Vietnam. Many thought Puller Sr. should have made it eighteen, including every man who had served under him.

Yet he never had.

Despite this, he had risen through the ranks swiftly. As a two-star he had gone on to command the illustrious 101st. He had left a mark bone deep on that fighting division that had stood the test of time. He had earned his third and final star and the rank of lieutenant general before his sixtieth birthday.

He was remembered as a soldier's general. He took care of his men but drove them as relentlessly as he drove himself.

As relentlessly as he drove his sons, thought Puller.

His men loved *and* feared him. Perhaps more fear than love, now that Puller thought about it.

And maybe that was just as true for the sons as the men under his father's command.

And now he lay sleeping in his bed at the VA. His world of command was gone, his sphere of influence nonexistent, his allotted time on earth winding down.

Puller turned to something that was deeply troubling him.

What his brother had said to him had been nearly as astonishing as what Hull and Shorr had told him.

How could he have misremembered the last day he had seen his mother?

His mother had been at that window. She had a towel wrapped around her head. Then she was gone.

But now Bobby had told him they'd had dinner together. And his mother had gone out. That the neighbor's daughter had come over to watch the boys. Puller didn't recall any of that.

He remembered that he had woken the next morning and his mother was not there. He remembered the MPs coming to the house. Then his father charging into the officers' quarters where they lived at Fort Monroe, bellowing at and bullying all those within striking distance.

And his father had lied to the police?

He stared over at the sleeping man.

Why would he have done that?

Because he had actually murdered his wife and Puller's mother?

It was pretty much unthinkable.

And yet Puller had seen enough in his career at CID to know that people were capable of just about anything.

He thought back to his early years with his parents. They had argued, but not to an excessive degree. The old man was harder on his sons than on his wife.

And Jacqueline Puller, known to all as Jackie, did not possess a submissive personality. If anything she was more than a match for her husband. The old man would be away and then he'd come home and try to change the rules of their lives that Jackie Puller had carefully constructed. As the boss of men rushing into combat, Puller Sr. evidently thought he was qualified and entitled to run everything. His wife had not been in agreement on that point.

So there had been arguments, words spoken in anger. But didn't most if not all marriages have that?

Puller didn't know for sure, never having been married. But he had conducted many investigations involving married couples. And he glumly recalled that more than a few involved one spouse murdering the other.

He left and went to his car. He got in and punched in the number.

"Shireen?"

"Puller? How's it going?"

Shireen Kirk had formerly been a JAG, or Judge Advocate General's, lawyer representing those in uniform. She had recently left the military and gone into private practice in northern Virginia. She had the rep of being a scorched-earth lawyer. And that's exactly what Puller required.

"I need a lawyer."

"Okay, so I guess it's not going too well."

"Well, my father needs one."

"I thought he was in a care facility with Alzheimer's?"

"Dementia, but yes, he is."

"If he did something that someone found out of bounds I think he'd have a pretty solid diminished capacity defense."

"It's not like that. This is from about thirty years ago when he was still in the military."

"Okay, what happened?"

Puller filled her in on the situation and the letter that Demirjian had sent to CID.

"That really sucks. You say they want to interview your father?"

"Yes."

"If he's been diagnosed with dementia he should have counsel there with him. I could even make a case that they can't question him because of his condition. He's liable to say anything and we don't want him to inadvertently incriminate himself."

"No, we don't."

"I can take the case."

"That's great, Shireen. But can they even charge him if he's not competent?"

"They can charge anybody, Puller. Competency is a matter for a court to determine. And even if he's not competent to stand trial they can hold the prosecution in abeyance until he becomes competent, if that ever happens. But that may be worse than him being tried for the crime."

"How do you mean?"

"At least if he's tried he can defend himself and maybe be acquitted."

Puller slowly nodded. "But if he's not tried because he's incompetent, people may assume he's guilty and is just getting off because he has dementia."

"Exactly. Being tried in the court of public opinion is often far worse than having your day in court. At least in the latter you get a judgment one way or the other. What's the name of the CID agent on the case?"

"Ted Hull out of the Twelfth MPs, JBLE."

He could hear her writing this down. "I'll contact him and tell him of my representation. I'll need you to sign a retainer agreement if your father can't. And I'll need to meet with your father at some point."

"I'm not sure how helpful that will be."

"I still need to do it. I can't rep someone without meeting them."

"Okay, I'll arrange that."

"Are you his guardian, Puller? Do you have a power of attorney?"

"Yes. We did that when my dad came to the VA hospital."

"Good, that simplifies matters. I'll have to request the CID file from the investigation they did back then. They must have talked to people, and I can get those statements, plus information on any theories or leads they might have been trying to run down."

"I want a copy of it when you do."

"Why?"

"Why do you think?"

"You shouldn't go there."

"Yeah, I've heard that before."

Her next statement surprised him.

"Did you ever look at any of the case files when you got to CID?" she asked.

"I tried to, but they wouldn't let me access them. Because of my personal connection to the case."

Puller had just told the woman a lie. He had never tried to access the case files. And right now he didn't really know why.

Shireen interrupted these thoughts. "What does your brother think of all this?"

"He's more analytical about these things than I am."

"Meaning he doesn't necessarily believe your father *didn't* do it?"

Puller had no response to that.

"I have some forms I need you to fill out so I can get going on this," she said. "I'll email them to you and you can sign and email or fax them back, okay?"

"Got it."

Puller went online and accessed a secure military database. He entered the name Stan Demirjian. There was only one since the last name was not common. Demirjian had retired as a sergeant first class. He had his military pension. It was mailed out to his home like clockwork. His address was in the file. They lived on the outskirts of Richmond, Virginia.

In his mind's eye Puller recalled a barrel-chested bald man with a gruff manner. But what sergeant first class didn't have a gruff manner? Your job was to mold men and women into fighting machines. You weren't there to be anyone's friend.

Puller hadn't had much contact with Demirjian when his father had been in uniform. Now that he thought about it, he had seen far more of Mrs. Demirjian than of her husband.

It was a two-hour drive from where he was to where the Demirjians lived. Should he go there and talk to them?

No one had told him to back off the case. And he could go and talk to them in a civilian capacity, not as a CID agent. It wasn't the best position, but at least it was something.

And maybe he should before someone told him not to.

The email with the forms to sign popped into his mailbox.

He drove to the CID offices at Quantico, printed them out, signed them, and faxed them back to Shireen. Now the legal ball could get rolling.

He drove home, threw a few things in to a bag, gunned up with his twin M11s, snagged an investigation duffel he kept in his apartment, changed the litterbox and filled the food and water bowls of his cat, AWOL, and hit the highway.

When he was on a case Puller always had a battle plan of how he was going to approach things. Now he had no idea what the hell he was going to do.

And if his father was guilty?

He shook his head.

I can't deal with that now. I can't deal with that ever.

And yet if it came to it, Puller knew he would have to.

CHAPTER

7

PAUL ROGERS HAD risen early and driven across the West Virginia border. He had stopped for dinner at a Cracker Barrel. There were big buses parked in the lot, and when he went inside he saw that the place was mostly filled with senior citizens, perhaps on some sort of tour or pilgrimage.

Pilgrimage. He could relate.

He ate alone at a table near the back of the rustic-inspired space.

The weather was clear now, but he had heard on the radio that a storm front was approaching and that it would bring rain and strong winds later that night.

He looked at his map and calculated that he would arrive at his destination in the afternoon, late or early depending on how soon he got on the road and how bad the traffic was.

He ate breakfast for dinner, cutting the sausage patties into four equal pieces and running them through his dense grits before putting them in his mouth.

In his mind he was placing his plan into quadrants too and then prioritizing each one. Military precision. If he ever needed his training, he needed it now.

He rubbed his head. It had become a habit so ingrained that sometimes he didn't even know he was doing it.

He looked around the large dining room once more and noted that many of the men had World War II caps on with stitched lettering signifying the military branches they had served in during the war. Some had pins on them representing specific units. They were all very old now, the youngest of them in their late eighties. Almost all were in wheelchairs or used walkers or canes to get around. They were gray, bent, but their features were proud, animated. They had fought the good fight and survived to have families and retirements and tour bus rides augmented with Cracker Barrel feasts.

Rogers thought, *I fought the good fight too. And I have nothing.*

Except he had a chance to make it all right. And he intended to give it the best shot he possibly could.

He finished his meal and hit the highway, driving right into the building storm.

He had something to get and he needed a special place to get it. Fortunately, he had passed a billboard that held the answer. And that would delay his reaching his destination. But that was okay. There would be time.

He slept in his car in the parking lot of a shuttered Walmart. Things must be getting bad, he thought, if Walmarts couldn't stay in business.

It was chilly and rainy and the Chevy's passenger-side window leaked. He watched the drips for a few minutes and then fell asleep.

He rose the next morning, drove off, and found a place to eat. At noon he headed to the gun show he had seen advertised on the billboard.

In some states gun shows had one big loophole. Private sellers didn't have to do background checks. Only licensed ones did. Despite political moves to close this hole, some sellers did not abide by the rules. Which was perfectly fine with Rogers.

Though things were changing, he could probably buy a weapon on the Internet without a background check, only he didn't have a computer, an email address, a credit card, or a physical address for them to ship the gun to.

He walked into the rambling tent that had been erected on the site and saw that dozens of dealers had set up small booths inside. The place was already packed, and he spent an hour simply walking around and observing. Most people didn't observe. They were too absorbed in themselves. Thus they missed nearly all that was actually instructive.

He could see that most people here were licensed dealers. Buyers were producing ID and filling out the background check forms that would be run through the FBI's NCIC database. The process took about ten minutes. There were a few private dealers, but they were selling shotguns and long guns and Confederate flags and cookies. And some of those didn't even have a booth. They were simply walking around with sandwich board signs inked with what they had to sell.

When the space in front of a particular seller cleared, Rogers walked over and looked at a pistol in its original packaging. The seller was a big flabby man in his forties wearing a camo shirt, jeans, and combat boots.

He eyed Rogers. "Beauty, ain't it?"

Rogers looked over the pistol. He said, "M11. Military use only."

The seller smiled and put out his hand. "Name's Mike Donohue, and I can tell you wore the uniform at some point if you know about the vaunted M11."

Rogers shook the man's hand, careful to avoid squeezing it too tightly.

Donohue took out the gun and held it up. "Collector's item. Explains the price."

"Why a collector's item?"

"Some time back the Air Force ordered a bunch of M11s but ended up not taking fifty of them. By contract Sig couldn't sell the M11 to civilians, like you said. But Sig Sauer could get a grand for each, and that was fifty thou potentially down the toilet, so they had incentive to get around that somehow. Then somebody had the genius idea that if you added another letter to the model number it would no longer technically be an M11, right? The A had already been taken for another M11 model, the M11-A1, so this became the M11-B." He handed the gun to Rogers and pointed out the letter. "Sig had it reengraved. You can see the B right there. And voilà, a civilian can own an M11. The manual that comes with it is military too. All the contents of the box are original. There's even a warning in there about radiation leakage from the tritium sights, but that's only for the Army and Navy versions, not the Air Force. So you'll have to find something else to kill you."

Donohue laughed and slapped Rogers on the shoulder.

Rogers fought back a nearly overwhelming urge to crush the man's face in retaliation.

Donohue continued, "Now, it's based on the original P228 frame, so it will only accept the thirteen-round mags. It comes with three. It won't work with the fifteen-round mags."

Rogers held the gun, sighted through it, checked the balance, slid his fingers along the grip, and slid back the rack twice to test the action.

Donohue said, "It's got the carbon steel slide instead of the milled version the P229 has. But there's only about a two-ounce difference between the two."

"You mind if I strip it?"

"Go ahead. I got nothing to hide. Just be gentle with her."

Donohue laughed and slapped Rogers on the shoulder again. "Damn, man, I bet you're older'n me, but I don't think you got an ounce of fat on you. Just muscle and gristle." He slapped his substantial belly. "Me, I'm just fat!" He laughed again.

Rogers nimbly field-stripped the pistol and then put it back together.

Donohue said, "Only four grand. It's a steal, really. Only fifty of these beauties in existence. Think about that."

"I *would* have to steal it," said Rogers. "Because I don't have four thousand dollars."

"I got others for a lot less."

Rogers looked some of those over and then withdrew as other potential buyers came along and crowded him out.

He backed about twenty feet away and watched Donohue. Periodically he saw him go out through a flap in the tent and come back with more merchandise.

Rogers went over to another booth and bought a Ka-Bar knife. No background check was required for this purchase, though a knife could kill too. He ran his finger lightly over the serrated edge and came away satisfied. He slid the knife back into its leather holder and attached it to his belt. He also bought a cheap plastic flashlight.

A few minutes later, he walked outside and around to the area from where Donohue had brought in more stock. He zipped up his jacket against the chilly wind. A big Dodge Ram was parked there. Attached to it was a small trailer. The truck was locked, the trailer padlocked. As Rogers watched from a distance, Donohue came out, unlocked the trailer, took out a few more boxes, locked the trailer back up, and went inside the tent again. Rogers moved forward, glad to have confirmed which vehicle was Donohue's.

In the bed of the Ford F-150 parked next to Donohue's ride, Rogers saw some cardboard boxes and old, rusted tools. None of it was any use to him. What he wanted was still inside the tent. He retreated to his car, pulled it around to that side of the tent, and waited.

Light grew to night. And the temperature continued to drop.

But time and cold meant nothing to him.

His stomach had rumbled once, and then he rubbed his head, focused, and the feelings of hunger vanished.

People streamed in and out of the tent for hours, until finally the stream grew to a trickle. And then the parking lot emptied. And then the dealers started taking down their booths and packing up what they hadn't sold.

Rogers watched as Donohue came out carrying several boxes. One of them, he noted, was the distinctive case of the M11-B. He wasn't surprised no one had bought it. Most of the potential purchasers he'd seen inside were working stiffs. He doubted any of them had four grand to throw down on a fancy-ass collector's pistol.

He rubbed his shoulder where Donohue had slapped him twice. He did not like people jacking him around like that. It was an insult.

Donohue finished packing and drove off. Rogers followed.

Donohue pulled into the drive-through of a McDonald's and bought some food.

Rogers had seen the man's Pennsylvania license plates. Maybe he was headed home.

Donohue then made it easy for Rogers. Instead of pulling over and eating in the parking lot of the Mickey D's, he headed on down the road. About a mile or so along he pulled off down a dirt road and into what looked to be an old picnic area.

Rogers cut the lights on his ride and slowly followed the truck. It turned off onto another dirt road and pulled to a stop.

Rogers didn't make that turn. He would finish this on foot.

Donohue switched off his lights and then must have cracked his window, because Rogers could hear music coming from the truck's radio.

Rogers killed his engine and got quietly out of his car. He approached dead center of the trailer so Donohue would not be able to glimpse him in the side mirrors.

He reached the door of the trailer. The padlock was a solid-looking Yale with a key entry instead of a combo. The metal clasp it was inserted through was stainless steel and about a half inch thick. It was designed, of course, so that all of the screw points on the two plates were covered when the door was closed and the lock engaged. But the designers had not counted on someone with Rogers's strength. He gripped the clasp and slowly pulled it and the support screws right out of the wood.

He quietly went inside the trailer and shone his light around. He saw the box and hefted it in one hand.

He stepped outside of the trailer.

"What do you think you're doing?"

Rogers stopped. Next he heard the click of a gun hammer being drawn back.

Using his peripheral vision, he could see Donohue standing next to the side of the trailer, gun in hand, a paper napkin stuck to the crotch of his pants.

"You can just put that down right now, asshole."

Rogers set the box down. Out of sight of Donohue, he slipped the knife from its holder.

"Good, now I can shoot your ass and you won't drop the box and damage that gun, dickhead."

Rogers pivoted on one foot, swung his arm back and around, and slammed the knife into Donohue. It went right through the center of the big man's chest and stuck into the wooden wall of the trailer, pinning him there like a moth to a corkboard.

After one long scream, the man died.

And still the screams continued.

For a moment Rogers couldn't fathom how the dead man could still be making noise, until he looked past the body and saw a small boy leaning out of the truck's driver's side, a Happy Meal in his hands, a smudge of ketchup riding on the outside edge of his mouth.

The boy must have been sleeping in the front seat when Rogers had been checking out the truck and trailer.

The boy was looking right at him. But it was dark. He couldn't possibly—

Rogers's brain jolted and jerked and misfired under his skull. He had contemplated every possibility except this one.

He had no choice.

He lunged, grabbed the boy's arm, and pulled him out of the truck. The boy dropped the Happy Meal and was still screaming until Rogers placed a hand over his face. He squirmed and struggled, but as his lungs and brain were deprived of oxygen, his thrashing slowed.

Rogers counted in his head, his gaze not on the boy but on the dead Donohue, probably the boy's father.

Eight...nine...ten.

As soon as the boy fell limp, Rogers removed his hand. He checked the pulse. It was there. Weak, but the lungs were inflating, the small chest rising and falling.

He was alive.

Rogers stared down at the little boy. The hair was blond, the limbs stick thin. The back of his neck covered in large freckles.

Rogers's brain misfired again.

What was he doing?

You never left witnesses behind.

You never left anything living behind.

Just finish it. It would only take seconds.

Instead, he put the boy back in the front seat of the truck and closed the door. He pulled his knife free from the dead man and Donohue slumped to the dirt. He wiped it clean on the grass and stuck it back into its holder.

He hefted the box with the gun and ran back to his car, got in, and drove off. He hit the main road and punched the gas.

As he roared down the road he ran his hand over the box containing the M11-B.

A collector's item.

The vaunted M11.

More than thirty years ago a revolver had been held against his head for five minutes. Only the M11 wasn't a revolver; it was a semiautomatic with a magazine to hold its bullets.

That's why Rogers had not simply taken the revolver from the woman he'd killed in the alley.

Unlike a revolver, which could only fire once the cylinder with a bullet in it lined up with the hammer, a semi would fire if there was only one bullet in the mag or thirteen. You couldn't play Russian roulette with a mag pistol, not unless you wanted no chance to live.

And Rogers wanted no chance for the person to live.

He was fifty miles away now and still didn't know why he had not simply killed the child.

There had been something in his head that had held him back. He thought he knew all there was to know about what went on up there.

Obviously he'd been wrong about that.

As he fled east with the spoils of victory, Paul Rogers wondered what else he'd been wrong about.

CHAPTER

8

PULLER PASSED THROUGH Richmond, where Lynda Demirjian was spending her last days in hospice, and continued on south and east. He was in his Army-issued black Malibu, which he liked because it had no bells and whistles, just an engine, four wheels, and something to steer it with.

He drove fast down Interstate 64 and arrived in Hampton in time to check into a motel and grab a few hours' sleep.

He was up with the dawn. He grabbed a cup of coffee and a bagel from the breakfast room in the motel lobby, climbed into his Malibu, and drove on to Fort Monroe.

The installation had been decommissioned in 2011. Part of it had recently been designated a national monument by President Obama. It had been named after the fifth president, James Monroe. Surprisingly, the fort had remained in Union hands during the entire American Civil War and was the launch pad for General Grant's successful assaults on Petersburg and the Confederate capital in Richmond that had essentially ended the war. Former Confederate general Robert E. Lee had been quartered here when he was still with the United States Army. And Confederate president Jefferson Davis had been imprisoned at Fort Monroe following the war. A memorial park there bearing his name had subsequently been created in the 1950s.

Puller thought it must have been one of the few times a prisoner was honored with his very own park.

The fort, at the southern tip of the Virginia Peninsula, had guarded the navigational channel between Hampton Roads and the Chesapeake Bay since the early 1600s. The seven-sided fort was the largest stone fort ever constructed in the United States. It had officially opened and been named Fort Monroe in 1819. The fort was built to prevent any foreign enemy from landing there, marching up the coast to Washington, and burning the city down, as the British had done during the War of 1812.

Fort Wool was across the channel and had been erected so that crossing fields of fire across the water could be deployed. That meant that ships trying to get through here could not hug one side of the channel in order to escape a pounding from the shore guns.

It was all a moot point now. Fort Monroe had never been fired upon in nearly two hundred years, and had never fallen into enemy hands. And it never would unless the completely impossible happened and a foreign enemy managed it.

Or, thought Puller, if America had another civil war.

With the current political climate, he thought that a more likely scenario than the North Koreans coming ashore onto Virginia soil.

With the post closing, the Commonwealth of Virginia had been given back much of the land the fort occupied. Most of the residential property had been sold or leased, though the commercial real estate side had been slower to come around.

Puller drove down the causeway leading to the fort's entrance, passing red, rusting ships in the water with names like *Sassy Sarah*. He found a parking space near the massive Chamberlin Hotel, which was now a retirement community, and proceeded on foot. He had snagged the camera he used at crime scenes from his duffel and hung it around his neck.

The sun had risen and the salt air filled his lungs as his long gait ate up ground. He passed homes on the waterfront. The largest residence of all had been reserved for the four-stars who had lived at Fort Monroe. Next to it were slightly smaller homes where three- and two-star generals had dwelled.

The street was quiet, tree-lined, and filled on both sides with large (at least for military quarters) two-story brick homes with porches that ran the full length of their fronts.

He found the one he was looking for, on a corner. It had a large backyard and the grass was neatly cut. The house looked well maintained, but didn't look occupied.

Puller walked around the perimeter of the property until he reached the rear yard. He came to a spot pretty much in the center of the yard and thought back to that day.

He'd been outside playing. A ball and a glove.

His brother had been somewhere else, probably at the library reading a book.

His father was, as usual, gone.

So he'd been playing catch with himself. He had spent a lot of time by himself. His brother was intellectually advanced far beyond his age. He liked to think, not throw balls.

He turned and looked at the window in the middle of the rear of the house. That was his parents' bathroom.

That was where the face was. His mother's.

He squinted because he was facing east and the sun was coming up.

In the crevice of his eyes he could see her smiling at him. The towel wrapped around her head. The contented look on her face.

But was she content?

Where had she gone that night? When she believed her husband would not be home?

The answer hit him like a Ka-Bar in the gut. Another man?

He took pictures of everything he was looking at.

He heard the voice as soon as he snapped the last frame.

"Hello?"

Puller turned to see a man staring at him from the corner of the yard. He didn't like it that someone could get that close to him and he not be aware of it.

The man was about five-ten. He looked to be in his late seventies and his upper torso was thickened, but he was still in decent shape. His hair was white and thinning on top, his mustache more salt-and-pepper. He was dressed in khakis, loafers, and an Army green windbreaker.

Puller walked over to him and the face came more into focus. And then it clicked.

"Mr. Demirjian?"

Stan Demirjian came forward, but he didn't have the same level of recognition on his features.

Then it hit him. "My God. Are you one of the Puller boys?"

"John."

The men shook hands.

Demirjian said, "You look like your daddy. But you're even taller."

"You still look combat ready."

The man laughed. "As if." Then he stopped laughing and his features became somber. "I guess they told you."

"It's why I'm here."

"I can understand that. I drove over this morning just to have a look around at the old place. Never thought they'd shutter Fort Monroe. Not with all the history and everything. Captain John Smith discovered the place. Point Comfort. First slaves came through here, you know, traded for damn supplies Dutch skippers needed."

"But even DoD needs to get with the times and save money," Puller pointed out.

"Yes, they do. We lived here on post housing. Took about a year to get."

"Right."

Demirjian took on a wistful expression, as though he were peering deeply into the past. "Monroe was where the big dogs lived. One- and two-stars didn't even have entourages like at other installations. Walked the streets by themselves. A hundred full colonels here when most posts were lucky to have a dozen."

"It was special in that way."

"But your daddy didn't need no entourage. Man was a damn load to handle all by himself."

"I wouldn't dispute that."

The two men stared uncomfortably at each other.

Demirjian blurted out, "Look, I just want you to know right off that I don't agree with Lynda. But she was insistent. And she's . . ."

"I know about her medical condition and I'm very sorry. I only have really good memories of her from our time here. She's a fine lady. And I hold nothing against her."

"That's real nice of you to say, John. Lynda's been a wonderful wife and mother and grandmother. But she just wouldn't let this go."

"When did it start?"

"About three months ago. Out of the blue. We'd just moved her into a facility to help her...needs."

"And she just started talking about my mother and father?"

"You have to understand, John..." He paused. "Heard you were in the Army too."

"CWO, 701st MP Group out of Quantico."

"That's an elite group," said Demirjian. "You get nominated for that group, not selected."

"Yes sir."

The older man waved off this form of address. "I never got the sir when I was in uniform because I wasn't an officer. And I sure don't deserve it now, Chief Puller."

"You were a top-notch SFC. Dad always said so. And as you know, he was a tough man to please. And call me John."

Demirjian looked around. "I remember coming over and barbecuing in this backyard. You and your brother running around playing Army soldiers. It was in your blood."

"You were a good friend to Dad. And to us."

"I would have run through a wall for your father, John. Hell, I *did* run through a wall for him. A wall of ground fire, mortar rounds, even napalm dropped by our fly guys. Happened about five times a day in 'Nam. And your daddy was right there beside me every time. And he was already a lieutenant colonel at that point. He didn't have to be running with the grunts like that." He rubbed his chin and continued. "When he got his second star they made him commander of the 101st. Best leader the Screaming Eagles ever had in my humble opinion. Then he got his corps command when they pinned on the third star."

"Helluva career," said Puller. He felt a bit awkward, unsure where this trip through his father's past was supposed to lead.

Demirjian looked down at his shoes for a few moments. "I have no idea what set off the notion in Lynda's head about all this. She was moved to the hospice part of the facility a month ago. That's when she told me she wanted to let the authorities know about this. That about gave me a heart attack. I begged her to just drop it. Thirty years ago? Who would remember anything? And your father and the way he is? Not able to really defend himself?"

"So you know about that?"

Demirjian stared over at Puller, his features crumbling. "I visited him up where he is now."

"I didn't know that," said Puller.

"This was about a year ago. He wasn't himself anymore. But he remembered me. He remembered some of the old days."

"He did back then. Not so much anymore."

Demirjian shook his head. "I'm one tough son of a bitch and I left that place bawling my eyes out. To see your daddy like that..."

Puller didn't say anything. He let Demirjian regain his composure, rub at his moistened eyes, and then continue.

"But Lynda wouldn't let it go. If I didn't help her she'd just get someone else to do it. That's what she said. Well, I figured that it would be better coming from my hand, so to speak." He glanced up at Puller. "Did they show you the letter?"

"They did."

"Well, I softened the tone a lot. I'm sure it still shocked the hell out of you, but her words, well, they were far harsher than what I wrote in that letter. Part of me felt like I was betraying my wife for doing that."

"It would be an awkward situation for anyone, Mr. Demirjian, and especially so for you. I wouldn't want to be in that spot."

"I don't want you to believe for one second that I agree with my wife on this, because I don't. But she's dying, John, and this was so important to her. I didn't want to open a can of worms for your daddy. He's the last man on earth I'd ever want to hurt. But like I said, if I didn't do it, Lynda would have found someone else."

"I understand." Puller paused and considered carefully his next words. "Do you think it would be possible for me to talk to her?"

"I thought you might ask that."

"I don't want to do it if it will upset her. I mean that."

"I don't think much could upset her now. And she's one tough woman. I wore the uniform, but she raised seven kids on an enlisted man's pay, largely on her own because I was always gone. And we moved fourteen times while the kids were growing up. I wonder which one of us is the real tough one?"

"So I *can* speak to her?"

"Way I see it, she's started all this. Now it has to be seen through. And he's your daddy. You have some rights in the matter."

"Thank you."

"I'll make the arrangements. You can come over later this morning. It takes her a while to get going these days. Give me your phone number and I'll call you in a bit."

Puller did so.

As the men walked back to their cars Demirjian said, "Could you give your daddy my best next time you see him?"

"I sure will."

"He doesn't know about this, does he?"

"No. I'm not sure he's in a position right now to understand it anyway."

"Maybe that's for the best."

"Maybe it is," agreed Puller.

"And I'm sure any investigation they do will clear your daddy absolutely and completely."

As Puller climbed back into his car, he wasn't nearly as certain of that as the old soldier was.

CHAPTER

9

WHEN PULLER RETURNED to his motel room he called his brother. Robert Puller answered on the second ring.

"Please don't tell me you're investigating this," Robert said immediately.

"Good morning to you too, big brother."

"It's the afternoon here. Where are you?"

"In Virginia."

"Right. Where in Virginia? Fort Monroe, perhaps?"

"You got a satellite tracking me?"

"No, but I can have one deployed. Or I can follow the chip in your phone. Or you can save me the paperwork and the cost of the sat time and tell me yourself."

"I just spoke to Stan Demirjian."

"Oh, you just happened to run into him," said Robert sarcastically.

"Actually, I did. I came down to look at our old quarters and there he was."

"You're shitting me."

"I'm going to talk to his wife later today. She's in hospice."

"And what exactly do you expect to gain from doing that?"

"Some answers, maybe."

"CID will have your ass if they know you're inserting yourself into this matter."

"They never ordered me off the case. And besides, I'm not here professionally. But it is my dad, so I don't see why I can't follow up on my end."

"You know the Army doesn't make distinctions like that. When you wear the uniform you don't have a 'personal' life. It's Army green all the way."

"I'm still going to talk to her."

"And she'll tell you that she believed that Dad killed Mom. So why bother?"

"I want to hear it from her, Bobby. The letter was the watered-down version, or so Stan told me."

"So you're going to interrogate a terminally ill woman about events from three decades ago?"

"I'm just going to listen. And she was the one who brought it up."

"And then what?"

"I don't know. I haven't really formulated a plan yet."

"The Army might formulate one for you. As in a court-martial."

"I haven't disobeyed any orders because I haven't been given any orders. I'm on leave, free to do what I want."

"As long as you're in uniform you are not free to do what you want. You know that!"

"Thanks for the lecture," barked Puller.

"John, I'm just telling you to be really careful about this—"

"Let's cut to the chase," Puller said, interrupting. "Do you believe that Dad did it?"

"How the hell am I supposed to answer that question? I don't know!"

"I think you suspect him."

"What do *you* think?"

"I think our parents loved each other and Dad would never have laid a hand on her."

Robert didn't answer this right away. In fact the silence drew on for so long that Puller thought he might have disconnected.

"Bobby? Did you hear wha—"

"I *heard*, John."

"And?"

"And time has a way of selecting memories we keep and memories we discard. At least for most people. The way I'm wired I remember pretty much everything as it actually happened, I guess, for better or worse."

"And what is that supposed to mean?" said Puller sharply.

"I thought it was fairly straightforward. I gotta go, John. I've got three-stars waiting on me. Just try not to crater your career, okay?"

The line went dead.

Puller stared down at the phone.

Selecting memories? What the hell was that about?

* * *

An hour later Stan Demirjian called. And three hours after that Puller was walking down the hall in the facility where Lynda Demirjian had come to die. A nurse escorted him.

Stan Demirjian had elected not to attend this meeting. Puller could not blame him. The old sergeant probably would have elected to try to retake Hamburger Hill over hearing his wife tell Puller his father was a murderer.

The nurse opened the door and ushered Puller in before leaving. Puller looked over at the bed. There was an IV stand and a monitoring unit and lines running from them to the shrunken form lying in the bed. The passage of three decades plus the terminal cancer had taken their toll on the woman.

Puller looked around the small room. It mirrored the one his father was currently occupying. He wondered what was worse: knowing that you were dying, or being oblivious to it?

He pulled up a chair and sat down next to the bed.

"Mrs. Demirjian?"

The woman moved a bit, her head turned toward him, and her eyes opened.

"Who are you?" she said in a croaky voice.

"John Puller, *Junior*."

Her eyes opened wide for a moment and then returned to slits, as though the lights overhead were too painful to fully engage.

"Last time I saw you, you were just a little boy."

"Yes ma'am."

Puller glanced at the bags on the IV stand and watched the liquids from them trickling through the lines terminating at a port in Demirjian's arm. From there they went into her bloodstream. He felt sure one of them was morphine.

"You're here...about...my letter."

"Yes ma'am."

"I loved Jackie very much. I respected her more than anyone I've ever known."

As did most with that name Jacqueline Puller had gone by Jackie. She also physically resembled Jackie Kennedy.

"And I know she liked you."

"I...I'm sure you aren't happy about what I've done." Her words marched slowly out of her mouth. Puller assumed that was just the way it would be with all the meds she was probably on.

"I would just like to understand it better."

"Did you read . . . it?"

"I did."

"What would you like to know?"

"You said in the letter that my parents fought a lot."

"They did."

"But I don't recall any of that."

"Do you remember when your mother would bring you and your brother over to my house?"

"Yes."

"That was so you . . . wouldn't see them fighting."

"How do you know that?"

"Your mother would tell me."

"But how would she know beforehand that they were going to fight?"

"Because your father was coming home from deployment. They always fought then."

Puller leaned back in his chair. "What would they fight about?"

"Mostly, your father wanting to control every part of her life."

Her voice had grown stronger the more she talked. She even boosted herself up a bit on her pillow.

She turned her head to the side and looked at him. "I know you don't want to hear this. I can imagine that to you, your father walked on water."

"My dad had faults," Puller said uncomfortably. "He could be rough."

"Yes, he could be. He was rough with Jackie."

"He never abused my mother."

Puller had raised his voice and then felt incredible guilt. The woman was dying.

"I'm sorry."

"Don't be. Your father was a hard man, John. He was used to commanding men in the most difficult thing there is, combat. He was used to whatever he said being done. That doesn't work in a marriage. That didn't work with your mother. In some ways she was even more strong-willed than her husband."

"But why would you think he would kill her?"

"Because Jackie was afraid of him. She was afraid he would do something to her." She paused for breath. "And your mother was thinking about leaving him."

Puller froze. "She was going to leave my father?"

"She wanted custody of you and your brother."

"She told you that?"

"She told me a lot of things, John."

Puller sat down again. "My mother went out that night. Did she come to see you?"

"No."

"Do you know where she was going or who she might have been going to see?"

"She had several other friends among the officers' wives. It might have been one of them."

"Might she have confided in them too?"

"It's possible. She was a very private person, your mother. But she was also getting desperate."

"Did the CID talk to you back then?"

"They came by and asked their questions, like you are now. But I could tell they were not focused on your father. They said he was out of the country."

Puller did not mention that Hull had found evidence to contradict this belief.

"Go on."

"Well, I told them that the Pullers had a marriage like many others. They fought. And they made up."

"You didn't tell them of the abuse? About her wanting to leave him and take my brother and me? That would have been a pretty powerful motive for killing her."

"No, I didn't tell them that."

"Why not?"

"Because my husband was in your father's command and wouldn't hear any words against him," she said bluntly.

"So you withheld information from the CID because of your husband?"

The words, perhaps now fueled by the meds instead of inhibited by them, came out in rush. "It was different back then. *I* was different. I had seven kids to raise. And I couldn't do anything that would jeopardize Stan's career. He was the breadwinner in the family, John. So, no, I didn't really tell them what I thought or knew."

"So why did you raise it all now?"

She ran a hand over her forehead and Puller could see that it was shaking.

She said, "I'm a devout Catholic. All of my children were raised in the Catholic faith. I've attended Mass every week for as long as I can remember." She paused to catch her breath. "So I cannot go to my death without doing something to right a great wrong. I wanted to avenge my friend."

"Your husband doesn't agree with you."

"Stan didn't know anything about it. Jackie would never have confided in him. And besides, like I said, he would never have heard a word against your father."

Puller could understand that this would very likely be true.

"But why are you sure that he harmed her? I mean, you must have been to write that letter all these years later."

Once more she lifted herself up on the pillow and focused on him.

"I said that the CID never focused on your father because he was out of the country."

"Right."

"Well, that was wrong. He was not out of the country. He was in Hampton on that day."

Puller felt his chest tighten. "How do you know that?"

"Because I saw him!"

"Where? How?"

"I was out running an errand. I saw your father drive down the street. He wasn't in your family car. He was driving another Army-issued vehicle."

"You're sure it was him?"

"I was six feet from him. He didn't see me but I saw him. And he looked quite upset."

"What time was this?"

"Around two-thirty in the afternoon."

Puller let out a breath. "Why didn't you tell the CID agents?"

She dropped back onto her pillow and shook her head. "I told Stan. But he told me I had to have been mistaken. He showed me your father's official schedule. It showed he was in Germany for another day. I guess he convinced me that I was wrong." She shook her head wearily. "But I knew I wasn't wrong. It *was* your father." She paused and gasped, "And that's why I wrote the letter."

Puller wanted to keep going but he could see that the woman was quickly tiring. And really, what more could she tell him? His father *had* been in town that day. He rose. "I appreciate your meeting with me. I really do."

Lynda Demirjian put out a hand, which Puller gently took.

"I'm sorry it came to this, John. It just seemed to me to be the right thing to do."

"I understand. Do you need anything?"

She shook her head. "When you get to the point I'm at, how much do you really need anyway? But I've got my faith. So I'm in a good place."

Puller quietly left the room and walked slowly down the hall. His spirits didn't brighten when he reached the sunshine outside. They actually faded.

Fights? Abuse? He and his brother shuttled off to friends so they wouldn't hear? His mother leaving his father?

It was like he had been listening to someone else's life. Someone else's childhood. This is what his brother must have meant about selective memory. He and Bobby couldn't have been shuttled off every time his parents had fought. That would have been impossible. So he must have witnessed some of it.

He walked to his car and leaned against the front fender. He sunk his chin to his chest and closed his eyes.

Somewhere in the dimmest recollections he had were buried things that apparently he would no longer allow himself to remember.

So how could he ever find the truth if he couldn't even admit it to himself?

CHAPTER

10

Paul Rogers opened his eyes and looked at the ceiling of his car. He had crossed into Virginia last night. It was now early morning.

And he had just realized he'd made a big mistake. In addition to letting the little boy live.

I hit the son of a bitch too hard. I killed Donohue too hard.

His hand slid to the knife in the holder on his belt.

How many inches through the chest? Donohue was big, thickset.

And the knife blade had hit the wall of the trailer and sunk into it, pinning Donohue to the wood.

He groaned, rubbed his eyes, climbed over into the front seat, started the car, and drove off.

He didn't have to do it that way. He could have struck with half as much force and killed the man. But he couldn't undo it, so he forgot about it.

He needed new wheels. If anyone had seen this car come out of the dirt road where the body and the boy were it would not be too good for him.

He drove his car behind a strip mall that was not yet open for business. He grabbed his bag, and put the vintage M11 into it. He tossed the box the gun was in inside a Dumpster, unscrewed the license plates from the car, slid them into his bag next to the gun, and walked off.

He slept under a bridge, awoke the next morning, and set out on foot. About an hour later he reached a small town in mountainous southwest Virginia. He found the local library, sat at a computer terminal, went online, and typed in a name.

Ballard Enterprises.

He got back a number of hits, some related to what he wanted and others not.

The company he was interested in had changed its name years back. It was now known as CB Excelon Corp. Chris Ballard had founded and run the eponymous Ballard Enterprises. When he tracked the man down online, Rogers found that he was still the chairman emeritus of Excelon, but had turned over the day-to-day operations to others. And Excelon's focus was now cyber security.

Thirty years ago it'd had an entirely different focus.

Rogers rose and left. He had printed out a picture of Ballard. It wasn't a recent one. The man was still in his fifties in the photo, the age when Rogers had known him. He wanted to know what he looked like now, but he had not been able to find a recent picture. Rogers hoped the man hadn't aged well.

Like I haven't.

But he wasn't chiefly interested in Ballard. There was someone else. A woman. He had not found her name in any of the materials. That did not unduly surprise him. Back then she liked to stay in the background. He imagined that hadn't changed.

He was hungry so he found a place to eat a block over from the library. Eggs, bacon, biscuits, and grits washed down with hot coffee.

This was a coal mining town. Rogers could see this in the

bent, blackened, and exhausted-looking men who came and went, the trucks hauling the black rock down the streets, the mile-long trains carrying the mineral long-distance, and the various plants parked around the area that dealt with turning the chunks of rock into electricity in faraway places.

He had read in a newspaper in prison that coal was dying. It looked like it was very much alive here.

He walked around the town, observing all the time. He was looking for something in particular, and many hours later he found it.

The white panel van pulled up to the bar with flashing neon signs and two men got out and went inside. Rogers followed.

The place was full. It was one of the few he'd seen in town that promised a bit of fun in the face of geographical isolation and backbreaking labor. Line dancing, nonstop drinking, pool, and video games.

Men and women hooked up and then parted. Glasses were lifted to mouths and slammed back down on the scarred wood of the bar. Pool balls were hit, aliens were killed on wide screens, and lips locked and bodies curved around each other in semiprivate nooks and crannies.

The two men hung their jackets on hooks on the wall and went directly to the bar. They were both big-bellied men with huge, callused hands and trim beards. Their hardscrabble lives were bolted onto every inch of them.

One of them had a knife in a holder on his belt. The other was armed only with a smile and hands that groped any woman who came within striking distance.

Rogers went to the bathroom. When he came back out he moved over against the wall to allow a group of drunken women to pass by on their way to the ladies' room to fix their makeup and perhaps their reputations.

His hand snuck into first the right and then the left pockets of the men's jackets. He cupped the car keys, watched the dancing for a bit, and then left.

He got into the van, started it up, and pulled off. He stopped outside of town to change out the plates.

He had already checked the van for distinguishing marks. There were none. It was relatively new. There were a million just like this one.

The name on the registration was Buford Atkins.

Well, Mr. Atkins would have to find new wheels.

The back of the van was filled with tools, both hand and power, and several pairs of work overalls. All that might actually come in handy.

Rogers drove for six hours, covering about one hundred and fifty miles. It was slow going because the roads were two-lane for the most part, twisting and loaded with switchbacks as he made his way through a chunk of the tree-laden Appalachians. He longed for a straight shot at interstate speeds, but that was still a ways off according to the map he'd found in the glove box.

He pulled off, slept for a few hours, and got back on the road. He finally hit the interstate and headed east. An hour later he stopped to eat.

He pulled out the photograph of Chris Ballard. Brilliant guy, Rogers had to give him that. Far ahead of his time.

But the woman who liked to stay in the background was even smarter than Ballard. In her twenties back then, she was head and shoulders above all others at the company in sheer brainpower and vision.

She would be in her late fifties now. He wondered where she was.

In fact, he was obsessing over that question.

Claire Jericho.

He hadn't said the name out loud in thirty years.

He reached down with his finger and nudged the ring. Jericho had given it to him. He had memorized the inscription carved on the inside of the band.

For the good of all.

Right.

She could be anywhere. She could even be dead. If so, he wanted to see her grave as confirmation.

And then he might dig through the earth with his bare hands, force open the coffin, and pulverize to dust whatever was left of her in there. If she was alive then he would send the woman to her grave.

He got back into the van and drove away.

A police car pulled up next to him at a stoplight. The officer glanced over.

Rogers kept his gaze straight ahead. He had no driver's license and the van was stolen. He had a knife that still held trace amounts of a dead man's blood. He had a stolen gun in his car that had belonged to the man he'd killed. He was wanted for a parole violation all the way across the country. He quietly contemplated how he would kill the cop if he pulled him over.

Luckily for the policeman, he pulled off when the light turned green.

Rogers accelerated slowly, and soon the cop car was out of sight.

He rubbed the back of his head. He did not want to confront the fact that the pains in his head were increasing and that they were also feeling different than they had previously.

What if my head explodes before I accomplish what I set out to do?

He flexed first his right arm and then his left. His knife wound was healing nicely.

His eyes scanned ahead. His night vision was better than his day vision, but the latter was still acceptable.

He cleared the mountains and entered the central part of the state. In another three hours he reached the Tidewater region of Virginia.

Then he pulled to a stop.

Fort Monroe was directly in front of him.

It was early in the morning. There was no one else around.

He had learned while he was in prison that Fort Monroe had been decommissioned.

That didn't matter to him.

All Paul Rogers knew was that, after all these years, he was finally home.

CHAPTER

11

He WENT BACK to the well once more. The water was still fresh.

His brother never forgot a damn thing.

The email had been returned within minutes.

Babysitter was Carol Andrews. Her father was Captain Russell Andrews in the Old Man's command. You know how to track that.

Puller did indeed know how to track that.

Uncle Sam always knew where former career soldiers were, for two very precise reasons: military pensions and health care benefits.

Puller accessed another secure database and discovered that Russell Andrews had retired as a full colonel and lived in Florida on the Atlantic side. He got Andrews's phone number and called him. After a few minutes of reminiscing and Andrews's asking about his former commander, Puller was able to learn that his daughter Carol, now forty-seven, was married with three teenage children of her own and lived in Richmond. Her married name was Powers.

The next call was to her. She didn't answer, but he left a message and she called him back a few minutes later.

"Talk about a voice from the past," she said.

"I'm sure you never expected to hear from me."

"I can't say that I did. I did hear about what happened with your brother, Bobby. I was glad that he was exonerated. I never believed he had done any of that."

"Thanks for keeping the faith."

"So what can I do for you?"

"My dad's in a bad way and I guess I've come to the point in my life where I just want to see things with a bit more clarity."

"I'm very sorry about your dad, but I don't know exactly what you mean."

"Carol, it wasn't until my brother told me that I remembered that you were over watching us the night my mom disappeared."

"Oh, God, John, I didn't know that. It was the most awful time. I still get the shakes thinking about it."

"Well, I'm a CID agent now and the case has never been solved, and I've decided I'm going to look into it."

"Oh, okay. Now I see what you meant. What do you want to know?"

"Pretty much everything. Because apparently I had what Bobby called selective memory when it came to all of it."

"Well, cut yourself some slack. You were just a little boy. So go ahead and ask your questions. It might be easier that way."

"So my mother went out that night?"

"Yes. I was going out that night too, but my boyfriend at the time called and canceled on me. He was always doing that, which is why I finally broke up with him."

"So you came over at what time?"

"Oh, jeez, let me think. It was so long ago."

"A ballpark is okay."

"Well, it was after I had my dinner, that I do remember. So, say seven?"

"Do you know where she was going?"

"No, she didn't say. She did say she expected to be home around ten or so."

"So she was definitely coming back?"

"Of course she was. What, did you think she was going to abandon you and Bobby?"

"But she didn't come back," said Puller slowly.

"I know," said Carol somberly. "Ten came and went. And then eleven. And then midnight. I called my mom and told her what was going on. There were no cell phones or anything like that back then. My mom didn't know what to do. But my dad was home and he called the MPs. Then he came over to stay with me and you and your brother. I remember every hour that went by I thought she would walk in the door. But she never did. The MPs took my statement. Then I guess they followed that up and searched for her."

"And my father?"

"He showed up that morning. We had brought you and Bobby to our house for the time being. I remember him bursting in our front door like he'd been fired out of a howitzer. He talked with my father, and then the MPs came by to talk to him. I wasn't party to any of that." She paused. "You say you don't remember any of that?"

"Not until now."

"Well, it might have been a defense mechanism, John. The brain is tricky. It can do stuff to protect us."

"What did you think happened to my mother?"

"There was a lot of speculation."

"Like what?"

Puller heard her clear her throat nervously. He said, "I've heard the rumors, Carol. About my parents not getting along."

"I want you to know that I never saw any of that, but I

wasn't really around when they were there together either."
She paused. "But I have to admit that some people thought
she might have left him, although I knew she would never
walk out on her sons. I'm not surprised that you wouldn't
have known about that. Adults aren't going to talk to little
boys about stuff like that."

"Was it that bad between them?"

"I don't know, John. I've been married for twenty-two
years and have three kids. My husband and I have had our
ups and downs, even gone into counseling a few times. And
I have to admit, some days I think about chucking it all. But
I never really would, because my kids are everything to me."
She paused and added, "And I do know that your mother
loved you and your brother more than anything."

"She said that to you?"

"She didn't have to. She showed it in the way she was
around you two. As a mother I know what to look for now.
Jackie adored you both."

Puller couldn't say anything for a few moments. "I appreciate you telling me that."

"So I can also tell you that the reason she didn't come
home that night had nothing to do with either of you."

"What about my father?"

Now Carol didn't say anything for a few moments. "I'm
not sure what you're suggesting."

"I've heard people *suggest* that my father might have
been the reason my mother didn't come home that night."

"But he wasn't even in town. At least that's what I was
told."

"What if he were? Was there scuttlebutt about that?"

"Not in my house. But then again, my dad thought your
father walked on water."

"My dad had that effect on people he commanded." He

paused, forming his next question. "Carol, how was my mom dressed that night?"

"Dressed?"

"Yeah, casual or... ?"

"Oh, no, not casual. Nice dress, heels, panty hose, some jewelry, her hair done up, makeup and everything. She was really beautiful. I remember thinking as she walked out the door that she was really put together. Funny, I remember that so vividly. But teenage girls are very much into clothes and accessories. I can tell you from experiences with my two daughters that *that* hasn't changed."

"So where could she have been going all dressed up like that?"

Carol didn't answer right away. "Well, it might have been some function. Or maybe dinner with a friend."

"But that would have come out in the investigation."

"I guess that's true. There weren't many places around back then to go dancing or drinking or anything," she said slowly. "Not that she would have anyway," she added hurriedly. "I meant for single people."

"Right. Not for *married* people."

I wonder if she was dressed to impress someone? Another man, maybe? And if my dad found out? Followed her?

He said, "So did you know some of the ladies back then who were her friends? Someone she might have confided in?"

"I'd have to give that some thought. My mother would have been one, of course."

"Your dad told me she had passed away a few years ago. I'm sorry."

"Thanks. That's the price of loving someone. You get ripped apart when they leave you."

Don't I know that, thought Puller.

She said, "I might be able to dig up a name and call you back. My family kept in touch with several of the folks at Fort Monroe."

"I'd appreciate it."

Puller gave her his number.

"Oh, John?"

"Yeah?"

"I hope you find whatever it is you're looking for."

"Me too."

CHAPTER

12

Paul Rogers had walked around the perimeter of Fort Monroe. He had done this a dozen times now and saw things on the last circuit that he had failed to see on the first. In some ways the place looked like a Hollywood back-lot set of a small town. The only thing missing was the film crew and actors.

This had been his playground of sorts thirty years ago. He'd been in his twenties, alone, confused, intimidated.

He was still alone. But he was no longer confused or intimidated.

He eyed the terreplein that ran around the fort. He had often run around this strip of grass and knew that it was one point two miles in length. Constructed over a sixteen-year period, the fort, also known as "the Gibraltar of the Chesapeake," had walls that extended over a mile and encompassed over sixty acres of land. The old rusted gun mounts could still be seen. These were the Endicott batteries that had replaced the cannon in the fort. Rifled barrels had led to the fortress cannons being rendered obsolete. Ships could fire from a long way away and the cannon could not match that range. The Endicott batteries had been brought in to fix that problem. Then with the invention of the airplane even the Endicotts became obsolete. After that the strategic and operational attributes of the fort were pretty much exhausted. It became more administrative and focused on "training and doctrine" after that, and indeed became the Army's center for those two intertwined disciplines.

As he looked down at the water in the moat, Rogers could see that nearly two hundred years of silt buildup had shortened the depth, already fairly shallow, to the point where at low tide he could see a sandbar.

He stared out over the narrow channel where the USS *Monitor* and the CSS *Virginia* had fought the first naval duel between ironclads. The channel was shallow and the deeper part was on the Fort Monroe side, so the ships coming in would hug the shore there. He remembered that the aircraft carriers would come so close to land they would shade the parade grounds.

Back then Rogers had learned as much about Fort Monroe's history as he could. Across that same channel three slaves had rowed across at the start of the Civil War and asked for refuge. The garrison commander, Major General Benjamin Butler, had agreed. When the Confederates, under a white flag, had shown up and demanded their return under the recently passed federal law about runaway slaves, Butler, a former lawyer, had given the rebels a lesson in the nuances of the law. Since they had seceded from the United States, Butler told them, they were no longer entitled to the protections of federal law. And since the slaves were being used in the war effort against the Union, Butler was treating them as contraband to be kept by the United States. Word of this reached the ears of many slaves, and thousands ended up seeking refugee status as "contraband" in what became known as "Freedom's Fortress."

Rogers's walk had taken him past the Old Point Comfort

Lighthouse. It had been built in 1802 and still worked, making it the oldest working lighthouse on the Chesapeake Bay.

Rogers remembered it well. As part of his training he had been required to climb the sheer walls of the lighthouse all the way up to the top railing. In the dead of night no less.

He had succeeded. He could remember standing on top of the lighthouse looking out at the vastness of the bay and the ocean beyond and thinking that his future was truly limitless. That he was special, when he never had been before.

On his walk Rogers saw the old arsenal that had made bullets and bombs for the Union. He passed the stone and arch-windowed St. Mary's Church where he had worshipped as a young man. A far different young man.

Afterward, he had not wanted to worship anything or anyone. It was all changed. *He* was all changed.

He clambered up on top of a wall to see the Chesapeake Bay better. He had spent days out there treading water, swimming, surviving in all possible weather. They had pushed him. Broken him. Rebuilt him.

And broken him again.

He hopped down off the wall.

After a while they hadn't bothered to fix him anymore.

He rubbed his head. But the pains were now more consistent and more frequent. He didn't know why. He walked back to the van and drove off, passing by a row of officers' quarters.

A world of memories had flooded back to him as soon as he had seen Fort Monroe. But none like the ones he had recollected when he stopped in front of what was known back then as Building Q. It was set off in a remote part of the fort. It had large buffers of empty land around it. There was a high perimeter fence with concertina wire. There were gates

with armed guards. Their job had been to keep some folks
out and other folks in.

He was one of the *other folks*.

Unlike many of the large commercial-sized buildings
around here, Building Q was not empty. The parking lot inside the fence was full of cars. The lights inside were on. As
he watched, someone came out of a side door, moved away
from the building, and lit up a cigarette.

The concertina wire remained on top of the fence. The
gates were manned by armed guards. He wondered if the
electronic security system was still active.

He didn't think about this for a casual reason.

He was coming back to break into the place.

After that Rogers was pretty certain of his strategy.

As he watched, the smoker threw down the butt of his
cigarette and walked back to the door. He used a key card
access to gain entry, pulled open the door, and went back to
whatever work he was doing inside.

So there is electronic security as well.

Rogers had seen enough for now. He left the fort and
went in search of work that paid cash and required no filling
out of any papers. He was tired of sleeping in cars. It might
be nice to have a bed. And a bathroom not connected to a
gas station.

As he left Fort Monroe he felt a sense of peace that he
had not experienced in a very long time.

It was a good feeling. Normally, he only thought about
hurting and killing. It was not his fault.

It was just the way he was wired.

Only others had done the wiring.

CHAPTER

13

Puller looked at the email, deciding whether or not to open it.

It had information he needed.

But it was also information that part of him didn't want to confront.

Shireen Kirk had not wasted any time. She must have already informed CID that she was representing John Puller Sr. And she had no doubt requested this documentation.

CID, being efficient even with a file three decades old, had promptly sent it to her. The fact that Shireen was a longtime JAG lawyer and knew pretty much everyone who mattered at all in the criminal investigative branches of the various services had surely aided her effort.

Nobody wanted to screw with Shireen Kirk, regardless of whether she still wore the uniform or not. She'd file a motion faster than you could discharge your sidearm.

After the drive from Fort Monroe, Puller sat down in a chair in his motel room and opened the file on his laptop.

The case heading for the file was daunting right off the bat.

Investigation into the disappearance of Jacqueline Puller.

He ran his finger over the letters of his mother's full name.

Jacqueline Elizabeth Puller.

Formally correct, though he had called her nothing other than Mom for the eight years he had had her as a mother.

After that? He had rarely used the term at all.

For several years when he was growing up, people would come up to him, their features full of sadness, and tell them how bad they felt for his loss.

He had no doubt they were being sincere, but for a little boy it was way too much to deal with. And Puller had started running the other way when folks headed toward him with "that look."

His father had not spoken of his wife from that day on. The family had just continued to exist with an enormously important piece of their world simply gone without any reason given.

Puller and his brother would speak of it sometimes, first as boys and then as men. But as the years passed and no word was ever heard about their mother, they began to talk less and less of her.

In his heart Puller felt sure that both his father and his brother believed that Jacqueline Puller had abandoned them and run off to a new and better life.

And that would be better, he thought, than his father's having killed her.

However, she had left no note, taken none of her clothes or other possessions. She had prepared dinner for them, arranged for a babysitter, and walked out the door, never to return.

As an investigator, Puller knew that when folks planned to leave—and he had traced several who had done so—they usually left some sort of note. If there were kids and it was the mother leaving, she invariably took the kids with her.

They also took a suitcase with clothes and other essentials. And they normally took the car. And they cleaned out bank accounts and maxed out ATM withdrawals.

His mother had done none of those things.

He believed she was planning to come back that night. But something had prevented her from doing so.

Or someone.

He read through the report, word by word, page by page. And then he read it twice more.

Pertinent people were questioned. Answers were received.

A few tangential leads had been run down.

And that was it.

Abject failure.

In less than two weeks.

Puller wondered if his father's status as the husband had had anything to do with the truncated investigation. Had they wondered if Puller Sr. had been involved and just didn't want to go there?

Perspectives about domestic abuse were different thirty years ago. Wife beaters were given time to cool off and sent back to battered women who were too scared to press charges. What was clearly illegal now was tolerated back then. A wink, a nod, a look the other way.

On an Army post three decades back Puller assumed things were different too. But to be fair, the CID back then was not aware that Puller Sr. had arrived home in time to possibly be involved in his wife's disappearance. He had not been a suspect.

Now, technically, he was.

Puller took out a notebook and a pen.

He needed to get a name from Carol Powers. One of his mother's friends whom he could talk to. That might lead to something else.

He needed to trace his mother's movements on the day of her disappearance.

He needed to see if there was any truth to the rumor that she was going to leave her husband.

He needed to find out why she was dressed up that night. Was it a date? Was it a function? If so, CID had been unable to determine what it was.

He put his pen down and closed his eyes, focusing his thoughts on the last day with his mother. The face in the window. The smile. Everything seemed good. That was not the expression of a woman about to abruptly change her life by walking out on her family.

Puller opened his eyes. He had learned that not only did time heal wounds, but it also played with memories. People often rejiggered memories to match what they wanted the past to look like, rather than how it actually had been.

He took the picture out of his wallet. It showed the three Puller men all in a row. Puller was the tallest, his father next in height, and his brother, at six-two, bringing up the rear. Age and deteriorating health had robbed Puller Sr. of two inches of his stature, so he would now be last in the height pecking order.

But Puller was looking to the left of the picture. Where his mother would have been standing had she still been with them.

This was the only family picture Puller had ever carried with him. In combat overseas, on every mission he had performed on behalf of the U.S. Army. On every investigation he had carried out as a CID agent.

He had no pictures of his mother.

He had had no choice in the matter.

His father had found and destroyed them all.

Puller slowly put the photo away, closed his eyes, and refocused...on that day.

The face at the window. Him playing outside. The smile.

A bead of sweat appeared on his forehead.

Come on, John. More happened. Bobby knows. Get past whatever is in your head blocking it. See it for how it really was.

He sat there for five more minutes, straining, his eyes scrunched so tightly closed that his pupils started to feel sore.

His eyes popped open and he sat there.

The wall had held.

He couldn't get through it.

He rose. Well, if not in his head, then with his boots on the ground.

One way or another he was going to finally get to the truth.

14

On the way to his car his phone buzzed. It was Carol Powers.

"Okay," she began. "It took a few phone calls, but I finally found Lucy Bristow."

"Lucy Bristow?"

"You probably don't remember her. She was friends with both our moms. They all volunteered at the Catholic church at Fort Monroe. St. Mary's."

"Okay. That was fast work. How'd you manage it?"

She laughed. "Women do these things differently from men. We keep phone numbers and addresses, and the ladies' network is a little more sophisticated than the beer-and-football phone circle. And we tend to keep in touch with each other."

"I guess that's right."

"She was around your mother's age. Her husband was under your father's command. Anyway, I just talked to her. She lives in Richmond now. Not that far away. And she said she'd talk to you."

"Did she remember anything from that day?"

"I didn't ask. I think it's better that she tells you directly, John."

"Okay, Carol, thank you. I really appreciate this."

She gave him the contact information and then clicked off.

Puller called Bristow and she agreed to meet with him later that day.

He drove off, heading northwest toward Virginia's capital city.

Part of him felt like he was playing the children's game of hot and cold. The farther away from Fort Monroe he drove, the colder the trail seemed to become. He assumed that whatever had happened to his mother, the answers would lie here. But to get to that point he would travel wherever he needed to.

Five minutes after he hit the highway his phone buzzed. He saw the caller ID. It was his CO, Don White.

He hesitated, not really wanting to answer and be told something he didn't want to hear.

But his training took over and he answered. In the Army your CO calls and you just pick up the phone no matter what. Otherwise, you would not be in the Army much longer. You'd be in a stockade.

"Yes sir?"

"Puller, got a call from the Twelfth MPs."

"Yes sir?"

"They filled me in on what's going on."

Puller felt his gut tighten a notch. "They came to see me when I was with my father."

"They told me that too. Agent Hull seems competent. I checked his record. Not a mark on it."

"I'm sure. He seemed good to me too."

"Damn shame all this is coming out now."

"Damn shame," parroted Puller.

"You got a couple days' leave, right?"

"Yes sir."

"You worked your ass off in Germany. Nailed those suckers to the wall."

"Thank you, sir. I had a good team over there. A lot of support."

"Right. Anyway, I was thinking you probably needed a little more R&R than a couple days. Go ahead and take a week. Check in when you can."

Puller could barely believe what he was hearing. "A week?"

"Check in. If you need longer, let me know. I can't remember the last time you took any time off, Puller. Even a soldier needs to recharge."

"Yes sir, thank you, sir."

"And Puller, step lightly. If things get hairy it's above my pay grade to backstop you. You do this with flanks uncovered, understood?"

"Understood."

The line went dead and Puller slowly pocketed his phone.

A mixed message. But one Puller heard loud and clear. First, the time off. Then the warning that his ass was exposed and no reinforcements would be coming.

He drove on.

* * *

Lucy Bristow did not seem familiar to Puller from across the width of her breakfast room table.

She was petite, slender, with short silver hair containing blonde highlights. Her eyes were large for her small, oval face, giving her a perpetually penetrating stare. A gold bracelet dangled on her wrist. She had made tea and given a porcelain cup full of it to Puller.

"I remember Jackie very well," she said. "I remember you

and your brother too. I doubt you remember me. You were just little boys."

Puller took a sip of the tea. It was hot and minty.

"And my father?"

She gave him a sharp glance. "Everyone at Fort Monroe knew John Puller Sr. He'd recently gotten his first star, brigadier general. I remember my husband told me your father's career was tied to a rocket but that he deserved it. He wasn't a paper pusher. He was a fighting man's officer. He'd paid his dues. He told me your father had more sheer courage than any flag officer above him."

"I understand your husband was in the Army?"

"Yes. He was a lieutenant colonel in your father's command. We saw your parents quite frequently socially."

"Is he still alive?"

"No, he's not. He died a long time ago."

"I'm sorry to hear that."

"We were separated shortly before, but it was still a shock." She put her cup of tea down and rubbed at her temple.

Puller watched her. "I'm sure."

"We didn't have children, so that made it a bit easier, if something like that can be made easier. My father was Army too, enlisted. Maxed out as an SFC. So an oh-seven was in the stratosphere for me," she added, referring to the official pay grade rank of a brigadier general.

"I'm an enlisted as well," said Puller.

"That's right. I heard you didn't follow your father to West Point."

Puller was surprised by this. "Who did you hear that from?"

"Army women keep in touch. Scuttlebutt as fine art, I like to say."

"Carol Powers told me essentially the same thing."

"I was very surprised to hear from her that you were look-ing into your mother's disappearance. I mean, it's been such a long time."

"I've been surprised by a lot of things lately."

Bristow sighed and picked up her cup again. "She was a beautiful woman. On the inside as well as the outside. She was very popular at the post. Everyone loved her. She could have put on airs, what with being a general's wife. But she pitched in and worked on projects, right in the trenches with all of us. And she brightened every room she walked into." She paused and added, "She was a help to both my husband and me when we were going through our...issues."

"I'm glad to hear that. I remember going to St. Mary's."

"I can still see her walking in with her two boys all dressed up in their Sunday best. You both were tall back then too. No surprise given how big your father was. And Jackie wasn't short either."

"He didn't go to church very much."

"You get to that rank the Army takes over your life."

"I guess so."

"Maybe that's why you didn't go to West Point," she said, giving him a shrewd look.

"Maybe," he said noncommittally.

"If I can speak frankly, I always thought it an odd match, your father and Jackie."

"Why was that?"

"Well, she was nine years younger, for starters."

Puller hadn't really thought about the age difference be-tween his parents. By the time he might have focused on it, his mother had long since vanished.

"And your father was the most focused man I've ever met. Commanded every room he walked into. The men loved and feared him."

"I wouldn't disagree with that."

"My husband said most of the enlisted under your father's command weren't sure if he was going to shake their hand or kick their ass."

"I wouldn't disagree with that either."

"Jackie commanded a room too, only with grace and elegance and just good vibes." She paused. "They met in Germany, did you know that?"

"Vaguely." Puller suddenly realized that he didn't know much about his parents' courting history.

"She was an Air Force brat. That was how I always saw her, floating above it all. Don't get me wrong. She was nice and polite to everyone, and like I said, she pitched in with all the work. But she was also reserved, keeping part of herself out of sight and reach of everyone. Now, your father at the time was a lieutenant colonel with a chest full of medals and bullet and shrapnel wounds from Vietnam. They met at some military function. I heard it was like fire and ice slamming into each other. But then within a year or so they were married."

"Opposites attract."

"Maybe. She had two miscarriages before your brother was born."

Apparently Bristow had made this abrupt segue to gauge Puller's reaction, because she was watching him closely.

His jaw dropping was all the answer she needed.

"So you didn't know?"

"No, I didn't."

"Parents don't often talk about that."

"I guess not."

"But I had several miscarriages too, and it was something that Jackie shared with me after she learned of my loss. That's why I know those details. When you called, I focused on that time in my life, and it was surprising how easily all our conversations came back to me."

They fell silent for a few moments.

"Can you tell me anything about the day she disappeared?" asked Puller finally.

Bristow gazed over his shoulder. "I really can't, John. You see, I had left my husband by then and moved into an apartment off the post."

"I didn't know that."

"It was for the best. Our marriage didn't work out. And then he died."

There was an awkward silence until Puller spoke up. "I was in the backyard playing when I saw her at the window. She was watching me and smiling."

Bristow nodded. "She was very proud of her boys." Her gaze dropped to his. "I'm sure you miss her very much. To not have her in your life all these years."

"Yes ma'am," Puller said dully. All these years without her. All that time gone. The things they could have experienced together.

"John, are you all right?"

Puller jerked back to find Bristow looking at him worriedly.

"I'm fine. So, the day she disappeared. It was a Saturday."

Bristow nodded. "Yes, that's right. The week leading up to that was a busy one. That Sunday there was going to be an Easter program at the church. A lot of details and planning. Your mother was on the committee, as was I. Even though I no longer lived on post, I would not have left them in the lurch on that."

"And she was looking forward to it?"

"Oh yes. We all were." She looked at him appraisingly. "You don't think that your mother just walked away from her family, do you?"

"I don't know what to think right now, ma'am. I'm just trying to collect the facts and see where they lead me."

Bristow nodded. "Your father was not the easiest person to live with."

"I can attest to that."

"But that would not have been enough of a reason for her to leave. And she never would have left her sons behind. Don't believe for one minute that she would have."

Puller considered this, his pen hovering over his notebook. "So if she didn't walk out on us, then something happened to her."

Bristow nodded. "That's what I always assumed. The MPs and CID agents came to talk to me, of course. And other people who knew your mother. Your father was out of the country, if I remember correctly."

Puller did not tell her that this was now known not to be the case. "Do you know anything that might have explained what happened?" he asked. "Something she might have told you that didn't seem important at the time?"

"They asked me the same sort of questions back then. I really didn't. And over the years I've thought about it from time to time, but nothing pertinent ever occurred to me."

"Carol Powers said that my mom was all dressed up that night. Like she was going somewhere special. Do you know where that might have been?"

"No, I really don't. She sometimes went out to dinner with some of the gals. But she usually didn't dress up for that. How was she dressed exactly?"

Puller told her what Carol had told him.

She shook her head. "That sounds like her Sunday best."

"I guess it does."

"I'm sorry I can't be more helpful. But I just don't know

what she might have been doing. It was just a typical Saturday night as far as I was concerned."

Puller asked a few more questions and then thanked her and left.

He sat out in his car for a few minutes pondering all of it. Then it clicked.

He put the car in gear and pulled off, heading back to Fort Monroe.

He finally had a potential lead.

Sunday best.

CHAPTER

15

PAUL ROGERS STARED up at the sign taped to the door of a bar called the Grunt.

Not a bad name in an area with a huge military footprint. He could imagine it was filled every night with rank-and-file Army grunts looking to drink away their troubles and have a little fun in between dodging bullets and IEDs and getting screamed at by sergeants.

Bouncer wanted.

That's what the sign said.

He opened the door and walked in.

At this time of day there were only a few people inside. He could tell most of them worked here and were getting the place ready for the nightly invasion.

He walked over to the bartender, who was stacking glasses behind the bar.

"I'm here about the bouncer job?"

The bartender looked him up and down. Rogers was rock-solid but he hardly had the heft one probably thought a bouncer should possess.

The bartender pointed at the other end of the room. "Office is back there. Knock on the door first."

Rogers headed that way, gazing around and taking in the

space in one effective sweep. Large dance floor, video game room, raised platform for a live band, lots of tables and chairs. And enough alcohol stacked behind the bar to sink an aircraft carrier with all hands on board.

Rogers thought back to the time he had been in a bar once. It had not ended well.

It had cost him ten years of his life, in fact.

A stupid mistake on his part. But the thing in his head had not let him make a better choice.

He walked down a short hall, reached a door marked *Office*, and knocked.

He heard footsteps and a moment later the door was opened by a man so large that he filled most of the doorway. He had a shaved head and was dressed in a black jacket, slacks, and a black turtleneck. He looked down at Rogers.

"Yeah?" he said gruffly.

"I'm here about the bouncer job."

The man took a step back and looked amused.

Rogers could now see into the office. It was a large room, twenty feet square with high-end built-ins and furnishings. Behind a sleek mahogany desk sat a woman in her midthirties, dressed in a beige pantsuit with a white blouse underneath.

The big man looked at her. "He's here about the bouncer job," he said derisively.

The woman stood. She looked to be about five-eight, slender with long blonde hair that held far darker roots at the top of her head.

"You have any experience?" she asked.

Rogers nodded.

"You're a little small for that line of work. And a little old."

"I can handle myself."

She came around the side of the desk and perched a hip on it. Rogers now saw that her heels bumped her height up several inches. Without them she was really about five-five.

She said, "You former military? You look it."

"Something like that. I don't want to fill out any paper-work. And I prefer cash. If that's a problem, I can leave now."

"You don't get to make the preferences," said the big man. "She's the boss. She calls the shots."

Rogers rubbed the back of his head, the sensation more a tingling than a pain. He looked up at the big man. "So why aren't you the bouncer? You're big enough. The *boss* afraid *you* can't cut it?"

The man looked ready to drive a fist right through Rogers's face. "Where the fuck do you get off—"

"Karl!"

The woman stood and walked over to them as Karl took a step back.

"Karl is my security chief. He stays with me."

"You need security?"

"I'm Helen Myers, Mr.?"

"Paul. Just call me Paul."

She looked at Karl. "He vets the bouncers. That's part of his job as head of security."

"Okay."

"And we normally run a background check on potential employees."

Rogers turned to leave.

"Wait," said Myers.

Rogers turned back around.

"Are you in some sort of trouble?"

"I had some trouble and I paid my bill on it. I'm a free man. And I really need the job. But I'm not going through a background check. No harm, no foul. Thanks anyway."

"Just hold on for a sec." She studied him for a few moments.

"Okay, Paul, I'm going to turn it over to Karl now."

Rogers looked at Karl expectantly.

Karl stepped forward and gave Rogers a smile that did not reach his eyes. "Let me see how you do visual sweeps."

Rogers turned his head to the right.

A second later his hand reached out and caught the haymaker Karl had planned to land on his chin.

Caught and held it.

Karl tried to pull free but couldn't break Rogers's grip.

"What the hell!" he exclaimed.

Next, Rogers gripped the fist so tightly that one of the man's knuckles popped out of joint.

"Shit," cried out Karl. "Let the fuck go, man."

"Please release him, Paul," said Myers.

Rogers let go and stepped back, putting his hands behind his back and standing at attention.

"Son of a bitch," said Karl, holding his injured hand. "What are you, some kinda freak?"

Rogers looked at Myers. "How much does the job pay?"

Myers said, "Five hundred a night. Hours are eight to two in the morning. We're closed on Mondays. We get a lot of soldiers and they can get rowdy. And none of them are lightweights. They all know how to fight. That's why the pay is what it is. I can't guarantee that you won't get injured. That's what happened to the last bouncer. You will have to sign off on that disclaimer."

"I haven't finished vetting him yet, Ms. Myers," said Karl, glaring at Rogers.

Rogers glanced at him. "I'll arm wrestle you, if you don't mind a blown-out rotator."

"I usually do a little boxing with the new guys," snapped Karl.

"I wouldn't advise that," said Rogers. "It would not be a fair fight."

"You little prick!"

Karl kicked out at Rogers, who sidestepped the thrust, clamped down on the leg, and effortlessly flipped Karl off his feet. An instant after Karl hit the floor Rogers straddled him, wrenched his arm behind his back, and put him in a chokehold that had Karl's eyes rolling in the back of his head.

"Stop, stop!" cried out Myers.

Rogers immediately let go and stepped back.

"Do I get the job?" he said calmly.

Myers looked down at the barely conscious Karl on the floor and then lifted her gaze to Rogers.

"When can you start?"

"Tonight."

"All right."

She added a bit shakily, "Do you have a problem I should know about, Paul?"

"I have no problems. And I'll do a good job for you."

"Okay, but we don't need you to kill anybody."

Rogers didn't answer her. He helped Karl to his feet and over to a chair. The big man wouldn't meet his eye.

"I'm sorry if I hurt you," said Rogers. "I just really need the job."

Breathing hard, Karl waved him off.

Myers led Rogers out of the office and into what looked like a workroom at the back of the bar. She gave him a set of clothes and shoes to wear.

"This is what the bouncer wears. They should fit okay."

"Thanks."

She asked, "Do you have a smartphone?"

He shook his head. "I don't have a smartphone and I don't have the money to buy one."

She opened a cabinet, pulled out a box, and tossed it to him. "It's a Samsung, hooked to the Web and all ready to go. The phone number is on the front screen. It's yours to use while you work here."

Rogers stuck it in his pocket. "Thanks."

"You'll also wear a headset and comm pack when you're on duty. I like my people to be in communication at all times."

"You sound like you were in the military."

"I'll see you tonight. Get in two hours early so you can be shown how we do things, understood?"

"Yes."

She glanced nervously at the door. "How did you do that to Karl?"

"I got a few tricks. And I figured I had to show him I got what it takes."

"Okay, I get that. But he has nearly six inches and over a hundred pounds on you. He's vetted a lot of bouncers a lot bigger than you, and none of them did what you just did. Karl usually had *them* on the floor."

"I'm stronger than I look," said Rogers.

"Obviously."

He left her there staring uncertainly after him.

He walked back to his van and drove to a motel that offered a twenty-nine-dollar nightly rate. It was a firetrap, but after ten years in a prison cell he had learned not to care where he slept so long as he could walk out the door of his own free will.

He paid for three nights in cash and went to the room after parking the white van in a space directly in front.

Five hundred dollars a night, off during the days, and he would still have time after he clocked out at two to do what needed doing. It was a good scenario for him all the way around.

He locked the door behind him, dropped his duffel on the floor, hung his work clothes up in the closet and placed the shoes directly underneath.

He sat on the edge of the bed and looked down at the smartphone. He'd never used one before. They were only coming into vogue after he had gone to prison. But he quickly figured out how it worked.

He went online and did some more digging on CB Excelon Corp.

His searches becoming more advanced, he skipped from one site to another until he found something interesting.

Former CEO retires and moves to the Outer Banks.

The story was about five years old. Chris Ballard had founded and run Ballard Enterprises and its successor, CB Excelon, for many years. The "CB" obviously stood for Chris Ballard. He had subsequently turned the reins over to a new regime. Now eighty, Ballard was retiring to a more leisurely life on the sandy beaches of North Carolina.

The story went on to bullet-point some of Ballard's successes and the work that his firm had done in connection with DARPA, the Defense Department's research arm. The article also gave a thumbnail history of the agency.

DARPA, created in the late 1950s by President Eisenhower, had started out as the Advanced Research Projects Agency. It had come into being in response to the Soviets sending Sputnik I into orbit. The organization had changed its name several times over the decades, before settling on

DARPA in 1996. With its new headquarters in Arlington, Virginia, it employed hundreds of people and managed a budget of $3 billion. Its mission was to nurture and support game-changing military technologies and to create surprises for America's enemies, although some of its project outcomes had had significant influence in nonmilitary applications. It funded numerous areas of development in the private sector and was known to give long leashes, short time frames, and overly ambitious—some would say impossible—goals to its contractors. It had had many successes but also spectacular failures. An independent agency, DARPA reported directly to DoD senior management.

Rogers already knew this about DARPA and didn't really care.

He found a mapping function on the phone and determined that the Outer Banks were only a couple hours from Fort Monroe.

His only lead to Claire Jericho was Chris Ballard.

North Carolina here I come.

CHAPTER

16

THE CAR HAD been in the driveway.

Puller sat on the hood of his Malibu staring at the old house on the grounds of Fort Monroe. The Puller family had owned a Buick four-door sedan back then, provided by the Army.

It had been in the driveway after his mother had left that night.

They had no other car.

She had to have walked.

Puller pushed off the hood and started to head down the sidewalk. He could have gone in one of two directions, but he had chosen the way that made the most sense to him.

Sunday best.

As he walked along he could not stop himself from imagining his mother making this same journey that night. His footsteps were following that same trek. His steps were hitting where hers had hit on this very same concrete. He visualized her all dressed up, her purse perhaps clutched at her side. Her gaze directly in front of her. Some purpose in mind.

Some destination.

When he reached St. Mary's Church, Puller stopped.

It looked the same as when he'd been a boy here. The trees around it were larger and fuller, but the church itself had remained frozen in time.

It was a beautiful little church. It would have made a great postcard picture, he suddenly thought.

Come here and worship God. It will get you in the spirit.

The Catholic church was still open and functioning. Its official name was St. Mary Star of the Sea Catholic Church. It had a school, also named St. Mary Star of the Sea, that catered to pre-K through eighth grade and was located across the causeway from the fort on Willard Avenue.

Puller had attended Mass here every Sunday with his mother and brother, and his father if he was in town. He had never gone back since she'd vanished. He had never seen the point to it, since God had ignored his teary pleas and never returned Puller's mother to him.

He stood out in front of the church for a few minutes, trying not to be overwhelmed by all the memories that had suddenly come charging headlong at him.

He walked up the steps and into the church. It was quiet and cool and a bit musty inside. He surveyed the interior, the blue carpeting and the sign over a shelf of written materials in the back that read *Thou Shalt Not Steal.*

He walked up the aisle and noted the stained glass windows on either wall.

One was a memorial to a soldier who had died in Korea. The words read, *He died so the kids next door may live.*

That seemed to be the lot of many a soldier, thought Puller.

You die so others don't.

Flags hung down from the ceiling on both sides. He looked up at them as he passed by.

Then his eyes finally reached to the small altar.

All the memories overcame him once more like an enemy overrunning his position on a battlefield.

He shut his eyes and let these images wash over him. Taking the seats in the pew, his mother always between his brother and him. They were little boys after all, and seated together they would have at some point during the Mass gotten into trouble.

He could conjure the smell of her perfume, delicate and barely there. The rustle of her skirt, the slight tap of her heel against the back of the pew in front of them. The methodical turning of the hymnal pages.

Standing up to sing, to pray, listening to the homily. Rising again. Genuflecting. Reciting the Lord's Prayer. Walking up to receive communion, Puller having qualified to do that only the year before his mother vanished.

Swallowing the host and wishing his mother would have allowed him to drink some of Jesus's blood in the form of the red wine.

Just once.

Putting the crumpled dollar bills in the offering basket.

Singing the final hymn as the priest and the altar boys walked down the center aisle bearing the cross and the Holy Book out into the foyer.

His mother lingering to talk to the priest and some friends, while he and his brother fidgeted, anxious to get home, change their clothes, and run wild outside. Or for Robert Puller to finish reading a book or complete a science project.

Puller blinked and his gaze went toward the altar. A door had opened on one side of it and a man in a white collar had emerged from an inner room. He was carrying some hymnals. When he spotted Puller he put the books down and walked down the center aisle toward him.

He was in his fifties, with a shock of fine white hair that neatly matched the color of the collar. He had on the usual black pants and a black clerical shirt with the white tab collar. His glasses fronted watery blue eyes.

"May I help you?" he asked, offering a smile along with his greeting. The man drew closer and held out his hand. "I'm Father O'Neil." He peered at Puller more closely. "I'm sorry, young man. Do you attend church here? I'm usually very good at remembering faces."

"I used to. About thirty years ago."

"Oh, then as a little boy?"

"Yes."

"Well, you go back much farther than I do. I've only been the pastor here for nine years. I came over from Roanoke."

"Father Rooney was the pastor when I came here."

"Father Rooney? That name sounds familiar. There were quite a few priests in between him and me. The Richmond Diocese likes to move us around."

"Would you have any idea where I could find him?"

O'Neil became slightly guarded. "Can I ask why you're looking for him?"

"My name is John Puller Jr. My father was in the Army, same as me. I used to come here with my mother and brother when we were little. My mother disappeared from Fort Monroe thirty years ago. She was never found. I'm just trying to piece together what might have happened."

The watery blue eyes softened even more. "Why now if so much time has gone by?"

Puller took out his CID cred pack.

The priest studied it. "CID? So is this an official investigation?"

"No, just personal. Some things have occurred recently that led me to want to finally find out what happened to her."

"I can understand that, Agent Puller. Not knowing is a terrible thing."

"So might you know what happened to Father Rooney? I don't even know if he's alive."

"Well, I can certainly try to find out. I can certainly make some calls. Do you mind waiting, or perhaps coming back later? I have a meeting coming up in about fifteen minutes that I have to prepare for, but I can do it right after that. Say about two hours or so?"

"I'll be back. And thank you, Father."

Puller left the church and checked his watch. He didn't like to waste time. The Army did not teach wasting time— quite the reverse.

Puller hadn't even reached his Malibu when he heard the man.

"What are you doing here?"

He turned to see CID special agent Ted Hull sitting in the driver's seat of his Army-issued Malibu that was a clone of Puller's. The Army bought in bulk with not a thought to diversity of the product. Indeed, in their eyes uniformity was a good thing, whether it was a soldier or a car.

Puller looked back at the church and then walked over to Hull's ride. "Just revisiting old times."

Hull eyed him suspiciously. Puller knew he would be doing the exact same thing if the positions were reversed.

"Is that right? At Fort Monroe, the scene of your mother's disappearance?"

Puller shrugged and leaned closer to the window. "You're the one who dropped this in my lap. Made me curious. What would you do if it was you and your mother?"

Hull nodded and tapped the steering wheel with his thumbs. "Probably the exact same thing you're doing."

Puller straightened. "Well, okay."

"You find out anything?"

Puller leaned back down. "I've talked to a few people. My mother was dressed up that night. She walked; our car was still in the driveway. The church was within walking distance. She was devoutly religious. Maybe she came here."

"Why here?"

"If she had a problem she might come here to talk about it."

"You mean like a confession?"

"They don't have any actual confessionals in the church, they just do it in one of the rooms. But no, I mean like just talking to a priest."

Hull eyed the church. "The same priest still here?"

"No, but they're trying to locate him."

"You think it might be a viable lead?"

"Since I have no others I'll take what I can get."

"I didn't see any record of the CID agents talking to a priest thirty years ago."

"They didn't really know my mother. I did. But then again, it may come to nothing." He looked around. "Place is really different now. I remember when it was full of uniformed people hustling somewhere."

Hull nodded. "Me too. But we got too many posts and not enough money. So there you go. When will you know if they found the priest?"

"A few hours."

Hull considered this. "You can't officially investigate this."

"I get that."

"So what are you really doing, Puller?"

"I'm just looking into my mother's disappearance. No law against that."

"If your father is a suspect there is. You're in uniform."

"But my father is not officially a suspect."

"Will you give me a call when and if this priest turns up?"

"Be glad to."

"Don't throw your career away over this, Puller. I understand a little about what happened with your brother when he was at USDB. Scuttlebutt was you got perilously close to the line there."

"I'm a soldier. Peril comes with the territory."

"There are different kinds of peril. And the one coming from your own side is sometimes a lot worse than anything the enemy can chuck at you."

Hull drove off.

Puller watched him go for a bit before turning his attention elsewhere.

He hadn't been completely truthful with Hull. He had another lead to follow up.

Part of it was real.

The other part was all in his head.

CHAPTER

17

PULLER SAT IN a chair in his motel room and stared at the duffel.

It was just an ordinary duffel.

Canvas.

Zippered.

Crammed with stuff that helped Puller do what he did.

Find the truth.

What he did. All he ever wanted to do.

Was that because his mother had left the house and never come back?

Because some evil had made sure she couldn't ever come back?

And was that evil his own father?

He covered his face with his hands, the impossible burden of this thought threatening to crush him without a gram of actual weight behind it.

Then he sat up straight and composed himself.

You're Army, John Puller. You're an Army Ranger. You can do the impossible. You're expected to do the impossible on a regular basis.

So open the bag, John. Open the damn bag and just let it out. Finally.

His fingers reached out to take hold of the zipper.

He imagined his father glowering at him.

Come on, soldier, you put your life on the line for your country. A damn zipper shouldn't be too hard.

He slid it down, spread open the canvas, and saw what he had put in there.

He touched the edge of the letter but didn't pull it out. Not right away.

He had to work up to it, as strange as that sounded. The gravitational pull of family dynamics; it left a black hole in the dust.

He finally eased it out enough to see the name written on the front of the envelope.

Written in his mother's hand.

John.

Not him, his father.

The letter had been for John Puller Sr. At the time he was a one-star busting his ass to add more silver to the epaulets. This meant leaving everything else in his life, including his family, in a distant second place.

Puller Sr. would finish his career with a trio of stars. There were only forty-three of those in the entire United States Army. But his old man wanted the fourth, which would have put him in the elite company of only nine people on earth at any given time. And because he never got there, he was a failure, at least in his eyes.

A failure in the mind he *used* to have.

Puller took the letter out and unfolded it.

He had never read it. He had found it when he was a little boy, his mother gone barely six months. His father had left it somewhere in the house at Fort Monroe. The envelope had been opened, but he had no idea if his father had read the contents.

He looked down at the writing that, despite the passage of years, he recognized as his mother's. She used to write many notes to him and his brother, ones of encouragement, support, sometimes just funny things to make them smile or, better yet, laugh, particularly when they were sad or uncertain or fearful.

The life of an Army brat was not easy. The life of a son of an Army legend could sometimes be pure hell.

The Puller brothers had learned that lesson vividly as they had grown into men.

People either assumed you were as good and talented and brave as your legendary father and never allowed you to fall below that supremely high bar, or they assumed you were nowhere near as good as he was because it was a rare family that could spawn multiple fighting legends. Thus you were instantly relegated to being parasites riding your father's coattails. Nothing you achieved would ever be because of what you did, but only because of who your father was.

So anything you accomplished, under either scenario, would never be good enough.

Because you would never be *him*.

The letter was brief but compelling, even heartwrenching in parts. What he would have given to have received letters from her when he'd been at college, or when he'd first joined the Army. Or when he'd been deployed overseas and was literally fighting for his life through some of the most hostile and chaotic situations imaginable.

Her words would have been his touchstone, his oasis in a sea of shit.

Puller felt his hand begin to shake as he read through the thoughts of his mother from three decades before.

Problems in the marriage. Problems with him. Problems with her.

But... she was willing to work things out.

Not for her or him.

But because of their sons.

Because that was what was truly important. At least to Jackie Puller.

But—and here was the crux of it—she wrote that she and the boys would have to go away for a while. To let John Puller Sr. see what his real priorities were in life. And then, depending on what he decided, they would go from there.

Puller folded the letter and slid it back into the envelope.

Words from the grave. Or if not the grave, Puller didn't know where.

Despite the obvious love and affection she held for her sons, as noted in the letter, Puller came away from reading it more depressed than he had been before.

Part of him had hoped that his mother *had* left her husband. Because that meant she might still be alive.

To Puller, this letter meant that his mother most likely was dead.

He would take bullets and bombs and jihadist fanatics trying to rip his life from him over that. You fought for the flag and country you represented. But you *really* fought for the guy beside you.

Here, Puller was alone.

It was just him and a vanished mother to whom he had given all of his heart.

As he stood there looking down at the envelope, depression was suddenly replaced with an even more powerful emotion.

Guilt.

Why had he waited all these years to do anything about this?

He was a trained investigator. Yet he'd never investigated

the one case that meant more to him than any he would ever confront. Even more than his brother being in prison.

Yet he had done nothing. Just let the time slip past.

He put the envelope back in his duffel and zippered it up, securing the fastener with a CID lock.

He pondered whether to call his brother.

But Bobby would probably just try to be logical and thus disdainful of every emotion his younger brother was feeling.

He didn't need logic or disdain right now.

He just needed someone to talk to about this who could see it from a side of life that had nothing to do with practicality and common sense.

He looked at his watch.

Hopefully he would have a lead on Father Rooney by the time he left and drove back to Fort Monroe.

He locked his room up and headed to his car.

When he turned the corner he saw her, perched regally on the hood of his Malibu like a flesh-and-blood ornament. He was so stunned he almost ran into a support post holding up the motel's porch.

Veronica Knox said, "I understand you might need a friend."

CHAPTER

18

Rogers showered, dressed in his new clothes, and slipped his smartphone into his inside jacket pocket.

He drove over to the Grunt and parked in the rear.

He entered through the front door, and the stares he got from the folks working there told him quite clearly that his beatdown of giant Karl had made the gossip rounds.

Anyone making eye contact with him quickly broke it off.

That suited him just fine. He was not here to make friends. This was all about the cash.

He was directed back to the office, where Helen Myers was waiting for him. She had changed into a sleek black pantsuit with stilettos. Her hair cascaded around her shoulders and her face was fully made up.

"Where's Karl?" he asked.

"He took the night off. He had to see to some things."

Rogers nodded. He imagined Karl had to see to a broken finger, a nearly crushed windpipe, a bad leg, and a wrenched arm. But that wasn't his problem.

Myers spent thirty minutes going over work details and the protocols and policies of the bar. "Half the IDs you'll see are fake. Twenty-one is the legal drinking age. No one under that age is allowed in. No exceptions. Most of the people in uniform are nineteen or twenty. You err on the side of keeping people out. The last thing I need is to be put out of business for promoting underage drinking."

"You'd think if you're old enough to fight for your country you should be able to drink a beer."

"I agree, but I don't make the laws. Weekends are our big nights, obviously. We're closed on Mondays to let everybody take a breather, but we're open every other night of the week."

"Anything else?" Rogers asked.

"You have to exercise discretion and good judgment, Paul. While we want to keep underage people out, we don't want a rep of being a place where folks get turned away unnecessarily or get hassled or beat up, okay? That's also not good for business."

"I understand."

"Each night we have a list of VIPs who you'll let bypass the line. I sent the list to your phone earlier. They'll come up and show ID. You match it to the name on the VIP list and in they come. They'll be escorted to a special section of the bar by people inside. You're to stay at the exterior door at all times unless you're called inside. You are the first line of defense."

"Who are the VIPs?"

"That's no concern of yours," she replied firmly. "Just clear them at the door. That's your responsibility, all right?"

Rogers rubbed the back of his head. "All right."

"You clean up well," she said, running her gaze over him. "You're in amazing shape. How old are you anyway?"

"Older than you probably think."

"You must work out a lot. Insanity? P90X? MMX?"

He shook his head. "Good genes."

She smiled. "Lucky you."

Yeah, lucky me.

"You do not drink on duty. You can have whatever you want after you get off, for free."

"I'm not much of a drinker."

"Suit yourself. Well, good luck tonight."

"Thanks."

Rogers walked out and sat at the bar, counting down the minutes to when the place opened for business. He asked for a glass of water with a lime and the bartender poured it out for him.

There was a TV on the wall behind the bar. The news was on. A man killed in West Virginia near the Virginia border. A young boy left fatherless. A rare gun stolen.

The newscaster looked particularly indignant as he recounted the cold-blooded murder.

The police were following up leads. A car might have been seen leaving the site of the killing. The little boy had survived but emotionally was not doing well, apparently having witnessed the entire thing.

The bartender had turned to watch the screen with Rogers as he wiped down glasses. "Friggin' sociopaths out there," he muttered, glancing at Rogers. "Death penalty's too good for 'em."

Rogers didn't reply. He had other things on his mind.

A car might have been seen.

He had ditched the car but used the same license plates from it. If someone had seen the plates?

Would the cops even look at a white van? They might. They might glance at the plates regardless; recognition might come. He would have to fix that.

He retreated to a corner of the room and sat at a table. He took out his phone and looked at directions to the Outer Banks. But he didn't have Chris Ballard's exact address.

A young waitress passed by and he said, "Got an old

buddy I'm trying to find. I've got his name and area where he lives but not the street address or phone number. Anything on this phone that can help me with that?"

"You can try a search on the area and name. And Google has street view so you can see the house too when you find it."

"Can you show me how to do that? I'm an old fart still uses a calculator. Just pick a name."

She grinned, then sat and went through the key clicks.

Rogers quickly picked it up. He thanked her with a twenty-dollar bill and she went off carrying a tray of clean glasses.

He put in his search and refined it as he went along, adding as much information as he could remember. Finally, an address came back. He used street view to see the place.

It was a mansion on the water behind high walls with an imposing steel gate. He saw what looked to be a security shack right outside the gate.

Ballard had obviously retired a very rich man after spending his career selling stuff to Uncle Sam.

Rogers committed the address to memory and cleared the search from his phone.

He next tried to find Claire Jericho's address. He found what he expected: nothing. He doubted that she had retired to the Outer Banks in a big house behind high walls.

Well, if he couldn't find her on his phone, he would have to rely on Chris Ballard to fill in the blanks.

Rogers didn't care if Ballard didn't want to tell him.

The man *would* tell him.

He sat back, closed his eyes, and counted off the time until his career as a professional bouncer began.

He rubbed the back of his head hard, as though to tell the thing there to cool it. He didn't need a loss of control right now. That would ruin everything.

And he had waited far too long to be stopped now.

CHAPTER

19

"WHAT ARE YOU doing here?" said a clearly stunned Puller.

Veronica Knox slid off the hood of his Malibu.

His gaze roamed over her. She was tall, around five-nine, with a lean, athletic build topped by auburn hair that had grown out some since Puller had last seen her. He also knew that she carried scars from a shrapnel wound on one of her hips and butt cheeks from a too close encounter with a mortar round in the Middle East.

She worked in American intelligence. Puller had never been fully clear for which agency. They had parted ways at Thomas Custer's tombstone at the graveyard at Fort Leavenworth in Kansas. In his dress blues he had invited her to spend a week's leave with him in Rome. She had politely declined. And he hadn't seen her since.

He had finally told himself he no longer cared. But seeing her, his gut was telling him that that was not true. Just the sight of the woman made his skin tingle a bit and his breath quicken.

She stopped within a foot of him.

Knox was wearing her usual official outfit, black pantsuit and white blouse with nearly every button buttoned and the collar turned up. He knew from experience that she was armed at the waist and with a throwaway at her ankle.

"Like I said, I heard you could use a friend."

"And who did you hear that from?"

"You should know by now that I can't reveal my sources."

He relaxed and studied her. "I thought I'd hear from you before now. I called a dozen times. I texted and emailed. If I had an address for you I would have been on your doorstep."

"I know, Puller. I'm sorry about that. Job gets in the way of a lot of things. I've been out of the country more than in."

He took a step back and crossed his arms. "How much do you know about what's going on?"

"Letter full of allegations against your father. The case of your mother's disappearance reopened. Your father perhaps the main suspect because of the new fact that he was back in the country that day."

"Your sources are pretty good," he conceded.

"And since you're here at Fort Monroe I assume that you are headlong into the investigation?"

"Not officially. But the CID agent on the case knows I'm around. I think he wants to collaborate."

"Ted Hull?"

"You know him?"

"No."

"So, again, Knox, what are you doing here? And don't use the friend line again. I'm not sure you have any."

Her features hardened. "I consider *you* a friend. You and your brother. We went through a lot together."

"Friends return calls. My brother, as busy as he is, returns my calls."

She assumed a pointed look. "Is this about Rome? My declining to go?"

"This is about you being here right now. I don't believe

you're here for me. So there must be another reason. I would just like to know what it is. Simple enough."

"I came here to help you, Puller. I know our last meeting was not a positive one. But your offer...it meant a lot to me. And you don't know how close I came to accepting it. And not a day goes by that I don't regret not going with you."

This frankness made Puller's features soften. "Are you being genuine, Knox? I want to know. Just tell me."

"Let me put it this way. I'm not supposed to be here. But I *am* here." She gazed over at the Malibu. "Care to go for a ride? We can talk?"

"I've got someone to meet."

"Still have to drive there, right?"

She opened the passenger door of his car. Puller shook his head and climbed into the driver's seat. They buckled up and he backed out.

"So who are you going to meet?"

"Somebody who might know something."

"And something always leads to something else. I remember that's your mantra."

"My brother actually invented it. But, yeah, it's how I think too."

"Your mother disappeared thirty years ago."

It wasn't spoken as a question.

He glanced at her as they drove along. "You looked at the file?"

"Of course I did. If I'm hooking up with you I come prepared. I know better than most that you don't like to waste time."

"Yeah, thirty years ago."

"You were eight years old, your brother nearly ten."

"Right."

"Your father was supposed to be out of the country but now we know he wasn't. Yet he wasn't at the house that night. The flight manifest said he was wheels down at Norfolk at one that afternoon."

"How the hell did you score that information?" he said, his frustration clear. "I don't even have it."

"Doesn't matter. That's what the information says. The question becomes this: Your mother left the house around seven-thirty that night. Your father was thirty minutes away from your old house at one p.m. Where was he in the intervening time? There was no account of him meeting with anyone official. So where was he?"

"What do you know about this flight? How did it get so buried that no one knew until just recently? And are they certain my father was on it?"

"That remains a big question, Puller. I can tell you that I'm not satisfied by what I've seen so far."

He pulled off the road and turned to her. "You know about the flight, that he didn't meet with anyone official? And you're not satisfied by what you've seen so far? How long have you been investigating this case?"

"Not that long. But I'm nothing if not efficient," she added coolly. "And I have the credentials to get answers from people who are not used to giving them so freely."

"I guess so," said Puller a bit enviously.

"So why did he come back early?" she asked.

Puller took the envelope from his pocket and handed it across to her. Then he pulled back onto the road.

She unfolded the letter inside and read it twice over.

"Did your father read this?"

"I don't know for certain. I know he had it."

"She wanted to work things out."

"Which means he had no motive to kill her."

"Well, we don't know that for sure," replied Knox. "And she says she wanted to go away for a bit with you and your brother. I bet your father was not happy about that."

"I'm sure he wasn't."

"And there could have been another reason."

"Like what?"

"The old story. Another woman?"

"My father *did* have a mistress."

She jerked and shot him a look. "What!"

"It was called the United States Army. He barely had time for his family, much less another woman in his life. But it would be nice to know why he came back early and didn't tell anyone."

"We'll have to dig into that. By the way, where are we going?"

"To see a priest."

She looked startled. "For what?"

"I'm going to confess my sins."

"Seriously, Puller."

"He's the something that might lead to something else."

She settled back in her seat. "Okay." She paused and then added, "I'm long overdue for a confession, actually."

"You're Catholic?"

She nodded. "But I won't do it today."

"Why not?"

"I doubt we have the time. It might take a few hours."

He gave her a look and she added, "I never said I was an angel, Puller."

CHAPTER

20

FATHER O'NEIL WAS putting hymnals in the backs of the pews when Puller and Knox walked in. Knox crossed herself as they walked up the aisle.

O'Neil walked over to them still carrying a stack of the songbooks. Puller introduced Knox to the priest.

"Very nice to meet you," said O'Neil.

He turned to Puller. "I made inquiries, and you're in luck. Father Rooney is still alive and he's in the area. He's retired now and lives with relatives in Williamsburg." He handed Puller a piece of paper. "Here's the address and phone number. I didn't call. I thought it better if you did so."

Puller said, "I really appreciate this, Father. You've been a big help."

"Well, one job of a priest is to help others." He looked around the interior of the church. "A beautiful sanctuary. I truly love being here." He glanced at Knox. "I saw you make the sign of the cross when you came in."

"Born and raised Catholic," said Knox.

"Where do you attend church?"

Knox hesitated. "Mostly in my head. I'm on the road a lot."

"There are many Catholic churches in this country."

"But not that many in the Middle East."

O'Neil smiled. "To which I think 'touché' would be the appropriate response."

Puller said, "On the drive over, Knox was talking about taking confession. Sounded like she had saved up a lot."

O'Neil brightened and said, "Would you like to take confession, Ms. Knox? We don't ordinarily do it at this time of day, but I'm always glad to make an exception for a world traveler in need of a sound Catholic ritual. We don't have formal confessionals, but we do have a private space that we can use."

Knox gave Puller a dark look and said, "I'll take a rain check on that, Father. But thank you."

O'Neil shook hands with them again and said to Puller, "I wish you luck in your search."

Outside, Knox said, "Okay, why do I feel like I need to say a hundred Hail Marys?"

"Confession might've cleared your soul."

She lightly punched him in the arm. "So, on to Williamsburg?"

"On to Williamsburg. But I need to call them first."

Puller made the call as they sat in the front seat of the Malibu. "The Clarks know we're coming, and Father Rooney will be ready to talk to us," he said once he was finished.

"How old is he now?"

"They said eighty," replied Puller.

"Is he in full possession of his faculties?"

"Apparently enough to talk to us."

"Have you seen your dad lately?"

"I was seeing my dad when Hull and a colonel showed up with the letter from my father's accuser."

"That must have been tough," she said.

"Not something I'd want to go through every day."

"Does your dad—?"

"Thankfully, he doesn't know anything. And for the first time I'm thinking that's a good thing."

"Did you speak to Lynda Demirjian?"

"First on my list. I spoke to her husband, Stan, too. He doesn't agree with her."

"But he served under your father."

"I know. He's not totally unbiased."

"What are you hoping to get from Rooney?" Knox asked

"Whether my mother was going to see him that night. She was dressed like she would for Mass."

"She might have been going out."

"She might have been. But if so, she probably would have mentioned it to the babysitter, and she didn't. I talked to her too."

"You really haven't been letting the grass grow under your feet."

"Not the Army way."

"Your mother might not have mentioned it if she was going somewhere she didn't want anyone to know about."

"Well, she walked wherever she was going all dressed up for everyone to see. How clandestine could it be?"

"I wasn't necessarily implying that she was having an affair."

"Sure you were. And trust me, I thought about that scenario, as much as I didn't want to. But in the end, I don't believe she would do that. A girlfriend would have known. It would have come out. None of the people I talked to mentioned anything like that. There would have been signs. And my mother was devoutly religious. Adultery is a mortal sin. I just don't see it."

"The way you state the case I think you're right."

They drove the rest of the way to Williamsburg in silence.

Kelly Adams was Father Rooney's niece. She had taken him in two years ago. His sister—Adams's mother—had lived with her daughter until she had died a few years back.

All of this Adams explained as she was leading Puller and Knox through the substantial footprint of her home not far from the historic area of Williamsburg.

"Very nice place," noted Knox. "Your yard is beautiful, everything in bloom."

"I love it here," said Adams, a petite woman in her late forties with short dark hair. "I went to William and Mary, right down the street. And my daughter goes there now."

"Great school," said Puller.

"One of the best," agreed Adams. "George is on the rear patio waiting for you."

"George?" said Puller.

"Oh, I'm sorry. You probably just knew him as Father Rooney. His first name is George."

She opened a French door and led them onto a rear deck made of stone pavers. There was a large wooden trellis overgrown with ivy that would give shade from the sun. Several comfortable seating areas were set up here. In the center of the space perched in a chair around a teak table was the retired priest. Adams led them over and made introductions.

Father Rooney's hair was snowy white and carefully combed. He was smaller than Puller remembered, but then Puller was a lot bigger now than he had been then. The old priest was dressed in slacks, rubber-soled shoes, and a white polo shirt showing off a bit of paunch. His skin was pale and his eyebrows were bushy. He had on tinted glasses though the sun was setting.

A pitcher of lemonade and glasses were on the table. Puller and Knox sat and Adams poured out lemonade for them and then returned to the house.

Father Rooney took off his glasses and rubbed them on a napkin. "John Puller." His voice held an engaging drawl that Puller instantly remembered from all the homilies.

"Yes sir."

Rooney put the glasses back on. "I haven't heard that name in a very long time."

"Referring to my father? I'm named after him."

"Oh, I know you are. And then there was your brother, Robert, or Bobby as folks called him."

"Yes."

"I read he was in trouble, but then it turned out he had been falsely accused. I hope he's doing well now."

"Very well. Or he was, until now."

Rooney took a sip of his beverage and sat back. "I take it this has to do with your mother's disappearance?"

"Yes."

Rooney nodded and glanced at Knox. "Do you work with John?"

"Yes," said Knox before Puller could interject.

Rooney nodded again and folded his hands over his small belly. "It was a long time ago. Why the sudden interest now?"

"Fresh developments. We can't get into those, but it has stirred renewed interest in the case."

"And you're with CID. Are you investigating this matter officially?"

Puller gazed at the retired priest a bit suspiciously.

Rooney smiled. "I spent nearly all my professional life working on military bases. You get to know the people, the process, how things are done. I had a great many friends among the CID community, John. You pick up on things."

"I'm here in a personal capacity, Father Rooney. Knox here is really doing me a favor."

"And are you with CID as well, Ms. Knox?"

She shrugged. "It's a bit more complicated than that."

Puller said, "The night my mother went out and didn't come back it was described that she was dressed in her Sunday best. St. Mary's was within walking distance and she didn't take the car. I wondered whether she came to see you."

Rooney took a minute to consider all this before clearing his throat and saying, "Jackie Puller was devout in her faith. As the wife of a one-star she was expected to participate in many efforts and organizations at Fort Monroe, and she did. But the efforts she expended at St. Mary's came solely from her faith. I can't think of one significant undertaking at the church for which she did not volunteer. She attended Mass every Sunday with you and your brother in tow. And your father occasionally. She also came several times a week to pray and perform her rosary. And she was a regular at the confessional."

At this last comment Knox shifted uncomfortably in her seat. If Rooney noticed this he didn't comment.

"So it would not have been unusual for her to show up at the church on any given day, or any given time?" asked Puller.

"No, it wouldn't. However, I wasn't expecting her that night. If I had been I would have told the police."

Puller nodded, slowly taking this in. He knew this probably was the case, but he still had had to pursue this lead.

"In your discussions with her did she seem happy? Were there problems with my father?"

Rooney held up a hand. "Although I'm no longer an active priest I will carry the sanctity of my conversations with my parishioners to the grave. So I'm afraid I can't discuss such matters."

"Even if we're trying to find out what happened to her?" said Knox.

"I'm afraid so. Exceptions soon destroy the rule." He looked over at Puller. "But I can tell you some of my conclusions without revealing anything that I discussed with her."

Puller sat up straighter. "Any information is more than we have now."

Rooney took a drink of his lemonade and leaned back in his chair. "Your mother, I believe, understood your father better than any person on earth. She understood the almost ferocious ambition that he displayed over the years."

"Based on what?" asked Puller.

Rooney settled his gaze on him. "Without getting into specifics, she often referred to the Puller family history. A generation removed from your father's," he added and then looked expectantly at Puller.

Puller thought about this for a few moments. "My paternal grandfather was a West Point grad too. He was in World War II."

"And what was the highest rank he achieved?" asked Rooney.

"Captain."

"And the reason for that?"

"He died on D-Day on the beaches at Normandy leading his platoon against the German fortifications. He was highly decorated and would have moved up in rank except for his death. He was considered for the Medal of Honor but didn't get it. Paperwork got lost, so I heard."

"And your father was how old when his father died?"

Puller quickly did the math in his head. "Eight."

Knox said, "So are you saying Puller Sr. felt abandoned by his dad and worked his whole life to achieve more than his father had?"

"No," said Rooney.

After a few moments of silence Puller said, "You think he was achieving all of it for his father? Because he never got the chance to do it himself?"

Rooney pointed at him. "That's what I believe."

"And did my mother think this too?"

"I can tell you that she had given it a lot of thought and more or less came to the same conclusion."

"I found a letter from my mother to my father. She wrote it shortly before she disappeared. She said she wanted to make things work out. Mostly for the sake of my brother and me. But that she wanted to take me and my brother away from him for a bit so my father could better understand his priorities. Meaning his family over the Army, I guess."

Rooney nodded. "That sounds like a decision Jackie would come to. She adored both you and your brother. And she loved your father. I'm breaking no vow to tell you that. But I could understand why she would want matters to come to a head. Taking his sons away from their father was a way for her to do that. She would force him to decide."

Puller sat there mulling all of this over. "Is there anything you can tell me that might help me to find the truth, Father Rooney?"

The old man sat there for such a long time that Puller thought he might have fallen asleep.

Finally, Rooney stirred. "Your father came to see me several days after your mother went missing."

Puller went rigid. "What did he want?"

"He wanted to take confession. And before you ask, I can say nothing about what he talked about."

Puller looked frustrated. "Well, I'm not sure that's very helpful, actually."

"What I can tell you is that your father was devastated by

her disappearance. I have never seen him so inconsolable. So if you're thinking he had anything whatsoever to do with whatever did happen to her, well, I would say that you're barking up the wrong tree. I'm afraid that's all I can tell you, but I hope it helped. I have witnessed much guilt in the confessional, Agent Puller. And the only guilt your father had that day was not being there for the woman he loved when she needed him."

Puller stood and held out his hand, which Rooney took.

"Thank you, Father. That was the most helpful thing I've heard in a very long time."

Behind the glasses, the old priest's eyes twinkled. "If you start going to Mass regularly you'll hear something uplifting like that every Sunday."

CHAPTER

21

Paul Rogers adjusted his shirt cuffs and then the headset, placing the mic an inch or so from the right side of his mouth.

He had added tinted glasses and a fedora covering his shaved head to his appearance, keeping in mind that somewhere a bench warrant had been issued for his arrest and cops here could very well know what he looked like. He was also growing a goatee.

Into the mic he said, "Rogers, checking in."

There was a squawk and then a voice came back to him. "Copy that, Paul. Loud and clear. Have a good shift."

He settled his back against the brick wall next to the entrance door. In front of the door were two metal stands with a red velvet rope strung between them, like at a theater.

It was thirty minutes until opening, but there was already a line of people down the street and around the corner. They were mostly young, many clearly military with their shaved heads and toned physiques. The ladies were dressed to impress; the men looked ready to drink and score with the aforementioned ladies.

Rogers looked down at his phone where the VIP list was up on the screen. Ten names. Bigwigs in some way, he supposed. At least locally.

He studied the people in line. Most of them were on their phones, tapping keys and, he supposed, communicating with someone. Some were taking pictures of themselves. He had heard about Facebook and that Twitter thing, although he had no idea what the purpose for either was. He had seen a young waitress inside posting something on her Facebook account. To Rogers it looked like a picture of what she'd had for lunch. But then there had been a photo of her nearly naked and he had turned away before she caught him looking.

The world really had changed a lot in ten years.

There were a few guys in line watching him. He knew what they were doing, because he was doing the same thing: sizing them up.

He could tell these guys were going to test him. Maybe with a fake ID, or a sob story, or a plan of misdirection to get some buddies into the bar unseen.

Rogers popped his neck and then rubbed the back of his head. It had started to tingle there. That was never a good sign.

Do not screw this up. Do not overreact. Do nothing to let them come and get you.

Using tools he'd found in the van and some black spray paint and tape, he had methodically doctored the license plates on the van, changing one letter and one number. He felt he was good to go there. So now he had to focus on the job at hand.

Finally, the thirty minutes were up and Rogers rose and unhooked the red rope.

"Single file, IDs ready. No problems, no trouble," he called out in a loud voice. "Any fake IDs are subject to confiscation at my sole discretion. If you don't like that rule, head somewhere else."

The line of people surged forward.

Rogers had been given a special light like the TSA used at airports. If the person looked anywhere close to the age limit, and most did, he pulled it out and hit the surface of the ID. Three times he held on to the ID because it was fake but good enough to fool almost anyone without the same equipment. The two girls and one guy affected by this did not want to go quietly, but Rogers gave them a look that made them turn and leave.

Then came a group of guys big enough to look like they played major-college football. Three blacks and three whites, and none looked over twenty.

He asked for IDs. The first two were obviously doctored so badly that Rogers didn't even bother keeping them. He just tossed them back. When they tried to pass by him, he put out an arm.

"Just to be clear, that was a rejection, guys. Try somewhere else, maybe where the bouncer is blind."

A black guy, the biggest of them, said, "Come on, man, we won't drink. We just want to dance and score quality time with some fine ladies."

"Sorry, no exceptions."

Another of the group, a slightly smaller white guy, stepped up.

"I tell you what, Grandpa. You let us in and you get to keep your teeth."

Rogers smelled the kid's breath. "You look like you been six-packing already. You might want to head back to the dorm and keep your scholarship."

"You must not have heard me, old man."

He took a swing, but Rogers had already moved and the fist caught nothing but air.

"Stop running, Gramps, it'll only hurt for a second," said the man.

Rogers turned to the other men. "I'm telling you guys to take your buddy out of here before something unfortunate happens."

The men all laughed. "You sound like a lawyer, dude," said the black guy.

"I'm nothing like a lawyer."

"How 'bout a doctor, then?" said the man who'd taken the swing.

Rogers turned to him. "I'm not following."

"Then you can heal yourself, asshole!"

He swung again, only this time Rogers didn't move. He stood his ground and, as he had done with Karl, clenched the man's fist. But he didn't just grip, he twisted and then jerked downward.

The man screamed and dropped to the pavement clutching his injured arm.

"You broke my fuckin' wrist," he wailed.

Rogers raised a fist to deliver a blow to the head that would have almost certainly killed the man. The spot on his head was burning like somebody had set it on fire with an acetylene torch.

No. Don't do it. Don't do it!

"Hey, man, come on, back off!"

Rogers stared up at the black guy.

"You proved your point, dude, okay?"

Rogers let go of the wrist and took a step back.

Instantly, on a sign from the black guy, two of the other men stepped up to take their shot.

Rogers didn't wait for either of them to take a swing. He grabbed the shirt of the bigger one, lifted him off his feet, and threw him against the wall. The man hit the brick hard and slumped down. When the other launched himself low at Rogers's belly, he brought a knee up and caught him right on the chin. The man fell to the pavement screaming with a mouthful of broken teeth.

Rogers stepped back and adjusted his hat.

"Come back when you're old enough," he said to the men who were still standing.

The other guys helped their injured friends up.

The black guy said, "Oh, we'll be back all right. Count on it, you son of a bitch!"

The group stalked off, with several of them supporting their injured buddies. The man with the broken wrist looked back at Rogers and screamed obscenities.

The other people in line looked stunned by what they had just witnessed. Even the ones who were obviously in the military. Some left. Most stayed.

Within fifteen minutes Rogers had passed all those twenty-one and older into the bar. All the rest were sent on their way. After seeing what Rogers could do, no one else gave him any trouble.

"Dude's a damn freak," one man muttered to his friend as they were turned away.

A minute later a stretch limo drove up and the driver got out, came around, and opened the door. Ten people got out. They were all in their twenties and thirties, split equally between men and women, dressed in casual clothes that would break the bank of most people.

One of the men from the group came up to Rogers. He was tall, good-looking, with thick, curly brown hair, and he wore a carefree, arrogant expression.

"Name's Josh Quentin. My party's on the VIP list."

Rogers looked down at his list and said, "I'll need to see ID from everyone."

"You're new."

"First night."

"What's your name?"

"Paul."

"Okay, Paul, fair enough. But from now on, remember us. We're regulars. And I don't like to wait."

He slipped a hundred-dollar bill into Rogers's hand.

They all showed ID and Rogers checked the names off on the screen on his phone.

"Have a good time, Mr. Quentin."

Quentin turned to look at him and smiled. "I always do." He grabbed the gorgeous woman next to him, who returned the grope with a smile and a flirty hip bump.

Some guys seem to have the Midas touch, thought Rogers. *And I wouldn't mind bashing in the brains of every single one of the pricks.*

He poked his head inside the door in time to see the group head up the stairs and into a room.

Rogers had not gone up there when he was inside the bar. It had been roped off. He did note that there was a security man posted at the bottom of the stairs who had let Quentin and his group pass.

Rogers wondered why people would come to a bar and then not go to the bar. Maybe they had their own personal one up there. Maybe they had something more than the peons below got.

As he was about to close the door he saw Helen Myers pass by the security man and head up the stairs. She went into the same room.

Rogers closed the door.

Four times that night he was called into the bar to handle a disturbance.

Four times he vise-gripped the arm of the offender just enough to get his drunken attention and led the person quietly out the door.

Twice he saw Myers watching him from the upper hallway. She seemed pleased with how he was handling things.

The place was packed until one a.m. with hundreds of drinkers, dancers, bad karaoke, and men grabbing ass and women sometimes letting them. Then people began leaving. At two he and another security man eased out the last few stragglers. Then the cleanup crew came in and started stacking chairs and mopping slickened floors. The bleach would probably come out in the morning, Rogers figured.

He didn't know how many drinks had been poured over the course of six hours, but he felt the Grunt had just made a ton of money.

He was sitting at the bar drinking a glass of water when Myers came over and sat next to him. She pulled out an e-cigarette and put the end between her lips.

"How was your first night?"

"Pretty much what I expected," he replied.

"I heard there was an altercation in line. With some big guys."

"They didn't understand the rules. So I gave a lesson. But I did it as nicely as I could. Like you said."

"I saw you do a couple of ejections from in here. They were well done."

"Thanks." Rogers took a drink of water and set his glass down. "Josh Quentin?"

Myers pulled out the e-cig from her mouth. "What about him?"

"What does he do to qualify as a VIP?"

"He owns his own company. Super smart. He's not a billionaire yet, but he will be. And he's barely thirty. A real mover and shaker."

"Good for him. Nice group of friends with him."

"He has lots of friends."

"Yeah, I saw him playing grab-ass with one of them. But she didn't seem to mind."

She shrugged. "He gets what he pays for."

"Almost a billionaire, huh? Then you'd think they'd be going to some fancy-ass club for high rollers."

She frowned at this comment. "This isn't Vegas. And we're not just a bar, Paul. We cater to lots of different interests and tastes. Some *fancier* than others. Good night." She rose to leave.

"What about my money?"

She turned back to him. "Payday is every Friday."

"The thing is I need some cash now."

She eyed him closely. Then she walked around the bar, opened the cash register, counted out two fifties, ten twenties, ten tens, and the rest fives and ones. She wrapped a rubber band around the cash and tossed it to him.

He slipped it inside his pocket. "Thanks."

"You're welcome. But that's a one-off. From now on payday is Friday."

"Understood."

"And even though you're not officially on the payroll, we'll be taking out something for FICA and income taxes. I'm not getting screwed by the IRS."

"What does that leave me, then?"

"Enough. Unless you want to fill out the paperwork? Full name, Social Security number, all that."

"No, I don't want to do that."

"Fine. Just so you know, I've never paid an employee under the table. I'm not a fan."

"So why me?"

She leaned against the bar. "You looked like somebody who needed a break."

"I appreciate that. So how's Karl?"

"I'm sure he'll be fine. And remember, he's your boss."
"Never forgot it. See you tomorrow. *Boss*."
Rogers rose and left.
It was nearly three in the morning.
It was time for him to go to work.

CHAPTER

22

ROGERS PARKED THE van well off the grounds of Fort Monroe and finished the trek on foot. This early in the morning, he was the only one out and about.

The salt air hit him from the channel, and far out in the water he could see the white lights of a passing ship. It was cool, quiet, and peaceful.

Depending on how things went, that could all change very quickly.

He knew exactly where he was going and wanted to get there quickly and unobtrusively. There were few who could move with more stealth than Rogers. That had been beaten into him for so long he could think of no other way.

The building was just up ahead.

He had passed it earlier.

Building Q.

He did nothing but watch for an hour.

It was now five minutes past four.

The private security did a sweep on the half hour, he noted. One went left, the other went right, and they crossed in the rear. A third guard remained at the front gate.

Standard protocols all the way around.

Predictable.

Which was what was wrong with the standard protocols all the way around.

As soon as all three guards were clustered once more at the front, Rogers moved. It took him ten seconds to scale the rear fence. He did so barely making any noise. He dropped within the grounds and looked around, keeping low.

He scuttled over to a set of rear entrance doors. They were metal below and chicken-wired glass above. He peered inside and saw the alarm system.

It glowed red. It was active.

You didn't waste guards and a security system on a building that housed nothing important.

The building was eight stories high, perhaps the tallest here other than the Chamberlin building. Back when the fort was being constructed, land was plentiful and elevators nonexistent. Thus the Army had opted for low-rise construction.

He took off his shoes and socks, tied the laces together, and swung them over his neck, each shoe dangling on either side of his head.

He found a handhold in the brick veneer of the building and gripped the masonry with a strength that would be unimaginable for even the best rock climbers in the world. His fingers and toes were actually digging into the hard surfaces. The skin there had been replaced with a synthetic tissue. That was the reason the police couldn't take prints from him. The synthetic looked and felt like the real thing, but it was far tougher than human skin, which would be bleeding from the friction with the stone.

He began to climb.

This was not the first time he had scaled this building, although not as part of his official training. He had simply done it on a bet.

He had won the bet. Ten bucks.

He reached the top ledge and vaulted over the edge and onto the flat, pebbled roof. The heavy HVAC systems that climate-controlled the building were housed up here. And there was, of course, an access door.

He hoped that his memory held up, for this was the critical point.

He reached the door. It was padlocked.

One pull and the clasp anchoring the lock tore free from the door.

He gripped the knob and turned it.

He took a breath and held it.

He was not experiencing fear. He could no longer feel that.

He was thinking about his exit strategy if an alarm went off.

Guards in front. Roof alarm. They'll secure the perimeter. How long will that take? I'll go over the rear side, down to the third floor, let go, and free fall to the ground. Over the fence and out. Twenty seconds. It will have to be enough. If I run into a guard, well, he'll be dead and I won't.

He opened the door.

He waited. No alarm sounded.

His memory had been good. They hadn't alarmed this door back then either. They imagined that no one could scale a sheer brick wall without the aid of a ladder. They were off by one on that assumption.

He shut the door behind him and moved down the stairs. The interior of the space outlined in his head from thirty-year-old memories, he made his way to the second floor and then out into the main corridor. He looked in the ceiling crevices for motion sensors but saw none. He looked for surveillance cameras but saw none of those either.

They had put all their marbles on the exterior security.

But that wasn't all. No cameras inside meant that who-ever operated this place wanted no record of what was going on in here.

It had been the same when Rogers had been here. Be-cause the things that went on here, well, they were not exactly pretty. Or maybe even legal.

He moved down the main corridor and saw that the place had been gutted and rebuilt. Old wooden doors with a top half of frosted glass engraved with department names had been replaced with sleek automated sliding glass doors ac-cessed by key card ports.

He couldn't get into any of these rooms without a key card. And if he tried, he was certain an alarm would sound. But the glass had one weakness: He could see inside the rooms. In one space he saw workstations with computers and sophisticated freestanding equipment.

In another room was a metal framework that looked fa-miliar to Rogers. It could be mounted on the exterior of something.

Or someone.

In another was a helmet with built-in goggles.

In yet another was a machine gun mounted on a metal platform with a seating area behind it. Next to the gun was a helmet with a surround that would cover the eyes and wires and cables coming out of the top of the helmet and leading to a control box attached to the wall.

Behind another glass door were enormous TV screens with grids and blocks of data running across them. They were evidently measuring some system that was currently running. Though the people didn't work around the clock here, the computer systems did.

Another space was set up as a chemical lab with burners

and test tubes and liquids running through pristine tubes. Set on work areas around the room were several iterations of what Rogers recognized as mass spectrometers along with some pieces of equipment that looked brand-new and that he didn't recognize.

He came away with a firm conclusion.

They're still at it here.

He looked down at his hands and then slid his sleeve up to look at the scars there. His whole body was a scar.

On the outside.

And on the inside. Maybe more on the inside.

I'm actually all scar tissue on the inside.

He left the second floor and went to the first, keeping well away from windows and doorways. There was a reception area near the front doors.

He had expected that.

And something else he expected was there.

Atalanta Group.

That was the name of the business that was housed here.

At first Rogers's brain automatically saw the name as Atlanta, but then he recognized that wasn't right.

Atalanta Group.

He had never heard of it.

But old companies faded and new ones took their place. And he had been gone from this world for a long time.

He checked his watch. He'd been in here a half hour.

He went back to the roof and peered over the edge. The guards were making their patrols. He waited until they had once more converged at the front before climbing back down the building after fixing the lock on the access door to hide any sign that he had breached it. He scaled the fence, landed on the other side, and made his way quickly back to his van.

He drove back to the motel and got there in twenty minutes. He went to his room, sat on the bed, and pulled out his phone. He put in the word "Atalanta." It did not take long to get hits.

Atalanta was a mythological *female* warrior of Greek descent, the only woman on board Jason's *Argo* and the lady who had killed the fearsome Calydonian Boar. She was the only female regularly listed among the greatest mythological warriors.

When he looked up "Atalanta Group at Fort Monroe, Virginia," he got exactly nothing. There was an Atalanta Group, but it had to do with specialty food and it was nowhere near Fort Monroe.

Rogers sat back and thought about this.

Secretive. Perhaps to a paranoid degree.

Atalanta, a great *female* warrior? The only one who ran with the male dogs?

He dropped his phone, lay back on the bed, and closed his eyes.

His lifetime of bad luck might have just turned to pure gold.

It was about damn time, he thought.

Claire Jericho was apparently up to her old tricks.

CHAPTER

23

PULLER HAD JUST walked into the lobby of the hotel where they were both staying. Knox was standing there, holding two cups of coffee from Starbucks. She handed one to him.

"Just like you like it."

He took a sip. "Thanks."

"Okay, Rooney pretty much said your dad was innocent. So now what?"

"Goal hasn't changed. We need to keep digging until we get to the truth."

"Okay, but sometimes the truth does not set you free, Puller."

She had followed him outside and over to his car.

He took out his keys and jingled them in his hand. "And what is that supposed to mean?"

"It's nothing I haven't told you before," she replied. "Despite what some people say, it's not always best to know versus not know."

He put his elbows on the Malibu's roof and scowled at her. "So if it was *your* mother, you'd rather not know what happened to her? Whether she's dead or not?"

Knox looked away from him but said, "If it were me I

would want to know. All I'm saying is, you want the truth, you better be prepared to handle it."

"Trust me, Knox. I'm prepared. I've had thirty years to get ready."

He unlocked the car door and climbed in. She did the same.

She looked at him. "So where to?"

"Rooney said he wasn't expecting my mother that night, but that doesn't mean she wasn't planning to go there. Something might have prevented her from getting there."

"Like what?"

"Like someone."

"You think someone snatched her? On an active military installation? With lots of people around? How could they possibly pull that off?"

"You'd be amazed at what I've seen people *pull off*."

A short time later they were back at Fort Monroe and parked in front of Puller's old home.

Knox peered up at the house. "Have you been in there yet?"

"No. Working up to it."

"Looks like a nice place."

"My dad was a one-star. It *was* nice. Nicer than anything I've been in since."

"Where did you and your brother go after your mother disappeared?"

"We lived with my aunt, my dad's sister, for a while in Florida. We visited her a lot when my mother was around. They really got along."

"Is your aunt still alive?"

"No, she was murdered."

"Good God, Puller. How? Why?"

"It's complicated. But suffice it to say I found out who did it and they were appropriately punished."

"Your aunt, your brother, and now your mother. Any other family members lurking out there for you to avenge?"

"I hope not."

"So after you stopped living with your aunt, where did you and Bobby go?"

"We moved with my father when he was reassigned. He was still our parent even if he wasn't around much. His staff helped to raise us. Dad always made sure we were taken care of. Nice ladies, housekeepers, people to help with homework and getting us places for sports and other stuff. Then Bobby went off to the Air Force Academy, and two years later I went to college."

They fell silent and both stared up at the house.

"So don't you think you should go in?" she asked.

He glanced at her. "Why?"

"Well, it might jog something in your memory that could help us."

"Knox, I don't remember anything—" Puller stopped and looked out the car window.

"What?" asked Knox.

Puller was thinking about all the things he hadn't remembered from that night, until his brother had set him straight.

"I...I seemed to have some selective memories from back then," he said.

"Then we should go in."

"It's locked up."

"I'm not sure that's ever stopped you before."

He looked at her. "Well, I know it's never stopped *you* before. Since I've seen you pick a lock on a house, go in, and shoot the person inside."

"That's hardly fair, since she was trying to kill me."

Puller opened the car door. "Let's go."

They approached from the front, and because the street was empty, Puller allowed Knox to quickly pick the door lock. They stepped inside and Puller closed the door behind them as Knox put away her pick tools. He looked around while Knox watched him closely.

"Changed much?"

He shook his head. "The Army's not much into decoration. The bones stay pretty much the same. You can change the paint, but when you leave you have to put it back to Army cream white. SOP."

There was no furniture left in the house. That made it seem bigger to Puller than it actually had been.

They cleared the first floor except for the bathroom. He went in there and peered out the window, which overlooked the backyard.

Knox looked over his shoulder. "Is this the window she was looking out when you saw her last?"

He nodded. "But the thing is, Knox, that was in the afternoon and she didn't leave until after we had our dinner."

"So you saw her again then?"

He closed the bathroom door. "Only I don't seem to recall it. Bobby told me."

"Okay, you had dinner, you said. Let's go into the dining room again and see if something hits you."

They walked into the small dining area off the kitchen. Puller leaned against a wall and studied the space.

He closed his eyes and thought back thirty years ago. The only thing was that people's memories were notoriously bad. That was why eyewitness testimony was so unreliable. Most couldn't remember what they were doing the week before at any precise time, much less three decades back. The brain wasn't really a computer, regurgitating pure facts. It was flavored with all sorts of human things, like embellishment, hope, sorrow, selective recall. Humans were the kings of re-visionist remembering.

We all want to look and sound better than we actually do.

But Puller was an Army investigator. Thus he held him-self to a higher standard than that.

His brow furrowed as he thought back. Nothing added, nothing subtracted.

Just remember, John. Just remember exactly as it was back then on that day, at that hour.

"There was a phone call," he said, opening his eyes.

"A phone call? From whom?"

"I don't know. But Mom was finishing up making dinner. The phone rang and she went to answer it. There were no cell phones back then. It was the landline." He pointed to a spot on the kitchen wall. "It was over there."

"Did you hear her talking on it? Where was your brother?"

"Bobby was outside. He might not have even heard it ring. And no, I didn't hear her talking on it. But I do remem-ber walking around that corner after she got off and seeing her face. She was upset." He grabbed his phone and punched in a number from memory.

Carol Powers answered on the second ring.

"Carol, it's John Puller. Listen, you said when we talked before that it was lucky you were home because your boyfriend canceled, otherwise you couldn't have babysat us?"

"That's right."

"So wherever my mom went that night, it proba-bly wasn't planned? I mean, it was last-minute if she called the same day?"

"I guess not. I mean she might have arranged previously with someone else to babysit and that fell through, but I sort of doubt it. I lived right there and your mom usually called me first."

"Did you tell anyone that when they were investigating her disappearance? That it seemed to be last-minute?"

"Um, well, no, no one asked me that specifically. They just wanted to know when I got there and if your mom had said anything to me about where she was going. And that's what I told them. Did I mess up, John? Should I have told them it wasn't planned?"

"It's not your fault, Carol. It's their job to ask. Thanks."

He put away his phone and looked at Knox.

"Cause and effect?" she said. "She gets the phone call and decides to go out. She calls the babysitter and dresses in her Sunday best."

"I wonder if they checked the phone records back then?"

"You'd think it would have been in the report if they had. And I don't remember seeing anything like that. And there's no way those phone records would be around now. Thirty years ago I think it was one of the Baby Bells running the phone service down here."

"So she got a call that made her change her plans and go out. And she never came back."

"You're sure you heard nothing that was said on that call?"

He shook his head. "I came in as she was hanging up. I just saw her face. She looked upset. But when she saw me she smiled. Then she had me help with making dinner."

"Your memory is definitely coming back since you walked in that door."

He nodded. "But I can't remember what I never knew. And I don't know who made that call or what was said." He looked at Knox. "I know it's a long shot, but can you check with some of your people and see if there's any way in the world we could get the phone number of who called her on that day?"

"I can try, Puller. But, like I said, it's a really long shot."

"And sometimes those pay off."

"But why not have CID do it? They can pull those records, if they exist, as easily as I can."

Puller didn't answer her.

Knox moved closer to him. "Do you think it's your sole responsibility to solve this case?"

"Well, I didn't do much work on it over the last thirty years," he shot back.

"You were a kid when it happened."

"But I haven't been a kid for a long time."

"And when you were in a position to do something about it, the case was long since cold. And it seems to me you had other things on your plate. Like fighting in two wars for starters. And then the Army isn't really well known for letting its people go off on a lark and try to solve a case on their own just because they want to."

"You can make all the excuses in the world, Knox, and so can I, but it still won't change things."

"But Father Rooney pretty much cleared your father of any involvement in her disappearance."

"No he didn't. He doesn't know that for a fact, and neither do I. My father was here on that day. He came back early and didn't tell anyone. And even if he is innocent I still don't know what happened to my mother. I let this mess sit for thirty years. No more, Knox. No more. Buck stops here. I get this done or die trying."

"But Puller, this could take a long time. You have a job. The Army is not going to let you indefinitely—"

He barked, "To hell with the Army, I'll resign if I have to, but this case is getting solved."

She looked to be about to make a response but then seemed to catch herself. She took a breath and stepped out of the room to make the call.

Puller went back into the bathroom and looked out the window.

Where did you go, Mom? Where?

She just walked down the street and disappeared.

Puller looked down at his phone. He and his brother and father had left Fort Monroe shortly after Jackie Puller disappeared. He had been back to the post a few times on official business, but never for more than a few hours at a time.

He did a search on his phone. The relevant search terms were "crime," "disappearance," "murder," "women," the year, and "Hampton, Virginia."

The search did its thing and Puller gaped at the result.

The first item said it all.

Police suspect serial killer in murders of four women in Williamsburg, Virginia.

The story was from the same year and month his mother disappeared.

And Williamsburg was thirty minutes from Fort Monroe.

Son of a bitch!

24

KNOX WALKED BACK into the room and said, "Okay, I've got the ball in motion on the phone call and we'll see what they can find."

She stopped because Puller was hunkered over his phone and hadn't even looked up when she had spoken.

"What's up?"

"Give me a sec."

He finished reading the screen and put his phone away. He quickly explained what he'd found.

"Serial murders in Williamsburg?" she said, her eyes wide in amazement.

"Same time period, and Williamsburg is only about a half an hour from here."

"But we can't know that they're connected."

"And we can't know that they're not," he retorted.

"Why'd you even think to look into something like that?"

"First rule of investigating a cold case: Were there other crimes in the area that might be connected to yours? I should have done it a long time ago."

"So a serial killer gets on a military installation, kills your mother, and, what, carries off the body?"

"I don't know. I just know that there's a possible lead

there. And yes, it was an active military installation. But at that time of year when my mother left, it was already dark. And there were never many people on the streets. The officer quarters weren't always full and there weren't a lot of young kids who would be out playing. My dad was an exception. He got married later. I can't think of many one-stars with really little kids. They tended to be older. The fact is this area was pretty isolated and away from the busy part of the post. And back then some of the buildings weren't used. She could have been dragged into one of them. So it might not seem that a killer could strike here, but he could."

"But how would he get on the post?"

"He might have already been on the post."

"You mean in uniform?"

"There were lots of people who worked at Fort Monroe that were not in uniform. But yes, he could have been in uniform."

"I take it the serial killings in Williamsburg were never solved?"

"They never even found a suspect to charge. Four murders. All women."

"And the bodies?"

"Found scattered around the area, mostly in isolated places and shallow graves."

"But if your mother was killed her remains were never found."

"No. But if he did kill her he might have done a better job disposing of her body."

"What was the timing of the murders? Meaning any after your mother disappeared?"

"No. They stopped. The last victim was three nights before my mother vanished."

"Was there any regularity to the attacks?"

"A couple weeks or so in between each."

"So your mother would have been an anomaly in that pattern?"

"Yes, but serial killers don't always stick to a pattern. Sometimes they seize an opportunity."

"Which you may be doing by latching on to this, Puller."

He stared down at her. "It's a potential lead, Knox. That's all."

"And it's a very cold case, so how do you propose chasing this lead down?"

"The police file would be a good start."

"And will you approach the local police in your official CID capacity?"

Puller didn't answer.

Knox added, "Because you're not officially tasked to take on that case. And you're not officially working on this one, so I'm not sure how that would fly."

"You could get those files."

"I probably could, but I'm not officially tasked to do this either. I have superiors to answer to, just like you."

"Really? So you're here on vacation time and nothing else?"

She stared at him and he just as resolutely glared back at her.

"We could run that in circles for days," she finally said.

"I can run for days. How about you?"

"You're not making this easy, Puller."

"Why should I?"

"Well, I guess it's hard to argue with that," she said sarcastically.

"So you'll do it?"

"I'll make a call."

"Say it may be in the interests of national security. That'll push you to the head of the records retrieval line. Otherwise we might be waiting for months. Tell them you'll send a CID agent to pick them up for you today if they can have them ready."

"Phone records from thirty years ago and now a file on four cold murders. My, how this case has evolved."

"Cases always evolve, Knox. They're like living things. And sometimes they turn into something truly unrecognizable."

* * *

Five hours later Knox learned that the phone records from thirty years before were impossible to access. But on the plus side, they were staring at ten file boxes filled with copies of everything the Williamsburg police and FBI had on the serial murders.

They had carried the boxes up to Knox's hotel room and stacked them against the wall. They ordered room service and started going through them.

Knox sat cross-legged on the bed. She had changed into black leggings and a pullover. Her feet were bare. Her hair was pulled back into a knot.

Puller had on the same clothes he'd worn that day, except he'd taken off his windbreaker. He sat at a small desk against the wall, intently poring over documents and photos and making notes on a legal pad.

The room had a balcony with a slider, which Knox had opened to let in the ocean breeze.

A minute later room service arrived with their meals. Puller had opted for steak and a baked potato, Knox for a salad with shrimp.

Puller was surprised to see the bottle of red wine.

After the attendant left, Knox uncorked the wine and poured out a glass. She sniffed it and then looked at him.

"I don't know about you, but I think a lot better with vino carbs in me."

He slowly nodded. "Okay."

"I don't think we need to let it breathe. It has all its got to give right now. Their wine list was actually pretty good."

"Above my pay grade. I'm more a beer guy."

She handed him a filled glass and they began eating their meals while still going over the files.

Puller took a bite of steak and said, "The locals didn't do a great job of processing the crime scene, and it doesn't seem that the FBI raised the bar much when they came on board."

Knox swirled the wine in her glass before taking a sip. "Well, we know the high standards you have, Chief Puller."

"This isn't a joke, Knox," he retorted.

She glanced up at him. "I never said it was. And unless you've forgotten, I've *seen* you process a crime scene, so it was actually a compliment. And just for the record, I'd appreciate it if you wouldn't bite my head off over everything I say."

Puller looked down. "I'm sorry. This case..."

"Is like no other, I get that, Puller. So let's keep digging and see what we find."

"Okay," Knox said a few minutes later. "The best I can make out, all the women murdered were single, professional types in their late twenties."

"Which is very unusual for a serial murderer," noted Puller. "The populations they often go after are prostitutes, runaways, people with little family support, risky occupations."

"And no one to care when they go missing," added Knox.

"But your mother fits none of those categories. And she also doesn't fit the young professional type."

"It could be a one-off," suggested Puller. "Or a wrong place, wrong time. If he saw my mother walking alone in her Sunday best? And while she was older than the murdered women, my mom looked a lot younger than her age."

"She was a beautiful woman, Puller."

He looked up to find Knox staring at him from the bed.

"You've seen a picture of her?"

"Like I said, I did my homework before I came here." She paused. "And I'm seeing her right now."

"What do you mean?"

"You have your dad's height but your mother's eyes, nose, and cheekbones."

Puller glanced down at the file he was holding, evidently uncomfortable with her observation. "I guess I never really thought much about that."

"Because it reminded you of your loss?" said Knox.

Puller didn't answer her.

She said, "It is a weird coincidence that a serial killer was operating barely thirty minutes away killing young women and it doesn't seem like the police here even made inquiries into whether your mother's case was connected or not. At the very least they should have done a little digging, particularly since they really had no other leads."

"It's more than weird. It's inexcusable."

He reached over and snagged another file he'd brought into her room.

"What's that?" she asked, finishing her wine and pouring herself another glass.

"CID file from my mom's case. If the special agent on the case is still alive maybe we should talk to him."

"You think he'll remember anything pertinent?"

"It's why we ask the questions."

They finished going over the files and then Puller made some calls and located retired CID agent Vincent DiRenzo. He left a message for DiRenzo, rose, and stretched out his tall frame.

"I think that's all we can do tonight, Knox."

Knox had taken off the pullover, revealing a tight white tank top underneath. She laid aside a file, sat up, freed her hair from the knot, tousled it, and looked at him.

"It's not *that* late," she said. "And we haven't finished our wine."

"It's after midnight," he pointed out. "We both need to get to bed."

"Okay."

He stared down at her and she back up at him.

"What?"

"You know what, Puller."

"Where exactly is this coming from?" he asked quietly.

"It's coming from a missed opportunity back in Kansas."

"So you're saying you made a mistake?"

"Yes."

He nodded, considering this.

She moved over to the edge of the bed and touched his arm with her hand. Knox's large eyes locked on his as she rubbed his arm. Puller felt a jolt of something go right through him.

"I want this, John," she said. "Right here, right now. I just want to be with you."

He said, "And you've thought this all the way through?"

"I don't want to think anything through. I'm leading with my heart, not my head."

He thought about this for a moment as she continued to

stroke his arm. "We're working a case, Knox. So I have to lead with my head. Good night."

He walked out the door.

Knox sat there looking devastated.

She let out a long groan and slumped back on the bed.

CHAPTER

25

I'M SORRY ABOUT last night."

A pale Knox glanced over at Puller, who was driving due west across Virginia. They were on their way to see retired CID special agent Vincent DiRenzo. He lived on Smith Mountain Lake near Roanoke.

Puller kept his eyes on the road. "I don't like getting played, Knox. I don't deserve that, not from you."

She tapped her toe against the floorboard. "Meaning what?"

"Meaning I would like to know why you *really* showed up on my doorstep."

"I already explained that."

"No, you *already* told me a bullshit story. I'd like the truth now."

She folded her arms over her chest and looked crossly out the window. "So I guess because of what I do for a living you always think I have a hidden agenda? That I'm never telling you the complete truth?"

"Couldn't have summed it up better myself."

"Screw you, Puller."

"Speaking of, your little maneuver on the bed last night? If that was your way of getting me to trust you, it seriously failed."

She sighed. "Okay, I guess I deserved that. And I'm sorry." She sat up straighter. "So, Vincent DiRenzo?"

Puller's shoulders relaxed with the change in direction of the conversation. "Had a solid career in CID. Nothing spectacular, but no big screwups either. He returned my call this morning and agreed to meet with us."

"You said he lives on a lake?"

"Smith Mountain Lake. I've been there before when I was working a case. Beautiful place. Mountains rise up right out of the water. It's a hydroelectric lake," he tacked on. "About forty miles long with more shoreline than the state of Rhode Island. Calling it a lake doesn't seem to do it justice."

She nodded. "Sounds great."

"We should also talk to the local police back in Williamsburg who handled the serial murders."

"I've already made calls. Waiting to hear back. And the FBI was involved too."

He nodded. "I was hoping you could make a call about that. You have more pull in that circle than I do."

"You expect me to make a lot of calls," she said sharply.

"Isn't that why you're here? To *help*?"

She looked out the window again and didn't answer him.

* * *

Vincent DiRenzo was a widower who lived in a three-bedroom gray shingle-sided cottage set on a small cove with mountain views in the distance. The yard was full of flowerbeds and neatly maintained.

They rang the doorbell several times and received no answer. Knox peered into the garage.

"There's a car in there."

Puller looked around. "Let's try the dock. It's a nice day, he might be down there."

"Nice place to retire," commented Knox as they walked to the dock.

"You ever expect to retire?"

"Neither one of us can do what we do forever."

"Some days it seems like it's the only thing I can do."

"Then you have my sympathy."

Though it was a freshwater lake, Puller could smell the brine in the air. A flotilla of ducks was making its way across the water as a boat pulling a slalom skier turned to avoid them. The ducks paddled quickly out of harm's way.

Puller and Knox went around a curve in the path and the dock came into view. It had two boat slips, a small enclosed kitchen and gazebo, and a storage shed, all on pilings with a pressure-treated wooden deck as the floor.

They spotted DiRenzo standing next to a boat up on a lift. Puller called out and DiRenzo turned and motioned them over.

The former CID agent was short and muscular. Introductions were made and he shook their hands with a firm grip. He was wearing jeans, tennis shoes, and a sweatshirt that read *Army Strong*. His hair was close-cropped and mostly gray. A matching mustache spread over his top lip.

He had the engine compartment open on a trim yellow-and-white Chaparral twenty-five-footer that was up on the lift.

"Nice boat," commented Puller.

"Handles the wake well and it's got a lot of pep when I need it."

"Sailor can't ask for more than that," replied Puller.

"You mind if I keep working while we talk?" asked DiRenzo.

"Not at all. Can I help you with anything?"

"You can hand me some tools when I ask you."

"Sure thing."

DiRenzo climbed into the boat and started taking off some bolts from the engine using a socket wrench.

"So, the Jackie Puller case," began Knox.

DiRenzo finished loosening one bolt and dropped it into a bucket on the boat's deck. He asked Puller for another size socket. Puller handed it to him and DiRenzo took a moment to pop it on before glancing at Puller.

"Notice you had the same last name."

"She was my mother."

"I actually remember you and your brother, although I'm sure you don't remember me. And everybody knew about your dad." He started loosening another bolt. "After you phoned, I made some calls to old buddies still in harness. You've got one helluva rep at CID, Chief Puller."

"I try to do my job like the Army taught me to do it."

"No argument there." DiRenzo wiped some grease off his hands and sat on the boat's gunwale. "Over the years I've thought about your mother's case from time to time. Damnedest thing I'd ever seen. It was like she vanished into thin air. No one saw, heard anything. I worked my ass off trying to get traction. A one-star's wife goes missing? You better cover all your bases. And it wasn't just any one-star. Hell, it was Fighting John Puller. You didn't want to face that man with no answers. Intimidating doesn't come close to describing your father."

"But you never reached any sort of resolution?"

DiRenzo shook his head. "We never even had one solid lead."

"I've looked at the case notes. You were thorough. Followed all the right procedures."

"But as you well know, some of it, maybe the most important parts of it, are what you feel in the gut. Probably eighty percent of the cases I solved were like that. You get a feel for the situation and then your instincts tell you when something doesn't smell right. But with that case I never got a feel for anything. I hit a total wall at the end. It was the most frustrating point of my career. I almost quit CID because of it. I felt like a failure. And it wasn't just me. They had other agents on the case. Again, it was Fighting John Puller. They were going scorched earth."

"Did you personally speak to General Puller?" asked Knox.

"Several times. As you know, he was out of the country when his wife disappeared."

Puller and Knox exchanged a subtle look that DiRenzo failed to notice.

"There was never any motive," continued DiRenzo. "That's what always bugged the hell out of me. There usually is. Random crimes, particularly on a military installation, aren't all that common. The people usually know each other."

"At the time my mother disappeared there was a series of murders in Williamsburg?" He paused and studied DiRenzo for his reaction to this.

The older man finished wiping off his hands and took up his socket wrench once more. But he didn't start loosening bolts. He just held it in his hand, tapping it against his other palm.

"We knew about that, of course. But your mother didn't fit that pattern, as I recall."

"She wasn't exactly the right age, but she could have passed for at least five years younger," pointed out Knox. "And she was well dressed that night. That's not so far off from the victims in Williamsburg. They were young professional women."

"But all those other killings took place in the Williamsburg area. The bodies were all found within five miles of the place."

"But Hampton is not that far away. And serial killers have been known to have one-offs. Seize an opportunity."

"Well, what you say is true," conceded DiRenzo. "But I remember back then that it was not deemed to be connected."

"Do you know who made that determination?" asked Puller.

"Well, it wasn't me. It came from higher up."

"In CID or somewhere else?"

"Just higher up. It filtered down to us grunts. Not sure of the origin. You know the Army. You follow orders."

Puller drew closer to the man. "Let me get this perfectly straight. Are you saying that you were told not to look into the Williamsburg cases as being possibly connected?"

"I never really looked into them, if that's an answer," said DiRenzo, avoiding Puller's gaze.

"And you never questioned that?" said Knox.

DiRenzo looked at her. "I did what I was told. I was an investigator, but I was also in the Army. And like I just told you, I followed orders. Because if the Army teaches you nothing else, it beats *that* into you."

Puller said, "And did you ever think of a reason why the higher-ups didn't want you to check into the serial murders to see if they were possibly connected to my mother's disappearance?"

"I thought about it. I thought about it a lot, actually."

"And?" said Knox.

"And any answer I came away with scared the shit out of me. So I finally stopped thinking about it."

CHAPTER

26

So this was how the other half lived. Well, the one-tenth of the one percent, anyway.

Rogers was leaning next to a tree off a road paralleling the beach.

The drive here had taken less than two hours. It was not even noon. He would have to get back in time for work. But he still had several hours to accomplish some things.

He was staring up at a home behind a high wall and steel gates that would have stopped a runaway Abrams tank. This was the palatial retirement home of Chris Ballard, the founder of what was now CB Excelon Corp.

Rogers had left his van back at a public parking lot just in case there were surveillance cameras posted by the front gate. He imagined they might film every car that went by the mansion. He did not want to be on that tape.

His eyes took in all points of the compound, for that's what it was behind the high walls. Multiple buildings, an internal road system, cars, people. He had found an aerial view of the place on the Internet.

Ballard had clearly struck gold sucking at the teat of the federal government.

There wasn't a whole lot of high ground here, but Rogers

managed to find what there was. He worked through several spots before he found a place that allowed him to see into the compound but provided him cover while doing so. He automatically took in all points of entry and exit, strengths, weaknesses, potential hiding places, and security configurations. He waited patiently as he watched fit men in khakis, polo shirts, and ball caps with holstered handguns and headsets making their rounds.

Four buildings, including the main mansion, which looked to run to over twenty thousand square feet, were set around an enormous infinity pool.

One of the buildings looked to be a pool house that was three times the size of a normal house that folks actually lived in. Sleek chaise lounges lined the pool, all positioned perfectly parallel to their neighbors. There was an outdoor bar, an elaborate fire pit, patios, flagstone walkways, and sumptuous landscaping.

Cars, mostly Mercedes and Bentleys, were parked in the bays of the eight-car garage. Rogers could see this because all the overhead doors were open and a couple of men were working on one of the cars.

Outside the stone walls and set up on the east side of the mansion was a helipad with a large "B" painted in the center. And behind that and running parallel to the beach was a three-thousand-foot paved runway. Parked at one end of the tarmac was a trim Falcon 2000 jet. As Rogers watched, a man in a pilot's uniform was doing a visual inspection of the aircraft.

All the accouterments of the super-rich down to the very last detail, thought Rogers. So many toys, so little time.

He made his way through a public access far down from the Ballard mansion to the beach. The Atlantic swelled and plunged in front of him as a strong wind pummeled the water. Salt air slammed into his lungs. Seagulls dipped and soared looking for meals. But none of that held Rogers's interest. He kept walking toward the mansion. The sand belonged to everyone and he wanted to see what the defenses of the estate looked like from the beach side.

He reached a spot directly in front of the Ballard property and saw that a high stone wall ran the entire length of the property. It was so high in fact that he could only see the upper floors of the main house.

In the middle of the wall was a wooden gate as high as the wall. He trudged along the beach after taking off his shoes and socks and rolling up his pant legs. When he was a hundred yards past it, he heard something. He turned to see the gate opening.

Out marched three beefy armed men, obviously security. Behind them was a sand-colored golf cart with cognac-colored seats driven by another security man. A second armed man sat next to him.

In the rear seat of the vehicle was an elderly man in a white robe and Panama hat with a black band. Next to him sat a young woman in a pale blue sheer cover-up.

The old guy was Ballard, Rogers was pretty certain. He was the right age, and who else here would get a chauffeur-driven golf cart ride to the beach?

They drove down near the water and parked. The security men laid out a large blanket, lounge chairs, a table, and a basket. Then they stepped back and formed a ring around the man and woman as they climbed out of the vehicle, the woman supporting the man.

She led him over to one of the chairs and helped him off with his robe. Underneath he had on bathing trunks and a T-shirt. His body was reedy and his chest sunken. He seemed particularly frail. She put sunscreen on his exposed skin and settled him in his chair.

She then took off her cover-up, revealing a sea-foam green string bikini underneath.

She looked like she worked out, not an ounce of fat to be seen. Her skin was tanned, but not too much.

She lay down on the blanket facedown in front of the man, her tight glutes only half covered by the bikini bottom. Ballard didn't seem to care. He just stared out at the water.

Yet Rogers caught one of the security men taking a peek at the woman before moving his gaze outward. By the time he spotted Rogers, the latter had already turned and was slowly heading down the beach. A hundred yards later Rogers stopped and walked over to the water, letting it rush over his feet.

Is that really Ballard? Probably. And the woman? Girlfriend? Trophy wife? Child? Grandchild? Nurse in a string bikini showing off her bod while grabbing some rays on duty?

The next sound made him turn and look back down the beach.

It was a sound of gathering power.

Then a rumble as that gathering power was set free.

About ten seconds later, the Falcon 2000 cleared the foliage that ran the length of the runway on the beach side, soared into the air, banked hard right over the water, straightened out, and continued its rapid ascent.

Rogers looked over at the man and woman.

The old man was still staring aimlessly out toward the water.

The young woman was up on her haunches and waved.

Rogers turned to follow her gaze and watched the twin plumes of exhaust from the jet's engines smear the otherwise clear sky.

So who is in the Falcon?

He walked a bit farther out into the water, letting the salt-water edge up his pale ankles. He glanced down and saw the remnants of the old scars on his calves. Every few seconds he would shift his gaze to the left and eye the little group on the beach.

The lunch in the basket was served, the woman dutifully taking care of the old gent. She had put her cover-up back on.

Glasses of wine were poured and drunk.

A bowl of fruit and a plate of cheese picked through.

Sandwiches nibbled.

And then everything was packed up and the golf cart along with the security team headed back up the beach, through the gate, and it closed behind them.

Apparently the king's sunbathing was over for the day.

Rogers waited a few minutes and then slowly made his way back the way he'd come. He left the sand behind, dried off his feet, put his socks and shoes back on, and trudged to his van. He rubbed the back of his head because it had started to throb again.

He wasn't sure how much he'd learned today other than that Old Man Ballard had a helluva retirement package, including a beautiful companion to see to his every need.

He had just climbed into the driver's seat when a car shot past him on the road. It was a silver late-model Mercedes convertible with the top down.

And the bikini woman was driving though she was now wearing a floral sundress.

Rogers hurriedly put the van in gear and pulled onto the road to follow her.

This might just be the opening he needed, he thought.

CHAPTER

27

T HEY DROVE FOR about five miles. The woman was a reckless driver, taking curves too sharply and often veering into the oncoming lane on the two-lane road before sliding back in the nick of time to avoid traffic coming the other way.

Rogers kept far enough behind her so she wouldn't grow suspicious, although in the five miles they had passed at least six other white vans. It was the vehicle of choice for the legion of contractors and service people who made their living catering to the homeowners and landlords around here.

At last she slowed and pulled into the driveway of a large stucco-sided home with a red-tiled roof set on the beach. It looked as if it had been magically teleported from Florida to North Carolina.

Rogers pulled past, rounded a bend, steered the van off the road, jumped out, and quickly made his way back to the house, settling in behind some high grass that was part of the perimeter landscaping.

The woman had climbed out of the car at the same time the front door of the house opened. The young man who stepped out was wearing khaki shorts and a white T-shirt. He was tall, young, and handsome.

And Rogers had seen him before.

Josh Quentin, he of the VIP room back at the Grunt with his own private room and pretty ladies who let him stroke their derrieres with abandon.

Rogers continued to watch as Quentin and the woman collided about halfway up the front walk. She kissed him tenderly and in return he grabbed her ass.

Such was life, thought Rogers. Mars and Venus.

They were already starting to undress each other as they staggered, limb-locked, up to the front door and then inside.

It was pretty obvious what the couple was about to do, and Rogers had no interest in witnessing it. He sat on his haunches and attempted to think this through.

What was Josh Quentin doing down here? Was this his house? And who was the woman? Was she married to Ballard and this was just a lover closer to her own age?

Rogers rubbed the spot on his head. The sun overhead was hot and that heat was intensified on the narrow patch on his scalp. He closed his eyes and imagined what was going on inside his brain right now.

They had talked to him about what it would feel like, what could possibly happen. But more had happened to him than they could ever have foreseen. As they had explained to him, this was virgin territory. It was risky. It was perilous. Some of it, perhaps most of it, could not be predicted.

As it turned out, there were very good reasons for this.

As it turned out, they had no idea what the hell they were doing.

His gaze floated up to a window in the stucco house. He had seen a flash of something. Perhaps it was the woman's dress being flung away.

He thought back to the slaughter in the alley after his bus ride from prison. The two young lovers, now both dead.

He didn't much care for young lovers.

Mostly because he'd never had the chance to be one.

He felt a searing impulse to break into the house and kill them both.

He rubbed his head vigorously, trying to force this thought away.

He still needed information and he had yet to get any.

He decided to rectify that.

He looked around, saw no one, and skittered over to the convertible. On the front seat was the woman's purse. She'd been in such a rush to lip-lock Quentin, she'd forgotten it.

He took out her wallet and snapped a photo of her driver's license with his phone.

Her name was Suzanne Davis.

He stole over near the house and looked up. He could climb it, no problem. The house was mostly shielded from the road by overgrown bushes. He peered into the window of the garage and saw one car. It was a Maserati convertible. He figured it was Quentin's ride. The prick seemed to like everything expensive.

He went around to the back. There was a swimming pool fenced in so it was private from anyone lounging on the beach.

He tried the back door. It was unlocked. He doubted Quentin had bothered to think about engaging any alarm before hustling the lady upstairs, but still, he was ready to run if need be.

But an alarm didn't sound.

He eased inside to find a room that was barely furnished.

The layout of the house was open and spacious, but the few pieces of furniture all looked generic. Rogers wondered if this was Quentin's home or simply a rental.

He looked around for a minute and found a piece of mail

with the house's address on it. The addressee was a corporation: VacationsNC, LLC. So this was probably a rental.

He headed up the stairs, conscious of every sound in the house.

From upstairs he heard what he expected to hear. Two young people screwing each other's brains out.

But they would finish at some point. People always did.

He reached the landing and followed the sounds down to the last bedroom on the left. There was another room catty-corner from that. He slipped in there and kept the door partially open. From this vantage point he could see into the bedroom across the hall.

A naked Suzanne Davis was astride Quentin.

Well, they'd be occupied for a while.

Rogers retreated into the room he was in and looked around.

He spied it almost immediately. A leather briefcase. He opened it and rummaged quietly around inside. He pulled out several papers and looked at each one. It was only when he reached the fourth one that his attention was held.

It was a document marked *Confidential*. It appeared to be an internal corporate document.

The writing on the document meant nothing to him.

What was at the top of the page meant everything to him. *Atalanta Group*.

Rogers looked in the direction of the bedroom.

Quentin was with Atalanta Group? Was this the company that Helen Myers had mentioned Quentin owning?

Did Jericho work for him? He shook his head. In truth, Jericho worked for no one except herself. He put the papers back, closed the briefcase, and stepped back over to the doorway.

His gaze reached the couple in the bed just as Quentin

flipped Davis over on her back so he was on top. He lifted her feet on top of his shoulders and quickly finished his business with a loud grunt before collapsing on top of her.

So much for romance, thought Rogers.

Quentin rolled off her and sat up against the headboard.

"Damn, that was good, babe," he said. "Wasn't it?"

Davis pulled the blanket up over her and leaned back next to him. "Yeah," she said automatically. "It was great," she added, her enthusiasm artificially pumped up, at least in Rogers's mind.

"How's the old man?" Quentin asked.

Rogers tensed.

"The same. Enjoying his leisure time."

"I bet." Quentin leaned over, opened the drawer of a nightstand, took out a small box, opened it, and rolled two joints, handing one to Davis. They lit up and both inhaled deeply.

He said, "She's one smart lady. I think I can hold my own, but some days I'm not sure."

Davis took another puff of the joint and settled back against the headboard.

"Did she get off okay?" he asked.

"Jet left a couple hours ago. She'll be back soon."

Rogers tensed even more, praying that they would say the woman's name.

Quentin took another drag on his joint. "Well, it'll be nice not to have her looking over my shoulder the whole time."

"Just don't screw up."

Quentin put an arm around Davis's bare shoulders and feigned a hurt expression. "Hey, babe, I know what I'm doing, okay?"

"I gotta go."

She rose and quickly dressed.

A minute later Rogers heard her heels clicking down the steps.

When he turned back to look into the bedroom, Quentin had finished his joint and lay stretched out on the bed. A few moments later the snores reached Rogers.

I could go in and kill him right now. But what would be the point? I need to know more. So he's more valuable to me alive than dead.

This is truly your lucky day, Josh. You got laid and you get to live.

He waited until he heard the car start up outside and then made his way back down the stairs and out the rear door. A few minutes later he was sitting in his van and staring down at the photos he'd taken.

Suzanne Davis.

He put that name in a search and added Chris Ballard to it.

He got many hits on Ballard, but nothing on anyone named Suzanne Davis who seemed to have a connection to him.

He next searched Josh Quentin. Lots of hits came up, but none that he wanted.

For a guy on the fast track, there was nothing about him out there.

But he *would* find Claire Jericho.

For Rogers, there was no Plan B.

CHAPTER

28

I'M NOT SURE what to make of that."

Knox looked over at Puller, who was staring out the windshield of his Malibu.

They were still parked in Vincent DiRenzo's driveway.

"Did you hear me, Puller?"

"I heard you."

"The guy basically said he was stonewalled on looking into the serial murders in Williamsburg."

Puller stayed quiet.

"Do you think he was telling the truth?"

Puller slid the car into gear. "I don't know. I haven't had a chance to check into it, have I?"

He pulled out of the driveway and pointed them on a route that would take them back to eastern Virginia.

"Why does it seem like this case is getting muddier the more we step into it?" said Knox.

"Maybe it was designed that way."

She shot him a glance. "Designed? What do you mean by that?"

Puller just stared out the window.

She glared at him. "Are you officially shutting down on me? Do I have to talk to myself all the way back?"

"You can do what you want, Knox. No one's stopping you. You always do what you want, right?"

She gazed at him stonily before saying, "You just keep piling on the insinuations, don't you?"

"Is that what you call them?"

"What do you call them?"

"I don't have to call them anything. I've got a case to investigate."

"You really do like to dance in circles, don't you?"

He kept his gaze on the road. Finally he said, "What would you do?"

She started to say something but then seemed to catch herself. "Talk to the Williamsburg cops who worked the case."

"We've seen the files."

"But we tracked down DiRenzo, and look what he delivered up that was not covered in the files. Maybe the Williamsburg cops will do the same."

"We need to find out who they are."

"I already did that. The two lead detectives are still on the force."

"From thirty years ago?"

"They were young when they worked it. They're close to retirement, but not quite there. I set up a meeting with them for later this afternoon."

"Without telling me?"

"I'm telling you *now*, Puller."

"And you wonder why I can't trust you?"

She stared at him for a moment and then broke it off and kept her gaze pointed out the window the whole ride back.

* * *

Always concrete walls, thought Puller.

Unlike on TV shows with all the glitzy bells and whistles, real cops lived on frugal department budgets that tacked far closer to painted cinderblock and dented gunmetal gray desks.

Puller was sitting opposite homicide detectives Jim Lorne and his partner Leo Peckham in a precinct building in Williamsburg.

They were both tall, thin, balding men in their sixties. Their faces carried the strain of having a job that required them to witness the dead bodies of the brutally murdered and then find out who had done it.

Lorne was twirling a pen between his long fingers.

Peckham gazed directly at Puller and Knox. He said, "We got your call, Agent Knox. And we know you requisitioned the files. You explained a little but not a lot. I'm afraid we're going to need to hear the whole story before we can jump into this again."

Lorne looked up from his pen-twirling. "And what's the Army's connection?"

Puller answered, "We're trying to see if your serial killer might have abducted someone from Fort Monroe about thirty years ago."

"He killed. He didn't abduct."

"And he might have killed this woman too, but her body wasn't found," noted Knox.

Peckham shook his head. "Don't think so. Way the bodies were disposed of, the guy *wanted* them to be found."

"So you're sure it was a man?" asked Knox.

"Four women murdered? Pretty sure it was a guy."

"The women weren't sexually assaulted," pointed out Knox.

Lorne shook his head. "But they were beaten to death, or

strangled, or their throats were cut. Now, granted, a woman could have cut a throat, but the beating and strangling, that's a guy's fingerprint."

Puller nodded in agreement. "We were curious why the investigation at Fort Monroe didn't connect up with yours back then. There were parallels and the two spots are barely a half hour apart."

Lorne shrugged. "I don't know what to tell you. I never even heard about the case you're talking about at Fort Monroe. No one from CID ever called us about it. And we had our hands full back then. Me and Leo were just young detectives at the time, but the force had had some attrition and we were the senior homicide guys. So we got the case. We busted our asses, spent every waking hour on it. Got to be an obsession if you really want to know."

"And we still didn't solve it," added Peckham. "And not that it matters, but our career path took a big hit. Promotions were slow in coming after that. But those poor dead women suffered far worse. The fact we never brought their killer to justice? I'll never get over that. No matter what else I did in my career, I was a failure."

Knox said, "Don't be too hard on yourself. Sometimes the bad guys get lucky and get away with it. I'm sure you did everything you could."

Puller added, "The file didn't have many clues. No real forensics."

Peckham nodded. "The guy didn't leave any DNA behind. And there was no sexual assault. And he apparently wore gloves."

"But no defensive wounds? Nothing under the victims' nails? If he strangled them there would have been a struggle, unless they were bound first. People don't just die without a fight."

Peckham glanced at Lorne and said, "They weren't bound. At least there was no evidence of that."

Lorne shifted in his seat. "You looked at the file photos?"

Puller nodded.

"Well, pictures couldn't really convey the actual damage. When I said strangled, that was probably not entirely correct."

"What would be more correct?" asked Knox quickly.

"That their throats, their windpipes, were completely crushed."

Puller stared at him. "Crushed?"

"Flattened would be a better description." Lorne shivered slightly as he said this. "I'd never seen anything like it and neither had the ME, and he'd been doing this work for forty years. And I've never seen anything like it since, thank God."

"Are you sure something else wasn't used? A rope, a metal bar, a board?"

"No, it was hands. Human hands. Even with gloves the evidence was pretty clear on that."

"So a big, strong guy," said Knox.

"Something more than that. It takes incredible force to do the damage we saw. The base of the spine was also crushed."

Puller stared at him incredulously. "The spine was crushed? Do you know how difficult it is to break, much less crush? That could happen with a long fall or some kind of car accident."

"I know exactly how difficult it is to crush a bone," answered Lorne. "Because I researched it afterward. Not even an NFL lineman would be that strong. He could break it, sure, but pulverize it?" He shook his head.

Peckham added, "And it was the same with the blows to the head that killed some of the women. The marks indicated a fist was used. But the skull was crushed. And the ME didn't think it was repeated blows. Only *one*."

Knox stared at him in disbelief. "One blow to crush a skull! Are you sure some animal didn't do this? You're talking strength like a bear or something."

"It was no animal. It was a human."

"Well, it's not any human I've ever run into," retorted Puller.

"Not any human I'd ever *want* to run into," replied Peckham.

"What about connections among the victims? We know they were all females, around the same age and professional types. But there weren't detailed records on exactly what their professions were."

Peckham said, "They all worked for government contractors."

"That might tell us a lot about the perp, then," said Knox. "He might have a beef against the government. He might have worked for the Feds or a contractor and been fired."

Puller said, "I'm sure you followed that line of inquiry."

"As far as we could."

"Meaning what exactly?"

Lorne answered. "Meaning most of what those women did was classified and we couldn't be 'read into it,' as they kept telling us. National security. That still means a lot today. Back then it scared the shit out of people. So we basically got zip on our inquiries because of that."

"In a serial killer investigation!" exclaimed Knox.

"Trust me, I wasn't happy about it either," said Lorne.

The four people sat there and stared at each other for a long moment.

"Okay," said Knox a bit breathlessly. "Where does that leave us?"

"I'm not sure," admitted Peckham. "At square one, maybe."

"What did the FBI conclude about all this?" asked Puller.

"I'm not sure what they concluded, because they never told us a damn thing. But I can tell you this." He paused, apparently wavering whether to finish the thought or not.

"We really could use whatever help you can give us," said Puller.

"Like you said, those women deserve justice," added Knox.

Peckham glanced at Lorne, who nodded.

Peckham turned back to Puller. "The FBI was hot and heavy over this right from the start. They acted like the Feds always do. The eight-hundred-pound gorilla come in to take over the investigation. And the glory that comes with solving it. We were just poor shmucks from the backwaters of Tidewater."

"Okay, and?" said Knox.

"And there came a day about three weeks after they'd joined the investigation where they pulled up their tent pole and went home."

Knox and Puller exchanged a glance.

Knox said, "They just left?"

Peckham nodded. "Out of the blue. There one day, gone the next."

Puller said, "And did they give you any reason for that?"

Peckham slowly shook his head. "I can tell you that the agents on the ground were pissed off. But there was nothing they could do about it."

"And were they ever given a reason?" asked Knox.

"If so, they never shared it with us," said Lorne. "But if you ask me, they got the same spiel we did."

"National security," said Puller, and Lorne nodded.

Knox said, "So presumably the orders came from higher up. Maybe as high up as the Hoover Building?"

Lorne shrugged. "I wouldn't know about that. But about two months later I got a call from some high up muckety-muck at the FBI. He asked how things were going. I told him what I knew, which wasn't much. Told him it didn't look like we were going to crack this sucker."

"And what was his reaction to that?" asked Puller.

Lorne licked his lips and started playing with the pen again.

"Detective Lorne?" prompted Puller.

Lorne looked up and let out a breath he'd been holding. "If you can believe it, the son of a bitch actually sounded relieved."

CHAPTER

29

Four photos.

Four dead women.

Puller stared at the pictures he had laid out on his bed at the hotel.

Was his mother the fifth?

Her throat crushed?

Her skull pulverized?

Never found?

Lying all these years in some makeshift grave?

He covered his eyes with his hands and tried to bring some calm to nerves that threatened to run away from him.

He had never felt this way on the battlefield. Certainly there was fear. Only a fool would not fear death while bombs and bullets were whirling all around like lethal snow. But his nerves had always held. That had allowed him to do his job as a soldier.

That had allowed him to survive.

He could not solve this case if his nerves would not hold.

He drew several long breaths and withdrew his hands and stared down at the pictures.

Victims of a serial killer usually had something in common. The killers picked their victims based on shared characteristics, at least in the person's demented mind.

Young. Professional. Female. Three characteristics.

And national security. A fourth characteristic.

Lots of things were classified back then, just like today, Puller knew. If the Feds had stonewalled a homicide investigation, the work the women did must have been really important. But they had to work somewhere. The problem was that the Tidewater area was home to a huge military footprint and thus DoD contractors were all over the place like ants at a picnic and had been for a long time.

So how had the killer gone about hunting for them?

And why Williamsburg?

Was it because the killer was from there? Or because he had migrated there from some other place?

Puller looked at the background sheets on each of the victims. He read through the bios of the slain women.

An engineer, a biologist, a chemist, and a computer programmer. Where they had worked had been redacted from the files. Puller shook his head. That was unheard of. How could the police establish a connection if they had no idea where the women worked?

However, it had been determined that they didn't shop or eat at the same places. They didn't live in the same buildings. They didn't get their cars repaired at the same shops. Two banked at the same bank, but that was all. This was before the era of smartphones and email, but hardline records showed no contact among any of the women.

If there was a common thread, it had escaped everyone's attention.

But the obvious connection was the national security tag. Only they hadn't been allowed to follow up that lead.

So maybe I should look at the case a different way, then. Not from the evidence. Not from the victims. But from the killer's perspective.

That was far easier said than done.

Getting into the head of a psycho was not going to be pleasant.

He had looked down at the pictures again when his phone buzzed. It was Knox.

"Yeah?" he said.

"You didn't say much on the trip back."

"I didn't have much to say."

"I've got to check out for a bit, then I'll be back."

"Problems?"

"Like you, my entire career is based on problems."

"Well, good luck."

"You too," she said, her voice a little strange, he thought.

Puller clicked off, set his phone down, and looked at the photos again. He was getting a sick feeling in the pit of his stomach. This whole case screamed cover-up. And he still didn't know if his mother's disappearance was even connected to it. He could be wasting time working on a case that might have nothing to do with what he had set out to accomplish.

But as he looked down at the photos of the dead women he also realized he could not just let this drop.

He pulled out his phone and called Ted Hull. He wanted to fill him in on what he'd found so far and hoped that the CID agent would reciprocate.

An unfamiliar voice answered. "Joyce Mansfield."

"I'm sorry, I must have called the wrong number."

"What number were you calling?" asked the woman.

Puller told her.

"No, that's right. But I just got this number assigned yesterday."

"The person I was calling works as a special investigator for Army CID. Are you with CID?"

The woman laughed. "I *do* work for the government. But

I'm with the Department of Agriculture. The only thing I investigate is soil depletion."

"And you just got this phone number? Are you in a new job?"

"No, been at the same desk for four years. I'm not sure why I got the number, but I wasn't about to turn down a new phone. It's a new Samsung," she added excitedly.

"Okay, thanks."

Puller clicked off and stared down at his phone.

What the hell is going on?

He was about to make another call when his phone rang.

Don White, his CO, sounded more anxious than Puller had ever heard the man before. And he didn't waste any time.

"Puller, you're being reassigned. There's a flight to Frankfurt tomorrow that leaves at zero six hundred from Andrews. You're going to be on it."

"I don't understand, sir. I thought I had leave time."

"That's been canceled," White said sharply.

"Why?"

"You don't need to know why."

Puller flinched at this rebuke. He and White had always gotten on well. "Can I ask what's the assignment in Frankfurt?" he said curtly.

"You'll get full particulars when you get there. I'll email the details of the trip."

"Sir, can you tell me what's going on?"

"I just did, Puller."

"And the case with my father?"

But White had already clicked off.

Puller sat back and numbly stared down at the photos on the bed.

Apparently the stonewalling had just picked up again after thirty years.

CHAPTER

30

SOMETHING WAS OFF. Rogers noted it as soon as he walked into the Grunt an hour before opening time.

No one would make eye contact with him. At first he thought it was because Josh Quentin had somehow spotted him back in North Carolina and conveyed that to Helen Myers, which would mean he was in big trouble.

But then he saw him sitting there, in the far back.

It was Karl, dressed all in black, with a cane leaning next to the table. Three of the fingers on his right hand were encased in splints. He looked stiff and in pain. A glass of whiskey was set in front of him. He had on sunglasses. Still, Rogers knew the man was looking straight at him.

He stood there for a few moments staring back. He held no sympathy for the man. Yet he was curious about how this was going to play out.

If Karl had simple revenge on his mind it would probably involve Rogers getting jumped by a bunch of guys. He would probably beat them, but that wasn't the point. That would almost certainly invite a visit by the police. Rogers could not afford that. A simple background check would send him right back to prison.

He made a decision.

He walked over to Karl and sat down across from him.

The man turned to gaze at him. Though his eyes were hidden by the shades, his features evidenced surprise that Rogers had come over. Then he looked away, as though determined not to play whatever game Rogers was up to.

"I had an uncle who told me something one time," Rogers began. "Always stuck with me for some reason."

Karl swiveled his head around to look at him once more. "And what was that?" he said sharply.

"There's not a man alive who hasn't had his ass kicked at least once. And for most of them it was a woman who did the kicking."

For a long moment Karl just stared at him. Then the big man burst out laughing. He laughed so hard he choked, coughing and gasping. Rogers rushed over to the bar, got him a glass of water, and helped him to drink it.

When Karl was sufficiently recovered he took off his sunglasses and eyed Rogers. "I've been married three times, so I can tell your uncle knew what the hell he was talking about," he said, grinning.

"I've been down the aisle too," lied Rogers. "It was like being hit by a freight train, and she never lifted a finger. It was all words. I would have taken Mike Tyson pounding me to a pulp over what that woman did to me."

Rogers was not lying now. This was what Claire Jericho had done to him.

Karl slowly nodded. "As God is my witness, I hear you, man."

Rogers eased back in his chair and assumed a contrite expression. "I really needed the job, Karl. I had nothing when I walked in here, just the clothes on my back and a couple bucks in my pocket. Desperate men, you know. They can do anything. I overplayed my hand. I went too far. I was trying to impress the boss. I lost control." He paused and pretended he was seated in front of the parole board for the third time.

"And so I'm sorry for what I did," he added, his expression one of deep embarrassment.

Karl slowly nodded. Then he turned and flicked a finger at the bartender and pointed to his glass. A minute later the man delivered another whiskey and quickly turned and left.

Karl slowly slid the glass over to Rogers.

"Apology accepted. Now let's drink to it."

Rogers picked up his drink and the two men clinked their glasses together and each took a sip.

"You ever do any of that cage fighting?" asked Karl.

Rogers cradled the drink and shook his head. "No, never did. Never really had the chance."

"You might want to try it. I think you could beat any son of a bitch I've ever seen. I think you could beat all of them together. You are one strong dude, Paul. I'm no weakling, but I never felt a grip like yours before."

"Good genes," replied Rogers. "My old man was smaller than me, but he could break me in two. Almost did a couple of times when he was drunk."

"Glad I never ran into him when he was drunk, then."

The two men drained their glasses and set them back on the table.

Rogers wiped his mouth. "I met Josh Quentin last night. Guy rolls in in a stretch limo with a bunch of beauty queens. He paws over the ladies like he owns them. What's all that about?"

In a low voice Karl said, "Guy's a prick."

"Ms. Myers said he's really rich, got his own company, printing money. And he's only like thirty. How can you not hate the dude? We'll be working men till we drop, while that guy just drifts off into the sunset on his yacht before he's forty."

"That's the God's honest truth." Karl looked pensive. "Now, what I heard was the jerk lucked into something."

"Pretty lucky guy, then."

"Hell, ain't that the truth. I've never been lucky like that."

"Me either. So what did he luck into?"

"Not sure. Some opportunity. Look, I'm not saying the guy's stupid. I don't think he's as smart as he thinks he is, but he's slick. He can grab the gold ring when it's staring him in the face."

Rogers nodded slowly. "I saw him walk into that room upstairs like he owned it."

Karl leaned in a little closer and pointed a finger at Rogers. "You pretty much nailed it there, Paul."

"Come again?"

"Josh Quentin is a good customer here, I mean a *real* good customer. He pays a monthly fee to the bar for that space upstairs. Comes and goes when he wants. Brings whoever he wants. *Does* whatever he wants up there. And that monthly fee? Pays for all of the bar's expenses. *All* of them. The other customers—and there are a lot of them—that's pure profit. So Helen is also printing money."

"Damn. Sounds like Ms. Myers is lucky too."

Karl shrugged. "Now, it made a living for her, sure. A good one. But when Quentin came along, that's when things really took off."

"How'd they meet?"

"Don't know. But they did. This was, oh, a couple years back."

"You been with Ms. Myers a long time, then?"

"Eight years this summer. She's a good lady. Fair."

"You two...?"

Karl pushed his whiskey glass away and shook his head. "No, nothing like that. Like I said, I struck out with women.

Three fastballs. I'm done batting. She wants more than a romp in the sheets with an old fat guy with bum knees. And I'm never getting hitched again."

"Maybe her and Quentin, then?"

"Never happen. Two different walks of life. And he likes his ladies a lot younger." He paused. "Although she usually goes up to the room when he's here. But probably just to check on things and make sure her golden goose is happy."

"I asked Ms. Myers about what went on up there, but she cut me off quick. I thought she was going to fire me for asking. And I was just curious. Didn't know what they had the separate room for and all. Not that it matters to me." He looked down at his empty glass, waiting for Karl to respond.

"Let's put it this way, Paul, whatever goes on up there stays up there. Believe me, I've tried to figure it out, but when I broached it with Helen, well, I was afraid I might get fired too."

* * *

Later, Rogers got his comm pack and received a report about a bachelor party coming into the bar. He was headed toward the door when Helen Myers stepped in front of him.

"I heard that you and Karl made peace. At least you were seen drinking together."

"I only had the one and it was before I was on duty."

"I'm not begrudging you two fingers of whiskey, Paul. And Karl doesn't drink with anyone he wants to kill."

She tacked on a smile to this.

Rogers didn't answer right away. He ran his gaze over her from head to stiletto heels. She was in beige tonight. Jacket, blouse, short skirt, bare legs, strappy shoes. Her hair had bounced across her shoulders as she walked.

Rogers said, "We reached an understanding."

"Glad to hear it."

"Will Mr. Quentin be coming tonight?"

Her eyes narrowed. "Why?"

"Last night I didn't know who he was. Now I do. I know he's an important customer. I just want to be ready to treat him right. Little extras, you know. Best foot forward for the bar. And I won't lie to you, he's a good tipper."

Her suspicious look faded. "Well, that's good you're thinking that way. He *is* an important customer. But no, he won't be coming tonight."

"It would have helped to have known who the guy was before," said Rogers. "Last night it was a little awkward, but it turned out okay. Won't happen again, of course."

"I'm sure it won't."

Rogers said, "Well, I better get out there."

"Good luck tonight."

"It's never really about luck, though, is it?" said Rogers.

CHAPTER

31

THE LINES WERE long again, but this time there were no disruptions. What had happened the night before seemed to have reverberated among those who frequented the Grunt.

Rogers saw Karl leave at around one-thirty, followed by Helen Myers at two.

Karl had waved to him. Myers had not.

At three the bar was empty and clean enough for the staff to head home. Rogers offered to lock up and set the alarm.

Finally, he was the last person in the place.

He had earlier noted the CCTV cameras. They were all around the bar area, and also posted outside.

But they were not, he had also noted, stationed at the stairs leading up to the VIP room. Nor were there any cameras on that level.

Someone didn't want a record of those heading up there, and he wondered why.

He took the stairs two at a time, jiggling the set of keys in his pocket. He arrived on the upstairs landing and looked around. There was only one door, although the room it accessed seemed to run the length of the corridor.

He assumed that this might have been the living quarters

of whoever had owned this building before it had become a bar.

He tried the door. It was locked.

He tried the keys in his pocket. The third one did the charm.

He opened the door and stepped into the room, closing it behind him. He didn't have a flashlight and didn't need one. His eyes were capable of seeing amazingly well in the darkness. He moved around the room, which was comfortably furnished.

It was actually more than one room. There was another room leading off it, separated by another doorway.

He opened this door and stared at the large bed. It was neatly made now. He figured it would not be so neat when Quentin and his ladies were here.

So was that what this was all about?

Just a place for Quentin to bed his entourage?

Yet he had been here with other men that night. So did the boys get equal turns between the sheets? Was that how Quentin paid his bonuses to executives at his company?

And why here? Quentin had the beach house not even two hours from here. And he must have a place in town somewhere. So why come to a room above a bar and spend a big sum each month for the privilege?

He made a search of the room and turned up exactly nothing. And Rogers knew how to search.

He closed the door behind him and locked it. Then he left the bar after setting the alarm and locking the exterior door securely behind him.

He had taken three steps down the alley leading to where he had parked his van when he saw them up ahead.

The players from the night before.

He turned around and looked behind him.

More big bodies had filled his rear flank.

The big black guy stepped forward, a malicious grin on his face.

"Told you we'd be back, asshole. And I keep my word."

Rogers looked to the man's left and saw the fellow whose wrist he'd broken. Next to him were the other two men he'd kicked the shit out of. One of them looked like he'd had his jaw wired.

Rogers looked back at the black guy, who had taken another long step forward. "Do you really want to do this?" he asked calmly.

"You got somewhere to go?" snarled the man.

"Actually, I do. So why don't you and I go one-on-one? I win. I walk. It'll save a lot of time."

The black guy stiffened and looked around at the men he'd brought with him. "I saw you were some kind of ninja, fuckface. That's why I brought reinforcements."

Rogers looked at the man with the broken wrist and the guy with the wired jaw. "If you come at me again, I will kill both of you."

The two men looked amused until they caught the expression on Rogers's face.

The black guy, perhaps sensing they were losing the upper hand, pulled something from his pocket. It was a knife.

"That's not going to change the outcome," said Rogers. "You just brought the weapon that I'll use to kill you."

"You really think a lot of yourself, dude. There's six of us. Count 'em."

"There's really only four, because these two"—he pointed at the two injured men—"aren't going to be part of it."

"You think you know 'em."

"I can read a face," replied Rogers.

"Still four to one. And we all came ready."

Rogers watched as one man took out a knife, one a chain, and another a baseball bat from behind his back.

Rogers sized up the situation. One of them might get a lucky strike in and put him down. It was fortunate none had brought a gun. He might lose. But he was probably going to win. The one thing he knew, though, was that he was going to fight.

"Trust me," he said to the black guy. "It won't feel like four to one in a couple of minutes. And I'll save you for last."

"Right. In case you didn't notice, we're all big and a lot younger than you."

"Well, you were bigger and younger than me last night too. How did that work out for you?"

"Your ass got lucky."

"Nobody's that lucky."

"Hell, we live for violence."

"Not the kind of violence you're going to see from me."

"You're full of shit!"

"Then let's get this started."

Rogers rubbed his head. He knew that once the fighting really started, he was not going to be able to control himself. The muscles in his arms, legs, and shoulders knotted. He was ready to strike. He would have to leave his job at the bar after this. He had no other choice.

He took a breath, let it out evenly. His nerves calmed, his heartbeat slowed, his blood flow grew steady. He popped his neck and was just about to deliver his first kill stroke of the night when a car's beams cut through the darkness.

They all watched as a police cruiser rolled to a stop. A moment later they got hit with a spotlight mounted on the side of the car.

A voice on a PA said, "What the hell is going on here?"

The black guy called out, "Nothing, Officer, we were just hanging out. But now we're heading on."

"Then *move* on. Now!"

The cruiser waited while the others hustled out the far end of the alley. The black guy looked back menacingly at Rogers.

Rogers was walking past the cruiser when the passenger window came down.

"What was all that about?" asked the police officer.

"I'm the bouncer at the Grunt. That was about some punks not getting to drink beer and wanting someone to take it out on. Namely me."

"Okay, I get that. Well, lucky for you we came along."

Lucky for them, thought Rogers.

"Thanks, Officer, good night."

Rogers walked off and the cruiser pulled through the alley, following the other men just in case.

Roger got to his van and drove off.

His plan tonight was fairly simple.

The Grunt was closed tomorrow night.

So tomorrow night he was going to have a chat with Chris Ballard.

CHAPTER

32

PULLER PACKED THE last of his things in the duffel and zipped it closed. It was like he had just zipped up the end of his life as well.

He had left AWOL with a family living in the same apartment complex. His cat did fine with long separations, but this time Puller had no idea how long he'd be gone. He didn't even know if he'd be coming back.

He looked down at the email he had received ten minutes ago. It had come from a two-star he had never met or even heard of. The message had been terse but to the point:

The investigation into allegations regarding the disappearance of your mother and culpability of your father has been concluded. No further action will be taken against any party.

Against any party.

That was telling him that his father was safe. The investigation was over.

But that was all bullshit, because there had never really been an investigation. Nothing had been discovered. The truth was still out there but no one was looking for it.

Well, one person is. Me.

He had already written his letter of resignation. He was leaving the Army and the only career he'd ever known.

The United States Army had done something Puller never thought it would do.

It let me down.

Still, as he had typed out the words, "I, Chief Warrant Officer John Puller Jr., 701st Military Police Group (CID), do hereby resign..." a knot had formed in his throat and a piercing pain had erupted in his gut.

He couldn't believe he was actually doing it.

But he had no choice. They had left him boxed in a corner with only one conceivable way out.

He had sent in the letter.

He was not waiting for a reply.

It didn't matter what they said to him. If they wanted to try to hold him for some reason, they would have to find him first.

So he was not going to Germany and his next assignment. He was going to continue to investigate this case whether the Army chose to or not.

His goal was simple. His goal was always simple.

It was how he had approached every case he'd ever undertaken.

Finding the truth.

He opened the door to his apartment.

Two men in suits stared back at him.

Five minutes later Puller sat in the back of a Tahoe and kept his gaze pointed out the window. The two men sat in front.

Their credentials had given Puller no choice but to accompany them. His sidearm had been confiscated for the time being. His cell phone had also been taken. He was uneasy about all of this, but he had to see it play out. He had no other option.

The SUV pulled through the guard entrance where the

men in naval uniforms checked IDs, scrutinized Puller, and then motioned them on.

Puller knew there was another wall of defense around the place that included men in suits with comm wires in their ears, like the pair in front of him.

The imposing house loomed up in front of them.

Puller had never been here. Most people had never been here.

The truck stopped in front of the house and they all got out. Puller was escorted inside, down a hall, and into a large room outfitted as an office and library. The men left him there.

He didn't sit. He had no idea what was about to happen, but he would take it standing.

He tensed when the door opened.

He came immediately to attention.

The man wasn't in uniform, but he once had been.

And more importantly, he was one beating heart removed from being the commander in chief of all the armed forces of the United States. That fact alone required Puller to treat him with military respect.

He was the vice president of the United States, Richard Hall.

Before that he'd been a U.S. senator from Virginia. And before that he'd been a one-star under Puller's father's command.

Puller knew all this. And he'd also met the man once, over twenty years ago, before Hall had traded in his uniform for a suit and the life of a politician.

Hall was about five-ten, and still retained much of the muscular build he'd had as a soldier. His hair was white and thinning, but his handshake was firm and his voice deep.

"Sit down, Puller. You look very stiff standing there."

Puller sat.

Hall went over to a table that held a decanter of whiskey and several glasses.

"Drink?"

"No thank you, sir."

"I'm pouring you one anyway. You look like you could use it."

Hall brought the drinks over and handed one to Puller. Then he sat down behind his desk.

"I heard that you resigned from the Army today."

"News travels fast."

"Certain news travels fast in certain channels."

Hall held up his glass and took a sip of his drink. Puller followed suit.

"And why did you do it?" asked Hall. "From all accounts you're one of the best investigators CID has ever had."

"I didn't think you'd been following my career."

"Your father was a good friend and a terrific mentor. So, yes, I have been following your career. And I know what you did in West Virginia. And in connection with your brother being unfairly imprisoned. You have done your country exemplary service both on and off the field of combat." He took another sip of his drink, set the glass down, and added, "Which is why you are here tonight."

"And why exactly am I here, sir?"

Hall leaned back in his chair. "There is something going on out there, Puller, that I'm not sure about."

"You're the VP, sir, what can you not be sure about?"

Hall gave a dry laugh. "You'd be surprised. This is a complicated country and a complex government, with many tentacles around the globe. No one can know everything about it. Not even the president himself, and certainly not his second in command."

"And how do I fit into the equation?"

"I'm going out on a limb, Puller. But in this instance, I'm glad to do it. Your father changed the direction of my life. I know his current circumstances, and I know of the letter with the allegation against him. I don't believe it for one moment. I know that your parents had their differences, but your father would have given his life to protect his wife. And his sons. I was deployed with him around the world. As a junior officer I had his confidences. There was not a day that went by when he did not speak to me about his family."

"He never said," replied Puller.

"That was not his way. Your father was a doer, not a talker. It made being under his command a bit difficult. He demanded Herculean effort from all of us. But I will say, without reservation, that he never asked any of us to do something he had not already done himself."

"Yes sir," said Puller. "That was how he was wired."

"Which brings us back to this situation and to you. For now, the Army has tabled your resignation, but you are on indefinite leave. What you do with that time is up to you." Hall held up a warning hand. "But mark this, you will not have the authority of the Army or the CID behind you, Puller. That was the best that I could manage."

Puller looked at him curiously. "Manage? With whom, sir?"

Hall rose from his seat.

Puller quickly stood.

"That's all for now, Puller. And just so you know, this meeting never happened. If you mention it to anyone, well, I would suggest that you don't."

Hall put out his hand. They shook. "Tell your father I said hello. I know he probably won't understand, but please do so anyway."

"I will, sir."

"I've wanted to go by and see him."

"He'd like that, sir."

"One more thing, Puller."

"Yes sir?"

Hall drew closer to him. "Watch all points on the compass, son. And I mean *all* points. You trust yourself. That's it. No one else. No one is your friend on this one. And after tonight that probably includes me. I did this out of respect for your father. But this is where my assistance ends. Just the way it has to be. It's going to be an uphill battle for you after this."

"But what about my brother? Are you telling me I can't trust him on this?"

"Good night, Puller. And good luck. I'm damn sure you're going to need it."

CHAPTER

33

THE TAHOE DROPPED Puller back at his apartment. His gun and phone were returned. He went inside and slowly sat down in a chair, his thoughts like confetti.

Puller had seen combat. He had killed and nearly been killed. He carried scars on his body earned in the defense of his country. He had worked hard to become a good investigator.

None of that had prepared him for what he was now facing.

All his life it seemed that he had been searching for something akin to the truth. And for the first time in his life it seemed that perhaps the truth didn't matter. It was an astonishing admission, and one he never thought he would make. He had gone from sitting next to his failing father's bedside to a quagmire that seemed to have no bottom at all.

He took out his CID cred pack and stared down at the silver eagle shield and his ID card.

For him this represented the culmination of years of sweat and blood. It represented the full force and effect of the United States Army, the greatest fighting machine the world would ever likely see.

But now?

He fingered the wings of the fierce eagle, as though hoping its touch would render all things clear.

It didn't work.

He put his creds away and checked his M11.

He had a spare in a gun case in his bedroom. He rose and fetched it and slid it into his rear holster. He felt a bit better being fully gunned up. But only a bit.

There were not many things that unnerved John Puller.

When you'd been through hell and back, when you'd seen pretty much every way one human being could kill another, it changed you in a way that was irreversible. In some ways it made you far stronger, able to act with confidence when the need arose, no matter the level of danger. People who were not so hardened became paralyzed in such dire conditions.

And they died.

Yet it also made you weaker in some ways, because it made you less compassionate, less able to forgive. Puller knew he suffered from that, but there appeared to be little he could do about it now.

He sat back down in his chair.

What the VP had told him tonight *had* unnerved him.

Don't trust anyone.

Not even the VP.

Not even his brother.

On any level it was a stunning revelation.

His phone rang.

He glanced at the screen.

His brother was calling.

He hesitated, but then decided his brother would just keep calling if he didn't answer.

"Yeah, Bobby?" He kept his voice casual, carefree, although he was right now wound tighter than the nerves of a drill sergeant on ten Red Bulls.

"I heard," said Robert.

"Heard what?"

"That you resigned."

"Who did you hear that from?"

"Messenger doesn't matter. Just got one question for you."

"What's that?"

"Are you insane?"

"Not the last time I checked."

"Resigning? Striking out on your own. For what?"

"For the truth, Bobby. Don't you think it's important enough?"

"What I think is important is for you to rescind the letter, get back on your horse, and start following orders again."

"Not sure I can do that."

"The Army will forgive and forget, Junior."

"It's not the Army I'm worried about. And I can't forget."

"Well, with this you have to. I know you want to find out what happened to Mom, but it was thirty years ago. It's an impossible mission. And you should just forget about it. Why set yourself up for failure?"

"Is that really your best advice?"

"Hey, I get it, you were Mom's favorite. So you want to avenge her. But this is not the way to do it."

Puller had stiffened when his brother said this. His attention became riveted instead of lackluster. "You really think so?"

"I know so. Look, I've given you advice in the past that turned out to be good, right?"

"Yes."

"Well, this is good advice too. Take it. Pull back the reins, take some time to clear your head. Hell, go on a vacation for a few days, or even a week."

"I'm not sure the Army will let me do that," said Puller. Did his brother know he was officially on leave with no end date?

"I think you'll find they will. So just *lose* yourself for a while, Junior. Then come back recharged. You'll see things a lot more clearly."

"Okay, Bobby. I guess you're right."

"I know I'm right. Now, don't make me come back there and have to kick your ass, okay?"

"Okay. And, Bobby, thanks."

"You're welcome."

Puller clicked off and had to smile.

His brother *was* on his side.

The phone call was being monitored. Robert had told Puller that by virtue of a lie only the two brothers would have known.

Robert Puller was his mother's favorite, not John. Though she had never showed it overtly, both sons knew it was true. It had been shown in a thousand small, sometimes barely perceptible ways. Their mother had favored the studious and shy Robert over John, who more closely resembled his father in toughness and with no lack of confidence in his abilities.

And though Puller shared his mother's sensibilities, it was also true that Jackie Puller had probably sensed that as the older son Robert Puller would be automatically judged by his father's accomplishments. And what little boy could measure up to that? Thus, her attention had been directed to him.

Robert had told Puller that the Army would be okay with him taking some time off. So he must have known about the official leave.

But Robert had gone a step further. He had told his

brother to *lose* himself. A seemingly innocuous statement, but John knew that Robert had been speaking quite literally. He could translate his brother's real message effortlessly.

The shit has really hit the fan. Go underground if you're going to tackle this sucker.

Puller could imagine that his brother had been ordered to make this call, had known that it was being listened in on, and had come up with a way to communicate his real intent to his brother, right under the noses of the listeners.

That was clear enough.

What wasn't clear at all was everything else.

CHAPTER

34

A CLOUDY NIGHT.

A mansion heavily guarded.

A frothing, pitching ocean right next door.

Paul Rogers took each of these things into account while he stared at the gates to Chris Ballard's refuge.

For he had decided that's what it was: a *refuge*.

Maybe from me.

Since he hadn't had to work tonight he had left Hampton at eleven and gotten here around one.

He knew where the guards were. And how high the walls were. What he didn't know was where Ballard slept.

That would take a bit of exploring. It would take a bit of risk. But he had no other options.

He scaled the wall on the north side of the compound and dropped lightly to the ground inside. He kept low for a few moments, scanning all compass points before heading toward the main house. The doors, he was sure, were armed. The grounds, he knew, were under video surveillance.

He had seen the camera positioning and spotted a narrow lane of invisibility that he used to reach the main house.

The walls were sheer, no handholds, at least for an ordinary person lacking climbing apparatus. The house rose four stories into the air.

The best views of the ocean were from the top floor. The sun would rise in the east, and he felt confident the owner of this place would want to see it do its thing.

He gripped an invisible crevice in the wall and started to climb, keeping his body tight to the face of the house. His fingers and feet pushed into the roughened surface, finding handholds where none existed.

The windows were dark on the second story.

On the third story he noted a dim light and took a chance looking through the glass.

Suzanne Davis, Josh Quentin's romp-in-the-sheets partner, was lying in bed, this time alone. The covers barely covered her and evidenced quite clearly that Ms. Davis opted for no clothing at bedtime even when she was riding solo.

Rogers kept going and reached the fourth floor. He veered horizontally against the face of the mansion until he reached the window. It was open a crack, no doubt to get the ocean breeze.

He looked down and saw a guard pass by. But the man's gaze never moved up. Rogers's fingers slipped under the wood and gently pushed up. The window, well oiled, slid open quietly.

In a flash Rogers was through it and inside.

He surveyed the darkness. He was not in a bedroom. It looked set up as a home office. Desk, shelves, a small conference table, several seating areas.

He spotted the door at the other end of the room.

In his head he visualized how the house must be set up internally.

The door to his left had to empty out into the corridor.

The door at the end of the room must open into an adjoining room. A bedroom?

He moved toward the door and noted the motorized wheelchair with a cane leaning next to it. This had to be Ballard's room.

He eased the door open. The bed was set against the far wall. A man was lying in the bed.

Rogers zeroed in on the face. Even in the darkness his eyes were able to see precisely what was there. And then his mind was able to whittle away three decades of wear and tear from the countenance.

Eventually, a man he recognized as Chris Ballard rose to the surface. A cheery, relaxed face that hid a personality filled with cruelty, a heart lacking the least bit of compassion.

He moved over to the bed and gazed down at the shrunken mass.

He thought about how best to do this. It was an issue of noise. He needed to have a conversation. And in order to do that he had to allow Ballard to talk.

He put a hand over the sleeping man's mouth. This had the effect he desired.

The man was jarred awake. He looked up into Rogers's face. His features went from fearful to curious.

And then the fear returned.

Rogers bent down and said in a low voice, "Where is she?"

He removed his hand from Ballard's mouth, but his fingers encircled the old man's throat and squeezed lightly.

Rogers's intent was clear. If Ballard tried to cry out, Rogers would crush his throat.

"Where is she?" Rogers said again.

"Who?" croaked the old man.

Rogers tightened his grip slightly. "Where?"

He tightened his grip a bit more. "Where?" he said again. The modulation of his voice was unchanged but his tightening grip around the neck told the old man of his urgency.

Ballard shook his head.

"Where?"

The old man shook his head.

Rogers squeezed the neck, but only for a second. The old man's eyes fluttered and then closed.

He had not killed, but merely incapacitated. He knew the difference.

He silently praised himself for not losing control and just killing the man. He checked the carotid pulse, just to be sure.

Life beat there, if but feebly.

He rose from the bed and listened intently.

He could hear nothing.

He looked back at the man and rubbed the back of his head.

The night had not turned out like he had wanted, but at least he had found Ballard.

Had Jericho been the "she" Davis had mentioned to Josh Quentin? The woman on the Falcon jet?

He touched the top of his head; his eye closed against the sudden, jarring pain.

Was I really that close to her?

He left the bedroom and walked into the office. He started going through papers, careful to put things back exactly as they were. He took some pictures of pages with the camera on his phone. He looked through the binders on the shelf and did the same with certain pages there.

Finished with that, he had one more thing left to do.

He walked back into the bedroom and lifted Ballard out of the bed as though he weighed nothing. And to Rogers the man *did* weigh nothing. And was nothing. Certainly not someone deserving of a life filled only with luxury.

He carried him over to the window that was set against one wall, put the unconscious old man down, and opened it. He peered out.

There was no one down there. The ground was cobblestone, as was the entire interior courtyard.

He stood Ballard up, gripped his shoulder and the back of his pajama trousers, lifted him off the floor, and pitched him headlong through the open window.

He watched as the man fell. Rogers wasn't sure if Ballard ever awoke to see death coming right at him.

And he didn't really care.

Ballard hit the stone headfirst. The crunch was audible up here. Rogers waited, counting seconds off in his head. Then he heard the running feet outside.

Security guards converged on the mass of bloody flesh at the bottom of the window.

He knew what they would do next.

He went into the other room, went back out the window he'd come through, and closed it completely. Then he made his way down the sheer wall even as lights inside the house popped on.

Passing the third floor, through the open window he saw Davis jump up and throw a robe on before rushing out into the hall.

Rogers's feet hit stone the moment the door to Ballard's office was slid open.

He had reached the perimeter wall when he heard someone open the window he'd just come through.

He was over the wall by the time the person looked out and saw...nothing.

Rogers hit the dirt on the other side and started to sprint.

He was back in his room in Hampton exactly two hours later.

He sat on his bed, took out his phone, and looked at some of the pictures he'd taken.

One was of Claire Jericho and Chris Ballard. Ballard wasn't as old as he had been tonight, but the man was still probably in his late seventies. So Jericho *was* alive. Or at least had been when this picture was taken.

Impulsively, he grabbed his keys and headed out.

He had a place he had to see. *Places*, in fact.

And he had to see them right now.

CHAPTER

35

I<small>T WAS A</small> window of opportunity.

That's all.

On the battlefield Puller had always referred to that as "the edge." If he and his unit could hit the edge at precisely the right time they could accomplish their mission. Not necessarily survive. The principal goal was executing the mission. Survival was a close second, but still second. That's why they called it combat.

Puller had left northern Virginia very late, and now it was less than two hours before dawn would break. He should have been asleep long ago, but sleep was the furthest thought from his mind.

He was ten minutes outside of Williamsburg. In the trunk of his Malibu was his big investigation duffel. Inside it was everything he needed to perform a professional and thorough examination of any crime scene. His only problem was that after thirty years there was no crime scene left to investigate.

But that wasn't necessarily true. Hence the trip to Williamsburg.

He reached the city limits, pulled off the road, and consulted a list with four names and locations on it. These were the names of the dead women and the spots where their bodies had been found.

Two were on the perimeter of the campus of the College of William and Mary, the second oldest college in the country behind Harvard. It was a place where very smart young people went to learn.

It was also where a serial killer had dumped half his victims.

The other two had been found at two separate locations, but both well within the city limits.

He reached the first site, pulled over, and got out. He took a camera from his duffel and walked over to the forested area where the body of the chemist Jane Renner had been discovered thirty years ago under a pile of leaves.

He walked to the spot and looked down. It was bare ground now. There was no special marker, nothing to denote that a young woman's body had been callously jettisoned here.

He took a few pictures of the spot and the surrounding area. It was lonely and probably was just as lonely thirty years ago. Within easy walking distance of the two-lane road he had driven in on.

Forensics had shown that Renner had not been killed at this spot. There had been very little blood. And lividity had demonstrated that the body had been moved after death. It was simple science. Once the heart stopped, blood ceased to flow and, due to gravity, settled in the lowest part of the body. If you died on your back, the blood settled and concentrated there, mostly in your back and buttocks, and some in your hamstrings and calves. If the body wasn't moved for a certain period of time, then even when it was transported elsewhere and turned facedown, the blood would remain right where it was.

Such had been the case with Jane Renner. Her killer would have had to carry her here. She was five-seven and weighed one hundred and forty pounds, so that would not have been easy.

A strong man carrying the woman over his shoulder could easily manage it for the distance involved. And a man who could crush spines was obviously strong enough to tote his victims.

Puller got back into his car and was about to start it up when he noted a white van passing by. It seemed to slow as it neared where he was. Then it regained speed and kept going.

It looked like a van that a workman would use. The driver was probably heading out to an early morning job.

He put the car in gear and drove to the next site. It was two miles away. The streets were deserted, the moon full, the air crisp. He reached the site and once more got out with his camera.

He took a few pictures and walked the area where the second body had been dumped. Gloria Patterson, twenty-four and an engineer. The killer had not even bothered to cover her with leaves.

He eyed the area. It was isolated although the campus of William and Mary was not very far away. Just through some trees, really.

He got back into his car and started it up. When he reached the third site, he saw it heading down the road away from him.

A white van.

But was it the *same* white van?

He couldn't be sure. It looked the same.

He snapped a few pictures of the area and then jumped back into his car.

The van was out of sight, but that didn't matter. Puller knew where he was going, and if this turned out to be the mother of all breaks, so did the person driving the white van.

He turned down the road leading to the fourth and last

site. As he drove up, he saw a glimmer of white as it reached a curve in the road and disappeared.

Puller didn't even bother to stop. He sped up, but kept back a bit. The last thing he wanted was to spook whoever was up there.

They passed the site where the fourth victim, the computer programmer Julie Watson, had been found, and the van seemed to slow. Puller was praying that it would stop and the driver would get out. Then Puller would do his questioning with an M11 pointed in the person's face.

But that didn't happen. The van kept going. And so did Puller.

The two vehicles reached a main road.

Puller snatched his camera and fired a few shots at the rear of the van.

They turned onto another road.

It was nearly five in the morning now and early-rising commuters were out in full force. This was a military community and those folks worked varying shifts, but the one coming up now was one of the biggest.

The van sped up and got on the entry ramp for Interstate 64 heading east.

Puller had to fall back because of the volume of traffic. It was still dark and now all he could see in front of him were winking red brake lights. He counted ahead to where he thought the van was located.

Soon he went through the Hampton Roads tunnel. It was lighted inside and he thought he could see the van far ahead.

By the time he came out of the tunnel and the overhead lights vanished, all he could see were taillights. And there was a white van right in front of him and one next to him. Neither was *the* van, because they both had stenciling on the sides and rear. One was a plumber, the other an electrician.

Puller looked up ahead. There were exits and the van could take any one of them, or none at all and keep going.

He decided to stay on the road.

He had driven many more miles, and traffic had gotten heavier as more and more cars piled onto the interstate. Finally, he gave it up and exited. He reversed course and headed west. He drove back to the hotel where he had stayed before and got a room.

He got out his camera and checked the pictures. He zoomed in on the shots of the van. He could just make out a license plate.

He wrote it down. It was a West Virginia plate. If he'd still been with CID, running the plate would have been no problem.

Had he just blown an incredible opportunity? Had the guy in the van been the killer thirty years ago, checking out his dumpsites at the very same time Puller had decided to do that too?

He was thinking what to do when his phone buzzed. He checked his watch.

Early call.

Puller didn't like calls this early. They usually portended bad news, and he'd already had enough of that lately.

"Yes?"

It was his lawyer friend, Shireen Kirk.

"Puller. I'm afraid I've got some bad news."

"About what?"

"No, about *who*."

"Then who?" he barked, his nerves frayed near their breaking point.

"Your father."

CHAPTER

36

FOR A MOMENT Puller thought that his heart had stopped.

Instantly appearing in his mind's eye was the image of his father in a coffin dressed in his blues and stars, he and his brother in full dress uniform standing off to the side while folks came to view their dad for the very last time.

"He's...dead?"

She said quickly, "No, I'm sorry, I shouldn't have said it that way."

"What the hell is going on, Shireen?" he shouted into the phone.

"Okay, just calm down. I can tell you're already having a bad day, though it's still morning."

"Is my father okay?" Puller snapped.

"Yes. And no."

Puller closed his eyes and with a massive effort willed himself to remain calm. "Just tell me."

"Your father got a phone call. I don't know how it got to his room or why it wasn't screened out. I mean, the personnel at the hospital know his condition."

"Who was the call from?"

"Lynda Demirjian."

"What!" barked Puller. "Did my dad answer the phone? How could he?"

"No one knows how he could, but apparently he did."

"What did she say to him?"

"Well, we couldn't ask your father that, of course. But we talked to Stan Demirjian. He told us. He didn't know that she was going to do that. But she told him afterwards what she'd done."

"Wait a minute, why ask Stan? Why not just talk to his wife?"

Puller could hear Shireen let out a long breath. "Because she's dead. She died right after telling her husband about the call."

Puller put his head in one hand and rocked back and forth on the bed. "And what did she say was my father's reaction to what she told him?"

"He started screaming things at her. Unintelligible, or so she said. And then he hung up."

"Well, that's great," said Puller. "How did you find out?"

"I'm your father's lawyer. I started my work. I called Stan Demirjian to get a statement from him before I talked to his wife. That's when he told me."

"And how was Stan taking it?"

"His wife had just died, so there's that part of it; the man was grieving. Plus he was sort of caught between a rock and a hard place—his wife dead, the man she had accused of this terrible crime a person Stan revered."

Yeah, I get being caught between a rock and a hard place, Puller thought. "Did you tell my father's doctors what happened?"

"As soon as I got off the phone with Stan. But they had already given him something to calm him. He was so agitated, they just didn't know why."

"Thanks for doing that."

"There's something else, Puller."

"What?" he said wearily.

"CID has dropped their investigation. Ted Hull—"

"Has been reassigned, I know." Puller paused. "Shireen, I want you to just drop the whole thing."

"What? Why?"

"The CID's been called off. So just drop it, Shireen."

"But I thought you wanted to find the truth?"

"I just...just forget I ever called you."

"Puller!"

He clicked off and tossed his phone down on the bed. He hoped that Shireen heeded his advice.

His phone rang. It was Shireen. He didn't answer.

It was then that he noticed the piece of paper on the floor. It was over by the door. He automatically pulled his M11 and skittered across the room, keeping low, halfway expecting the door to be kicked in at any moment. He slowly reached down and picked up the paper.

The note was handwritten.

Meet me outside in ten. VK

This could be a trap. His first instinct was to climb out the window, make his way down, bypass the parking lot where an armored Humvee might be waiting, and hoof it on foot for a few miles. But then he looked at the note again.

That's when he saw there was faint writing at the bottom. *Not the Fort.*

He had to smile. This was a line he had given her when they had been working together on his brother's case. He had called her "Fort Knox" because she seemed impenetrable. This was her way of confirming her identity.

But still, it could be a trap.

The Vice President's warning came back to him.

Don't trust anybody.

Knox was in the clandestine world. Puller had found they were the toughest people of all to trust, because it seemed they could never, ever tell you the complete truth.

But Knox had risked her life to save his several times. She had helped to clear his brother and been nearly killed in the process.

He kept his M11 out and checked his watch. His musings had burned five minutes of the ten.

He went to the window that looked out on the front parking lot. Dawn had come and it was light enough to see clearly.

What he didn't see was a mass of black SUVs waiting to snatch him away. The lot was quiet. There were many parked cars because the hotel was large, but he only saw a couple of people there.

One was a man in military uniform carrying a briefcase. He got into his car and drove off.

The other was a woman who had just gotten out of her cab and was walking to the front entrance, rolling her suitcase behind her.

Puller looked at his watch.

Two minutes to go.

He grabbed his bag and pulled it over one shoulder. He had a feeling he wouldn't be coming back here. He slid the gun in the other pocket of his windbreaker but kept it gripped in his hand. He hit the elevator and made his way down.

The lobby was empty except for the woman he'd seen earlier checking in and the sleepy-looking front desk person helping her.

He eyed the doors leading out. If Knox was outside he wondered why. He also wondered where she had been.

He crossed the lobby and walked outside. It didn't take him long to find her. That was because she drove up in a black sedan.

She rolled down the window as he looked at her.

"What are you doing?" he said.

"At the present moment, saving your ass. Get in."

"My duffel's in my car."

"No it's not. It's in my trunk."

"The key is in my pocket."

"I don't need a key," she said. "Just get in."

"Why not take my car?"

"It's tainted goods, Puller."

"You mean they're tracking it?"

"I'll explain. Get in!"

He threw his bag into the back and climbed into the passenger seat.

She hit the gas and they shot out of the parking lot.

"What the hell is going on, Knox?"

"I'll tell you what I know, but you're not going to believe a word of it."

CHAPTER

37

Rogers had kept checking the rearview all the way back to where he was staying.

There had been a car back there. It had been at the first dumpsite, and then he'd spotted it at the third and the fourth sites. Then he had driven straight to the interstate.

He cursed himself for going to where the bodies had been. But the thing in his head had made him do it. And the thing in his head, he had found, could make him do anything.

He was now sitting on the bed in his motel room thinking all of this through.

Who could have been back there?

The thing was, the person had been at the first dumpsite *before* he'd gotten there. Now, that might have been a coincidence, but to be at the third and fourth too? And maybe he was at the second, but Rogers might have left by then.

Was it the police? Were they investigating the murders once more? They had never been solved. It might be one of those cold case investigations.

And I might have stumbled right into the middle of it.

He pulled out his phone and checked the newsfeeds.

What he expected to see wasn't there.

For all the world knew, Chris Ballard was still alive and well behind his fortress walls. Certainly by now the police would have been called and an investigation commenced. And the news outlets certainly would have been informed.

Rogers had tried to make it look like suicide. Even if Ballard couldn't walk, he could have crawled to that window and levered himself through it.

But with either murder or suicide there should have been something about it in the news by now.

For the next two hours he kept flipping through all the late breaking news sites.

Zip.

It was fully light now. He changed clothes and went down to the motel diner and had some breakfast while checking his phone constantly.

There was still nothing, which could only mean one thing: They were covering it up. Either the police hadn't been called or they had been and higher-ups had put a stranglehold on any leaks to the media. Perhaps they were trying to figure out if this really was a suicide or murder.

And if they concluded that it was a murder they might conclude that he was back to deliver his revenge.

And more to the point, *she* would know of it.

Claire Jericho's brainpower had been something to behold. But she had a dark side too.

Rogers no longer had compassion. It had been taken away from him, along with many other things. She, on the other hand, apparently never had any compassion at all.

This was the person who had created him. Perhaps in her own image. He lacked the capacity to dig any deeper into the psychology of it.

He went back to his room, lay on the bed, and closed his eyes. But he didn't sleep.

His mind went back thirty years and then stopped on *five* women.

He hadn't chosen them at random. They had *something* in common.

Me.

It had taken a lot of work on his part, but he had gathered the necessary information and then done what he had set out to do. It was all he had thought about for the longest time.

And right before they died, they knew exactly how I felt about what they had done to me.

And with that thought he fell asleep. He didn't wake until it was time for him to go to work. He got ready and drove to the Grunt.

Helen Myers greeted him in the back hall of the bar.

"Did you have a good night off?" she asked.

"It was pretty uneventful," replied Rogers.

"Nothing too exciting, then?"

"No."

Rogers was telling the truth. There had been absolutely nothing exciting about throwing Chris Ballard out a four-story window and watching his head smash into the cobblestones.

"I wanted to let you know that Josh will be in tonight with a party," Myers went on.

"Right, thanks for the heads-up. He'll be going up to his room?"

"So you know about that?"

"I saw him head up there last time. I figured that's where your VIPs go. They're not going to be in general pop, are they?"

"General pop?"

"Just a term I've heard used. Should I just clear his whole

party in without checking IDs? He seemed a little ticked off when I did that the first night."

"Yes, just let them in. I'll vouch that they're all legal," she added with a smile tacked on.

"Will Karl be in tonight?"

"He's already here. In the back."

"I'll stop in and see him before I go on duty."

"Good."

He left her there and continued on to the back to see Karl. The big man was seated at a table and looked better. Rogers saw no cane. And Karl wore no sunglasses.

Karl motioned for Rogers to take a seat. He did so.

"I heard about the 'incident' the other night."

"How?"

"Cop on the beat is an old bud of mine. He told me. These punks are starting to be a real problem."

"I can handle it."

"I have no doubt of that. But the thing is, we don't want that kind of trouble. You kick the shit out of some of these college boys, or maybe even kill one, it's not good for business. See what I mean?"

"I see. And I won't do anything to mess it up for the bar."

"Good man."

Rogers left him and went back into the bar area in time to see Myers ascend the stairs, unlock the door to the VIP room, and go in. He drew back and watched. A minute later she reemerged and shut the door behind her. In her right hand was the door key. But she had something in her left hand that hadn't been there before.

He backed up and then came around the corner as though just emerging from the back hall.

They met at the bottom of the stairs.

She said, "How's Karl?"

"Like a new man," said Rogers, glancing down. Myers was gripping something in her left hand, but he couldn't see what it was.

She looked back at him. "Anything else?"

"No. I'm good to go."

CHAPTER

38

"ARE YOU GOING to tell me, or are you just going to keep driving?"

Puller was staring directly at Knox.

"I'm trying to process it all in my head so I can give you an efficient version," she replied.

"Where have you been?"

"Finding out things."

"And did you?"

"Processing, Puller, give me a sec. I was wheels down just an hour ago. It's still a bit garbled in my head."

He waited until she pulled off the highway and into the parking lot of a 7-Eleven. She put the car in park, undid her seat belt, and said, "I need coffee. You want some?"

"Okay."

She got out, went in and bought two large coffees, came back to the car, presented one to him, and took a sip of hers.

"Are you done processing?" he asked.

She nodded and sat back. "There was a lot about this case that didn't add up. The FBI pulling out of a serial murder case? That's unheard of. The forensics not being professionally done. Investigators getting stonewalled. No leads at all with four women dead. And the playing field being manipulated by so-called 'higher-ups,' which is very convenient because it lets anonymity reign."

"Agreed on all points," said Puller. "Just so you know, Ted Hull got reassigned and his phone number was given over to a woman from the Department of Agriculture, so no one could contact him. And I'm supposed to be on a flight to Germany because I got pulled off the case too."

"So why aren't you on the plane?"

"Because another *higher-up* intervened, this time on my behalf."

"Which higher-up."

"I can't tell you because I was ordered not to disclose it."

"Ordered, by someone in the military?"

"This isn't a guessing game with clues, Knox. We were discussing what you found out?"

She took another sip of coffee and he saw a vein pulsing at her temple. He also saw her hand quiver just a bit as she set her coffee in the cup holder.

"We might have stumbled onto something so big I'm not sure I can even comprehend it, Puller, much less deal with it."

"Let's start small. Give me some details."

"I spoke with a man named Mack Taubman. He was my mentor. He was the reason I survived my early years in the field. He served his country in the intelligence field for over forty years and did it better than anyone I know. He's retired now, but he was square in the middle of things in the 1980s."

"Meaning what?"

She met his eye. "Mack told me that on the Fort Monroe installation back then there were some highly classified— some might say disturbing—research projects going on."

"By the Army?"

"You heard of DARPA?"

"Of course," he said.

"They finance some interesting projects."

"Like the one at Fort Monroe?"

"Yes. There was a facility there. A Building Q."

"Sounds like a James Bond thing, "commented Puller."

"It might have been, actually."

"What does this have to do my mother?"

"I don't know. All I know is a man I greatly respect didn't want to even talk about this in hypotheticals. When I brought up the murdered women in Williamsburg, I thought Mack was going to have a heart attack."

"He thinks they were connected to whatever was going on at this Building Q?"

"Yes."

"And what exactly was going on there?"

She shook her head. "Mack either didn't know or, more likely, did know but wouldn't tell me. Mack always took the oath of confidentiality very seriously."

"So you're telling me that some government project resulted in the deaths of four innocent women?"

"It could be the case, Puller."

"But it wasn't like they were injected with some super-secret new poison as guinea pigs and died from that. They were attacked and murdered, Knox. By someone!"

"I read the reports, Puller. And I'm sitting right next to you, so you don't have to shout."

He thumped the dashboard and looked out the window. "And my mother? How is she connected to this?"

"She may have been the fifth victim."

He turned to stare at her dully. "Did your *friend* tell you that?"

"No, he didn't actually know about Jackie Puller's disappearance. That's just speculation on my part."

"We need more than speculation."

"Well, let's see where this all logically leads us. Your mother disappeared from Fort Monroe. Building Q is located there. Whatever happened to those four women seems to have emanated from Fort Monroe. Your mother disappears right in the middle of all that and is never seen again. Just a coincidence?" she added sarcastically.

"No, probably not."

"So if a government project went haywire and resulted in four, or five, murders including the wife of a one-star no less—that means there was a cover-up of massive proportions."

Puller said, "Do you think the women could have been killed by someone on our side, and then it was all made to look like a serial killer's work?"

"For what reason?"

Puller said, "The women might have known something incriminating. They might have all had a connection to Building Q."

"Well, that's something we'll never know, since their places of employment had been deleted from their files. But remember what the Williamsburg homicide detectives said about the injuries. Like an animal, only human. Crushing."

"So maybe the disturbing and classified research at Building Q thirty years ago had to do with building some sort of…"

"Fighting super freak?" suggested Knox.

"Yeah."

She hiked her eyebrows. "This is all speculation, Puller."

"That's all we have, Knox! Speculation! That's what happens when you have no damn facts to work with. But my theory is no more out there than yours. You think a cover-up happened at very high levels. That's why your friend clammed up."

She looked down at her hand and then up at him. "I'm not used to having my side against me."

"You think I am?"

"This is scaring the crap out of me, Puller."

"Okay, let's get back to investigative basics. We have some facts to work with. Something happened at Fort Monroe in Building Q. The results of that were four women being murdered, and the powers that be covered it up. And if that is the case, the powers that be are probably no longer in power. They might be dead after thirty years."

Knox shook her head. "Even if they are, there is no way the government wants this to come out. Think about what it would do to current projects. Even if these guys aren't around, it would ruin their reputations. And some of them might still be around. And in power."

"Which would explain the stonewalling, the shuttered investigations, Hull and me getting pulled off the case. They don't want it to be solved."

"Four murders unresolved," said Knox. "Four families with no closure because someone's rep might take a hit."

"Five families, maybe," said Puller quietly.

"Yeah, maybe five," she replied, looking at him closely. "I know how hard this must be for you."

They were both silent for a while until Knox said, "So how and where do we start?"

"I told Shireen Kirk to get the hell out of Dodge."

"Why?"

"For the same reason I'm telling you to do the same thing."

"You're not serious?" she said, obviously stunned.

"I'm very serious, Knox. I have a reason to follow this

up. You don't. I'm not going to let you put your career and maybe your life on the line for this. You nearly died already helping me and my brother. I'm not going to risk that happening to you again."

"Puller, I'm already involved. I'm already here."

"I appreciate what you told me. It gives me a place to start. But it's just going to be me from now on."

"Puller!"

He opened the car door, took out his duffel, popped the trunk, grabbed his investigation bag, hoisted them over his shoulders, and leaned back into the open car door.

"Thanks, Knox. I owe you."

"*John*, please don't do this."

He pushed the car door closed with his knee and set off down the sidewalk.

CHAPTER

39

Rogers assumed his post outside where the line was already fifty deep. The IDs came out and his work began.

Two hours later the stretch limo arrived and out popped Josh Quentin and what looked to be the very same entourage. With one significant addition.

Suzanne Davis was there in a tight mini and crop top. He noted that her bare shoulders and arms were toned. She had a tat of a dragon on her right triceps. She had a plastic cup in hand. Rogers doubted it contained soda.

She didn't seem to be mourning the passing of poor Chris Ballard, he observed. Neither did the smiling Quentin.

"Paul, right?" said Quentin as they approached.

Rogers nodded. "You can go right in with your group, Mr. Quentin."

The young man slipped a hundred-dollar bill into Rogers's hand and clapped him on the shoulder. "Good man."

"Thank you, sir."

Quentin squeezed Rogers's shoulder. "Whoa, you're solid as a rock, Paul. You work out?"

"A little."

"I do an extreme fitness routine. It's more a young person's thing. Strong as you are, you might not be able to keep up. Ton of cardio."

"I'm sure it's too tough for me, sir."

"Age catches up to us all."

Davis glanced up at him as she passed by.

"Nice tat," said Rogers.

"Nice hat," she shot back.

At two o'clock in the morning the limo came round. Rogers held the door open as Quentin and his group came out.

Quentin pressed another hundred-dollar bill into his palm.

Rogers counted off the group and saw that Davis was not there. "Aren't you missing one?" he asked.

"Suzanne's passed out upstairs," said Quentin in an annoyed tone. "I thought I'd let her sleep it off. I'll send a car for her in the morning."

"I can take her home, Mr. Quentin."

"It's in North Carolina."

"Not a problem. I'll just wait here until she wakes up."

Quentin slapped him on the arm. "Thanks, Paul. I'll email her and let her know the plan. She'll give you the directions."

He climbed into the limo and it pulled off.

Rogers watched it go. Either Quentin was a very trusting man or a very stupid one. He had just left an unconscious lover of his alone with a complete stranger. Or maybe he just didn't care.

Rogers went into the bar and helped clean up. Myers and Karl had left earlier.

If anyone else knew that Davis was passed out upstairs they didn't let on.

Then everyone else left and Rogers held the keys to the Grunt in his hand.

He locked the front door, walked up the stairs, and found the door to the room unlocked. He opened it and flicked on the light.

Davis was not in the first room, so he passed through into the bedroom. And there she was, sprawled on the bed and without a stitch of clothing on.

He drew closer, looked around, found a blanket draped over a chair, snatched it up, and threw it over her.

Then he sat down in the chair and waited.

He heard a ding from somewhere and instantly sat rigid in his seat.

Then he noticed her phone on the nightstand. It had lighted up when the text came in.

He looked at the screen.

Had to leave, babe. Early meeting tomorrow. Paul the bouncer taking you home to NC when you wake. See you soon. J

Rogers sat back down and watched her. She tossed and turned in her sleep and several times pulled the blanket off herself. Each time Rogers put it back on.

Finally, at about four in the morning she sat straight up, pulled the blanket off her, and looked straight at him.

"Who the fuck are you?"

She didn't seem to be embarrassed that she had no clothes on.

"Your phone will explain."

"What?"

"A message from Mr. Quentin."

She looked around, seized her phone, and accessed the message.

"You're Paul?" she said groggily.

"I was at the front door when you came in. I'm the bouncer."

She looked down at her bare chest. "Where the hell are my clothes?"

"I don't know. I covered you with the blanket."

He got up and looked around. Then he got on his knees and pulled her skirt, top, and a bra and underwear out from under the bed. He dropped the articles of clothing on the bed and said, "I'll wait for you in the other room while you get dressed."

He closed the door behind him.

He heard her get up. He also heard her stumble, apparently hit her knee, and loudly curse. A minute later the door opened. She was still zipping up her skirt.

"Any idea where my shoes are?" she said crossly.

He reached behind a sofa pillow and pulled out a pair of stilettos.

"Thanks." She sat and put them on.

As they walked down the stairs he said, "I'm afraid I've only got a crappy van."

"If they had Uber in this shithole I'd use them. I'm in North Carolina. It's two hours."

"Mr. Quentin told me."

"*Mr.* Quentin just fucking left me?"

"Looks like it."

"Asshole!"

"Do you want me to drive you to a hotel here instead? You can make arrangements to go home tomorrow. Well, it's already tomorrow, but I mean later in the day."

"No. I'm wide awake now. Let's just get on the road."

He locked up the bar after setting the alarm system and they walked to his van. They climbed in and, to her credit, she didn't complain about the condition of the interior. She curled up in her seat and closed her eyes.

"I'll need directions," lied Rogers.

"Get on Sixty-Four going towards Norfolk. I'll tell you from there."

"Okay."

He drove onto the interstate and settled back in his seat.

She gave him directions as needed, though he knew the way and they were soon nearing the Outer Banks. Traffic was nonexistent at this time of morning.

"Have you known Mr. Quentin a long time?" Rogers asked.

She looked at him with puffy eyes. "Why?"

"No reason. Just making conversation."

"Well, stop. I don't know you."

"Sorry."

He gazed out the windshield at the coming dawn, thinking that she was right around the same age as the dead women.

"About five years," she said abruptly.

He glanced at her. She was staring at him.

"I've known him about five years."

"Ms. Myers says he's very successful. A real up-and-comer."

"I guess you could say that."

"Guy obviously has money."

"Oh, he's got money all right."

"How'd you two meet? Must have been after college. I know he's thirty."

"Why do you think I went to college?"

He shrugged. "Don't most young people these days go to college?"

"Did *you* go to college?"

"If I did I probably wouldn't be a bar bouncer at my age."

"How old are you?"

He told her. "How old are you?" he asked.

"You're not supposed to ask a woman her age."

"Didn't know that."

"I'm thirty-one." She reached out and felt his shoulder. "You look old in the face. But you're jacked like an athlete. You ever think of having a face-lift?"

"May be hard for you to believe, but it's never crossed my mind."

Her interest obviously growing, she felt his bicep. "I'm serious, I bet you don't have any body fat at all." She tugged at his shirt. "You got a six-pack under there? Guys your age always have potbellies. But not you." He felt her fingers flit over his crotch.

He gently nudged her hand away and said, "How's your head?"

She straightened and stared out the windshield. "I don't get hangovers. I just pass out when I drink too much. I'm fine. And I'm hungry." She looked out the window. "There's an IHOP a half mile up ahead. Let's get some breakfast."

He pulled into the parking lot and she led him into the place, which was about half full at this hour. They ordered coffee and food. She played with her paper napkin and stared over at him.

"Why are you a bouncer?"

"Only job I could find."

"I don't have a job, not really."

"What do you do with your time, then?"

"Pretty much whatever I want."

"Must be nice."

"You think?"

"I don't know. I've always had to work. But I guess it's good to have some purpose."

"Josh is a dick."

"I thought you were friends."

And lovers, he thought.

"We are, but he's still a dick. Don't you have any dick friends?"

Rogers shook his head. "I don't have any friends."

Their coffee came, followed by their food a minute later.

As they ate Rogers said, "Why is he a dick?"

"He thinks way too much of himself."

"But you hang out with him."

She shrugged. "We sort of got thrown together. We're sort of in business together."

"Really? I thought he had his own company."

"He's the head guy. But that doesn't mean he actually runs it."

"What's the company?"

"None of your business," she snapped.

"You're right. It's not."

"Damn, hey, baby!"

They looked up to see three large young men in jeans and T-shirts standing next to their table. One of them said to Davis, "I know you, sweet cheeks."

"I don't think you do," she said sharply and turned back to her cup of coffee.

"I *know* I do. A party couple weeks ago at a frat house at East Carolina. We got it on. You telling me you forgot?"

"I'm telling you I don't know you."

His face flushed and then creased in anger. "Is that right? Shit, all you talked about was how big and hard I was. Screaming like a bitch. You telling me you don't remember that?! Your name's Suzy, right?"

She stared back up at him. "Go away! I don't know you."

"Look, you—"

Rogers interjected, "Just move on, guys, the lady's not buying."

Now all three men turned their attention to Rogers. The first one said, "Did I ask for your two cents, Gramps?"

"No, but I'm giving it anyway."

Their waitress, who had been watching all of this, rushed over. "Look, we don't want no trouble here. Just leave these folks alone or I'll have to call the cops."

The man turned, gripped her face with his hand, and shoved her away. She staggered back, hit a table, and fell to the floor. The lady working the cash register picked up the phone and punched in 911.

The man turned back to Rogers. "Well, let me give you some advice, old man." He put his big hands on the table and leaned in close. "Mind your business before you get hurt."

Rogers sighed and rubbed the back of his head. He'd been having a nice breakfast and was finally getting some useful information when the Three Stooges had shown up.

Just dial it back. Only enough to get their attention.

When his hand came back down on the table, it landed on top of the young man's.

And he pressed down.

"Shit!" yelled the man. "Let go. Fuckin' let go of me."

Rogers pressed down even more.

The man dropped to his knees screaming.

Rogers finally let go, gripped the back of the man's head, and slammed it against the table. He fell to the floor unconscious.

The other two men leapt at Rogers.

He caught the first one with a punch in the gut. He had to

consciously pull back most of the force, so the man merely fell to the floor holding his belly and throwing up.

The third guy got behind Rogers and put him in a choke-hold.

Rogers reached a hand up, effortlessly peeled the man's fingers away from his throat, stood, and turned. He planted a vise grip on the man's wrist, spun him around, and torqued the arm up so high that the man's shoulder popped out of joint. He fell to the floor howling in pain.

Rogers put some cash down on the table. "You ready to go?" he asked Davis.

She looked up at him openmouthed and nodded.

Rogers had seen the lady at the cash register phoning what he knew was the police. He did not want to be here when they arrived.

Some of the customers, mostly elderly folks, clapped in appreciation as they passed by.

They reached the van and got in. Rogers put it in gear and sped out of the parking lot.

"That was freaking amazing," gushed Davis. "Where did you learn to do that?"

"School of hard knocks, I guess."

"What's your name again?"

"Paul."

"Paul what?"

"Just Paul."

She sat back and looked out the windshield. "I did know that guy."

"Okay."

"I sort of make bad choices with men."

"You wouldn't be the first."

"Where do you come from?" she asked.

He shot her a glance. "What, family, you mean?"

"Whatever you want it to mean."

"Then I don't come from anywhere. I'm just...here. I've got nobody. Just myself."

She nodded. "I can relate."

"Come on, you're way too young and pretty to be alone."

She waved this off. "My dad died in prison. He popped a drug dealer who gave him some bad coke. My mom smoked crack for breakfast till she croaked."

He shot her another glance. "You're shitting me?"

She grinned. "Maybe I am." Her smile vanished. "Or maybe I'm not. I know I've been on my own since I was thirteen."

"So you didn't go to college, then?"

"I went to East Carolina. And let an idiot screw me because I was bored. But then you know about that."

She laughed but then turned serious. She reached her hand across and laid it on top of his. The look on her face was crystal clear as to her intent.

Still, it took Rogers a few moments to pick up on this. He was taken aback. "Come on, I'm an old ugly fart who needs a face-lift. Said so yourself."

She just continued to stare at him and stroke his hand.

Rogers looked back at the road.

"When was the last time you were with a woman?" she asked.

He glanced over to find her watching him.

"It's been a while."

"I could tell."

Rogers looked back at the road. He didn't know this woman. She was working for Ballard. She was screwing Quentin. Apparently she was screwing whoever wanted to do her. He didn't know why he'd defended her at the breakfast place. It was none of his concern. But he had done it nevertheless.

"Paul?" she said. "Maybe we should pull off the road."

He parked behind a boarded-up strip mall, put the van in park, and looked at her. For the first time he really looked at *her*. Not as a potential lead. Not as a way to get to Jericho. Not as someone he might kill. He looked at her the way a guy is supposed to look at a woman in certain instances. And he found a beautiful young lady who wanted him, staring back.

He blinked. A memory flickered across the horizon of his brain. A young man. A young woman. Flesh on flesh. Bodies as one. The rise, and fall, and the aftermath. All…something wonderful. Something he'd never experienced since.

Her hand stopped stroking. She leaned over and kissed him. "Come on," she said. She slipped between the seats and into the back of the van.

Rogers slowly followed. She turned around, kissed him again, and started to undress. Rogers looked around at the cluttered interior of the van and then stared over at her as her clothes hit the dirty floor. He eyed something on a shelf, pulled out the cloth tarp, and laid it down.

"How gentlemanly of you," said Davis with a smirk. She crawled over to him.

He looked down at her. He had seen her naked twice now. But this was different. Her body was…beautiful. Even the dragon on the triceps was arousing him.

Davis pushed her breasts into him as she reached up and slipped off his jacket. When she started to undo the buttons on his shirt he stopped her.

She looked uncertain. "You don't want to?"

He was thinking, *No, I don't want you to see the scars.*

"Better this way," he said.

They lay down on the tarp, he above her.

He started breathing more quickly. And his brain seemed to be misfiring.

She said, "Um, you can keep your clothes on, but you *do* have to unzip your pants."

She helped him with this, and then he settled down on top of her. But his brain was still misfiring.

In frustration he gripped the edge of a shelf built into the van's wall so hard it broke off and a heavy tool toppled down and almost hit them.

"Shit, what was that?" exclaimed Davis, who half sat up.

"It's... it's nothing." He slowly settled her back down.

"Paul, everything okay?"

His heart was beating so fast he thought it might burst. He couldn't remember how to do this.

I can't even remember how to make love to a woman. How pathetic is that?

"Paul," she said again, squirming under him.

He felt a strong impulse to grab her neck and break it. Desperate, he racked his brains and suddenly hit on it.

Davis and Quentin in the bedroom. He rolled over and brought her up on top of him, settling his hands around her taut waist. He was careful to grip her very gently.

She smiled down at him. "How'd you know I like it this way?"

"Lucky guess," he muttered.

Ten minutes later it was over.

Because he had failed and grown soft.

She lay down next to him.

"That was great."

"Don't bullshit."

"It *was* great for me. I'm sorry it wasn't for you."

"It was great for me, even if..." He looked away from her.

"I liked the way you were holding me. You're so strong, but you were so gentle. I like that. I liked that a lot."

He looked at her searchingly. "Really?"

She kissed him on the lips. "Yeah, really."

She nestled closer to him and put her bare leg over him. A minute passed and he heard her soft snores.

Then he closed his eyes and joined her.

CHAPTER

40

Rogers slowly blinked himself awake.

Next to him, Davis slept on.

He rubbed the back of his head and tried to make sense of what had happened between them.

But he couldn't. He had always imagined that he had left humanity behind when they had changed him. And he had thought having sex with a woman impossible.

Before he'd viciously killed a man in a bar fight and gone to prison for ten years, he had killed others. Only he'd never been caught. He had no fear. But he also had nothing else that would inhibit him from taking another's life.

He had read of serial killers who were missing something critical in their frontal lobes. It was the significant difference that made one normal or made one a monster. Just a piece of DNA lacking or forming the wrong sequence. Or a lobe not quite as developed as it should be. You went from mainstream to Jeffrey Dahmer.

And that's what they did to me. I was born right and they made me wrong.

But ten years in prison had given Rogers something he thought he would never have. An opportunity to be away from anyone he might have otherwise killed. A buffer of bars and guards. It had given him time to think, to regain a measure of control.

He turned on his side and studied the sleeping Davis.

What had surprised him, when he finally thought about it, was that he had no impulse to harm her. But he had to remind himself that he had killed the couple in the alley only when they tried to kill him. And Donohue the gun dealer would still be alive if he'd just stayed in his truck eating his Mickey D's.

And I let the boy live.

He rubbed his eyes and wondered whether what was apparently happening to him was a good thing or not. After five minutes he had no conclusive answer.

He looked at his watch. It was nearly eight o'clock. The sun was shining brightly. Davis was still sound asleep next to him.

He once more marveled at her beauty. And then he looked down at his hands. Scars. He lifted his shirt. More scars. He touched the incision on his head. The biggest scar of all.

The analogy was obvious, Rogers thought: *Beauty and the Beast.*

He climbed back into the driver's seat and looked at himself in the rearview mirror.

For so long as he could remember he had looked just like this.

Not his features. That was obvious enough.

No, it was the look in his eyes.

Haunted. Crippled. Hungry for something I'll probably never get.

"Paul?"

He turned to see Davis rise and start dressing.

"Yeah?"

"I need to get home."

"Okay. I'm ready. Let's go."

She climbed into the passenger seat. As he started the van she reached over and kissed him on the cheek.

"What was that for?"

"Do I have to have a reason?"

"I guess not."

"We need to do this again. Really soon."

"You think that's smart?"

"I don't care if it's smart. It's what I want."

She gave him directions to the destination. He didn't know if it would be the rental on the beach or the fortress where the owner had taken a dive into expensive cobblestones.

It turned out to be the fortress.

As they neared the destination, Rogers began to panic a bit. What if Jericho was here? What if, despite all the years, she recognized him?

When Davis directed him to the front gates he said, "Damn, after what you said about the problems with your parents, I wasn't expecting something like this."

"It is a little much. But I hit the jackpot. The people who adopted me are really, really rich."

He stared at her, dumbstruck. Ballard had adopted her? So he'd killed her father? "So you live with them here?"

"That's right."

"But I thought you said you were on your own? That you didn't have anybody?"

"I didn't really know you back then. Now I do. A girl has to be careful."

"I guess so."

He couldn't fathom why Ballard's death seemed not to have made a dent in her. And he didn't see one cop car or one bit of police tape. Weren't they investigating the man's murder? What the hell was going on?

The gates opened as they approached. A guard came out,

and when he saw Davis he motioned for Rogers to drive through.

Rogers didn't look at the security guards as he passed by, though he noted in his peripheral vision that they were scrutinizing him.

Davis directed him where to park. She opened the door.

"Can I pay you for taking me all this way?"

"I think you already paid me more than I deserved."

She smiled. "That was a nice thing to say. You want to come in?"

The panic returned. "No. I better get back. But thanks."

"Okay, I'll see you at the Grunt, I'm sure."

"You better let Mr. Quentin know you got home safe."

"Like he cares," she scoffed. She leaned across the seat and placed a firm kiss on his mouth and then inserted her tongue into it.

Rogers had the impression that multiple eyes were watching this. Still her lips felt sweet and salty and seemed to perfectly mesh with his.

The next moment the car door closed and she disappeared inside.

That's when Rogers heard the knock on the glass.

He turned to see one of the security team there.

"You got a minute, sir?" the man asked crisply, the expression on his face unreadable. He motioned for Rogers to get out of the van.

When Rogers looked around he saw five more men all carrying MP5s along with serious expressions. They had surrounded the van in the few seconds between the kiss and Davis going inside. That was impressive, he thought.

He wondered if what was going to come next would be equally so.

Rogers opened the door and stepped out.

CHAPTER

41

Rogers FACED THE man who had requested his exit from the van.

"Can I see some ID?"

Rogers shook his head. "Not unless you're cops."

The man tapped his finger against the barrel of his MP5. "How did you end up with Ms. Davis?"

Rogers managed a smile as the men closed ranks around him. "I drove the lady home at the request of Josh Quentin. You can call him and check. He'll vouch for me. The name is Paul."

The man said, "Who are you?"

"I just told you. Paul."

"Paul what?"

"I'm the bouncer at the Grunt. Mr. Quentin and Ms. Davis were there last night. Ms. Davis became...ill. Mr. Quentin had to leave and he asked me to drive her home. And I did. Safe and sound."

"The Grunt closes at two. It's a two-hour drive from there to here. It's eight o'clock in the morning. What happened to the other four hours?"

"We didn't leave right at two. She was still indisposed. We left around four. And we stopped for breakfast at the

IHOP, at her request. We took our time. She seemed to be in no rush. And I'd worked all night. I was tired, so I wasn't trying to break any land speed records."

He pointed toward the door Davis had entered. "Just ask her if you don't believe me."

"What's going on?"

They all turned to see Davis's head poking out of what Rogers knew was her bedroom window.

The security man looked up. "Just checking to make sure everything is all right, Ms. Davis."

"Everything *is* all right. He drove me home. I wasn't feeling well. Okay? He works at the Grunt."

"Yes ma'am. Thank you, that's all we needed to know."

The man turned back to Rogers. "Well, thank you for getting her home safely," he said smoothly, his demeanor now friendly, though Rogers saw his finger flick toward the round selector of his MP, so his friendliness was purely for Davis's benefit and the flick was for his benefit.

"You're very welcome," Rogers said. "I'll be heading on now. I could use some sleep."

Davis called down from the window, "Paul, you can crash here for a few hours. It's probably not safe for you to drive right now." She added with an impish smile, "You must be *exhausted* after our little detour."

Rogers glanced at the security man and could read his expression clearly.

She slept with you?

Yeah, I can't believe it either, thought Rogers.

"You know, Ms. Davis, that's actually a good idea. Just a couch or something will be fine."

"I'll have them make up a room for you. We have enough of them. And you'll be back in plenty of time for work."

The room he was given was right next to hers on the

third floor. As he closed the bedroom door behind him he wondered again how everyone here could appear so normal when the owner of the place had just died. He lay on the bed but did not close his eyes. Finally, his eyelids did flutter as the breeze from outside swept in and embraced him.

He had seen that as he had grown older, his stamina, while still Herculean by most standards, was not what it used to be.

He awoke with a jolt and immediately checked his watch. Four hours had passed. The sun was high overhead.

He heard movement in the room next door and then the shower started to run. He imagined Davis naked with the water streaming over her.

He looked out the window that faced the beach. From up here he could see over the walls, down to the sand.

And Rogers was hard pressed to not cry out at what he was seeing.

A team of security was leading the old man, who rode in the same cart, out onto the sand. The only difference was, Davis was not with him. He got out of the cart and was helped to a chair that was set up for him on the sand.

The bodyguards formed a ring around him, their faces pointed outward.

Rogers looked down at his hands.

Who the hell had he been holding?

Who the hell had he been talking to?

Who the fuck had he thrown out the window?

He didn't hear the water stop next door.

Or hear a hair dryer start up.

He just sat in the chair and stared out the window at a man who should by all rights be dead.

He *did* hear the knock on the door a few minutes later.

He turned toward it as the door opened.

Davis stood there dressed in white capri pants, sandals, a pale blue striped shirt, and a wide-brimmed sun hat. A pair of sunglasses dangled from her fingers.

"I'm heading down to the beach. You want to come?"

"I have to get back. It's getting late."

"When can I see you again?"

He stood. "Look, I'm old and you're young. I'm poor and you're not. You can have any guy you want. Rich, handsome ones like Mr. Quentin."

"I'm not looking to marry you, Paul. I just want to know when we can hook up again."

"I work tonight. You planning to come to the bar?"

"I wasn't. But I am now."

"Okay, I'll see you then. If you're in the VIP room I can't go in there. Only Mr. Quentin's guests can."

"Stop calling him Mr. Quentin. You make him sound far more important than he is."

"Well, he's a very important client of the Grunt."

"Whatever. I'll see you tonight."

Rogers pointed out the window. "I see a man on the beach with a bunch of guards. Is that where you're going?"

She nodded.

"Is that the person who adopted you?"

"You ask a lot of questions," she said, but in a humorous tone. "I'll see you tonight."

"Okay, sounds good."

"Thanks for breakfast. And the rest," she added, flicking a smile at him.

She left and he watched a few minutes later as she walked out to the beach and joined the old man.

Rogers drove back to Hampton more confused than he'd ever been.

CHAPTER

42

AFTER LEAVING KNOX, Puller had hoofed it to a rental place and a half hour later driven out in a Mitsubishi Outlander.

He had not discounted anything that Knox had told him. In fact, he believed every word.

If this project at Building Q had ended in the murders of four women, and possibly his mother as well, that would be a secret the government would go to great lengths to bury. And for very good reason.

Money drove the Defense Department as much as anything else. If this story got out, Puller could see billions and maybe tens of billions of dollars of defense spending drying up. And shoulder stars, promotions, and retirement packages might be eviscerated as fingers were pointed and blame placed.

And a lot of private contractors who made their living off Uncle Sam would see their bottom lines crash and burn, their stock prices crater, and their huge executive paychecks disappear.

What would folks do to prevent that?

Pretty much anything they have to.

He got a room at a motel, paying in cash. He'd had to use

a credit card for the rental because there was no other way. They could track him that way, but he needed wheels. He hunkered down for the night while he thought over everything Knox had told him.

He was tempted to call his brother but didn't want to do anything that might get Bobby put back in jail.

He ate breakfast the next morning at a place near the motel. After that he drove straight to Fort Monroe, parked, and hoofed it the rest of the way on foot.

He had a map of the fort and quickly located Building Q.

The first thing he noted was that it was obviously still active. The parking lot was full, the perimeter fenced and guarded. People came and went. Trucks arrived, unloaded or loaded, and left.

What he couldn't see was what the hell they were doing inside there.

Over the hours he watched many people come and go. Some were older. Some younger. Men and women, with the majority being men. He read their body language and processed the possibilities.

He had counted nearly fifty people arriving and leaving when he settled on the one he wanted. He had seen her come and go twice now. Perhaps for a break. She had gotten into her car one of those times and headed out.

He snapped a picture of her with his phone as she was sitting idle at the security gate. As she passed by his hiding place, he noted her appearance up close. Around thirty, petite, unassuming. She had avoided direct eye contact with the security guards. Perhaps an introvert? She drove a beige Ford Fiesta that was as nondescript as she was.

Those were all good things for what he wanted to do.

Six o'clock came and a large group of people headed out the doors of Building Q. Puller found her in the crowd and hustled back to his car. When she passed by in her Fiesta he dropped in behind her.

They drove to what was most likely her apartment. She went directly inside.

Puller stayed in his car contemplating what to do. He could make his flanking maneuver now, or he could wait.

She came back out dressed in a short skirt, a low-cut blouse, and three-inch heels.

That was interesting.

He continued to follow her.

He looked at his watch. It was nearly eight p.m.

Puller wondered where the lady was headed.

She drove about a mile across town and parked her car on the street.

Puller did likewise.

He followed her down the street and around a corner.

And ran into a long line of people waiting to get in somewhere.

He looked up ahead and saw a sign over a door.

The Grunt?

He'd never heard of it, but then he'd never spent much time down here since he'd been a child.

The woman he was following was in the line ahead of him. Puller had two soldiers and a Navy guy in uniform behind him and a gaggle of college-age women in front of him. And the two groups were flirting with each other. Puller finally stepped behind the guys in uniform so they could more directly carry on their flirting with the ladies.

They finally worked their way up to the front, where a tall, well-built man in his fifties wearing a hat, glasses, and black clothing was checking IDs.

The woman Puller was following was cleared in, as were the young women behind her.

Then the soldiers stepped up to the line and presented their IDs.

The man checked them, held a light up to them, and handed them back.

"Nice try, guys," he said.

"These are legit," said one of the uniforms, a tall, thin male. "I'm twenty-two."

"Maybe in another life."

"This is crap," snapped the man.

"My light says it's a forgery, and the light is the judge," said the bouncer.

"Listen, old man—"

That's when Puller stepped in. He put a hand on the soldier's arm.

When the guy whipped around, ready for a fight, he was staring at the clawed eagle on Puller's CID badge.

The grunt stiffened.

"Bad luck for you all around, son," said Puller. "Now, I have no jurisdiction over the water boy there," he said, indicating the man in the Navy uniform. "But I sure as hell do over both of your butts. So turn back around and tell the man you're sorry, and get back to your post. And consider yourself lucky I don't haul your asses down to the stockade for using a fake ID, soldiers!"

Puller's voice had steadily risen as he was speaking, and by the time he was done he was in full-on drill sergeant mode. The two uniforms jumped out of line and tried to do their best imitation of world-class sprinters. After a moment's hesitation the Navy guy followed. They turned the corner and were soon out of sight.

Paul Rogers looked up at John Puller and put out his hand. He said, "Thanks for that. I never want any trouble."

"That's always a good way to look at things. And by

the way, I'm old enough to drink." He showed his ID card.

"Works for me, Mr. Puller. Have a good time."

Puller walked past him and into the bar.

Rogers flicked a glance at him and then turned back to his work.

43

THE GRUNT WAS already three-quarters full, but Puller had little difficulty finding the woman. She was at the bar with a drink already in hand.

Over the next hour he watched her work the room. Flirting, drinking, dancing, flirting some more. Finally she ended up in a corner with a guy who had his hand on her butt and his tongue down her throat. And in a show of equality, she was returning the favor.

Around ten, Puller's gaze shifted to the front door when a group came in led by a tall young man dressed in what looked to Puller to be a suit that maybe cost more than his Army-issued Malibu, kicking in the government discount. He and his group walked past a security guard and up the stairs. They passed through another door and it closed behind them. The security guard moved his bulk back in front of the staircase.

Puller assumed that no one else was going to be allowed up.

A good-looking woman passed in front of his field of vision. She was dressed professionally, unlike most of the other women here, and seemed closer to Puller's age than the rest of the clientele. He watched as she had a word with one of the bartenders and then went over and checked the till. Owner or manager or both, thought Puller.

He checked the woman he was following. She was still lip-locked in the corner.

He walked over to the bar where the woman was just closing up the cash register.

"Looks like you got a gold mine here," he said.

She stared up at him and smiled. Then she saw his empty hands.

"But you're not contributing to the gold," she said. "Won't you have a drink?"

"Sure. I can get it from the bartender."

"No, I'll pour it for you. On the house."

"Not much gold in freebies."

"One good deed, you know."

She drew the pint and handed it to him.

"I'm Helen, Helen Myers."

"John Puller."

"You're a bit…"

He looked around and grinned. "Older than your usual clientele."

"That's very delicately put."

He took a sip of his beer. "Is this your place?"

"What makes you say that?"

"You look like a lady in charge."

"Well, I am as a matter of fact."

"Good for you."

"How about you? What's your line of work?"

"Uncle Sam."

"You look military. What branch?"

"Army."

"My father was in the 82nd Airborne."

"Hell of a division."

"That's what he said, right up to the day he died. He was career military. That's where I got the idea for the Grunt. He was enlisted. Guy in the trenches."

"Me too. I'm sorry I had to pull a couple grunts out of line. They had fake IDs."

She frowned. "I know. I hate that. You'd think if you're old enough to fight and die for your country, you're old enough to buy and drink a beer. It's stupid."

"Preaching to the choir."

"Then you probably saw our bouncer, Paul."

"I did. He looks like he can take care of himself."

"Oh yes he can. Have a second beer. On the house."

He raised his glass. "No, that one I'll pay for."

She smiled, walked across the room, and went past the security guard and up the stairs, passing through the door, which she closed behind her.

Puller watched all of this and then turned his attention back to the woman. Her "friend" had left her and she was fumbling with something in her purse.

He walked over to her.

"Got a minute?"

"Excuse me?"

She glanced up at him as she pulled out her lipstick and redid her mouth. Puller figured most of what had been on her lips had ended up on the guy's face or down his throat.

"I'd like to talk to you."

"You can talk. And you can also buy me a drink. That's the price."

He pulled out his CID shield and held it up. "Let's talk. And you can buy your own drink, though I think you've had enough, so make it a Coke."

She froze with her lipstick poised a centimeter from her mouth. "You're an Army cop?"

"Yes I am. Building Q?"

"W-what about it?"

Gripping her arm, he said, "Over here, please."

He led her around a corner and down a hall that led to the kitchen. It was probably the quietest part of the place right now. Most people were drinking, not eating.

Puller said, "You work at Building Q?"

"What if I do?"

"Highly classified work. And yet here you are, getting drunk and letting young punks paw you? Where the hell is your brain?"

Her face flushed. "Where do you get off—"

Puller held up his badge again. "This is where I get off. You're under the jurisdiction of the Department of Defense. Your work is directly related to the United States Army. And my job is to protect the United States Army."

Puller didn't know if the Army was paying her salary, but the Army was by far the largest component of the military and it had its fingers in pretty much all pies. "And the national security interests of this country," he added.

"I-I know that. I'm not doing anything wrong."

"Your contract has a morals clause, correct? And listed behavior that you can and cannot do. One of those prohibited activities is putting yourself in situations where you could be blackmailed." He looked down at her. "Do you think if someone took pictures of you dressed like this with a guy's tongue down your throat and his hands on your ass, that you could be compromised?"

"Who the hell would do that?"

"Let me see some ID." He barked, "Now!" when she seemed to hesitate.

She produced her driver's license.

"Anne Shepard?"

"Yes."

"Confirm for me your employer's name. Unless you're too drunk."

He shot a hand out and steadied her as she rocked back and forth on her stilettos. Her lip trembling, she said, "Atalanta Group."

"That's right," said Puller, who up to that point had never heard of Atalanta Group. "And are you aware that your being here places you in a position to be blackmailed by enemies of this country?"

"But I'm just here having fun. I work twelve-hour days, pretty much every day. I'm just here to blow off some steam."

"There are smart ways to do that. This is not one of them. The guy with his tongue down your throat?"

"He's just some guy."

"That *some* guy will be arrested when he leaves here. He's an American-born spy in the employ of the Chinese looking to steal DoD secrets."

"Oh shit! That guy! You're kidding, right? He just wanted sex, like all guys."

"What did you tell him? Did he ask about work?"

"No, I mean—" She stopped, flustered. "I mean, he asked what I did."

"And what did you tell him?"

Shepard started to breathe heavily. "I think I'm going to be sick."

"The restroom is down that hall. I'll be here when you come out."

It didn't make Puller feel good that he was doing this to the young woman, although there *were* strict rules about what such folks should and should not do in their off hours. And this bar, filled with military and presumably private contractors, actually would be a great place for a spy to operate. He told himself he was teaching her a tough lesson.

He pulled out his phone, did a search on Atalanta Group, and came up with exactly nothing. How was that possible? Every company these days had an online identity.

He didn't even know if Atalanta Group was in business in the 1980s. Or ran the project that was currently being conducted in Building Q. This could all be a wild-goose chase, but somehow Puller didn't think so.

Vincent DiRenzo, the former CID agent, had talked about gut feelings being part of any investigation. Well, Puller's gut was burning right now. He was getting warm. He just needed to keep going.

When Shepard came out a few minutes later, she looked green.

"Let's go somewhere else," said Puller.

CHAPTER

44

Puller led Anne Shepard outside where there were still people in line waiting to get in. He waved to Rogers as he passed by, and the latter waved back.

"Thanks again," said Rogers.

"No problem."

Puller escorted Shepard to his car and they climbed in. "Am I really in trouble?" she said.

"That depends," said Puller. "We've actually been watching Atalanta Group for a while now."

"Why?"

"Irregularities."

"What kind of irregularities?"

"How long have you worked there?"

"Four years."

"Well, Building Q has been operational since at least the 1980s."

"I don't know anything about that."

"How is the work coming?"

"Are you read in for this?"

"Shepard, I wouldn't be here talking to you if I weren't." Her face fell. "Okay. Well, we've made big strides."

"Any issues?"

"Not really."

"Management treating you okay?"

"Mr. Quentin is supportive and he gets whatever we need."

"Quentin?"

"Josh Quentin. He runs the program. He may own the company for all I know. I'm not at a level that needs to know that." She looked across the seat at Puller. "Just so you know, he was at the bar tonight too. He goes there a lot. It's how I found out about it."

"What does he look like?"

"Tall, young, handsome. The ladies really go gaga over him. You might have seen him going up the stairs to the second-floor room."

"I did. What goes on up there?"

"I've never been up there. Only Mr. Quentin and his group are allowed up there."

"Are the people coworkers?"

She laughed. "Did those women look like science nerds to you?"

"So what are they, hookers?"

"I don't know. I doubt it. Josh is young and rich. He can get women without having to pay for them."

"Okay."

"Were you referring to Mr. Quentin when you mentioned 'irregularities'?"

"Why?" When she didn't answer immediately he added, "Shepard, if you have something to say, say it. The Army does not pay me to waste time."

"It's just that Mr. Quentin doesn't seem to have much of a science background. I mean, when he comes around to check on things the questions he asks are pretty basic. I would have expected him to know more, that's all."

"Maybe he's just a business guy."

"But every project I've ever worked on the leadership are serious scientists in their own right."

"So maybe this project is different."

"Maybe it is."

"What part of the project do you work on?"

"Are you really read in for this?" she asked nervously. "I don't want to get into trouble."

"You're already *in* trouble. And I'm trying to save your ass."

"Okay, okay. I'm just freaked out." She took a deep breath. "I work on the exos and liquid armor programs."

"Exos?"

"Exoskeleton hardware. Lightweight systems worn on the outside of the soldier's body, powered by lithium batteries. It increases their strength multifold. And we're working on a concept that would increase that multiple dramatically. A lot of this research was done by DoD starting in the 1960s, but the science and materials weren't there yet. The exoskeleton suits back then reacted unpredictably. I heard some people were even hurt."

"Is that right?" said Puller. "And the liquid armor?"

"Armor that's flexible until the impact of a bullet triggers it to instantly harden into a shield as impenetrable as steel. Then it repairs itself after being damaged by enemy fire."

"Sounds like a Marvel movie."

"Only our version isn't special effects. It actually works."

"So you're basically building the super soldier?"

"Yes."

"And you're funded by DARPA, right?"

"Yes, although I think our direct link is DSO, the Defense Sciences Office. But they report directly to DARPA's director. Before I came to Atalanta, I worked at another contractor on TMS projects."

"TMS?"

"Transcranial magnetic stimulation. There's also its counterpart, transcranial direct current stimulation. The differences are pretty much outlined in their names. One uses magnetic fields, the other electrical currents."

"And the goal?"

"In the military, to increase alertness and make the soldier in the field think better and faster in adverse conditions. It's well past the concept stage. It may be near deployment."

"I was in combat. I could have used that."

"Well, it's coming."

Puller considered all of this. "I'm going to need your help, Ms. Shepard."

"What can I do?"

"You can be my eyes and ears on the inside. We'll exchange contact information and you can report to me at regular intervals."

She looked panicked. "I . . . I don't know if I can do that. They might charge me with spying or something. Or treason. I . . . could be executed."

"Just calm down. Nobody's getting executed. You have the weight of the CID behind you. We take care of the people who help us." He paused and considered another tack, because Shepard did not look convinced. "Let me lay this on the line for you, Shepard. There *is* something going on at Atalanta Group that smacks of espionage."

"Holy shit! Are you serious?"

"I wouldn't be here otherwise. You noted it already. Your suspicions about Quentin? His lack of scientific background? His coming to this place and going to that room to do what? You telling me that's not making you think twice?"

She nodded slowly. "You're right. It doesn't add up."

"And if a spy ring is going on over there, we need to stop

it. If you help me, your back is covered. If you don't there are no assurances and it might very well be guilt by association when the hammer comes down. Then you're on your own."

"Omigod!" she exclaimed and rubbed a drop of sweat off her forehead.

Puller reached over and gripped her hand. "This is not my first investigation like this. I know what I'm doing, Shepard. You just have to trust me, okay? You'll find out I'm a good friend to have. So, will you do it?"

She finally nodded. "I'll do it."

They exchanged contact information.

Puller said, "Now go home and hit the sack. And don't go back to that bar."

"I won't. I swear. Thanks."

"Are you okay to drive?"

She nodded. "I am now. I don't think I've ever been this sober in my life, actually."

Puller watched her hurry across the street, get into her car, and quickly drive off.

Puller was about to get out of his car when he heard it.

Screams and gunfire.

Coming from the vicinity of the Grunt.

He jumped out of his car, pulled his weapon, and, like he always did, sprinted toward, not away from, the violence.

CHAPTER

45

IN SOME WAYS it could have been a street in Tikrit or Mosul.

Gunfire, smoke, screams, the darkness broken by the bursts of fired rounds. The only thing missing was the ear-splitting bang and concussive punch of an IED.

Puller came around the corner and immediately narrowed his target silhouette by shifting to the right. He also kept low, gripping his M11 with both hands. He did arcs with his weapon, looking for targets and trying to discern who was dangerous and who was a victim.

There were people lying in the street.

He stopped, took cover, and punched in 911. He identified himself to the dispatcher, taking only two short sentences to report who he was and what he was seeing. She told him to stay safe and that reinforcements were on the way.

She had obviously never been in the military. Staying safe was not in the job description. Quite the reverse, actually.

People were running past him, away from the gunfire. Puller checked each one to see if they had a weapon. None did. They were obviously frightened and simply trying to get away alive. Mass shootings had seemingly become ubiquitous in America, but that didn't make it any easier to deal with when you happened to be smack in the middle of one.

Puller drew closer to the entrance to the bar, which appeared to be the epicenter of the gunfire. As he went he passed figures on the ground, knelt, checked pulses, and kept going.

Some were alive; some were dead. He had nothing to triage the living. His only plan was to try to prevent any more dead or wounded.

He saw the flash of movement to his right a split second too late.

The gun was kicked out of his hands.

He turned to see the knife coming at his throat.

Anyone else would have simply been killed.

Puller blocked the blade by gripping his attacker's forearm, then sliding his hand down to the elbow and cranking the limb inward, against the body and not in the direction an elbow was designed to go.

The man screamed and his knife clattered to the pavement.

The guy was Puller's size. He kicked out at Puller and caught him in the oblique. It hurt like hell, and he staggered back, but the blow didn't stop Puller from executing his plan.

Puller lunged forward and drove his elbow straight into the guy's face. The man screamed again and grabbed his face with his one good arm, an arm that was about to be rendered not so good.

Puller ripped the arm up, bent it against the joint's natural range of motion and jerked it behind the man's back, torquing the limb past its breaking point.

He hooked an ankle around the man's right foot at the same time as he slammed his knee into the guy's spine. The man tripped over the foot, and with his left arm bound behind him and his right arm useless from Puller's elbow twist, he hit face first with Puller's weight full on top of him, his knee still at the base of his spine.

He was down for the count. Still breathing but bloodied and unconscious and missing several teeth. Puller rose, found his gun, and kept moving forward.

The door to the bar was wide open. Paul, the bouncer, wasn't anywhere that Puller could see.

He kept sweeping his weapon and listening for sirens.

More gunfire was coming from inside the bar.

He reached the doorway and looked inside. His training allowed him to size up stressful and violent situations quickly.

He could observe, by quick count, about thirty people inside. Four men were on the floor. What their status was, he couldn't tell. Three were young. One was a big guy dressed all in black and with what looked to be splints on one hand. He was older, as evidenced by his white hair.

As Puller gazed more closely he could see the man was dead, his eyes wide and glassy under the harsh lights of the bar. The other men's backs were to him. He didn't know if they were dead or simply injured.

Paul the bouncer was in the process of disarming one guy who was far bigger and younger than he was. As Puller watched, Paul whipped the guy around, clamped two hands around his neck, and jerked to the right. Puller could imagine the neck snapping cleanly in two with the move.

The man died without making a sound. Paul let him go and the man slumped to the floor.

Puller stepped into the doorway, pointed his gun, and fired two rounds crisply at the man who had his gun pointed at the bouncer's head. The man caught both rounds in the torso and fell forward, as dead as the other guy, only with a lot more blood.

Rogers stared over at Puller and then turned to see the dead guy, his gun still in hand.

Puller called out, "Any others?"

Rogers shook his head. "Don't think so. Four in here and three outside."

Another shot rang out a moment later. Puller whipped his gun in the direction. Rogers ducked down and looked that way too.

A man fell forward, the pistol still clenched in his hand.

Behind him was Suzanne Davis. She lowered the gun she'd just used to kill the man.

Rogers slowly rose.

"You owe me," said Davis.

"Yes, I do," said Rogers. He jerked a thumb at Puller. "I owe him too."

Puller kept his weapon out and looked around at the others. They were young, drunk, puking, crying, some bawling. All on the floor, the living shit scared out of all of them.

Only he, Davis, and Rogers were standing.

"I'm Suzanne Davis."

Puller nodded and introduced himself. "You handle your weapon well."

Puller suddenly saw a flash of movement behind the bar and swung his gun that way.

Helen Myers emerged from under the bar, shaky and pale.

Puller lowered his weapon.

They could all hear the sirens now.

"What the hell happened?" said Puller.

Myers came around the corner of the bar. "These men came here…" She looked down at the body of the big man with the white hair.

"That's Karl," she mumbled. "He's my head of security. *Was* my head of security." She fell silent and covered her face with her hands.

Puller looked over at Rogers questioningly as Davis came to stand next to him. She put the gun away in her purse and slung it over her shoulder.

Rogers touched the body of one dead man with his foot. "These guys were professionals."

Puller had already come to the same conclusion.

"And Karl?"

Rogers cocked his head and listened intently as the sirens drew closer. He looked back at Puller, the muscles tight around his neck. "Two of these guys burst in with Karl between them. I went to help him and they shot him right in front of me."

Myers said, "Karl called. He was coming in late tonight. I think...I think he must have run into these guys maybe in the parking lot. Maybe he tried to stop them."

"Wrong place, wrong time," commented Davis.

Rogers looked at her. "Where'd you learn to shoot?"

"Same place you learned to fight, school of hard knocks."

Rogers nodded, his eyes once more looking over Puller's shoulder, in the direction of the sirens.

Puller slowly lowered his weapon. "So you took out...six armed men with just your hands?" he asked Rogers.

"I got lucky."

Puller looked at Rogers's arm. "You're bleeding."

Rogers didn't even look at the wound. "It's fine."

The door from the upstairs room opened and Josh Quentin cautiously peered out, his face ashen. "Is it...is it over?"

Puller looked up at him and then saw the women crowding in behind, all looking disoriented.

"Who are you?" asked Puller, though he knew the answer.

Myers answered. "That's Josh Quentin, a customer."

"You better get down here," said Puller. "The police will want to talk to all of you."

"Oh, shit, the police?" said Quentin.

Rogers looked over at Davis in time to see her do an eye roll at Quentin's comment.

Outside, Puller heard the racking of automatic weapons, and the thick pounding of combat boots on pavement. He put his gun away before the cops accidentally shot him. He moved toward the door to face them.

The lead assaulter poked his shielded head around the edge of the door.

Puller had his badge out and loudly identified himself. "We've got wounded people outside and in here. You're going to need multiple ambulances."

The assault team, ten strong, swept into the room and quickly secured it. Josh Quentin and his group, once drunk, now stone cold sober, were quickly escorted downstairs.

Those not wounded were sequestered and the initial interview process begun. The dead were identified by IDs in their wallets and purses. The shriek of ambulance sirens filtered into the bar.

The team turned to triage as they moved among the wounded, while others checked that the shooters really were dead and that there were no more of them lurking around.

Puller helped with this, and when the ambulances arrived he assisted in lifting the wounded onto gurneys and then into the waiting rescue vehicles.

Homicide detectives showed up about twenty minutes later and started to officially process the scene. Puller offered to help, but they politely declined.

Sitting on a stool at the bar, he also provided as much information as he could about what had happened.

The detective said, "There's no ID on any of these guys.

They look Eastern European if you ask me. I've looked at some of their weapons and the serial numbers have been professionally removed. These guys are pros. Some kind of criminal hit team."

"Why would a professional hit team from Eastern Europe attack a bar?"

The detective shrugged. "Right now, I couldn't tell you. Maybe because it's a military hangout?"

Puller leaned back in his barstool and stared off, thinking about this.

The detective's words brought him out of these thoughts. "I guess it was lucky you were here, Agent Puller."

"I really didn't do that much. The guy you really want to talk to is—"

Puller looked around the room for Rogers.

The man had disappeared.

Puller looked over at Josh Quentin and his party. And then at Helen Myers, who was being questioned by another detective.

And Davis was nowhere to be seen.

"What was that?" said the detective, who had been distracted by his partner's calling out to him about a piece of bagged evidence.

Puller said slowly, "It was nothing. It'll keep."

He walked over to the bodies of the men inside the bar. The ME was examining one of them.

Puller showed her his badge and said, "You got a cause of death yet?"

The woman nodded and pointed to the two men lying next to the one she was examining. "The guy on the left has a crushed carotid. The guy on the right has a fractured windpipe. The guy over there had his skull cracked."

Puller considered this and said, "The shooters outside?"

"Same sort of crushing injuries. Don't know what sort of weapon was used."

"I don't think you're going to find a weapon," said Puller.

"Why's that?" she asked.

Because the weapon is gone, thought Puller.

CHAPTER

46

*S*HIT.

Rogers slammed the white van into gear and drove off.

Luckily he had parked well away from the bar, and thus outside the perimeter the police had set up. He had managed to slip out the back of the bar before the police could get there.

Cops everywhere. People who had seen what he had done. Bodies all over the place. And the tall guy who had saved his ass?

John Puller. Army CID. Military cop.

Had his appearance merely been a coincidence, or had he fed Rogers a bunch of crap?

Yet Puller *had* saved his life.

Rogers wanted to go back and find out exactly who John Puller was and what he was doing here. Yet as more sirens filled the air he decided retreat was the better choice. He punched the gas and drove on.

He got to the motel, packed his few things, carried them out to the van, and drove off. His heart was racing so fast he thought it might explode.

He traced the scar on his head, pushing down hard where the thing was. He looked at his arm where he'd been wounded.

He'd lied to Puller. It was a bullet wound, not a blade. But it was in and out. He could feel no pain and he noted that it was already starting to heal.

He rubbed the thing in his head. He hated it, but he loved it for the things it could do like that.

I'm a science-fiction freak.

But with billions of dollars to burn through, even science fiction could become reality, however fleetingly, and with all sorts of side effects and adverse consequences.

Adverse consequences.

That's how they had described it in the report. They hadn't given him a copy. He'd stolen one.

And when they fully realized what they had created? How adverse the truly adverse could be?

He focused on the road up ahead. His short-term goal was to relocate somewhere. He couldn't go back to the Grunt, but he had some money.

The next moment he had to pull off the road, slam the car into park, bend over the steering wheel, and throw up.

The pain seared through every one of his limbs. If ten was the top of the normal pain scale, this was a hundred.

Or a thousand.

Over the first twenty years it had happened only once a year.

When he'd been in prison over the last ten years the frequency had increased to once every six months.

But the thing was, the last time it had happened was less than a month ago. He'd been sitting in his cell staring at the wall. He didn't know what time it was, only that it was somewhere in the stretch between late at night and the wavering darkness right before the dawn. It had taken all of his immense strength and self-control not to scream out loud.

He had gripped the bars of his cell and actually felt the

metal begin to move a bit in his hands. He had immediately released them because the last thing he needed was the guards seeing that he was strong enough to actually damage the steel bars of his cage.

He had thrown himself down on the floor, gripped the concrete foundation that was his bed with a thin mattress thrown on top, and held on for dear life, his body curling into a fetal position in his silent agony.

He had emerged from that episode with every nerve in his body feeling like it was on fire.

Rogers did not feel pain. The thing in his head had taken care of that.

But this, this was beyond pain.

And he felt everything about it.

Ten minutes passed as his body convulsed without ceasing. Finally, he sat up and discovered that he had cracked the steering wheel in his hands.

He slumped back against the seat, his lungs heaving as he struggled to regain some sense of composure. But all the while he was thinking of only one thing.

Less than a month!

It had happened again in less than a month.

From year intervals, to six-month intervals, to less than thirty days.

What next? Weekly? Daily?

He touched his carotid and felt the blood racing through the vessel at a potentially lethal clip. He breathed in and out, deep, calming, settling.

Finally, he started to come out of it, his physiology going back to normal, or as normal as things got inside his skin.

He put the van in gear and awkwardly steered with the broken wheel. He would have to get some duct tape and fix that. There was some in the back of the van.

As he drove, his mind settled on another report, again one that he was not supposed to read but had. One line in particular had stood out to him.

The latest metrics strongly indicate that the underlying infrastructure does not appear to be sustainable long-term in a humanoid environment due to chemical, physiological, and biological incompatibilities.

Underlying infrastructure?

Sustainable in a humanoid environment?

Due to...?

"Fuck!"

He pulled off the road again and just sat there staring at his hands.

Infrastructure.

They were part of that.

He touched his arms and legs.

Them too.

His head.

Yep.

He knew exactly what that line of the report meant.

He was dying. It had been thirty years and the time was coming. Everything was accelerating. The piper needed to be paid. And he was the only one who could do it.

He was the dark side of Superman.

And his kryptonite was right inside him.

My kryptonite is me.

They had designed him to eventually detonate, spontaneously combust, fall apart, wither and dissolve. He didn't know what it exactly would entail. And really didn't give a shit.

The result is the same.

No more Paul Rogers.

It will be the end of me.

When the hand touched his shoulder he whirled and his fingers seized around the person's neck.

It was Davis.

Rogers had rarely been more stunned in his life. Then he realized he was squeezing her neck, because her eyes were beginning to bulge.

He quickly let go and she collapsed, breathing hard.

"Where the hell did you come from?" he barked.

She couldn't answer until she had regained her breath. Then she sat on her haunches in the space between the bucket seats and the back of the van.

"I knew you weren't going to hang around for the cops. And I knew your van. So I came out and climbed into the back and hid there before you left the bar."

He looked at her warily. "Why?" he asked.

"Why did I know you weren't waiting around for the cops? I saw your face when the sirens started up. I saw the arteries in your neck swell as they got closer and closer."

"Why are you in the back of my van?"

"Because I like you. And I'm trying to figure you out."

"You need to get out of here."

"Why? Because I might get in trouble hanging out with you?"

He started to say something, but it wouldn't come out.

She said, "Are you okay? You were really, really sick." She paused, looking him over. "Do you have cancer or something?"

He didn't answer. He was trying to process how all this was going to spin out.

He looked at her neck. It was bruised from his fingers.

Just finish the job. She can't be here.

"Paul, are you okay?"

"I'm fine. It's not cancer. Just some food poisoning."

"Well, thank God for that. Food poisoning passes. Look, it's late, we should find a place to stay."

"You can't stay—"

She cut him off. "Just for tonight. Then you can drop me." She added, "I did save your life tonight. Isn't that worth something?"

* * *

After he found another motel and paid in cash they went to the room. Rogers took off his jacket and Davis slipped off her shoes.

"Your arm's still bleeding," she said.

"It's nothing," he said distractedly as he sat down in a chair, his gaze flitting to the window.

"Listening for more sirens?" she asked as she perched on the bed, drawing her legs up under her.

He shot her a glance and then looked away.

"If it makes you feel better I have a rap sheet too," said Davis.

"Before you found the pot of gold with your adoptive parents?" he said.

"Something like that. How about you?"

"I never found a pot of gold."

"I mean the criminal part."

"I'll sleep on the floor." He rose and took off his shoes.

Davis stood, unzipped her dress, and stepped out of it.

Rogers froze. "What's going on?"

She didn't look at him as she took off her bra and underwear. "Don't get crazy. I can't sleep with clothes on." She smiled. "The guys usually don't mind. And it's not like you haven't seen me naked."

She went into the bathroom, washed her face, came back

out, and crawled under the covers. Rogers watched her turn on her side and close her eyes.

"Good night, Paul."

He hit the wall switch and the room became dark. He looked down at the floor and then walked over to the bed and lay down on top of the covers.

Davis turned to face him. "We're two peas in a pod, right? Damaged goods trying to make our way?"

"Where'd you learn to shoot like that?"

She gripped his hand. "Things will look better in the morning," she said. "They always do."

"But what about the rest of the day?" he said dully.

"Well, that's why I learned to shoot like that."

She closed her eyes and fell asleep.

CHAPTER

47

WHILE THE POLICE continued to process the crime scene, Puller took the opportunity to go upstairs and inside the room where Josh Quentin had been.

The police had questioned and then released Quentin and his group. They had hightailed it out of here so fast one of the ladies had run out of her high heels.

Puller looked around the space. Bottles of beer and whiskey and wineglasses littered the place. So they *had* been partying.

He went through the door into what was set up as a bedroom. The bed was unmade, the pillows on the floor.

So they had been doing more than drinking. Were the women with Quentin hookers? Was that what was going on up here? Was that why Quentin was so scared about the cops coming? Big executive for a defense contractor caught with his pants down in a sea of hookers? And why would Helen Myers, who seemed to Puller like a sensible and responsible business owner, take that sort of risk? This was not Vegas. Prostitution was not legal in Virginia.

He walked back down the stairs to find Myers watching him from the bar. He walked over to her.

"What were you doing?" she asked.

Her mascara had run from her crying. She seemed to catch what he was gazing at, turned to the bar mirror, saw the damage, and used a wet bar towel to rub off the mascara.

"I guess I look a mess," she said.

"You're alive. Count your blessings."

She slowly put down the towel. "You're right."

"Who's Josh Quentin?" asked Puller.

"I told you, he's a customer."

"He uses the upstairs room."

"He does."

"What for?"

"A private space."

"What does he need a private space for?"

Her expression became guarded. "I wouldn't know. That's why they call it private."

"There's a bedroom up there. And it looks like some action took place there."

She shrugged.

Puller looked around at the cops and detectives working the bar area.

"These guys will eventually work their way up there. And they're going to have the same sorts of questions."

"Upstairs had nothing to do with what happened downstairs."

"Doesn't matter if something illegal was going on up there."

"Nothing illegal was going on up there," she retorted.

"How do you know? You just said you don't know what goes on up there."

"I meant that I know Josh, and he would engage in nothing illegal."

"Prostitution is illegal."

"Oh, for God's sake. Those women are not hookers."

"You're sure of that?"

"Yes!"

"How? Because Quentin told you? I know for a fact that they're not coworkers of his."

She crossed her arms and stared back at him. "I really don't have to tell you anything."

"No, you really don't." He pointed to the cops and detectives. "But those guys you do. And I'd have a better story prepared than the bullshit you just tried to feed me."

Myers rose. "I need to attend to some things."

"I'm sure. Calling a really good lawyer should be first on the list."

She hurried from the room and disappeared down the hall to her office.

On a hunch Puller went over to the bar where one of the waiters was sitting looking exhausted. He held up his set of keys and said, "Ms. Myers asked me to get something from her car, but she was so distraught she forgot to tell me what make and model."

The man said, "Oh, it's the blue BMW 750. License plate says 'Grunt.' She parks it in the back lot."

"Thanks."

He went outside and got into his car and positioned it so that he could see the big Beemer.

Fifteen minutes passed and then he saw Myers rush out from the back of the bar, climb into the BMW, and fire it up. She drove out of the lot and hit the street.

Puller moved in behind her but kept well back. There was enough early morning traffic that he had some cover behind other cars.

The drive was not a long one. But it was surprising for Puller.

Myers drove into Fort Monroe and made her way along the waterfront before cutting a sharp left away from the channel. A few minutes later she pulled up to the gate at Building Q.

Puller stopped, got out his camera, and snapped some shots of Myers, who after being vetted by the guards was waved through. She parked in a free space.

Before she even got out of the car one of the exterior doors of the building opened and there appeared Josh Quentin. He was still dressed in the same suit and still looked shaken by the night's events. He and Myers hugged and then he led her inside.

Puller managed to get shots of all this. Then he sat in his car thinking about what to do next.

He had no authority to gain access to Building Q. If he tried he'd either be thrown out on his ass or arrested. Or both.

Two hours passed and he had decided to drive back to his hotel and try a different tack in solving this case when Myers came out of the building. Quentin was not with her.

She drove out of the parking lot and Puller fell in behind her. She apparently was so focused on where she was going that she never once looked back.

He followed her onto Interstate 64 heading west. She got off at the exit for historic Williamsburg.

Puller checked his watch. It was now after eight in the morning.

Puller followed her to the Williamsburg Inn, a stately building a short walk from the downtown shopping area. She opted against the valet and parked her Beemer in the lot on the right side of the hotel's entrance.

Puller did likewise and pulled out a ball cap and sunglasses and exchanged his jacket for a blue windbreaker he kept in his duffel. He put those on just in case she turned around and spotted him.

She walked past the top-hatted front doorman and into the lobby of the inn.

Puller flitted in after her.

She must have called someone from her car, because Puller watched as she walked straight through the elegant lobby and out through a set of French doors on the other side that emptied into the rear grounds of the inn. There was wrought iron furniture set up there with aged brick underneath forming the patio.

A man rose from one of the chairs. He was tall and thin, with longish graying hair, and dressed elegantly in a dark suit and red tie with a matching pocket handkerchief.

Myers immediately started talking but the man held up his hand, apparently to calm her. He took her by the arm and they walked off together down a brick path. Before they were out of sight Puller followed.

He saw a sign that read *Spa*. He followed about fifty feet behind.

Then he saw them turn into what looked to be a private garden enclosed by a high brick wall.

He did a turkey peek through the opening and saw them settle on a bench about halfway down the garden. There was no one else there. He hurried down the path until he was right on the other side of the brick wall from them.

Puller listened as closely as he could, but they were whispering, so he couldn't make out what they were saying. Frustrated, he rushed back down the path to the entrance into the garden. He poked his head around the brick column in time to see Myers reach into her pocket and take something out. He snapped several pictures as she handed it across to the man.

The man pocketed it and they both stood and headed toward where Puller was hiding. Puller nipped around a large holly tree just before the pair appeared at the garden entrance.

They passed by him and reentered the inn's lobby. Puller followed and saw the man head up the stairs while Myers left by the front entrance, no doubt headed back to her car.

Puller debated what to do next. Follow the man or follow Myers?

He finally concluded that he knew where Myers had come from. He figured he needed to find out more about the man.

Puller sat in the lobby and waited until the man came back down rolling a small suitcase and carrying a leather briefcase over his shoulder. He headed to the front desk. Puller got up and went out to his car. He watched a minute later as the man came out and said something to the doorman. The doorman waved at a waiting cab. It pulled up and the man got in.

Puller followed the cab to the Amtrak train station. The man got out of the cab and Puller quickly parked. He followed the man inside the small station and took a seat two down from him.

The man opened his briefcase and took out a laptop computer. He slid the device Myers had given him out of his pocket. Puller could see that it was a flash drive. The man inserted it into the USB port in the laptop and clicked some keys.

Puller rose and went around behind the man, standing about fifteen feet away. He took out his camera and shifted slightly to the right so that he could see the man's screen. He adjusted the lens, zooming in as much as he could, and started taking photos as the man flicked through several screens.

The man then pulled out his phone and keyed in a number. Puller returned to his seat to see if he could overhear the conversation.

He couldn't make out the words, not because he couldn't hear them but because they were in another language that he recognized but couldn't speak.

French.

He glanced over when he heard the train coming in. A voice on the PA said it was destined for Washington, D.C.

He looked over. He had no authority to arrest the man, or even detain him. And if he did try to stop him he would give away that he had been following him. And Myers.

He kept himself from leaping up and tackling the man and instead watched him board the train. As it pulled from the station, Puller headed to his car. There, he checked out the pictures he'd taken of the man's laptop screen.

They were technical drawings and formulas that were too advanced for him to make much sense of. Still, it looked like Myers was passing secrets to this gent. And it was also clear to Puller that Josh Quentin had been passing those same secrets to Myers. That explained the room at the Grunt.

It was ironic that Puller had used a story of possible espionage at Atalanta Group to enlist Anne Shepard's help, only to find out that the espionage was apparently all too real.

Now the questions were many.

What were these secrets?

Where and *what* was Paul the bouncer?

And what the hell, if anything, did my mother's disappearance have to do with any of this?

48

Four faces stared back at John Puller.

Four women.

They were young. They were professional.

And they were all dead.

He had looked at these photos before, without much success.

He leaned back in his chair in his motel room and did another search on the name Atalanta. According to mythology, Atalanta had been left on a mountaintop by her father to die. Only Atalanta was cared for by a she-bear and survived. She became an exemplary fighter and huntress and a committed virgin, spurning advances from all men and even challenging them to footraces, with death to the loser. But a clever fellow enlisted the aid of Aphrodite and beat Atalanta in a race. They married and had a son. Then Atalanta and her husband were turned into lions by a goddess who felt they had disrespected her.

Puller rubbed his eyes and wondered where any of this crap was getting him. He had never once in his life used mythology to track down a criminal, and he really didn't want to start now.

He settled on his other possible lead. Crushing injuries. The women had all suffered crushing injuries.

He closed his eyes and thought back to the crime scene at the Grunt.

The medical examiner had used that word several times. *Crushing.*

Paul the bouncer looked to be in his fifties. He had completely destroyed a group of big, strong men. Manhandled them in fact. Puller had been jumped by one, and though he had beaten the guy with his superior fighting skills, he hadn't crushed any part of the man. And it had been a tough fight.

And Paul had clearly wanted to get out of there before the police arrived. So who, or what, was this guy? Was he the super freak that he and Knox had speculated might have come out of Building Q? Thirty years ago he would have been in his twenties. But if so, why would he be a bouncer at the Grunt? Had he remained in the area after all these years? Why? It made no sense.

Puller's phone rang. He looked at the screen.

It was Knox.

Puller hesitated. But if he didn't answer, he supposed she would just call back until he did.

"Hello?"

"Where are you?" she said immediately.

"Why?"

"Because all hell broke loose last night in Hampton." She paused. "What do you know about that?"

"I heard the sirens."

"Don't lie to me, Puller! I'm staring at a police report that has you listed as being on the scene and shooting and killing someone."

"Well, that was quick work on your part."

"So what do you know?" she persisted.

Puller hesitated and looked at his watch. "You have time for some breakfast?"

She didn't respond at first. "Just like that? After kicking my ass to the curb?"

"We all have to eat."

"Where and when?"

He told her.

He grabbed a shower, changed his clothes, and drove to the hole-in-the-wall diner he'd spotted previously. He didn't want to do this, because he didn't fully trust her. But another part of him realized he needed Knox's resources if he was to have any chance of solving this case.

Knox was already seated at a booth in the back with a cup of coffee in front of her. She wore jeans, a black blazer, three-inch boots, and an expression that could have melted titanium.

He sat down across from her, ordered a coffee, and fingered the plastic menu she slid across to him.

"You look good," he said.

She took a sip of coffee, gave him a blank stare, and said, "Don't try to play nice. You are already on my last nerve."

"Didn't know that."

"Like hell."

He sat forward. "You eating?"

"I'm close to pulling out my gun and shooting you."

He looked down at the menu. "Let me order first. I'd rather die on a full belly. I'm going to have the All-American. Lots of carbs and protein. From your expression I'm going to need it."

She watched him order and then shook her head when the waitress turned to her for her order.

The waitress left and Knox sat forward. "Well? You called the meeting."

Ten minutes passed and Puller talked the whole time, telling Knox in information-filled paragraphs *almost* everything he had learned since he had last seen her, including following Helen Myers to Building Q where she had met up with Josh Quentin. And the French gent who'd taken a morning train to Washington, D.C. And about Paul the bouncer and his extraordinary fighting abilities. He pulled out his camera and showed her the pictures he'd taken. When he got to the more technical frames Knox focused even more intently.

"Puller, this one has to do with cell mutation." She forwarded the frame. "And this one looks like it's some sort of organ regeneration concept."

"Well, I'm glad you can make some sense of it."

"If they were passing secrets I thought it would be dealing with the exoskeletons and liquid armor the woman told you she was working on there. This stuff isn't military-grade material."

The next moment his breakfast showed up.

He glanced at Knox, who was staring at him. "You look hungry all of a sudden," he said.

"I'll have the pancakes," she said to the waitress.

The woman walked off and Puller dug into his meal. As he lifted his fork to his mouth, Knox put out a hand and gripped his arm.

"Okay, Quentin is passing this stuff to Myers and Myers to the French guy. It's not military secrets, but it's obviously something valuable."

"Right. I wish I could have stopped the guy, but I had no grounds."

"But you have his picture and the fact that he speaks French. That's something. I can get his image into a facial recognition database. It's not just criminals but also people of particular interest to our government. If the guy is on that list we'll find out who he is."

"Sounds like a start. And we can also lean on Myers to cooperate if the database comes up zero."

"This bouncer guy. Where is he?"

"I don't know. His name is Paul. We have his description. We can get a BOLO out. He wanted no part of the cops."

"But do you really think he's the guy who murdered those women? I mean, what are the odds?"

"Longer than I can calculate. But that still doesn't mean it couldn't happen. People do win the lottery. Maybe this is just our turn."

"So he killed all those guys with his bare hands?"

"Yes. He *crushed* them, in fact."

Knox drew in a quick breath. "Like the murdered women?"

"Yes."

"Did you ask the people at the bar about him?"

"I intend to. Last night was a little chaotic."

"Right, of course. But if we can get to this Paul guy."

"Might be the tip of the iceberg. And we're not the only ones after him."

"What do you mean?"

"The attack on the bar? They were after Paul, I'm sure of it."

"Why would a gang of killers target him?"

"They might have been paid to do it." He sat forward. "And now you can tell me why you suddenly called out of the blue."

He expected some sharp retort. He didn't get it.

"Puller, we have a situation."

He lowered his fork and said, "I understand we have a situation. You told me that when we last met."

Knox drew a breath. "Right." She said nothing else.

Puller took a bite of food and a sip of coffee, then set down his cup. "Well?"

"Not here."

"We can go back to where I'm staying."

They arrived there thirty minutes later.

Knox leaned against the wall while Puller sat in the one chair looking up at her.

When she said nothing he spoke up. "First you show up out of the blue. Then you disappear. Then you show back up with a story about this friend of yours scared to death and tell me about this possible cover-up."

"I came back to help you. And you just walked away," she added bitterly.

"I was trying to protect you."

She barked, "I can protect myself, in case you hadn't noticed."

He nodded and said in a rapid-fire manner, "Okay. Agreed. So you're back. I need your help. What can you tell me?"

She seemed about to bark at him again, but she swallowed, ran a hand through her hair, and with that movement all of the anger seemed to drain from her.

"The situation?" prompted Puller, who was watching her closely.

"Remember Mack Taubman?"

"Your friend who almost had a heart attack when you told him about what we were investigating?"

"Yes."

"What about him?"

"He's dead."

CHAPTER

49

Puller rose and stared at Knox.

Knox kept her gaze on the floor.

Puller said, "How?"

"They're not sure. It could be suicide."

"Gun?"

She shook her head. "They don't know what exactly. But from the little I heard there was no outward wound or signs of foul play. Mack might have taken poison."

"Or someone might have fed it to him," countered Puller.

"I don't know," said Knox distractedly.

"Was he found at home?"

"Yes."

"Did he live alone?"

"Mack's wife had died. His kids were grown."

"If they suspect suicide, was there a note?"

"I don't know, Puller."

"Did he ever strike you as suicidal?"

"No, but I hadn't seen him in a while. And I told you this had rocked him. Maybe our conversation led him to kill himself."

Knox slumped down and sat on the floor.

"If it did, Knox, you had no way of knowing. It was on him, not you."

"Easy to say."

"Yeah, it is. But it's also the truth."

"Mack Taubman was a tough guy, Puller. He'd seen it all. I can't believe he would kill himself over this."

"Did he contact anyone before he died?"

"I wish I knew. But that's out of my hands."

"No way to find out?" he asked.

"I've made calls, but the gates have already shut."

Puller stared down at the floor for a few moments. "Okay, Knox, I'm going to tell you something I shouldn't."

She gazed up at him. "Why?"

"Because I know how hard this has been on you. And I know you've told me more than you normally would. And I appreciate that."

She wiped at her face and continued to look at him.

"It was the Vice President who got me back on the case."

Knox stood unsteadily and placed a hand against the wall. "The VP? *The* VP!"

"Yeah, the guy who takes over if the President goes down."

"Holy shit. You met him?"

"He called me over for a drink, a free ticket back on the job, and a warning."

"But why him? Why the hell did he get involved?"

"That one's easy. My father was his mentor. He was repaying a favor. But that's as far as he'd go. And just so you know, he's scared too. And he's not privy to everything. And he will never officially acknowledge his intervention."

Knox stared at him dumbly. "The Vice President of the United States is scared?"

"Everybody gets scared from time to time, Knox, even the Vice President. But we need to focus. Some thoughts are coming together for me. Want to hear them?"

"Yes," she said. "But I have to tell you something first."

She crossed the small room and sat on the edge of the bed.

"I didn't exactly show up on your doorstep for the reasons I said I did."

"Astonishing," replied Puller coolly.

"When the allegation came out about your father killing your mother I was called in by my boss. He obviously knew that we had worked together."

"And was it his idea to have you try to seduce me?" asked Puller, his gaze never leaving her face.

Her face flushed. "No, that…that was on me."

Puller looked a bit taken aback by this. "Okay. Go on."

"I just thought they wanted me to see if the allegations were true, although I didn't understand why it was any concern of my agency's."

"And did there come a time when you began to understand?" asked Puller.

"It's why I left when I did. Things were not adding up. We were getting into areas that smacked of a black hole. Federal investigations do not get shit-canned for no reason, Puller. The FBI does not go home with its tail between its legs. A serial murder case doesn't go up in smoke. There *is* a cover-up, at the highest levels. So it's clear now that a government project *did* go sideways thirty years ago and it resulted in the deaths of those women."

"Meaning Building Q?"

She nodded.

"They're still doing stuff in there, you know."

"I wouldn't be surprised."

"Is it the same stuff?"

"I'm not cleared for that."

"Well, I know, even though I'm not cleared."

"You said you told me everything," she said, obviously annoyed.

"I lied. How's it feel to be on the receiving end?"

She let out a long sigh. "It feels shitty."

"Good."

"Will you tell me now?"

"They're building exoskeletons to make soldiers run faster, jump higher, and be far stronger. They're going to make their brains work better while under stress. They're going to put them in liquid armor that stiffens to titanium when a bullet hits and then repairs itself. And that's probably just the tip of the iceberg."

"Super-soldier stuff, then?"

"It's not exactly a secret. You can Google DARPA and find out that stuff too. At least generally. They don't tell you how they're doing it, of course. But they do have pictures. The woman who works at Atalanta Group told me about it."

"But *how* they're doing it is the key. And you can't just Wikipedia that. At least not the specifics."

"But this isn't about stealing DARPA secrets. This is about women who died thirty years ago. So, did a guinea pig go wild and become Ted Bundy, only with super powers?"

"You mean did they have a super-soldier program three decades ago?"

"I think they did. And I think he might have been the bouncer at the bar."

"We have got to find this guy."

Puller had a thought. He called the number for the Grunt and was surprised when someone answered. It was one of the bartenders whom he'd met while he was there. He identified himself. "How's it going?" he asked.

"Well, we won't be open for a while. In fact, I'm not sure

we'll ever open after what happened. Stupid, senseless violence. If you want to talk to Ms. Myers she's not here."

"I know that. I was actually calling about Paul, the bouncer. Is he there?"

"Paul? No. I haven't seen him since last night. Why?"

"I was just trying to see if he needed anything. He was wounded and then he just disappeared. I don't think he received any medical attention."

"Damn, I didn't know that. There's just so much going on..." The bartender's voice trailed away.

"I know, and I don't mean to add to your burden. I can try to locate him. You happen to know what car he drives?"

"Car? Yeah, I saw him pull into the parking lot last night when I went to take a smoke before my shift started. It's a white van."

Puller tensed. "A van. You mean like a soccer-mom van?"

"No, like you see workmen or contractors use. Although there were no signs on it or anything."

"You wouldn't happen to know the license plate? I can trace him that way."

"No, I don't. I don't even know his last name. I don't think anybody here does."

Puller clicked off and looked at Knox.

"What was all that about a van?" she asked.

He quickly explained about seeing the van at some of the locations where the bodies had been found.

"Holy shit, Puller. He has got to be our guy!"

"It's looking that way. Now we just have to find him."

"You know this could cost us both our careers," she said.

"Personally, I think if that's all we lose, we'll be lucky."

"I was actually thinking the same thing."

"And knowing all that, why did you come back?"

"I thought that would be obvious."

"Not to me."

"I've grown accustomed to having you around." Before he could respond she added, "And I would never go over to the dark side, Puller. I might bend the rules to get the job done, but I didn't join up to do bad things. Or to see really bad things covered up. Like the deaths of four women. Or the disappearance of your mother."

A long moment of silence elapsed.

"I appreciate that, Knox."

"But you still don't trust me?"

"I didn't say that."

"You didn't have to. The look on your face says it all."

"You risked your life to save my brother. Ordinarily, that would be enough for me to always believe you're on the up-and-up."

"Ordinarily."

"Part of your job is to lie, to deceive. I never know when I'm on the receiving end of one of those mortar rounds, Knox. It's just how I see it. I'm sorry. It's just how I'm wired."

She nodded. "I guess I can understand that. So where does that leave us?"

Before he could answer his phone rang. He looked at the screen. "Don't recognize the number."

"You better take it anyway. Maybe it's Super Paul."

"Hello?"

"Agent Puller, my name is Claire Jericho. I'm with Atalanta Group. And I believe we need to meet."

CHAPTER

50

ONE BREATH, TWO breaths, three breaths, four breaths.

Rogers had turned the water on in the shower until it was near scalding. He was rubbing the soap so hard against his skin that he could feel the flesh tearing and starting to bleed.

He was trying to erase all the scars.

He finally realized he couldn't, dropped the soap, and leaned his forehead against the fiberglass wall of the shower. A few moments later he reached down, turned the water off, and just stood there, his head against the wall. His eyes were scrunched closed, his lungs heaving, his muscles twitching.

Five breaths, six breaths, seven breaths, eight breaths.

That was the ritual they had instilled in him when they were making him what he was.

It was painful. All of it was painful. Even when they put him under to do the innumerable surgeries he would wake up in the most incredible pain.

Breathe, they had told him. Count the breaths. Focus on the numbers, not the pain.

He was told painkillers were not an option because they had to accurately measure what he was feeling. And the only way to do that was to make him experience it the whole way.

When he asked they told him it was all about *replication* and *scale*, two terms with which he had no familiarity.

In his mind's eye a thirty-year-younger Claire Jericho looked down at him as he lay on the hospital bed, writhing in so much pain that they'd had to shackle him to the bed like a prisoner.

And it had become clear fairly soon thereafter that he *was* a prisoner.

She had taken off her glasses, wiped a spot clear, put them back on, placed a small hand on his bucking shoulder, and told him in the calmest tone possible that what he was doing was for the greater good. That philosophy had become like a second heartbeat or an additional way to breathe.

When he had finally risen from the hospital bed and gone back to his room, he found a small box there. Inside was the ring. He opened his eyes and held up his right hand. He gripped the ring there with his other hand and wrenched it over the lumpy knuckle, leaving a trail of ripped flesh and blood in its wake.

He looked at the engraving on the inside of the band.

For the greater good. CJ.

CJ. Claire Jericho.

She had given him the ring when he'd recovered from the surgeries.

It symbolized their bond, she had told him.

She was his mentor. He was her prized pupil. Together, they could accomplish great things. Books would be written about them. They were, together, the tip of the spear in a brave new world.

And I bought every fucking line of the poison she spewed.

He had come from nothing, having traveled over an ocean as a stowaway in a cargo ship to get there. He had no friends, no contacts, and no prospects. No support.

And then he felt his luck had changed when he'd answered an ad for a job and run smack into Jericho.

He didn't know he was to become a guinea pig as a way to achieve *her* vision for what the world in the future should look like.

He put the ring back on, dried off, changed into the only clean clothes he had, sat down on the bed, and gazed at the still sleeping Suzanne Davis.

It really all came down to Building Q. Jericho was there. She had to be there. He had tried the mansion in North Carolina. He had killed—or at least thought he had killed—Chris Ballard.

He had two possible leads to Jericho.

One was Josh Quentin.

The other was lying right in front of him.

Quentin worked for Atalanta, which meant he worked for Jericho.

And what exactly was going on in that room? Not just sex, drugs, and alcohol, surely.

If he could find out? And if it was something illegal or something that Quentin would not want to be made public he could possibly use that to get to Jericho.

It was a long shot, he knew. But right now all he had were long shots.

Davis had been adopted, or so she'd told him. Had Ballard been the one? If so, could he use her to get to Ballard and then to Jericho?

He rubbed his head. *But I killed Ballard. Or did I?*

"You look like your head might explode."

He looked up to find Davis awake and watching him.

"Just thinking through some things."

She sat up against the headboard. "Can I help?"

"Don't think so."

"Okay. You hungry? I'm starving."

"There's a place around the corner."

"Give me a couple minutes."

She washed up and put her clothes on. They walked to the diner. Davis ordered half the menu and ate it all. Rogers could only manage coffee.

"You still have food poisoning?" she asked, a forkful of scrambled eggs poised in front of her mouth.

He nodded and went back to his thoughts.

Quentin might be a better track to Jericho than Davis. He apparently didn't bother locking up the house on the beach. Rogers could get in and make him do what needed doing. And what could he really do with Davis? Go to the Ballard mansion and hold her hostage until Jericho walked out? That wasn't going to happen. He needed subtlety here. Problem was, he was engineered for brute action. He started counting in his head again.

Jericho is one smart lady. She's playing chess, you can't play checkers. Brains, not muscle, will get you there.

Yes, Quentin over Davis made a lot of sense. He would use him to get to Jericho.

He glanced up at Davis as she bit into a piece of toast. And the truth was—he couldn't quite believe he was actually admitting this to himself—he didn't want to do anything to get Davis hurt. It was an astonishing revelation for him, because Rogers had long, long ago ceased caring about anyone.

But now?

"You need a ride home?" he asked.

She shook her head. "I didn't go to the bar last night with

Josh. I drove. You can drop me. I'm at a parking lot across the street from the bar."

"Okay."

"Okay," she parroted back. "So we're done here?"

He fiddled with a paper napkin and glanced up at her. "Meaning?"

"Meaning are we done here? You and me?"

"Yeah, I think we are."

She reached into her purse and put some cash down on the table. Inside the purse he could see the pistol.

She saw him looking at it. "Beretta," she said. "Mini Cougar model. Fits my hand really well. Double-stack mag chambered in nine mil. And I'm partial to Italian made. They've been in business since 1526, did you know that?"

"No."

"So they must know what they're doing, right? I mean, come on, all that time? Nearly five centuries? I mean, shit."

"Right."

"Took that guy out last night with it, right? Dropped him on the floor, right?"

"Right."

"Else you'd be fucking dead. Right?"

He looked at her and she looked back at him.

"Right," she said, answering her own question. "Don't forget that." She stood. "Let's go."

He dropped her off back at the parking lot and watched her get into the Benz convertible. She put the top down, slid on her sunglasses, and drove off without acknowledging him.

Rogers sat in his van and then reached into the glove box and pulled out the M11-B. He held it in his right hand. Looking in the rearview mirror, he pressed the muzzle against his temple. He thought back to that night, long ago, when a revolver had been held by Jericho against this very temple. She told him she was going to pull the trigger again and again at random intervals. She told him she didn't know if the gun was fully loaded or not.

The test was to demonstrate whether the emotion of fear had been fully eradicated from his brain.

He was strapped into a chair with wires and electrodes measuring every part of his mental activity, including all emotional points.

He had endured five minutes and five trigger pulls of the six-shot weapon, three of them rapid-fire.

No bullet had erupted from the barrel. Otherwise he would not be here.

And he had never once flinched.

After the test was successfully concluded, he had been released. Jericho had handed him the gun. He had aimed it at a dummy target and pulled the trigger.

The bullet blasted a hole in the dummy's head.

Part of him believed that Jericho knew exactly how many bullets were in the gun and had no intention of killing her prized creation.

The other part of him believed her to be a purist when it came to testing and the sacrifice of his life would be but a small price to pay to maintain that high quality of scientific validation.

He got into his van and drove to near Fort Monroe. He knew he would have to get another ride because the van might have been seen. He trekked on foot to Building Q and took up surveillance. With any luck he might spot Quentin, or even *her*.

And if he did see her, he might not be able to control himself. He might just attack.

He didn't care if he died, so long as she did too.

Him staring down at her, his hands around her throat. Hands that she knew better than anyone could crush the life out of her in a second.

He wanted to see her looking back at him. He wanted her to know that things had come full circle. That he had come back and done what needed doing.

Ridding the world of her.

CHAPTER

51

JERICHO COULD NOT meet with them until that evening, so it was after nine and well dark when they arrived at Fort Monroe.

Puller and Knox were escorted into Building Q by one of the armed guards who had been posted outside. The building was clearly closed for the night, the workers having apparently all gone home; the parking lot was empty of cars.

They passed down a long corridor and were led into a small conference room and left alone. They heard the guard's heels tapping on the floor as he went back to his post.

They sat side by side at a small round conference table. Knox glanced at Puller and then her gaze drifted to a small camera lens sunken into a corner of the ceiling.

Puller had already noted this. He nodded at her.

They waited in silence until the door opened again.

Framed in the doorway was a petite woman in her late fifties with short graying hair, dark glasses, and dressed in a navy blue skirt and matching jacket and a white high-collared blouse. On her feet were low-heeled black shoes. She looked to Puller like a veteran banker or lawyer.

She nodded to them both before sitting down across from the pair.

"My name is Claire Jericho. I was the one who called you, Agent Puller."

Puller nodded and then indicated Knox. "This is—"

"I know who she is. Very nice to meet you, Agent Knox. Your reputation precedes you, as does your colleague's."

Knox and Puller exchanged glances before settling their gazes on Jericho.

She looked back at them impassively, cleared her throat, and said, "May I offer some refreshments? Tea, coffee, bottled water? I believe we also have sodas."

They both declined.

She leaned forward and rested one hand on top of the other.

"I know that both of you are exceptionally busy, so I won't waste your time. The fact is your interaction with one of my employees, Anne Shepard, has been reported to me. I have interviewed Ms. Shepard personally. The result was she was terminated this morning."

"Why?" asked Puller.

"For the same reasons you told her last night, Agent Puller. She was frequenting an establishment and behaving in a way that breaches the terms of the contract she had with us. There was no remedy other than immediate termination."

"Is that why you called? To tell me that? You could have done that over the phone."

"I like to convey important information face-to-face."

"Josh Quentin works here, doesn't he?" asked Puller.

"He does."

"Well, he was at the bar too. Apparently he goes all the time. He has his own room upstairs. He goes there with a bunch of women. There's a bedroom up there. Does that violate his contract?"

"I wouldn't know, not having seen his contract. He's the CEO of Atalanta. So he outranks me."

"And yet you're certainly older than he is," noted Knox.

The inscrutable face turned to her.

Jericho said, "Titles are not based on age. They're based on many factors. Mr. Quentin has an impeccable reputation in the field. He has risen quickly no doubt, but solely on his merits."

"And what do you do here?" asked Puller.

"We do contract work with DARPA. Our mission is solely military support. It's no secret."

"It's actually very secret," said Puller. "I couldn't find anything on Atalanta Group at all. You don't even have a website."

"We have no need for any of that. We have our work and we have our client and we do our job."

"After you called I checked on you. I couldn't find anything on you either. And I know where to look."

Jericho stared impassively back at him. "I just wanted to let you know that the matter with Ms. Shepard has been dealt with."

"She was lucky," said Puller. "Right after she left a bunch of guys shot up the bar."

"Really? Was anyone hurt?"

"You hadn't heard about it?" asked Knox. "It didn't happen that far from here."

"I was focused on other things."

"Well, as a matter of fact, quite a few people were killed and injured."

"That is tragic," Jericho said, her features still impassive.

"Were you aware that four women were murdered in this area thirty years ago?" asked Puller.

"I don't really understand the segue, Agent Puller. I thought we were talking about the present."

"The murders were never solved."

"That is unfortunate, but I don't see the relevancy to what we were discussing."

"We're looking at a possible connection between the Army and the murders," said Knox, the remark drawing a quick glance from Puller.

"And why would you be doing that?" asked Jericho.

"Because we think the killer might be connected to the military in some way. Perhaps to this installation."

"This is no longer a military installation."

"But back then it was. And this building was operational back then, wasn't it?"

"This connection, do you have any idea what it might be?"

Knox looked at her, bemused. "It's an ongoing investigation. I'm not at liberty to speak about details."

Jericho let out a small sigh. "I rather hoped this would not be necessary, but I see that it is." She focused on Puller. "There is no investigation. Neither of you have been authorized to perform any such investigation having to do with any murders that may or may not be connected to this installation."

"And how could you possibly know that?" asked Knox.

Jericho continued to stare at Puller. "I would have hoped, Agent Puller, that you would have had more respect for the institution for which you wear the uniform than to try to smear its reputation in a misguided attempt to clear your father of murdering your mother."

Puller said nothing, while Knox glanced back and forth between the two.

Jericho continued, "It gives me no pleasure to have to say

these things to you. I am aware of your father's current condition. I know of the allegations made by Lynda Demirjian. I know that your father arrived back in this country a day before he told authorities he did. I make no judgment on his guilt or innocence. I would hope that he is innocent, though, because his heroism while in uniform is indisputable. And one Puller being in prison was one more than necessary, wasn't it?"

"My brother was cleared of all charges," said Puller tightly. "He was wrongfully convicted."

"And his exoneration was due largely, I am told, to your extraordinary investigative skills and tenacity. And therefore I wonder why you're not exerting those same skills on behalf of your country during the course of *authorized* casework."

"My father—"

She cut him off. "You were told that matter has been dealt with and the inquiry concluded. Mrs. Demirjian is deceased. Your father's reputation will not suffer in the least." She looked at him inquiringly. "I knew your father. Did you know that?"

Puller felt like she had slapped him in the face. This odious woman had known his father?

"No, I didn't know," he said tersely.

"Although we didn't exactly see eye to eye on things, he was an outstanding soldier. I understand you are too. Which brings me to the point: Why are you doing what you're doing?" She glanced at Knox. "And why is this very valuable agent of our country wasting her time helping you do it?"

Puller said, "My mother was never found. I want to know what happened to her."

"So why then has it taken you all this time to delve into the case? Surely you've had many opportunities to do so."

"The letter from Lynda—"

Again she cut him off. "So your desire to seek the truth had to have a catalyst, then? An allegation against your father triggered your sudden desire to know what happened to your mother? Then I take it you cared for your father more than you did your mother if her fate meant nothing to you for three decades until an allegation by a dying woman threatened the reputation of *Fighting* John Puller." She paused. "Were I to have a son, I would expect better treatment."

Puller's hand actually moved an inch toward his M11.

Knox stood and barked, "You are way out of line, lady."

Jericho stared blankly up at her before settling her gaze back on Puller. "Do you think I'm way out of line, Agent Puller? Or do you think I am the only person to actually speak the truth to you about this matter? I don't often tell people what they want to hear. I tell people what they *need* to hear. You said you wanted the truth? Well, here it is. You need to give up this foolishness, get your head back on straight, and move forward with your life and career of service. If you don't, things will not turn out so very well for you."

"Is this where I'm supposed to ask if you're threatening us?"

"No. A threat implies that something *may* rather than *will* happen. I don't wish there to be anything but clarity between you and me."

Puller said nothing to this, but by his look her words had resonated deeply within him.

Knox just stood there staring at her.

Jericho said, "By training I am a scientist. I only care about the facts. You are an investigator. You should only care about the facts. In that way what we both do is very much alike. Facts are irrefutable. Truths coming from those facts can be difficult to accept, particularly when they are of a personal nature. But truths, Agent Puller, cannot be ignored. Any more than lies can. And people do lie to themselves. All the time. We dupe ourselves into believing that our motives are pure, our actions purer still. But at some point, one has to face up to them for what they are. But one fact does exist here, and I will reiterate to you exactly what it is: If you pursue this it will not turn out well for you." She abruptly rose. "Thank you for coming to see me. I doubt we will meet again."

Claire Jericho turned and left.

52

KNOX EXCLAIMED, "I have never met a bigger bitch in my life. The crap that came out of her mouth? And the arrogance? I wanted to kick the shit out of her. And she's working for *our* side?"

They were sitting in his car in the parking lot of Building Q, the lights of the facility the only thing breaking the darkness.

"I just wanted to shoot her," said Puller quietly.

He stared up at the façade of the old building and then gazed at the high fence and armed gate.

"You noticed they didn't let us see anything that was going on in there?"

"I guess they'd say we weren't cleared for it."

"I would bet that few people are."

"So the real purpose of her wanting to see you was to tell you to back the hell off or it will not turn out so well for us," said Knox.

"I don't think she left any possibility of misinterpretation."

"And are you going to back off?"

"What do you think?"

She smiled. "So what's our next step?"

"Finding Paul."

He put the car in gear and drove out of the lot. They headed out of Fort Monroe.

There were no other cars about at this time of night. Across the water were Fort Wool and Naval Station Norfolk.

They had just passed through the entrance to Fort Monroe along the waterfront when the car jerked, slowed, and then suddenly accelerated to nearly eighty miles an hour. Knox was thrown back against her seat by the force.

"Puller, what the hell are you doing?"

"It's not me," he snapped. "It's the car."

He slammed on the brake and then tried to shift into park. Neither maneuver worked. He dug his foot under the accelerator pedal to try to pry it up but it wouldn't budge.

The speedometer clicked to a hundred and they were still accelerating.

"Omigod!" screamed Knox as the car veered sharply to the left and cut across the oncoming lane, very nearly flipping in the process before the rubber regained firm traction.

What was about to happen would make them both wish the car had flipped.

The vehicle hit a bump, went airborne, cleared the low wall, sailed into open space, and then gravity forced the nose of the car down and they slammed into the dark waters of the channel.

The air bags deployed and Puller was stunned by both the impact of the water and the gas-filled bag slamming into him. The car started to quickly sink into the brackish water of the channel.

Puller shook his head clear and looked over at Knox. Her eyes were closed and there was blood on the side of her head. Despite the front and side air bags she must have hit something.

Puller had been trained to never panic under any circumstances. And thus the water rising and the car sinking did not cause him to lose his nerve.

He unsnapped his seat belt and reached over to do the same to Knox's.

It was jammed. He pulled out his Ka-Bar knife from its leather holder on his belt, put the blade under the harness strap, and cut away.

By now the car was under the surface and water was pouring in from crevices all over the vehicle. Puller was now operating in near-total darkness. It was like he was flying through fog without instruments.

He reached up, felt around, and hit the button for the inside light and it miraculously came on. He kept cutting away, his mind jumping ahead to what he would have to do next.

The water was not deep here, he knew, about thirty feet. But it was deep enough to kill them if they couldn't get out.

The harness finally gave and he pulled the unconscious Knox free. The water was now up to their waists.

Keeping the slumping Knox's head above the water, he turned and kicked out against the door. But having to push through the water was weakening the strength of his kicks, and the water was now up to the bottom of the window.

He held Knox in one arm, bracing her head against the ceiling of the car as he gripped the door handle with his free hand. He opened it and pushed his shoulder against the door. He could feel it give just a bit. If he could put his full bulk against it, he was sure he could get it open.

The only snag was that to do that he would have to let go of Knox.

And she would fall into the water, which was up to his chest now. Despite his training, he felt panic rising.

He maneuvered Knox on top of him, her face pointed to the ceiling, and then he slid over to the door and pushed against it. He could feel it give some more, but the water pressure was now too great.

Shit.

A few moments later the water was up to his neck and rising every second. He felt the car level out as it hit bottom.

They were now thirty feet down. Swimming to the surface was not impossible, but they had to get out of the damn car first.

"Knox! Knox! Wake up!" He reached up, shook her violently, then slapped her face. "*Knox!*"

He heard her sputter and then choke as water entered her mouth.

"What . . . what?" she began groggily.

Puller had to arch back to keep the water out of his mouth.

He pulled his gun but knew it was no good. He should have done that sooner. A mistake. Probably now a fatal one.

Unlike in the movies, guns immersed in water did not fire. But with nothing to lose, he pointed it at the car window and pulled the trigger.

Nothing happened.

The water was now up to his eyes. Even arching back he couldn't keep his mouth out of it. He started to sputter and choke on the foul stuff.

He rammed his big feet against the glass, but he couldn't get any momentum pushing through the water.

Holding Knox up, he put his back against the steering wheel, torqued his body, put his feet against the door and pushed, slowly, methodically. He was using every ounce of his considerable strength. He could feel the door give, but only a bit.

So this is how it's going to end?

He felt Knox move above him and then she fell into the water next to him.

He frantically reached for her, but she came up beside him and, mimicking his movements, put her feet against the door and they pushed together, their backs arched to keep their mouths out of the water.

They pushed as hard as they could, synchronizing their movements. The door began to open a bit more.

But it wasn't nearly enough, and if they moved to try to get out, the water pressure would slam the door closed. For good.

The interior lights of the car were still feebly on. They could dimly see each other. Their dual fates were imprinted on their resigned features.

As they both passed under the water, she reached out and touched his cheek.

The panic in her eyes, he was sure, was matched in his.

But he was feeling an even more powerful emotion.

Failure.

He had failed.

And he had died.

And most damning of all?

He had allowed Veronica Knox to die alongside him.

You didn't do that to a comrade. You saved them, even if you died yourself. That was just the Army way. That was the point of being a soldier.

Sacrifice.

They were past saving at this point, he knew. Even if someone had seen them go into the water, which he didn't think they had.

But Puller was not going to give up.

He turned back to the door and pushed with all his might.

This took a lot of air, but it wasn't like he was going to need it much longer anyway.

He looked at Knox, clenched his teeth to keep out the water, and mouthed the words, "I'm sorry."

She nodded in understanding.

They were going to die. But at least they would die together.

Still pushing against the door with his shoulder, he reached out with his hand and she took it in hers.

He felt her hand tremble and he clinched it tight.

His air nearly gone, he turned to look back at her.

Her eyes were fluttering as the hypoxia took over.

In another moment their mouths would open and the water would rush in, fill their lungs, and that would be that.

He stopped pushing and turned to her, traced her jaw with his finger.

And then Puller held her tight.

And they died.

CHAPTER

53

ANY MOMENT NOW he thought his head would explode.

Paul Rogers wiped at his eyes and refocused.

Building Q was across the street. He was hidden in a large clump of bushes.

He had decided he would stay here until he saw Claire Jericho walk either in or out of the place. And when she did he knew exactly what he was going to do.

If she didn't, he was going to head to North Carolina and torture Josh Quentin until he had what he needed to get to Jericho.

It was getting dark now and he had watched workers leaving over the course of about two hours.

Jericho and Josh Quentin were not among them.

The guards made their patrols and Rogers kept his vigil.

Then around nine o'clock he saw the car pull down the street, pass his hiding place, and turn into the gate. It was directed to a parking space next to the gate.

He tensed as the two people got out.

One was the tall guy. Puller with CID. An Army cop. He was with a woman. They were led into the building by a guard.

"Son of a bitch," muttered Rogers. So Puller *was* working

with them. He was probably reporting to Jericho right now his interaction with Rogers, his dismantling of a team of killers at the bar. Jericho would know now that Rogers had returned.

Puller and the woman were spies for her.

Rogers rubbed at the spot on his head so hard that he could feel some of his scalp peel away. It started to bleed. He took no note of it. It didn't matter.

He settled back in his hiding place and waited.

Less than thirty minutes later, Puller and the woman came out and got into the car. They didn't drive off right away but just sat there.

Rogers couldn't see their expressions from this distance, but he figured they must be feeling pretty good right about now. He imagined Jericho rewarding them somehow for having put her on to him.

He ran to his van and climbed in when they started their vehicle.

He dropped in behind them with his headlights off as they passed by where his van was parked, hidden by the corner of a building.

They drove out the main road leading out of the fort.

Rogers debated what to do. He could punch the gas and ram them, overpower them, and make them tell him what they had told Jericho. He thought he might do that before they reached the small downtown area just over the causeway.

He was just about to hit the gas when he stared straight ahead, amazed at what Puller was doing.

The car shot forward.

Has he spotted me? Is he trying to get away? Is the woman dialing Jericho right now? Will the choppers soon be appearing in the sky?

He started to accelerate when the sedan cut a sharp left, almost flipping over, hit a slight rise in the earth, and sailed over the wall and into the channel.

Rogers skidded to a stop and watched from his van as the car immediately began to sink.

What the hell is going on?

The car disappeared from view, a slight frothing of the water the only sign that it had been on the surface moments before.

As he watched his thoughts whirled.

Okay, they're dead. That'll save me the trouble.

But then something else occurred to him.

Puller saved my life. But I didn't ask for his help. I owe him nothing.

Shit.

Rogers counted off three seconds in his head and then kicked the van door open, leapt out, ran straight toward the channel, jumped high in the air, and dove into the water after taking a lungful of air.

It was very dark down here, but he was following the vertical current caused by the bulk of the descending vehicle.

He was moving so fast his head nearly collided with the top of the sedan.

He felt along the edges and then downward until his fingers closed around the door handle. It was partially open but the pressure of the water wouldn't let it move another inch.

Through the window he could make out two figures inside. He couldn't tell for sure, but they seemed to be facing each other.

Rogers planted his feet against the rear door of the car, gripped the front door handle with both hands, and gave a titanic tug.

The door opened fully.

He reached inside and grabbed Puller's arm and next the waist of the woman. He didn't know if they were unconscious or even alive. But if they were still alive they wouldn't be for long unless he got them out of the water.

He kicked off hard to the surface. A few moments later he broke it cleanly and hauled them up, one on his right, one on his left. He used his legs to kick to shore, careful to hold their faces out of the water.

Both were wheezing and spitting up water, but their eyes remained closed and they made no move to free themselves from his grip or try to swim on their own.

He set them both on land. Then he rose, dripping wet, and examined them more closely.

Puller was breathing hard. He turned to the side and upchucked water. When his eyes fluttered and he looked like he might try to sit up, Rogers reached down, gripped his neck, and gave a squeeze firm enough to cut off a substantial part of his airflow. The weakened Puller gave a shudder and passed out.

Rogers turned to the woman. Her eyes were closed and she did not appear to be conscious. He checked to make sure she was breathing and then effortlessly lifted her over one shoulder and used his free hand to grab Puller by the scruff of his jacket. Carrying the woman and dragging the large Puller like he weighed only as much as a child, he got them over the wall and hurried over to the van.

He loaded them both in the back, climbed in, and gave a long searching look in all directions. He saw no one.

He leapt into the back of the van and checked the pulse of each, just to be sure. He was afraid he might have squeezed Puller's throat a little too firmly. But he found that both were alive and breathing, though the woman turned to the side and threw up, as had Puller, before slumping back, unconscious.

Rogers used some rope from the back of the van to securely tie them. Then he closed the driver's door, put the van in gear, and drove off.

CHAPTER

54

H E WAS DEAD.

And he knew she was dead because he had watched her die.

But dead people were not capable of thinking, were they?

Puller slowly lifted his head and looked around.

Tools, shelves, ropes, and the smells of paint, oil, and old food met him head-on.

To his left was Knox, her eyes still closed, but she was breathing.

Puller shook his head clear with difficulty.

How was this possible?

The car. The water. The last breaths.

He had been prepared to die.

He thought he *had* died.

Then he realized he was tied up.

He felt a hand on his shoulder. He felt the fingers grip and then dig slightly into his skin.

Puller felt the otherworldly strength in those fingers.

He shook his head again and felt that same grip on his arm, pulling him from a car submerged in thirty feet of water.

The hands lifted him up and turned him around so the men were facing each other.

He looked up into the countenance of Paul Rogers, though he only knew the man as Paul.

Rogers's features were rigid, though Puller could see momentary flashes of pain, represented by grimaces, flit across the man's features.

"You got us out of the water," said Puller.

Rogers rubbed the back of his head but said nothing.

"My car went out of control. It was driving itself. Drove us right into the water."

Rogers continued to rub the back of his head as Knox stirred, her eyelids fluttered and then opened fully. She saw Puller, then Rogers, and then looked down at the ropes binding her.

"Paul saved us," Puller said.

Knox processed this and nodded. She too could see the look on Rogers's face and knew that Puller was trying to keep things calm, trying to keep Rogers calm.

"Thank you," she said.

Rogers moved his hand away from his head and sat there on his haunches.

"You work for her, don't you?" said Rogers.

"Who?" asked Puller.

Rogers slammed his fist into the side of the van next to Puller's head and drove a dent three inches deep into the metal. He removed his bleeding hand from the pit he'd created and looked back at Puller.

Knox looked desperately at Puller, but he kept his gaze directly on Rogers.

"We met with a woman named Claire Jericho because she called and told us she wanted to meet."

Rogers inched closer to Puller so their noses were barely centimeters apart. "Why would she want to meet with you unless you were working for her?"

"To tell us to back off our investigation. And if we didn't that something bad would happen to us."

Something occurred to Puller and he glanced at Knox. "They bugged my car. They heard me tell you that I was going to continue the investigation."

"And they remotely took over the car and ran us right into the channel," added Knox.

"They tried to kill you?" said Rogers.

Puller said, "Well, I didn't drive myself into the water to die."

Rogers sat back against a shelving unit built into the interior wall of the van.

Puller said, "You know Claire Jericho?"

Remaining silent, Rogers nodded.

"From a long time ago?" asked Puller.

Rogers glanced up at him.

Puller said, "I think she also tried to kill you. I mean very recently. At the Grunt."

Rogers kept his gaze on Puller.

"Those guys who attacked the bar? I don't see them doing what they did that night unless they were paid to do it. And the only thing worth killing there was you."

Rogers eyed him suspiciously. "Why do you care?"

"We know about the four women who were killed," said Knox. "And their bodies buried around this area."

"Five," said Rogers. "It was five women, not four."

Puller went rigid and Knox gave him a nervous glance.

"Five?" said Knox. "But only four bodies were ever discovered."

"They took her. They took the fifth one."

"Where was this?" asked Puller.

"Fort Monroe."

"Who took her?" asked Knox.

"Them! They took her."

"Did you kill those women?" asked Knox.

Rogers said nothing. He just sat there taking measured breaths, his head bowed, his hands clasped in front of him.

"Did you know that her name was Jackie Puller?" asked Knox. "The fifth person that was killed?"

Rogers looked at her from under hooded eyes. "No, it wasn't."

Puller stiffened some more and then relaxed. "Then who was it?" he asked. "What was her name?"

"Audrey Moore."

"Why did you kill her?" asked Puller.

"Who said I did?" Rogers said sharply.

"Assuming that you did, would it have been random?"

Rogers started to rub the spot on his head again.

Puller licked his lips and said, "Do you know what happened to Jackie Puller?"

"She has your last name. Who was she to you?"

"My mother."

"None of the women were mothers."

"In my wallet there's a picture of her from the investigation file. Can you look and tell me if you ever saw her around here?"

"Why do you think I care?"

"Will you just please do it? Please?"

Rogers stared at him for a few moments and then took the damp wallet out and found the picture.

"Do you remember her?" asked Puller.

Rogers put the picture back into the wallet and stuffed it back into Puller's jacket. "I never saw her. And I would have remembered her."

Puller gave an imperceptible sigh of relief. "So these other women worked with you?"

Rogers said nothing.

Puller said, "This was three decades ago. Why are you back here now?"

"Unfinished business."

"Claire Jericho?"

"Unfinished business."

"We're not working with her. If anything, we're working against her."

"But you're also looking into the murders of those women."

"Did you kill them?" Puller asked.

Rogers rose. "I need to decide what to do with you two. But no decision is going to turn out right for you."

"So you saved us to kill us?" asked Knox. "How does that make sense?"

"You think any of this is supposed to make sense?" Rogers paused. "Was Jericho really in Building Q tonight?"

"Yes," replied Puller.

"And she tried to kill you?"

"Yes. But I doubt there's any way we can prove she hacked into my car's computer."

Knox said, "What did they do to you, Paul?"

"Why do you give a fuck?" snarled Rogers.

"It's our job to give a fuck," barked Puller.

Rogers rubbed the back of his head again. "I...I was the test."

"The test? For a super soldier thirty years ago?"

Rogers nodded dumbly.

"Was Jericho in charge of the program?" asked Knox.

Rogers shook his head. "Not technically. It was Chris Ballard's company."

Knox said, "I know that name, Ballard. He's retired now."

"To the Outer Banks in North Carolina. Big mansion on

the beach." Rogers paused and then added, "He's dead. Or he should be."

They both looked at him, startled. "Why do you say that?" asked Puller.

"Because I threw him out a window four stories up. But then he came back to life."

Puller glanced at Knox, who was staring at Rogers, her face drawn in concern.

Rogers saw her look. "I'm not screwed in the head, lady. It couldn't have been the same guy, of course. But another guy who looked like the one I killed was out on the beach the next day. I don't know what the hell is going on."

"Why did you go there? And why did you throw who you thought was Ballard out a window?" asked Puller.

"To get information on Jericho. And when he told me squat I chucked him out the window. He deserved it after what they did to me."

"Why didn't you just leave the test program?" asked Knox.

"You think I had that option? I was a prisoner."

"But you did eventually get away," pointed out Puller.

Rogers nodded. "I planned it for months. They never saw it coming. See, they built me too good. They didn't figure in cunning and my ability to lie. They gave me that and I used it against them."

"So they messed with your mind too?" said Knox.

"They messed with everything. You know how strong I am. But that was nothing compared to what they did up here." He tapped his head.

"How so?"

In answer Rogers picked up a screwdriver from a can on the shelf, placed the tip against the palm of his hand, and pushed it in. Blood spurted out as the tip disappeared into his hand. He gave no reaction.

Puller eyed him. "They took away your ability to feel pain."

"They took away *everything* that made me human."

Puller said slowly, "They made you...the perfect killing machine."

"Only they forgot that your target might not always be the enemy," said Knox breathlessly.

"My *enemy* became whoever was in front of me," said Rogers dully. "I had no control over it."

"Josh Quentin works for Atalanta Group. That's Jericho's new company. It's in Building Q."

"I got in Building Q the other night. Climbed one of the walls up to the top."

"How the hell did you do that?"

"I'm just strong. And I have artificial skin on my palms and fingers, and on the bottoms of my feet, so I can dig into whatever I'm climbing."

Knox exclaimed, "Why doesn't anyone know about any of this?"

"Because four, or rather five, women died," said Puller. "So they buried it."

The next instant the jolt of pain hit Rogers so fiercely he bent over and threw up. He staggered back, clawing at his torso.

"Paul, what's wrong?" shouted Puller. "Can you cut us loose? We can try to help you."

Rogers tore at his clothes, ripping them off his body until he stood before them in only his skivvies. Both Puller and Knox stared at the hideous scars up and down his body.

"Omigod," exclaimed Knox.

Rogers was bent double by the agony. He tore at his

head, pulling a hunk of his scalp free. Blood poured down his face.

He looked up at them.

"They did that to you?" asked Puller, eyeing the scars.

Rogers moaned, leapt over them, and threw open the back doors of the van. First he picked up Knox and hurled her through the opening. Then he did the same with Puller. They rolled and tumbled before coming to rest still bound tightly and groaning in pain.

When Puller managed to look back the van had started up. The next instant he heard tires squealing. The van roared off, turned a corner, and was gone.

CHAPTER

55

Kɴᴏx ᴡᴀs ꜰᴀʟʟɪɴɢ through open space, so fast that she knew she would die as soon as she hit something solid. It was not survivable. This was it.

She opened her eyes and saw Puller staring down at her.

"What the hell?" she managed to say in a garbled voice.

He held up his Ka-Bar knife. "Lucky I was able to reach this."

He helped her up.

"Where are we?" asked Knox.

"Not sure." He pulled out his phone. "But let's see."

"It still works?"

"Waterproof," he said, hitting some keys.

"Williamsburg is a mile that way," he said, pointing to his left.

They started walking in that direction.

"Should we call somebody, let them know what happened?" asked Knox groggily.

"Who exactly would that be?"

She looked at him. "I...I guess you're right." She glanced back over her shoulder. "Paul was...it was so terrible, Puller."

"They screwed with his brain so he could kill and not feel bad about it."

"You mean they made him a monster."

"But the monster didn't kill us. He saved us."

"So he could get information."

"He got information and he still let us live."

She nodded slowly. "Does that mean the mind control thing they built into him is wearing off?"

"I think more likely that whoever Paul was before is re-asserting itself."

"So what do we do now?"

"Clearly Jericho tried to kill us tonight. She's afraid of what we might find out. So I say we keep working to justify that fear."

"She may not know that we're alive."

"That's right."

Puller's phone buzzed. It was a text. From his brother.

In all caps it said, CALL THIS NUMBER NOW. NO MONITOR. BTW RICKY STACK HAD NO CHANCE.

Knox was looking at the screen. "Who is Ricky Stack?"

"The biggest kid in third grade who tried to take my lunch."

"What happened?"

"He learned the error of his ways. That's Bobby's way of confirming that it's him on the other end of the text."

He called the number as they walked along. His brother answered on the first ring.

"Are you okay, Junior?" he asked immediately.

"Why wouldn't I be?"

"Because three hours ago an unauthorized use of a DoD satellite was made in Hampton, near Fort Monroe. In fact on the grounds of Fort Monroe. That was too much of a coincidence for me."

"So that's how they took over the car."

"Come again?"

Puller quickly explained what had happened.

"Claire Jericho," Robert said in a hushed tone.

"You know her?"

"I know *of* her. She's at the very highest levels, John. I mean, she meets with the Joint Chiefs. She goes to the Oval Office. I've heard her lecture. She's brilliant. Beyond brilliant. Once-in-a-generation intellect."

"She's also a monster, Bobby."

"How so?"

"Are you sure there's no one monitoring this?"

"I've bounced this signal off so many pieces of sky hardware and encrypted it to such an insane degree that I'm surprised we can even understand each other."

"Okay." Puller took five minutes to tell him about Paul. When he was done his brother was silent for so long that Puller was afraid someone had intercepted the call and taken his brother away.

"John, this is not good."

"Tell me something I don't know. The thing is the women that were killed? I think they all helped build Paul. And this last victim, Audrey Moore, I'm sure will have the same sort of connection."

"So he killed them in retaliation?"

"I'm sure he would have loved to kill Jericho, but he probably couldn't get to her. The five women were the next best thing."

"Jesus," said Robert. "Talk about guilt by association."

"Bobby, if this Jericho is such a rock star, how come Knox and I have never heard of her?"

"She wants it that way. Even when she comes out and speaks it's only to a select few. No publicity at all. She's always in the background. She has people run the companies she ostensibly works for."

"Like Chris Ballard thirty years ago and Josh Quentin with Atalanta Group now?"

"I know about Ballard, and I know a little about Atalanta Group. I don't know Quentin."

"Well, Quentin is passing government secrets to a bar owner in Hampton. And she's passing them on to some French-speaking guy in Williamsburg."

"What?" exclaimed Robert. "Do you have proof?"

"I have pictures. I can send them to you. Maybe you can run this French guy down. Knox was going to try, but you might have a better shot."

"What sort of government secrets?"

"I'll send you the screen shots I took. Knox says it looks like it has to do with cell mutation and organ regeneration."

"Okay."

"And the woman's name is Helen Myers. She owns a bar called the Grunt in Hampton."

"Send me the stuff and I'll see what I can find."

Robert gave him a secure site to send the photos to.

"Okay. But this Paul guy said he didn't remember seeing Mom?"

"That's right."

"Do you believe him?" asked Robert.

"Yeah. He basically confessed to killing five women. What was one more?"

"I suppose."

"You said there was unauthorized satellite use. Can you trace it? Can you tell if they were able to remotely take control of my car? I know that's possible."

"If someone was good enough to hijack one of our birds, they're sophisticated enough to cover their tracks.

We might be able to reverse engineer a trail from your car's computer."

"Doubtful. It's under thirty feet of water. I'm going to have a lot of explaining to do to the rental car company."

"You really think it was Jericho?"

"Five minutes after leaving her and talking in our car about not abandoning the case, someone drives my car into the channel? Let's not make this too complicated."

"One thing is really puzzling me," said Robert.

"Just one? You're way ahead of me, then."

"Paul said he killed Chris Ballard. Or who he thought was Chris Ballard."

"That's what he said."

"And he couldn't have been mistaken?" asked Robert.

"He said he threw the old guy headfirst out a four-story window."

"Then it was a double."

"Right, maybe for security reasons."

Robert said, "Ballard could afford enough security to keep would-be murderers out of his fortress on the beach. If he felt so insecure in his protection that he thought he needed a double handy to take on a potential attacker, then he should have just spent the money on a new protection team."

"So what can you do with that?"

"I can dig, that's what," replied his brother.

"You mentioned the fortress on a beach. I didn't tell you that."

"I have access to satellites, little brother. And Ballard, though retired, personally owns a slew of patents that are very important to our defense efforts."

"Is there any connection between his old company and Atalanta?"

"I'll check."

"When do you think you might have something for me?"

"When I know, you'll know. And John?"

"Yeah?"

"Every flank you have is exposed and no reinforcements are being dialed up. You're rolling solo, bro."

Puller glanced over at Knox, who had clearly heard this.

"Copy that," said Puller. It was pretty much the same thing his CO, Don White, had previously told him.

He clicked off and looked at Knox.

She smiled weakly. "Well, the good news is we're still alive."

"And the *bad* news is that's all the good news we have," replied Puller.

CHAPTER

56

SIX HOURS.

For six hours he had counted his breaths like an insane man, waiting for the pain to stop.

He was lying in a bed in a motel he didn't remember checking into.

He had stolen another car and switched plates with a second car he'd happened upon.

He rubbed his face. He'd washed up at a gas station. But he'd dug a hole in his head; it was now covered by a ball cap.

He sat up but immediately bent over as another jolt of pain pounded him. But the frequency had subsided.

Another hour passed and he was pain free. He took a shower, put his clothes back on, and headed out.

He was running out of time now.

Puller and the woman hadn't mentioned that they'd told Jericho anything about him, but they might have.

He tapped his ring against the car's steering wheel.

For the greater good.

Yeah, right. If I can find you, I'll show you the greater good, or at least my version of it.

It was dark when Rogers drove south. He crossed into North Carolina and headed on to the Outer Banks.

He reached Quentin's beach house, drove past, left his car in a small public parking lot, and stole back to the house.

There were no cars out front, but there might be one in the garage.

He checked.

The Maserati wasn't there.

Rogers stepped back and looked up at the darkened house. He knew Quentin was not at the Grunt since it wasn't open. Was he at Building Q? Had this trip been for nothing? When he had no time to lose? Maybe the man had a place in Hampton. That would make sense, only Rogers had no way to find out where it was. He should have checked the registration on the Maserati the last time he was here. That might have given him an address other than this one, because he recalled the car had Virginia plates.

The flash of a car's headlights made him leap behind a large bush just in the nick of time. The car pulled into the driveway and the garage door started to wind its way up. As the sleek vehicle pulled past him and into the garage he saw who was driving it.

Helen Myers.

She looked distraught. She got out of the car and headed to the house through a connecting door. She punched a keypad on the wall as she passed through. The garage door came down, but not before Rogers was able to slip inside. He skittered over to the door through which Myers had passed and listened at the wood.

Heels clicked on tile. He heard a thump.

Her bag being dropped on the kitchen island?

Then the footsteps headed upstairs.

He waited another few seconds and then opened the door and slipped through.

The house was quiet, the first floor mostly dark. The only light was coming from the hall leading to the second floor.

He saw her bag on one of the kitchen counters. He searched it but found nothing of interest.

Rogers headed up the stairs. When he reached the top floor he heard the water start up.

He counted down the bedrooms, passing the one where Davis and Quentin had screwed each other's brains out. Now that he had slept with Davis that memory caused him anger. He wanted to share nothing with Josh Quentin.

There was a light from under the partially open door on the last room on the hall.

Rogers crept there, knelt, and put an eye to the crevice.

Myers was just finishing undressing.

She undid a clasp at the back of her hair and it cascaded down to her freckled shoulders. She stretched and Rogers could see small clusters of muscles in her arms and back. Then she disappeared into the adjoining bathroom.

He waited until he heard her step into the shower and close the door. Then he crept in and looked around. The bedroom was large, with decorations made of seashells strewn throughout and a couple of beach prints on the wall.

When Rogers heard the water being turned off, he sat on the bed and waited. Then a hair dryer started up.

When the dryer stopped running, he pulled out his vintage M11-B pistol and held it in his hand.

The door opened and she appeared wrapped in a towel. When she saw him she leapt back and screamed.

He said nothing, did nothing.

When she saw who it was she stopped screaming and stared incredulously at him.

"P-Paul? W-what are you doing here?"

Her gaze fell on the gun and she took another step back.

He stood and gripped the pistol.

"What are you doing here? How do you even know about this place?"

"I followed someone here once."

"Why?"

"Because I needed information."

"Information? About what?"

"About me."

"I-I don't understand."

"Where is Josh Quentin? Isn't this his place?"

"No. It's my place. He just stays here sometimes."

"And Suzanne Davis stays here with him sometimes."

Her features darkened. "What do you mean?"

"Do you know Davis?"

She nodded mutely.

"They come here to fuck. They do it very energetically."

Myers didn't move a muscle. She just stared at him.

"I need to find Quentin. Where is he?"

"I don't know. But why do you need to find him?"

"He knows somebody I need to find."

"Who?"

"He works for Atalanta Group. Did you know that?"

"I-I might have heard him mention it."

Rogers took another step toward her. She drew back. He rubbed the back of his head, trying to push back the pain that was rising in him again. This was getting very inconvenient.

She said, "I don't know what you want me to say. You've broken into my house, Paul. I could call the police. But if you leave now, I won't. You might still be messed up from what happened at the bar. I know I am. I still have no idea why those men attacked the place."

"They were coming to kill me."

Myers caught a breath and stared at him. "How do you know that?"

"I just know."

"But why would anyone want to kill you?"

"Because I am what I am, and she is who she is."

"Who is this person?"

"Claire Jericho."

He watched her closely for a reaction to the name. And got it.

"So you know her?"

"She works with Josh. Is she the person you want to find?"

He nodded.

"Why?"

"She made me."

"Excuse me?"

In answer Rogers took off his shirt. When Myers saw the scars she slumped back against the wall. "Omigod. What... Omigod."

"She made me," he said again.

She started to tear up. "I'm so sorry, Paul. I—"

He cut in, "You can help me."

"How?"

"You can help me get to her."

"How!" she wailed.

"Through Quentin."

"I don't know how to do that."

"You just need to acquire the target. I'll take it from there."

"Look," she pleaded, "I really don't want to be involved."

He gripped her shoulder. "You already *are* involved. Now compose yourself and then contact him. Tell him you want to meet. Here."

"What reason would I give?"

"I'll leave that to you. Come up with a good one. And I'll be watching while you do it."

"And if he doesn't come?"

He squeezed her shoulder just enough to make her wince. "You better pray to God that he does. Because I'm running out of time and patience."

CHAPTER

57

CLICK. CLICK. CLICK.

While Robert Puller was digging, his brother was doing the same thing.

In his motel room he was tapping away at the keys on his computer.

He had no idea of the hour.

Knox had fallen asleep on the bed.

But Puller was not tired.

He was pissed.

And when he got pissed, he worked even harder.

Right now he was doing something he should have done earlier. Seen if anything unusual had happened at Fort Monroe around the time his mother disappeared. Anything out of the ordinary that might be tied to that disappearance. There might be nothing, certainly. But right now he would take anything.

He had gone through pretty much every possible event, and there weren't many, when his gaze froze on the name.

He checked the date.

He checked the location.

He rechecked the name. And the other name listed with the first one.

Son of a bitch.

Is that why she played so coy?

He closed his eyes and thought back to the night his mother disappeared. His brow creased as he strained to remember something.

She had made them dinner. She was dressed to go out. He had followed her into her bedroom as she went to get something.

She didn't know he was there. She had paused at a dresser.

A drop of sweat appeared on his brow, so intense was his concentration.

She had reached down for something there.

He scrunched his face up.

Her fingers touched the frame. It was a photo.

She picked it up, looked at it.

Then she put it back down.

But Puller had seen enough.

He opened his eyes and swore under his breath.

He hadn't asked the obvious follow-up question because he didn't think it was relevant and he was also trying to be tactful.

Well, the hell with tactful now.

"Knox? Knox!"

He rose, gripped her shoulder, and gently nudged her.

"Hey, wake up. I might have something."

She stirred on the bed, mumbled something, and then sat straight up and looked at him crossly.

"What?"

He said, "Why would one woman know the history of another woman?"

She rubbed her face and then gave him an even crosser look. "I don't even understand the question."

He grabbed his laptop and sat next to her. "Here are my

notes on a conversation I had with someone. Read through them."

Knox yawned, stretched, and refocused. She read down the page and scrolled to the next.

"Okay," she said. "That is a little unusual. I mean, she said they talked, but some of these things, at least it seems to me, the woman did her own research. I mean, they aren't the sorts of things that would come up in normal conversation, certainly not between two women."

"She said my parents and she and her husband frequently socially interacted. And that my mother helped *them* through their issues. She spoke reverently about her."

"But she also said that your mother sort of floated above everyone else. You could read that two ways. Jealousy being one of them."

"And there's something else," said Puller. He showed her the news article.

"Her husband committed suicide?" exclaimed Knox.

"His body was found the morning after my mother disappeared. But he could have died the same night that she vanished."

"You think they might be connected?"

"I don't know. But I also don't know they're *not* connected."

"So this might explain what happened to your mother that night?"

"Let's hope so, because I'm fresh out of leads and ideas."

* * *

This time Puller did not phone ahead.

They arrived at eight o'clock in the morning on the woman's doorstep.

Lucy Bristow answered the door in her bathrobe. She didn't look happy, but then neither did Puller.

"What do you want?" she said brusquely.

"Answers," said Puller bluntly.

"About what? I've told you all I know about your mother."

"Can we do this inside?" asked Knox.

For a moment Bristow looked like she might slam the door in their faces, but then she stepped back and motioned them in. She led them into the kitchen and said, "I'm making some tea, would you like some?"

Puller declined, Knox accepted.

Bristow poured out two cups and they sat at the kitchen table.

"Now what exactly is this about?"

"You didn't tell me that your husband committed suicide," said Puller.

"I didn't know I had a responsibility to do so," she retorted.

"He most likely died on the very night my mother disappeared."

"So what?"

"Who found him?"

"I did."

"But you were separated," said Puller. "You weren't living together."

"We were supposed to meet to go over some details of the divorce. He didn't show up. I called. He didn't answer. No one knew where he was. I drove over there... And found him."

"How did he die? The article I read didn't say."

"Why is this any of your business?"

"If it's connected to my mother's disappearance it is my business."

"How could it possibly be?"

"Please, Mrs. Bristow, just answer the question," said Knox.

She sighed, took a sip of tea, and said, "He overdosed. Painkillers. He'd suffered an injury and had a big supply of them in the house. He apparently used a whole bottle of them to commit suicide."

"You said that my mother helped you work through issues."

"She did."

"You also said she helped your husband."

"Earl and Jackie were friends," she said stiffly.

"I'm not suggesting there was anything deceitful going on between them," said Puller.

"I don't see where this is going," said Bristow sharply.

"My mother got a phone call the night she disappeared. I was there. I remember she looked upset, agitated. Then she got dressed and went out somewhere. Could the call have come from your husband? Would he have called my mom if he were in distress? If he needed to talk?"

"Particularly if he were contemplating suicide," added Knox.

"And if he did, don't you think it likely that my mother would have gone over there to talk to him?"

When Puller had mentioned the phone call, Bristow's face had paled and she had put her teacup down because her hand had started to tremble.

Knox said, "What is it?"

Bristow put a hand to her mouth and tears emerged at the corners of her eyes.

"Mrs. Bristow, please, tell us," implored Puller.

She composed herself. "Earl called *me* that night."

"You?"

She nodded, wiping at her eyes. "He was distressed. He sounded drunk. He..." Her voice trailed away and she fell silent.

"Did he ask you to come over?" said Puller.

She looked at him and nodded.

"And what happened?" asked Knox.

"Nothing. Because I didn't go over. I went out with some friends instead."

She let out a gush of air and leaned forward, put her forehead on the table, and started to sob.

Knox and Puller just stared at her. Finally, Knox put a supportive hand on the woman's shoulder and said, "It's okay, Mrs. Bristow. You had no way of knowing."

The sobs racked the woman for another minute before she sat up, grabbed a napkin from the holder in the center of the table, wiped her eyes, and blew her nose.

She sat back, let out a long breath, and said, "Well, I might as well get it all out." She blew her nose again and wadded the napkin in her hand.

"I told Earl that I wasn't coming over and..." She stopped and looked at Puller.

"And what?" asked Puller.

"And that he should call Jackie."

"Why my mother?"

"Because he was infatuated with her. Besotted, head over heels in love, that's why. It was a bitchy thing to do, I know, but I was just fed up."

Puller sat back looking surprised.

Knox glanced nervously at him and said to Bristow, "Was that the problem in your marriage? Is that why you separated?"

Bristow nodded. "That along with the fact that Earl drank too much."

Puller said, "Are you saying they were having an affair?"

Bristow shook her head. "Earl clearly wanted to. He would have married Jackie if he could have."

Puller exclaimed, "She was already married. To his commanding officer! And my *father*."

Bristow looked at him from under hooded, reddened eyes. "Do you think someone in love gives a damn about that?"

"And my mother?"

"Your mother had no interest in anything like that. She was a devout Catholic. When I told you earlier that she floated above the rest of us, I meant that in a divinely spiritual way."

"You seemed to know a lot about Mrs. Puller," said Knox. "More than you would get simply from conversation with her."

"When it was clear my husband was in love with her I did some research. I don't know why. I just did. I wanted to hate her, I guess. Find some flaw to make myself feel better. But when I realized that Jackie had no interest in breaking her marriage vows I actually became closer to her. She knew what was going on. She knew how Earl felt. And she gently but firmly made it very clear to him that it was never going to happen."

"So when you declined to go over there that night, you told him to call her?"

"Yes. And if she got a call that night I'm sure it was from Earl. But I had no idea she had gotten a call that night, so I never thought that Earl had contacted her."

"She didn't go right away. She made us dinner, my brother and me, so I doubt he told her he was thinking of killing himself. She would have called the police immediately."

"Do you remember what time the call was?"

"Around six, I think."

"Then it was after he called me." She glanced at Puller. "Why did you think about this connection?"

"The date of your husband's suicide. Your knowledge about my mother. And I remembered that before she left the house that night she picked up a photo off her dresser. In that photo were my parents, and you and your husband."

Bristow sighed and closed her eyes.

"So my mother goes to meet him," said Puller. "She disappears. And later he commits suicide?"

Bristow's eyes popped open. She seemed to sense where he was going. "Do you...are you alleging that Earl murdered your mother? He loved her."

"And love can turn to hate when it's rebuffed," said Puller grimly. "As an Army investigator I've seen that happen more times than I can count."

"Omigod!" Bristow said. "But what would he have done with...?"

"With her body? I don't know. Did he call you again that night?"

"No."

"Why didn't you go to see him?" asked Knox.

"Because I had nothing to say to him. I was mentally and emotionally exhausted. So I just told him to talk to the woman he really loved, which wasn't me!"

"Did my father know about all this?"

Bristow looked at him contemptuously. "Do you think if he did know he would have let things stand like that? Your father would have come over and kicked the shit out of Earl. And Earl knew it. He feared your father, like most of the junior officers."

"But those officers didn't have the hots for my mom," retorted Puller. "And if he couldn't control himself, and he couldn't have my mom, then maybe he decided no one else could either," said Puller.

"I can't believe that Earl would have harmed her."

"And I can't take the chance that he didn't without thoroughly checking it out."

"What do you mean?"

"I mean getting a search warrant for your former house."

"You can't think that—"

"I'm a criminal investigator. What you think and what I know people are capable of are light-years apart."

Puller had called his CO, Don White, explained the situation, and White had gotten a search warrant. It was fairly easy because the house the Bristows had lived in back then was now vacant.

A team of agents had come in and spent all day tearing the place apart. Cadaver-sniffing dogs had been brought in to go over the house and grounds.

It had taken time, and money.

And the result was zip.

Puller had seen the resentment in the CID agents who performed this work. They were overworked as it was without this time-waster. That's what he read in their looks.

Puller had been so sure, but the dogs would have found something if there had been anything.

He leaned against his new rental, surveying the property, while Knox stood beside him.

"Well, it was worth a shot," she said.

"We may be the only ones who think that. And now we're back to square one," he replied.

"We need more information," said Knox.

"The thing is, if Earl Bristow wasn't involved in my mother's disappearance, who was?"

"You don't think the wife was, do you? Maybe she was feeding us a bunch of bull. Maybe she wanted to get back with her husband and was jealous of your mother."

"I checked. She had an alibi for the time in question. And people I talked to seemed unanimous in their recollection that Lucy Bristow wanted the divorce."

"So maybe we're barking up the wrong tree."

Puller glanced up and down the street they were on. "Shit," he muttered.

"What?"

"Come with me."

He started walking and Knox fell in beside him. "Where are we going?"

"If my mom came to visit Bristow that night she would have come this way. It's really the only way to come from our house."

"Okay."

Puller kept going, his long, purposeful strides eating up ground. Knox, tall as she was, had to hurry to keep up.

He stopped when he got to a heavily wooded area, and took a picture of it with his camera.

"What was that for?" asked Knox.

"You'll see."

They rounded a bend in the road and Puller stopped.

"Damn," exclaimed Knox.

Building Q was just up ahead.

Knox looked behind her and then back at Building Q. Then she stared up at Puller.

"So you think she passed Building Q on her way to the Bristows'?"

"She had to. And even at that time of night Building Q would have had guards posted outside."

"Wait a minute, then some of them should have seen your mother pass by."

"I'm sure they did."

"And the wooded area? Why did you take a picture of that?"

"Because it would have provided cover for someone waiting to jump her. So if something happened to her, I'm betting it would have happened there. And if no one from Building Q reported seeing my mom pass by, although she would have been in full view of the perimeter guards, then whatever happened to her must be connected to Building Q."

"And what, the guards were told to say nothing?"

"Exactly."

"But what do you think happened?"

"Paul told us about his last victim, Audrey Moore."

"Right. But her body was never found."

"I checked on her. She was a chemist. And she disappeared on the same night my mother did. No one connected it because no one knew from where Moore had disappeared."

"What are you getting at, Puller?"

He didn't answer for a long moment. "My mother was taken because she saw Audrey Moore being killed by Paul."

Now Knox seemed unable to find her voice.

Finally she said, "But Moore's body was never found. All the others were."

"That's because he didn't have time to dump her body."

"You think your mother frightened him away?"

"No. I don't think anything could frighten that guy. I think Paul had to run for it because he was interrupted by people who could kill him or imprison him. Again."

"Building Q. Claire Jericho!"

Puller nodded. "Paul never saw my mother. He never laid a hand on her. It was the people from Building Q. She saw things she couldn't possibly be allowed to tell anyone."

Knox let out a gasp. "So you're saying she was just in the wrong place at the wrong time?"

Puller nodded. "Yeah."

Knox's brow furrowed. "And Bristow? When she never showed up at the Bristows' he probably assumed she didn't care about him."

"And he killed himself," finished Puller.

"The problem is, how do we prove any of this? We'd need a miracle."

"Maybe I have a way to get one."

He pulled out his phone and punched in a number.

Anne Shepard, the recently fired scientist from Atalanta Group, answered on the second ring. She did not seem pleased to hear from him.

"You promised me that if I helped you—" she began.

"I had nothing to do with your being fired," interjected Puller. "That was all Claire Jericho's doing. I never even talked to anyone at Atalanta Group. Then she called me in and told me she had fired you. She must have found out some other way."

"Well, either way, I'm out of a job."

"Maybe I help you, you help me."

"How?"

Puller arranged for them to meet Shepard at a café in Hampton. She was waiting for them at a back table.

He sat down across from her with Knox next to him. They ordered coffees and Puller plunged right in.

"Do you know the owner of the Grunt, Helen Myers?"

"No."

"But you knew Quentin had the room upstairs?"

"Well, yeah. I wasn't the only one who knew that. He would bring other people from the company there sometimes. In addition to the *ladies*."

Knox said, "Did they ever tell you what went on up there?"

She looked at Knox. "I don't know who you are."

Knox pulled out her official creds.

Shepard's jaw dropped and she assumed a more contrite expression. "I'm sorry, I didn't know."

"Did anyone at Atalanta Group ever talk about what went on up there?" Knox asked again.

"Some of the women. It seemed like only the really good-looking ones got to go with Josh. I never made the cut."

"And what did they say?"

"That things got a little wild. Too much alcohol."

"Drugs?"

"No, they never mentioned that, but then they probably wouldn't have. They have contracts too that forbid that."

"They forbid too much alcohol too," noted Puller.

"Yeah, you pointed that out to me already," said Shepard sarcastically.

"Sex?" asked Knox.

"There was some, yeah."

"The women and Quentin?"

"No one ever said they'd had sex with Quentin. But there was a bedroom and couples would slip off there. It was all consensual," she added hastily. "And no one was paying for sex."

"Did any of your friends ever mention Myers coming into the room?"

Shepard thought about this. "Once," she said. "It was kind of weird."

"What was?"

"Well, my friend said that Quentin spent a lot of time with her."

"Well, so what? Maybe they're friends."

"Yeah, but Quentin likes the young babes."

Puller took out his phone and showed Shepard the screen grabs he'd taken from the laptop of the man who'd met with Myers at the Williamsburg Inn.

"Look familiar?"

Shepard gasped. "Where did you get these?"

"Never mind. Just tell me what they are."

"They're stuff Atalanta Group was working on."

"Cell mutation? Organ regeneration? I thought you were into exoskeletons and liquid armor, for the military."

"I am, but we have a number of related projects. And in the past I worked on those two."

"Cell mutation?" said Knox. "How does that help the military?"

"Well, cell mutation isn't always a bad thing, like with cancer. There are lots of positive attributes to the technology. For instance, it can be used to help soldiers heal faster by bulking up levels of white blood cells."

Puller thought about this and something seemed to click in his head. "Would any of this have a *commercial* application, outside the military?"

"Oh yes. Take the cell mutation. They can be engineered so you can live off your fat more efficiently. You do that, the forty-billion-dollar weight loss industry disappears. With regeneration you can heal faster, have a better immune system. We can take on Alzheimer's and heart disease. Old people can potentially have the energy, physical, and cognitive levels of the young. Pain blockers that last up to a month. The health care industry is a three-trillion-dollar beast. Some of this stuff could make people wealthy. I mean Bill Gates wealthy."

"But not Atalanta Group?" asked Puller.

"Well, we're a military support contractor. And you know

the military isn't really permitted to pursue commercialization of products."

"But you do undertake this sort of research?"

"Well, yes, we have to in order to do the work we're contracted to do. But it stops with the military applications."

"But someone could commercialize it?" said Puller.

"It would have to do with who controls the patents. The IP rules my world. You control that, you control everything."

"And you don't know about that? The ownership of it?"

"You'd have to talk to legal about that."

"Right," said Puller, tapping his spoon against his cup.

"Is someone stealing technology? Is that what this is about?"

Puller fixed his gaze on her. "I don't know. Can you steal from yourself?"

Shepard never had a chance to answer.

Puller had grabbed her arm and thrown her under the table.

The bullet hit right where Anne Shepard had been a second before.

CHAPTER

59

JOSH QUENTIN WAS driving fast.

And he didn't look happy, because he wasn't.

He could have been killed at the Grunt. Just the thought made him want to pull his Maserati off the road and throw up.

He feared death because he simply had too much to lose.

Hell, I have everything to lose.

He was young, handsome, charming, and the ladies loved him. On top of that, he was wealthy. On top of that, he was on the cusp of far greater wealth. And he was only thirty-two.

No one was going to take that away from him. He had come from nothing and there was no way in hell he was going back there.

He pulled into the garage of the beach house and saw her car parked in the next bay.

Well, this had better be good. He was a busy man.

He opened the door into the house.

A moment later everything went dark.

* * *

Quentin slowly opened his eyes and saw his knees and then the floor.

He raised his head slowly. The pain shot through his skull with just this simple movement. He felt like he might be sick.

Then something grabbed the back of his neck and jolted him straight up. He cried out with the pain before his gaze came to rest on Rogers.

"What the hell are you doing?" he screamed.

"You took your time getting here. Myers called you last night."

"What the hell business is it of yours?"

"I have some questions for you."

"Questions? For *me*? You're a fucking bar bouncer."

Rogers tightened his grip on the man's neck just enough to see the slight bulge in Quentin's eyes.

Quentin swung a fist at Rogers, who easily deflected it.

"Questions," said Rogers again. "And you take another swing at me, I'll break every bone in your body."

Quentin's gaze fell on Myers, who was seated across from him and tied to the chair she was in. "You bitch! You set me up."

"He was going to kill me, Josh," said Myers pitiably.

"Great!" spat Quentin. "Now this psycho's going to kill us both!"

Roger cuffed him on the jaw. "Shut up."

Quentin howled in pain until Rogers gripped him by the chin and twisted him around so they were eye to eye.

"Questions. You answer them, I don't kill you."

"Bullshit. You think I'm stupid?"

"I don't want you. I want her."

"Who?" said a bewildered Quentin.

"Claire," answered Myers. "He wants Claire Jericho."

Quentin took a moment to process this and then a wary look came into his eyes. "You want to kill Claire? Why?"

"I have my reasons."

"Josh, don't be crazy," barked Myers.

"Shut up, Helen," snapped Quentin. "I'm not giving up my life for hers."

Rogers looked at Myers. "It's your only way out."

"And you won't kill us if we deliver Jericho to you?" said Quentin.

"That's what I said."

"But we can identify you," pointed out Myers.

"I'm not going to be around."

She looked at his pale face. "Those scars. Are…are you dying?"

Rogers didn't answer her. He turned back to Quentin. "Where is she?"

"Not so fast," said Quentin. "If I'm talking about my life, I need to have some assurances."

Rogers gripped Quentin's neck harder.

Quentin gasped, "Look, if you kill me you've got no shot at her."

Rogers relaxed his grip. "Where is she?"

"She's in one of two places. Chris Ballard's place near here. Do you know where that is?"

Rogers nodded.

"Or at Building Q at Fort Monroe. Do you know it?"

"Intimately," replied Rogers. "But which one?"

"I can find out. It'll take one phone call."

Rogers was about to say something, but Quentin added, "You can listen in. I'm not screwing around with my life, okay?"

Myers said, "Quentin, please don't do this."

He ignored her. "But she has security. There's nothing I can do about that."

"That's not your problem, it's mine." Rogers held up

Quentin's phone, which he'd taken from his coat jacket. "*Text* her. Tell her you need to meet her here."

"I'm not sure she'll—"

Rogers gripped Quentin's neck again. "Be persuasive."

Rogers watched as Quentin took the phone, gave his message a few moments' thought, and then started to type.

When he was done he looked at Rogers for approval.

"Send it."

Quentin hit the send button and Rogers took the phone away from him. "Now we wait," he said. He looked over at Myers, who was quietly sobbing. "Look, if Jericho shows up I'm not going to hurt you."

"I know."

"Then why are you crying?"

"Because you're going to kill her."

Rogers looked puzzled. "What do you care?"

Myers didn't answer.

CHAPTER

60

PULLER, KNOX, AND Shepard were under the table in the café. Puller and Knox had their guns out. Shepard was screaming hysterically.

The café, which had been quiet moments before, had erupted into chaos as the customers screamed, ran, jumped, and shoved trying to escape.

Puller reached a hand over and gripped Shepard's shoulder. "You're okay," he said in a calming tone. "The shooter's gone. You're okay. Do you understand me?" He squeezed her shoulder reassuringly.

She finally quieted and gave him a jerky nod. "Okay."

"I want you to stay right here. The cops will be on their way. You're safe, okay, Anne? You're safe."

She gave him another nod and then a tight smile. "You...you saved my life."

"I'm glad I was here."

"Me too."

"We'll be back."

Puller and Knox reached the front door of the café. Puller did a turkey peek through the opening, found it clear, and they raced out into the street.

"How did you manage that?" she asked.

"I saw the shooter reflected in the mirror at the back of the café."

A woman was squatting down on the pavement crying. She saw Puller and Knox with their guns out. She put up her hands and said, "Please, don't shoot me."

Puller whipped out his badge. "I'm a cop. Are you hurt?"

She shook her head.

"Did you see the shooter?" asked Knox.

She pointed to her left. "Down that alley. Tall guy in a black hoodie with a rifle."

Puller and Knox raced off, turned the corner, and headed down the alley. They could hear police sirens in the distance. It was well dark now and Puller was listening to the pounding footsteps ahead of him.

They reached another street, turned left, and raced down it. They saw a shadow of movement dart down another alley.

They reached the opening, paused for a few moments, and then entered. They kept going, following the steps ahead. But when they stopped, so did Puller. He held up a hand for Knox to do the same.

Puller was in full combat mode now. And he wasn't liking what he was seeing.

He looked back at the other end of the alley. In the dark there wasn't much to see. But he had senses honed to such a fine degree that he could see what others couldn't.

"What is it?" Knox said in a whisper, hunkered down next to him.

Puller shook his head slightly. He could no longer hear the sirens. The police must have already reached the café.

It had been risky. Done in a public place. And the shooter letting himself be seen in the mirror? A rookie error? Or a calculated maneuver?

Because here we are, blocks away from the scene, in the middle of a dark alley with both flanks exposed.

Puller pulled out his second M11 from the holster in his rear waistband. He leaned into Knox. "Trap," he muttered. "Keep your eyes and ears open and your pistol ready."

She looked behind and then up ahead. "The woman back on the street?"

"Part of it," said Puller in a tone so low only she could hear. "Most people aren't that observant when shots are being fired. Should've seen that. She led us right here."

"What do we do now?"

"We move."

Keeping low, he led her twenty more feet down the alley, even as they both now heard footsteps behind them.

They were in a pincers trap that Puller knew well because he'd used it many times in combat. Whoever was back there had some military or at least paramilitary training.

If whoever was tracking them had NV goggles and/or laser sights, this would not be a long fight.

Which was why Puller did not intend to stay on the field of battle.

He looked over at the building adjacent to where they were and calculated something in his head. Then he and Knox ran another ten yards down the alley.

When Puller saw the door he suddenly hurtled sideways and slammed his thick shoulder into the wood. It gave under his two hundred and thirty pounds, the lock broke off, and the door swung inward. He and Knox dove inside a split second before a dozen rounds slammed into the exterior walls and through the open doorway.

Puller kicked the door closed behind them and looked around. They were in what looked to be an abandoned commercial building. The space was empty except for some boxes, a few odd pieces of furniture, and a lot of dirt and grime. The walls were brick and the windows were set high, their exterior sides covered with rusted metal grillwork.

There was a light switch set next to the door. Puller tried it. The building had no juice.

He took out a small but powerful flashlight and shone it around. There was a door on the other side of the large space.

Puller looked quickly around, found a long piece of wood, and used it to jam closed the door they had come through.

"That won't hold them long," pointed out Knox.

"But it will tell us when they enter the building," rebutted Puller.

They raced across the space and reached the other door. But Puller grabbed Knox by the arm to stop her before she went through.

He pointed both his M11s at the door they'd entered and emptied a half mag each through the door.

She looked at him questioningly.

"That just bought us another thirty seconds. The counter-fire will start up in about five clicks."

They hustled up the steps and a few more moments later heard the bullets ripping into the door Puller had fired through.

"Good combat instincts," said Knox as they high-kneed it up the stairs.

"You either gain them or you don't make it," said Puller.

"Someone has to hear the gunfire," said Knox.

"They're using suppressed rounds," said Puller. "The technology has gotten a lot better. This area of the town is deserted at night. And by the time someone does hear, we'll probably be dead."

"So what do we do?"

"We keep moving. Stationary targets are easy targets. That's why they use them on shooting ranges, so wannabes can feel good about themselves."

He kicked open the door and they were confronted by a set of steps. They took them two at a time and came to a hall that went off in both directions.

"That'll take us to the front of the building and that way to the rear," calculated Puller.

"So which one do we take?"

"Neither. They'll have them covered."

"This is nuts. I'm calling the cops."

She pulled out her phone and looked at it in disbelief: She had no bars.

Puller glanced at her. "I already checked mine. They're jamming the signal."

"Great. So you say we don't go fore or aft? Then where do we go?"

"We go up."

"What, so they can trap us on the roof?"

"Come on."

Puller led her down the hall until they reached a door marked *Stairs*. He pulled it open and they headed up.

They had heard the door they had initially come through open as the wood Puller had jammed there was broken. The sounds of footsteps had carried across the open lower floor.

Now the footsteps were echoing through the building. The men after them apparently didn't care if Puller and Knox knew they were coming. That was the confidence gained by superior numbers and firepower.

Puller led Knox up one flight of stairs after another until they reached the roof eight stories up. Puller forced the door and then used his Ka-Bar knife as a wedge on the hinge side of the door to jam it.

"Now what?" asked a perplexed Knox.

"You told me you ran track in college."

"Are you drunk?"

"Did you?" .

"Yes."

"Ever practice the long jump?"

"Yes, I was pretty good at it."

"Glad to hear that."

"Puller, what the—"

They heard footsteps racing up the steps to the roof.

He grabbed her hand. "Let's go."

"What?"

They sprinted flat-out toward the edge of the roof.

Knox's eyes bulged as she finally saw what his plan was. She started to scream but it died in her throat.

Puller's hand still clamped around hers, they reached the small ledge, pushed off, and soared over the alley below.

For a long moment it seemed like they were suspended in the air, moving neither forward nor back.

Their momentum carried them over the multistory drop.

They hit the roof of the adjacent building, tucked, and rolled.

Before Knox could even catch her breath, Puller jerked her up and pulled her toward the access door on the building's rooftop. He busted through it and pulled her inside and closed the door just as the men broke through the door on the roof of the building they had just been in. The armed men raced over the expanse of the roof looking for them.

Meanwhile, in the other building Puller and Knox clattered down the steps. They reached the ground floor and Puller found an exterior door leading to the side opposite the building they'd just leapt from. They pounded down the street.

Puller's unerring sense of direction led them back to their car about twenty minutes later. They climbed inside and Knox finally let out a deep breath.

He looked at her. She was pale and shaken, her eyes staring straight ahead, as though she were in a trance or on the edge of hysteria and trying desperately to hold it together. Her face was bruised, her arm badly scraped, and her jeans and shirt torn.

"You okay?" he asked anxiously.

She slowly nodded. "Thanks for saving my life." She paused. "And if you ever do something like that to me again, I swear to God I'll fucking kill you."

CHAPTER

61

PULLER BLINKED AWAKE the next morning. He had slept in his clothes. As he sat up he looked out the window of the motel room on the outskirts of Williamsburg, Virginia.

The sun was starting to rise. The angle of light hit him in the eyes and he turned away.

He heard water running. He sat up and looked around.

Knox was in the bathroom. They had decided to only take one room. There was safety in numbers.

Knox padded out of the bathroom. She had taken her jeans off and the T-shirt was too short to conceal her pale thighs.

"How's your arm?" asked Puller.

"Fine," she said curtly.

"You feeling sore? We hit pretty hard."

She didn't respond.

They had not talked last night. Knox clearly was too angry to do so and Puller couldn't come up with the words to initiate a productive discussion. He decided to try again, with a universally appealing opening.

"I'm sorry," said Puller. He paused and added, "I thought if I told you what I was planning you might freak out and not do it. Then we'd be dead."

She sat down on the corner of the bed and glared at him. "Have more faith in me next time," she said, though her tone was more conciliatory.

"I will."

She scooted up next to him and laid her head against the pillow. She closed her eyes and scrunched up her brow as she rubbed her injured arm.

"So they tried to kill Shepard and then tried to kill us. Led us right into a trap."

"Which tells me they're worried we're getting close to the truth."

"Who do you think those guys were?"

"My guess is mercenaries. They're a dime a dozen now. Probably brought in from another country. Even if we managed to track them down they could tell us nothing. Money wired to an offshore account from an untraceable source. I've seen that enough times."

"I get that when they're operating in the Middle East, but here? Hiring killers to come to this country and kill a DoD contractor?"

He glanced at her. "Well, some assholes came to this country and knocked down buildings using planes, right? So in my book anything is possible."

She sighed. "Right."

"We need to find Paul. And we need to get to Jericho."

"We have no idea where he is, and we have nothing on Jericho."

Before he could answer his phone rang. It was his brother. He put it on speaker and laid the phone between them so Knox could hear.

Puller took a minute to fill his brother in on what had just happened. Robert listened in silence that he let linger for a few moments after Puller was finished speaking.

"Things are coming to a head, John."

"Yeah, that I get. I just don't know whose head is going to be left on their shoulders."

"The guy you saw with Helen Myers is Anton Charpentier."

"Is he a spy?"

"No, he's a businessman. He's not the big force behind all this. That's my best estimate, anyway. But he is wired into some fairly substantial global business interests, and not all of them are allies of this country."

"Shepard told us that some of the things Atalanta Group was working on have enormous commercial applications. Billions, maybe trillions."

"They do. And which Atalanta Group is barred from exploiting. They don't have the rights to do so."

"She says it comes down to who holds the patents."

"Shepard was exactly right. And the person who holds all those particular patents is Chris Ballard."

"Ballard!" exclaimed Puller. "But he's retired now."

"But he locked up all the patents for years. In fact, they were issued personally to him as the inventor. Now, I doubt he was, at least for all of them, but the lawyers probably papered it that way. And any employee he had would be contractually bound to assign any IP rights over. Just the way it works."

"How do you know Ballard has the rights?" asked Knox.

"After I deciphered what was on the screen shots you took, I checked at the Patent Office."

"But why would you have thought to do that?" asked Knox.

"Because there has to be a *motive* behind all this. And nine times out of ten the motive is financial gain. And as you already pointed out, the patents issued to Ballard are potentially worth enormous sums in the commercial field."

"So could he exploit them commercially?" asked Puller.

"Yes. Atalanta Group is solely engaged as a defense contractor to build the technology they were working on in support of the Army. They're licensing technology from Ballard to do that work."

"Okay, but is *he* exploiting it commercially?" persisted Puller.

"Not that we know of. As you pointed out, he's officially retired."

Knox said, "But he has a corporation. Just because he's retired doesn't mean he can't build this stuff, right? And if it's so valuable, why wouldn't he?"

"I don't know. But I could find nothing that shows the Ballard organization is working on any of this. There may be a sub out there I'm missing, but I don't think so."

Puller said, "But Helen Myers is slipping the technology to this Charpentier guy. And Myers is getting it from Quentin, who works at Atalanta Group. The same place Jericho works. And she told us he's essentially her boss."

"Don't believe that for a minute," said Robert. "I think the only true boss Jericho has ever had is herself."

"So how is Quentin getting this information and why is he passing it to Charpentier?" asked Knox.

"I don't know," said Robert. "But we need to find out. This is a national security issue now, John."

"Can you get your folks to dive into this?"

"Doubtful. Even with what you showed me it's just not enough to bring out the cavalry yet. There are lots of issues to consider, not the least of which is the French are pretty strong allies of ours."

"But it's probably not the French government behind this, Bobby. It's the corporate side. And just because Charpentier is French doesn't mean he's not selling this stuff to the Russians or the Chinese. Like you said, it's a national security problem. And he's mixed up with people who are not allies of ours."

"Doesn't matter. We still have to tread very carefully."

"I don't see why," said Puller.

"Because we don't know how far this goes. Or how high the corruption is. These things don't tend to exist in a vacuum. There was a corruption case involving a Malaysian businessman and the Seventh Fleet. I think all told about two dozen officers, including ten or so admirals, were implicated. People had suspected before, but with so much firepower behind the corruption all attempts at intervention got whacked until it got so bad that the water boiled over and that brought everybody down. We might have a similar situation here. And if so, we can't run around screaming about it or everyone will cover their tracks."

"But what about Shepard and us nearly getting blown away? That doesn't make the water boil?"

"Proof of a connection, John. Do you have it?"

Puller let out an exasperated sigh. "So what now?"

"Any lead on this Paul guy?"

"No. But he wants Jericho badly. So maybe we reverse engineer it. We look for her and he might turn up."

"She spends time at the Ballard estate in North Carolina, that I know. They're still apparently very close."

Knox said, "I can track down property that Quentin might own."

"And do the same with Helen Myers," said Puller. "She's up to her neck in this too. And let's see if we can get a handle on where they are right now."

"Sounds like a plan," said his brother.

The line went dead. Puller glanced over at Knox. She was working away on her phone.

"Got any databases that will help us?"

"I'm doing my best," said Knox.

"Well, let's try an obvious place first."

He tossed her the ripped jeans. She sat up and started to pull them on. Puller watched as her legs slipped into them. She stopped with the pants halfway up her thighs and looked at him.

"What?"

"Nothing."

He quickly turned around and fumbled with his knapsack.

* * *

They drove to the Grunt.

"No one's going to be there this early," pointed out Knox as they walked down the alley toward the bar.

"I don't care. I'll break inside and look around."

However, as they approached the front of the bar they saw a light on inside. Puller knocked and the door was answered a few moments later by a young man.

"Can I help you?"

Puller flashed his creds. "I was here the night of the shooting. You were working behind the bar, I think."

"That's right. I remember you."

"What are you doing here this early?"

"Ms. Myers asked me to come in when the police released the bar. I'm just checking on stuff, cleaning up."

"Thinking about reopening?" asked Knox.

"That will be up to Ms. Myers."

"Speaking of, any idea where she is?"

The man shook his head. "She has a house in town, but I know she's not there. It's on the way here. When I passed it the place was dark and her car was gone."

"She have another place?" asked Puller.

"Yeah, a beach house in North Carolina. She might be there. It's only a couple hours away."

"You have the address?"

"I do, but I don't think I should give it out."

Puller held up his creds again. "It says United States Army. We're the good guys. And she might be in danger. We think she might have been the target for the shooters."

"Omigod, really?"

"Really. The address?"

They left the Grunt a minute later with a piece of paper with the beach house address. They got into the car and Puller drove off.

Knox was looking at her phone. She hit some keys, plugging in the address.

"The guy was right, it's only about two hours from here. And there's something else."

"What?"

"This address is only about thirty minutes from Ballard's estate."

"Interesting and probably not a coincidence."

"You think Myers is working with Ballard?" said Knox.

"Why would Ballard steal his own secrets and hand them off to this Charpentier guy?"

"Crap. This case is a real mess."

"And getting messier all the time."

CHAPTER

62

ONE BREATH, TWO breaths, three breaths.

Myers was asleep, still tied up in the chair. Her head drooped on to her chest, her hair hanging limp. She mumbled sometimes but he couldn't make out any words.

Josh Quentin was asleep too, and, like Myers, bound to another chair.

They had gotten a text back last night from Jericho that she was busy but would be able to meet with them in the morning. The important thing was she was coming here. And he knew exactly how he was going to kill her.

He felt it coming on, so he got up and rushed from the room. He reached the bathroom just in time and threw up in the toilet. He got out of his clothes because his body felt literally on fire. He climbed into the shower and turned the water on as cold as it would go. It still felt like he was in a steam bath. Or a furnace. It was as though the water was hitting his skin and evaporating from the heat.

He grabbed the pipe stem of the shower head and squeezed. He felt the metal give under his grip and let go before he crushed it.

He slumped against the tile, counting his breaths but

still losing control, feeling the enormous weight of hopelessness settle down on him.

He was Atlas without the requisite strength.

For the first time in his tortured life, Paul Rogers wasn't sure he could actually do this. He didn't know if he would survive long enough. It would be a cruel irony if he were to drop dead at the woman's feet, inches from his decades-long goal of snuffing out her life.

He climbed out of the shower, toweled off, and sat on the toilet. The pain finally subsided, the internal fires lessened in their intensity. He put his clothes back on and returned to the room where Myers and Quentin were still sleeping.

He sat down and was surprised when Myers lifted her head, opened her eyes, and looked at him.

"I know you have good reason to hate her," she said.

Rogers glanced at her, held her gaze steady for a few protracted moments, and then looked away, staring at the gap between his feet.

She glanced over at Quentin. "I wouldn't trust him."

"I don't trust *anyone*," said Rogers, looking at her so fiercely that she changed color and looked down.

"What are you going to do with me?"

"I told you. Jericho gets here, you're free."

"I saw what you did to those men at the bar. I don't think that's the first time you've killed someone."

He looked up at her. "I was created to kill. It's really the only reason for my existence."

"I'm not sure I've ever heard anything more awful than that."

He said nothing to this because he had nothing to add.

"Those scars? What did they do to you?"

"The scars made me strong." He tapped his head. "But this is what made me a killer."

Myers started to say something, but Rogers held up a hand. "No more talk."

Time ticked away.

Night passed to morning.

Myers fell asleep again.

Quentin had never awoken, perhaps safe in the belief that his treacherous actions would allow for his survival.

Rogers just stared at the floor.

Until eight o'clock in the morning came.

When the sound of the approaching car made him go to the window.

It was a black SUV. It pulled into the driveway and she got out.

Claire Jericho, in the flesh. She was dressed in a dark pantsuit.

He gasped and then drew a long breath. He could barely believe she was here, that he was, after all this time, only a few feet away from the woman who had destroyed him. He felt his body heat up like someone had lighted a fire under him. It was all he could do not to jump through the window, grab her, and finish it.

Rogers raced over to Quentin, roused him, untied him, and told him what to do. Then he ran into the bathroom, got a washcloth, and stuffed it inside Myers's mouth so she couldn't call out.

Her panicked eyes looked back at him.

"It'll all be over soon enough," Rogers said.

He turned and grabbed Quentin by the arm. "You step one inch out of line I will crush your skull."

Quentin nodded, smoothed out his shirt, ran a hand through his hair, and headed downstairs, with Rogers right behind him.

They reached the front door right as the knock came.

Rogers peeked out the sidelight. It was just Jericho. Whoever else was in the SUV had remained there.

Quentin opened the door and motioned Jericho inside. She stepped through the threshold.

Rogers closed his eyes and in his mind everything the woman had done to him came roaring back like a tsunami inside his skull. He opened his eyes. He was done counting breaths.

He pulled the vintage M11-B from his waistband.

He would point it against her head.

He would see how she liked it. Then he would put the gun down and cram the ring down her throat.

And finally he would strangle her with the hands she had made stronger than a gorilla's.

For the greater good. You can carry it to eternity.

Rogers was about to strike when the gas hit him in the face.

He remembered those eyes staring at him, just as they had three decades ago.

They were probing, piercing, and missed nothing. They were X-ray eyes if there ever was such a thing.

She didn't smile. She didn't laugh. She didn't look gloating or triumphant.

She simply looked mildly curious.

Rogers's body tensed and then relaxed as the vapor settled in his lungs for an instant before his bloodstream sent it barreling to his brain.

And a moment later everything shut down. Unconscious, he dropped to the floor at her feet.

Jericho looked down at him and then nudged his rock-hard shoulder with her foot.

"It's good to finally see you again, Dimitri."

CHAPTER

63

I T SHOULD BE this one," said Knox.

They had crossed over into North Carolina about ninety minutes ago. It was now after nine in the morning as Puller turned into the driveway of the large beach house.

"The Grunt must be a cash machine," said Knox as they got out of the car.

"I think selling stolen government secrets is probably more lucrative," replied Puller dryly.

They walked up to the front of the house.

"Puller, the door is open," said Knox.

Puller already had his gun out; Knox followed suit.

He looked down at the asphalt drive. "That looks like a fresh oil spot," he said, pointing to a dollop of liquid.

They stepped to the side of the front door and Puller gave it a nudge with his foot. It swung open and he did a quick look inside.

He eyed Knox and motioned with his head.

She ducked into the house, her gun pointing center left. Puller followed her performing his arc center right. They cleared the first floor and then checked the garage.

"That's Myers's BMW," said Puller. "I don't know whose Maserati that is."

Knox opened the door to the Maserati, popped the glove box, and took out the registration.

"Josh Quentin."

"Okay, this is starting to make sense."

"Do you think they're here?" asked Knox.

"We have more house to search, but I didn't hear anything."

"You think they're dead?"

"I think we'd better check."

They moved up the stairs and went room by room on the second floor. In a bedroom, Puller reached down and picked up a length of rope and a balled-up washcloth.

Knox said, "Looks like someone was restrained. Who do you think it was? Myers?"

"I don't know."

They split up, with Knox taking half the floor and Puller the other half. Knox cleared her section and then found Puller in one of the bathrooms.

"Find anything?"

He pointed around the toilet. "Looks like someone was sick to their stomach."

Knox wrinkled her nose. "Smells like it too."

"And then there's this." He led her over to the shower. "Check out the pipe."

She looked at it. "Someone nearly crushed it. Did you check for a tool mark?"

"It doesn't look like a tool was used. From what I'm seeing it was someone's fingers."

"That pipe is metal and it has to be thick enough to withstand the water pressure."

"I can think of only one guy who could make metal seem like putty."

"Paul. So he was here. Do you think he was the one tied up?"

Puller shook his head. "That rope never would have held him."

"So he had someone tied up. Myers?"

"It's her house. But it could be Quentin."

"I wonder how Paul found out about this place?"

"I don't know. But he apparently was here."

"But why would he think Myers has anything to do with Jericho?"

"I don't know, Knox! Unless he stumbled onto what they're doing in that upstairs room at the bar."

"I guess he could have. He worked there."

Puller examined the couch and then focused on something. "It's a few strands of hair fiber." He picked them up. "Doesn't look like Myers's. Maybe Josh Quentin's? His car's in the garage too."

"Maybe that's who Paul was looking for? Maybe he followed Quentin down here. And didn't even know Myers was going to be here."

"That could be."

"And we know he and Myers are working together to pass secrets. It would make sense that they might meet here," noted Knox.

"So Paul, Myers, and Quentin were all here together. And people tied up with washcloths balled up in their mouths so they couldn't cry out and warn someone."

"So Paul was holding them both? And now where are they? Did he take them somewhere?"

Puller nodded. "It's certainly possible. Maybe to get to Building Q? To get to Jericho?"

"Okay, but if so, how do we get in there without an invite?"

"Maybe we need to make our own invitation."

"How?"

"We have a two-hour drive to come up with one."

CHAPTER

64

ROGERS SLOWLY OPENED his eyes. He felt like a tank round had been fired right next to his brain. Cloudy, fuzzy, unfocused. Like he and Johnnie Walker Black had been on a drinking binge for a month.

And he couldn't move his arms or legs.

Slap.

The hand hit him lightly on the jaw.

He blinked rapidly and focused on the person next to him.

Claire Jericho stared back at him.

He was lying on a gurney. He was not bound, but he couldn't move. He licked his dry lips.

"What did you do to me?" he asked quietly.

"Nothing too remarkable. Anesthetic gas. How are you feeling?"

"I can't move my limbs."

"Nerve blockers. Brachial plexus and femoral nerve, among others. We used those before on you."

"And why did you do that?" he said, his teeth gritted.

"Well, there aren't many restraints that can hold you. I thought this best. It's not painful. And it does wear off."

He looked around. "What is this place?"

"This place is safe, Dimitri."

"My name is Paul."

"That's right. Paul Rogers."

She pulled up a chair and sat down next to him.

"How did Quentin tip you off?" he asked.

"He didn't. He followed your instructions to the letter."

"How did you know I'd be there, then?"

"Josh Quentin never summons me," she said simply. "But I was already on my guard."

"Why?"

She slipped a small notebook from her jacket pocket and opened it to the first page. "You were convicted of second-degree murder. You served ten years of a fifteen-year sentence and then were paroled. Unfortunately, you were paroled a day early because of a clerical error."

"How did you know? They couldn't take my prints."

"DNA," she interjected. "They took DNA from you. And when that DNA sample was eventually picked up by us four years ago we knew where you were."

"If you knew four years ago why didn't you come for me then?"

"We couldn't very well do that. You *had* killed someone. But we kept watch and we are very glad to have you back."

"Why?"

"For testing, of course. When we designed the system we had no real idea of its longevity. But with you here now, we can run precise tests that will tell us exactly the durability of what we placed inside you."

Rogers said, "I've been back to Building Q. Nothing has changed."

"If only that were true, Paul. What we're doing now is mundane and unimaginative and, quite frankly, dull. Exoskeletons? Nano–muscle fiber for a paltry thirty percent strength boost? We more than *quadrupled* your strength

NO MAN'S LAND   407

metrics. And exos are cumbersome, heavy, severely limited. Better NV goggles? Who really cares? Now, the liquid armor concept is something different, but not that terribly innovative. With bionic boots we get past the limiting factors of the spaghetti strap we call our Achilles' heel, but, again, that's not a game changer." She rubbed her hand over his immobile arm. "Nothing comes close to what we did with you, Paul. You fulfilled our mission of creating a meta-biologically dominant soldier." She removed her hand. "But the Pentagon shut down the whole program. It really was the most misguided decision and has set us back decades. The wars in the Middle East would have been far different if we'd had a division made up of soldiers like you. Far different." She reached up and touched the spot on his head. "And this, this was the crowning achievement. This made everything else we did to enhance you secondary." She paused and then added in a reverent tone, "A fighting machine who has no fear. It was the greatest attribute one could bestow on a soldier."

"Fear is necessary in a war, if you're the one fighting it," said Rogers through clenched teeth.

"Nonsense. Fear makes one weak. A soldier who feels is not a real soldier."

"I wasn't aware you knew what it was like to be in combat."

She shook her head again, her expression now one of disappointment. "That's hardly the point, is it?"

She looked back at her notebook. "Two people were found murdered in an alley near the depot where the bus you took from prison dropped you off. We also found your parole papers in the trash can. Then you no doubt made your way across the country. Stolen cars, probably. And then we come to West Virginia."

She turned the page.

"A gun dealer, Mike Donohue, was murdered in West Virginia. The police report said that a knife had been driven through his chest with such force that it had pinned him to the wall of his trailer. An astonishing feat of strength. Donohue was a large man with a deep, thick torso."

She reached over to a table and picked up the M11-B. "And this was the only thing the police could find that was missing from Donohue's truck. I take it you were going to hold it against my head, as I did you that one time. Revolver versus semiautomatic. You obviously didn't want to leave my death to the whims of chance."

Rogers said nothing. He just stared at the ceiling.

She put the gun down and turned back to her notebook.

"The one thing that truly disturbed me, Paul, had to do with the boy. Donohue's son, Will."

"I didn't kill him."

"*That's* what disturbs me."

With a roar of rage Rogers managed to flip himself off the table. He landed at her feet but couldn't move an inch after that.

She stared down at him. "Now what did that accomplish? Really?"

She pulled a phone from her pocket, made a call, and four men arrived. They lifted Rogers back onto the gurney and this time strapped him down. With a wave of her hand she dismissed them and they were alone once more.

"Are you able to have a civil conversation now?"

"What the fuck do you want with me?"

"I already told you. Testing. I can't stress enough how critical this is."

"Why? You're not building *freaks* like me anymore."

"Granted, we're not building *soldiers* like you now, but I

strongly feel that we should. And you will help me to make others see that."

"I went out of control. I murdered people."

"That was unfortunate. But every grand vision has sacrifice."

"Those women? I was murdering you over and over. Because I couldn't get to you."

"I'm well aware that the killings were symbolic. But those women were all doing their jobs, Paul. We lost a lot of talent. I was very disappointed that you did that."

"*You* were disappointed!" he screamed. "You made me a fucking killing machine!"

She put a calming hand on his shoulder. "You're right. It wasn't your fault. It was an error on our part. But we were in brand-new territory. That comes with risk. Look at the science of flight. Do you know how many pilots died so that we can now safely travel from one side of the world to the other in a matter of hours?" She paused. "But now, with you back in the fold, we can find out where we went wrong. If we find the right answers and make the required adjustments, then we can restart the program and do this the right way. You know, for the longest time I thought you were dead. And then to find you in prison, well, it held a lot of potential. We just had to get you out of there."

"I was paroled. *I* got me out."

"Well, that's not exactly how it happened. Your first two parole hearings did not go well, as I understand it. But we pulled a few strings and made sure the third time did the trick."

He stared over at her.

"We really wanted you back, Paul. But then we lost track of you. After you escaped you must have gone underground. And it's not like we had the resources back then that we have today to find you. And we couldn't very well call the police and list you as a missing person."

"I got as far away from you as I could."

"I didn't realize you were working at the bar as a bouncer until very recently."

"You sent those men to kill me."

"No. I sent them there to bring you to me."

"They were trying to kill me!"

"No, at least not at first. One of them managed to get away. He later told me that things got out of hand. Someone tried to stop them before they got to the bar, a very large older man."

"His name was Karl."

"Yes, Karl. Then when they got to you, well, you started killing them. And then it was kill or be killed. I thought I had sent enough men, but I was wrong apparently. His description of your fighting prowess was quite detailed. If this had been a test, you would have passed with flying colors. It was quite exciting."

"Innocent people died," he snapped. "Because of what you did."

"Yes, well . . . as I said, sacrifice."

"Go to hell!"

She patted his shoulder again. "I want to understand how you came to control the impulse to kill, Paul."

He looked away from her.

"Please, this is very important."

She waited but he said nothing.

"How did you not kill the boy, Will Donohue? If you can explain to me your process for doing that I believe that we can make the necessary adjustments that will ensure we will never have that problem again."

He looked at her. "A super soldier that doesn't want to kill? How exactly does that work?"

"You misunderstood me. I meant *programmed* to kill only the enemy."

"And who exactly decides who the enemy is?"

"That's not part of my mission. Others decide that. Political leaders."

"That makes me feel much better."

"It needn't be complicated, Paul. Just tell me how you did it."

Rogers suddenly moaned, and if his limbs hadn't been useless he would have clutched at the spot on his head.

An excited Jericho rose from her seat, raced across the room, and rolled a monitoring machine over to the gurney. She hurriedly attached electrodes to Rogers's temples, and then opened his shirt and placed sensors on his chest and one at his neck.

She turned on the machine and studied the screen. She clicked some buttons on the attached keyboard and studied the results. All the while Rogers moaned and screamed. Then he turned his head to the side and threw up.

Jericho did not appear to notice.

"Fascinating," she said. "But we really need to hook you up to 3-D imaging, body scanners, that sort of thing. The equipment we have today is light-years ahead of what we were using thirty years ago. That will give us the clearest picture of what is going on. And a full blood workup, of course. It will take a long time, but I'm going to get this right. I promise you that."

She made the call and twenty minutes later Rogers was being rolled into another room, still in intense pain. He was laid in a tube and run through a scanner.

Jericho studied the screen showing the inner workings of his body. "What level of pain are you feeling, Paul? Please be as precise as you can. And what is the frequency of the attacks?"

"Fuck you!" he screamed.

"We're wasting valuable time. I don't know when you might have another episode like this."

Rogers didn't answer. Evidently frustrated with him, Jericho continued to study the screen.

"This is truly fascinating," she said. "I can already see where improvements can be made." She began to jot down some notes on an electronic tablet. "I'm going to pull up your old records and compare them to what I'm seeing now. This will allow me to dig further into the progression. Do your joints hurt? We were using composites before anyone knew what they could really do. Stronger than steel, more malleable than plastic. But the scan does evidence some breaking down of the limb structures. But the brain implant is the most fascinating."

"Shut up!" screamed Rogers.

She went on as though she hadn't heard him. "Do you know that your brain has woven a nerve circuitry around the implant? And also *pierced* it." She paused and then added excitedly, "Your *brain* is inside the implant. That may be the source of—"

"Shut up!"

She fell silent, but her lips moved as she apparently was talking to herself. Her eyes shone with the wonderment of all that she was seeing, while Rogers lay there in utter misery.

As the pain began to subside he looked over at her engrossed in the screen.

He just wanted to put an end to the madness.

To her.

And then to himself.

"That wasn't Ballard," he said.

This got her attention. She turned to him.

"So it *was* you who threw him out the window."

"And I don't think the other guy is either. So where is he?"

"Don't worry, Paul, it'll all be over soon."

"A lot of things will soon be over," he said.

Including you.

"I'll be back," she said. "I just need to check on some things."

She left the room and Rogers stared up at the ceiling. He tried to move his arms and legs, but nothing worked.

Shit!

He was running out of time and options.

When the door opened again he didn't even turn to look at her.

"Paul?"

Now he did turn.

Suzanne Davis was standing there.

She walked over to him and looked down.

"I'm sorry," she said. "I wish I could do something to help you."

He shrugged. "Is she the 'rich' one who adopted you?"

"Yes."

Rogers looked away and shook his head. If he could move his arms right now he would reach into his head and rip the thing out.

"She ever give a reason?" he said.

Davis looked away. "Maybe she was lonely."

Rogers turned to stare at the ceiling again. "You need to think about that some more. At some point, she'll get tired of you. And then...?"

"Can you move?"

"They got me shot up with shit. Where are we, by the way?"

"Same place."

"Where's Ballard? The real Ballard?"

She shook her head.

"Can't or won't tell?"

She just shook her head again.

"It doesn't matter, I'm dead anyway."

She ran her finger down his arm. "Why did you come back? You could be anywhere else."

"Do you know what she did to me?"

"A little."

"Then you should understand that I had to come back."

"I guess I do."

They heard a noise from somewhere nearby.

Davis leaned down and kissed Rogers on the cheek. "I'm really sorry." Then she turned and left.

Rogers slowly looked back at the ceiling.

And started to count.

CHAPTER

65

"Y OU THINK HE'S in there?"

Knox was watching Puller, who was looking through binoculars at Building Q from a hiding place across the street.

"Maybe." Puller lowered his binoculars. "If he is, Jericho has to be there too. But we have to be sure."

"Okay, how do you propose doing that?"

"Well, the direct approach might be best." He handed her the binoculars. "If I'm not back in twenty minutes, call the cops."

She looked startled but nodded.

Puller hustled across the street and up to the front gate. When the guards headed out to confront him he held up his creds and badge.

One of the guards said, "You were here before."

"That's right. To meet with Claire Jericho. She called and asked me to meet her right now."

The guards looked puzzled. The one who had recognized Puller said, "But she's not here."

"Are you sure?"

"I've been on duty since oh six hundred. She checked out last night and she has not signed back in."

Puller looked confused. "I don't get it. She called maybe thirty minutes ago and said to meet her at Fort Monroe." He looked over their shoulders at Building Q. "This is the only facility she works at here, right?"

"Far as I know."

"How about Josh Quentin? I know him too."

"No. He hasn't come in yet."

"Thanks."

Puller hustled back across the street and joined Knox. He quickly explained what the guard had told him.

"Where, then?" asked Knox.

"She needs a private, secure place."

Knox snapped, "Ballard's place."

"That's what I'm thinking."

* * *

Two hours later they were back in the Tar Heel State. Puller had called his brother and filled him in on what they had found and where they were going.

"Please tell me you're not going to break into Ballard's mansion," said Robert.

"Okay, I won't tell you," replied Puller.

"Holy shit, John, will you just take a breath and think about this? Now instead of screwing your career, you could go to jail. Or even be killed."

"Thanks, Bobby. God knows I'm not used to putting my life on the line," he added dryly.

Puller put the phone away and checked his watch. "We'll wait until dark and then recon the place. I'm sure it's well guarded, but every facility has weaknesses."

Day drifted to night. They sat in their car in a public parking lot off the beach.

Puller checked his watch. It was eleven.

"Let's go."

He popped the trunk and pulled out from his duffel a set of NV goggles.

"Good thing I didn't have my duffel in the car when we went into the water."

"Yeah, good thing it was just *us* in the car," shot back Knox.

They hoofed it as close to Ballard's place as they could without the possibility of being seen. Hidden behind a sand dune, Puller powered up his goggles and took a sweep of the place.

"Initial conclusions?" asked Knox a minute later.

"My brother was being quite literal when he called it a fortress."

"Great."

"High stone walls. Big gate, exterior security, and I'm betting internal sweeps. No doubt they have electronic surveillance as well."

"Just another quiet, relaxed day at the beach."

"Paul said he got in there."

"Yeah, well he's Superman *and* Spider-Man rolled into one, remember?"

"Let's time the security sweeps for the next hour and go from there."

Puller shimmied up a tree and viewed the interior of the compound's courtyard.

A few minutes later an SUV pulled down the road and the gates opened to admit it. Puller watched as it swung into the courtyard and backed up to a set of French doors. Men got out of the vehicle and opened its rear doors.

The French doors opened a moment later and Puller watched as a gurney was rolled out. It was quickly loaded into the back of the SUV.

Puller climbed back down. When his boots hit sand he grabbed Knox's arm.

"What's going on?" she said.

"They're transferring a 'patient.'"

"What patient? Ballard?"

"Not Ballard. Paul."

"You're sure?"

"I saw him."

They reached their car as the SUV passed. Puller slipped in behind the other vehicle.

"Where do you think they're taking him?" asked Knox.

"We're not going to find out."

"What!"

"Hold on."

Puller sped up, cut to the left, hit the gas, paralleled the SUV, and rammed it with his car.

"Shit, Puller!" exclaimed Knox as she grabbed a hand-hold on the ceiling of the car.

The SUV veered over and rammed Puller's car back.

The bumpers locked, which was what Puller had been hoping for. He hit the brakes and forced the other vehicle to slow and then go off the road. He slammed the car into park and jumped out, gun in one hand and his badge in the other.

"Federal officers, get out of the vehicle. Now!"

Knox had emerged from the passenger side and had her gun out too.

"Now!" barked Puller. "Or we will open fire. You are completely surrounded and we have a chopper coming in."

The two front doors of the vehicle opened and two men got out, hands up.

Puller said, "On the ground, facedown, hands behind your head, fingers interlocked. Do it. Now!"

The men hit the dirt and did what he ordered.

Knox cleared the rest of the car. It was empty except for Rogers in the far back.

Puller cuffed the two men and then ran to the back of the SUV and threw open the doors. Rogers looked at him groggily. "What are you doing here?"

"Saving your butt. Can you walk?"

Rogers shook his head. "Temporary nerve blockers."

Puller hefted Rogers over his shoulder and carried him to their car and put him in the backseat, buckling him in.

"Hey!" screamed one of the cuffed men on the ground. "What about us?"

"Hire a good lawyer," replied Knox.

Puller managed to disentangle the bumpers and then he pointed the vehicle back toward Virginia.

From the backseat Rogers said, "They took Josh Quentin and Helen Myers. They were with me when Jericho came and gassed me."

"Why were they with you?" asked Puller.

"I wanted to use them to get to Jericho. But she tricked me. She took me somewhere and performed all these tests on me. She wants to figure out what went wrong and then restart the program. She's fucking nuts."

"Where were you when she took you?" asked Knox.

"At Quentin's, or now I know it's Myers's beach house. You know where that is?"

Puller nodded. "Yeah, but what time was that?"

"Around eight in the morning."

"We got there at nine and searched the place. There was no one there. But we did see Myers's and Quentin's cars in the garage."

His phone buzzed. It was his brother.

Puller took a couple minutes filling him in, but it appeared his brother was just waiting for him to finish before conveying his own information.

"We just found out something," said Robert.

"What?"

"Josh Quentin's body washed ashore on the Outer Banks this afternoon."

Puller sucked in a quick breath. "Homicide?"

"Clearly."

"Cause of death?"

"Appears his skull was crushed in." He paused. "Maybe like some of the dead women."

Puller glanced in the rearview at Rogers.

"Thanks for the info, Bobby."

"What are you going to do with him?"

"Right now, I'm not sure."

CHAPTER

66

PULLER CLOSED THE curtains in the motel room in Hampton and turned back to Rogers, who was lying on the bed, still immobilized.

Knox was sitting in a chair next to the bed, gun in hand. Puller had filled her in on what his brother had told him.

Rogers eyed them. "What is it?"

Puller told him about Josh Quentin.

"I didn't do it."

"And we should just accept that as gospel?" retorted Knox, gripping her pistol.

His gaze drifted to the gun. "Aim for the head or the heart. Otherwise it won't stop me."

"Son of a bitch," said Knox, shaking her head. "This is like sci-fi."

Puller sat down in another chair and faced Rogers. "Okay, we need to have a come-to-Jesus meeting. Where have you been all these years?"

"Wandered around. Did some really bad shit but didn't get caught. Then I was in prison for the last ten for manslaughter. Then I got paroled."

"So you're in violation of that parole."

"I'm in violation of a lot of things."

"Have you killed anyone else since you left prison, other than those guys who attacked you at the bar?"

"What do you care?"

"I'm trying to understand you, Paul. So I can decide whether to help you or throw you in a cage forever."

Rogers looked away. "Two people in an alley who tried to rob me after I left prison. Then a gun dealer in West Virginia I stole an M11 pistol from. I wouldn't have killed him, but he was going to shoot me."

Knox and Puller exchanged glances. Puller said, "Why would you need a gun?"

"I wanted to return the favor for something Jericho did to me."

Puller said, "A gun dealer? West Virginia? I heard that on the news."

"That's right."

Knox said, "But his kid was with him. And he wasn't harmed."

Rogers said nothing.

Puller said, "Why didn't you kill the boy too? He was a witness."

"I...I just didn't."

"So you *can* control your...impulses?"

"I did then."

"Do you know where they were taking you?"

"Probably to dump me in the ocean like Josh Quentin. Jericho had finished her tests and I'd told her what I knew about Ballard."

Puller tensed. "You told us you'd tossed an imposter out the window but there was another man on the beach later. That must be the real Ballard."

"I think the real Ballard is dead."

"So why would they pretend that he's still alive?" asked Knox.

Puller was quiet for a few moments before saying, "My brother told us that Ballard personally controlled all the patents for the technology that Jericho was selling off to private interests." He looked at a quizzical Rogers. "That's what was going on in the upstairs room at the bar. Quentin passed the secrets to Myers and she slipped them to some French businessman. Stuff was worth a fortune."

Knox said, "So let's say Ballard really is dead. I wonder where the ownership of those patents goes?"

Puller said, "His will would tell us that. But I don't think they were going to Jericho. So if he is dead they might use the decoy old guys to keep up the impression that Ballard is alive. Maybe they performed plastic surgery to make them look like Ballard. I guess when you have that much at stake, you'd do pretty much anything."

"But when people visited wouldn't they know the person wasn't Ballard when he started talking?"

"Not if they said he had Alzheimer's or dementia or something like that. Then nobody would expect him to...to be able to be who he was."

Knox looked at him and seemed to understand that Puller could easily have been talking about his father.

Knox looked over at Rogers. "This guy has already admitted to killing one of the decoys plus others. We don't know that he didn't kill Quentin. I think we need to go to the co—"

Knox didn't finish her sentence, because Rogers had leapt up, stripped Knox of her gun, spun her around, and held the weapon to her head.

Puller swung his pistol around, but Rogers said, "Put it down or she's dead."

"You don't have to do this, Paul."

"Just call me Rogers. Neither one is my real name, so who cares?"

"You can't go it alone," said Puller.

"Put the gun down, Puller. I won't ask again. And I don't care if I die. But I think your partner here does."

Puller slowly lowered his gun.

Rogers immediately let go of Knox and handed her gun back to her. He sat down on the bed and rubbed the back of his head while they both gazed down at him.

He glanced up at them. "The nerve block wore off before we even got here."

"So why didn't you kill us when you had the chance?" said Puller.

"And why give me my gun back?" added Knox.

"I didn't kill Quentin."

He got up and went into the bathroom, where they could hear him being violently sick.

Puller looked at Knox. "I believe him."

"So do I."

"He seems to be falling apart."

Rogers staggered out of the bathroom a few minutes later and fell on to the bed.

"You going to be okay?" asked Puller.

"No, I'm not, but I'm still going to get Jericho."

"Quentin is dead. Maybe Myers is too. Jericho might be tying up loose ends."

"That doesn't mean she's not dead. And there's another gal too, Suzanne Davis."

"The one who saved your life back at the bar?" said Puller.

"Jericho apparently adopted her. She was at Ballard's. She knows what's going on too. She sort of babysits the old guys."

Puller glanced at Knox. "If we can get to either of them, Myers or Davis, we could use them to nail Jericho."

"That's a long shot, since we don't know where they are, or whether they'll cooperate."

"It's the only shot we have." Puller looked at Rogers. "How *have* you controlled the impulse to kill over the years, Rogers?"

Rogers took a chest full of air and let it go. "At first I thought it was something that I worked through when I was in isolation in prison. But Jericho took a brain scan during her testing. She said my brain had rewired itself both in and around the implant. So maybe that was it. I don't know. I'm not a scientist. I'm just the guinea pig."

"So maybe who you used to be is coming back?" suggested Puller.

Rogers gaped at him. It was clear he had never considered this possibility.

"I'm not sure I even remember who I was," he said quietly.

"But why all these painful attacks?" asked Knox.

Rogers rubbed his legs. "They installed an endoskeleton made of composites. Made me the strongest person on earth."

"So what's happening to it?" asked Knox.

"After thirty years it appears to be dissolving. Or maybe my body's finally rejecting it, I don't know."

"Is there any way to reverse it?" asked Puller.

"Not so anyone's told me."

Puller and Knox exchanged a glance. Puller shook his head.

Knox said, "Okay, then we need to get to Davis and/or Myers. I have to believe that if they're alive they're at Ballard's."

Rogers said, "I got into the place before. I can do it again."

"But this time we'll be with you," said Puller.

CHAPTER

67

"YOU SCALED THAT wall with no rope?"

Puller, Knox, and Rogers were flat on their bellies on the beach looking up at the Ballard compound. They had on black ski masks pulled down over their faces.

Behind them the ocean surf beat on relentlessly, covering any noises they might have made.

Rogers held up his hand and flexed his fingers. "This is all I need."

Puller carried a loop of rope over one shoulder.

Their plan was fairly straightforward. Rogers would scale the wall and then use the rope to get Puller and Knox to the top of it.

They had watched the sentries making their rounds. The guards had changed it up from the last time Rogers had been here, but there were still gaps in the system.

"They're going to be on higher alert," said Knox. "They know you got away and that you're with us."

"And we're not going to kill any of them unless we have to," Puller said to Rogers.

The man shrugged. "If they try to kill me, I will kill them. You got a problem with that, stay on the beach."

Puller stared at him for a long moment. "Actually, that's the same rule I have."

They had chosen the far left corner of the wall to make their ascent. Rogers had given his shoes and socks to Puller, who'd put them in his small knapsack.

Puller and Knox watched as Rogers, the rope looped around his shoulder, scaled the wall like he was walking down the street. He reached the top, scanned all around, and then lifted himself onto the top of the wall and lay flat.

Knox looked at Puller. "Okay, now I've seen everything."

"You might see even more in just a few minutes."

Rogers let the rope down, wound the other end around his waist, and gripped the edge of the capstone as he served as the anchor point for the other two.

Knox went first, and within ten seconds she was lying next to Rogers.

Puller joined them in about the same amount of time.

They peered into the courtyard, saw that their way was clear, and used the same process to descend into the courtyard. They raced to a far corner of one of the outbuildings and took stock of their situation.

They shrank farther back as an armed guard came into view and met up with another on rounds. The men briefly spoke before moving on separately.

Rogers pointed to an upstairs window on the main house. "That's Davis's room."

"How do you know that?" asked Knox.

"I brought her here after she went on a bender at the Grunt. Ballard's room is at the top. He's got most of the floor. Or whoever it is up there. I don't know where Myers might be."

"And they know you killed the 'fake' Ballard?" whispered Puller.

Rogers nodded. "I told Jericho."

Puller nodded and pulled from his knapsack two metal objects roughly the size of his hand. "Ready?"

They both nodded.

"Go."

Knox and Rogers crept around the interior of the courtyard, closely following the track of the guards making their rounds. When they got near the front entrance they stopped.

Knox looked at her watch, counted down, and then gave a thumbs-up to Rogers.

A second later the quiet was broken by glass being shattered, followed by twin explosions. Smoke started pouring out of the upstairs windows of the main house.

Screams were heard, an alarm went off, and Knox and Rogers shrank back into the shadows as the guards ran pell-mell toward the main house.

An SUV pulled up to the main gate and the driver leapt out and rushed over to the main house, leaving the vehicle running.

A minute later four guards rushed outside. Suzanne Davis, in a bathrobe, Helen Myers, fully dressed, and an old man in a wheelchair were with them.

They headed straight for the SUV.

And ran right into Rogers and Knox.

And Puller on the backside.

Rogers took one of the guards and threw him so hard against another that they both hit the wall and slumped down unconscious.

Knox had her gun aimed at the head of a third guard. "Put it down," she said.

He dropped the gun and Rogers walloped him on the head, sending him unconscious to the cobblestones.

Puller knocked out the fourth guard.

Knox pushed Davis and Myers into the rear seat. Rogers lifted the now agitated old man from the wheelchair and into the front seat.

Puller took the wheel of the SUV and drove it straight out of the gates, which opened automatically from a sensor on the inside.

Myers looked at each of them. "What the hell is going on?"

Rogers pulled off his ski mask.

"You!" she said, obviously stunned.

"Me," he said simply.

"And your friends?"

"Here to rescue you," said Rogers.

Puller and Knox took off their masks.

Myers smiled. "Thank God for rescuers."

Rogers glanced at Davis.

"I wasn't aware I needed rescuing," she said bluntly.

Puller drove to where he had parked their car and the group transferred to that vehicle.

Once they were on the road again, Rogers asked Myers, "What happened after I got knocked out?"

"Men came in and took me out. I don't know what happened to Josh."

"We do," said Puller. "He's dead."

"What?" said Myers.

"Washed up on the beach with his head bashed in."

Rogers eyed Davis again. "How do you feel about that?"

"Probably the same as you do. Nothing."

Knox looked at the old man, who was unfocused, his head tilting to one side. "I'm thinking plastic surgery on the face and other stuff to make him look like Ballard."

Puller glanced in the rearview at Myers and then Davis. "Work with us and maybe you get a deal."

"A deal for what?" said Myers sharply. "I wasn't aware I'd done anything wrong."

Knox said, "Anton Charpentier. And we have the pictures

to prove it. The Feds are already working up their indictments."

Myers paled and glanced out the window.

Rogers said, "They want Jericho. Not the small fish. You talk, maybe you walk."

Myers said, "I . . . I don't know."

"You don't know?" said Knox incredulously. She looked at Davis. "Okay, so we nail her ass for espionage and she goes away for life. How about you? You want to deal?"

Rogers glanced at her. "Don't be dumb."

Davis shrugged.

Puller added, "Cooperate now and it will only help you down the line."

"They just hired me to look after this guy," she said, indicating the old man. "Other than that, I don't know squat."

"*Guys*, don't you mean?" said Knox.

"I don't know, do I?"

"You play games, you're going to do some hard time."

"Well, I guess that's why they have lawyers."

Knox glanced at Rogers. "Is she stupid or tougher than she looks?"

"She killed a guy, so I'd opt for the latter." He looked at Davis. "They *hired* you? I thought you said that Jericho had adopted you."

Myers gaped and said, "What?"

Davis kept her gaze on Rogers. "Nobody adopted me. I got the gig through Josh. I told you I knew him before."

"How did you know him before?" asked Knox.

"We had some good times. And we had some bad times."

"And you're not sorry he's dead?" said Knox.

"Like I already said, I don't care one way or another. I can tell you that Josh wouldn't have cared if I were the one dead. That's sort of the relationship we had."

"You had enough of a relationship to screw him," said Rogers. "At the beach house."

Davis appraised him. "Well, I screwed you too. Does that mean we have a relationship?"

Knox and Puller exchanged a quick glance.

Rogers shook his head, "I think it was just sex."

Davis and Rogers looked away from each other.

Puller kept driving.

CHAPTER

68

THEY REACHED THE motel in Hampton at three in the morning. They got the old man into the bed, leaning him up against the headboard because he was having a little difficulty breathing. He had said nothing the whole trip and now immediately fell asleep.

Knox looked at Myers and Davis and motioned to two chairs. "Sit."

Davis said, "You can't just keep us here against our will. It's kidnapping."

Puller said, "I'm a cop."

"Yeah, I saw you at the bar with your *Army* creds. Guess what, I'm not in the military, so you have no jurisdiction over me."

Puller looked at Rogers. "You didn't tell me she was a lawyer."

"I'm not a lawyer, but I want to call one. So even if you think you can hold me, you can't stop me from talking to a lawyer."

Myers said, "Why don't you shut up and listen to what they have to say?"

Davis gave her a withering look. "I'm not the one passing government secrets, am I? So why don't *you* shut the hell up, Little Miss Spy?"

An exasperated Myers said to Puller, "What kind of deal can I get?"

"Depends on how much information you have."

"If I give you Jericho *and* Charpentier?"

"Then we may be talking minimal prison time in a federal country club. You'll be out and setting up a new bar in no time."

"Okay."

"So is that a yes?"

She nodded while Davis looked disgusted.

Knox said, "How did you get involved with all this?"

"Through Josh. He came to me. Jericho had brought him in to 'run' Atalanta Group, but really to ferry the information to Charpentier. She had a prior relationship with him."

"So Claire Jericho handpicked them both?"

"Yes."

Knox said, "Makes sense to use the bar as a transfer spot. Lots of military there, no one would be suspicious."

Puller nodded and looked at Myers. "And the secrets? Were they commercial applications of the patents that Ballard held?"

"Yes. They were worth an unbelievable amount. But like you said, Ballard controlled them."

"And what's the deal with Ballard?"

"He got Alzheimer's."

"And is this Ballard?" asked Puller, indicating the old man.

Myers started to say something but then stopped. She glanced at Davis.

Puller looked at her. "You want to get in on the deal too, or are you going to let your friend here get all the goodies?"

"Ballard's dead," said Davis. "He was dead before I came on board."

"How did he die?" asked Knox. "Natural causes?"

"If you call a bullet to the head natural causes."

"And who killed him?"

"Jericho, at least I think. I wasn't there. Josh thought it was her."

"And how did you get involved?"

"I already told you that. Through Josh." She eyed Rogers. "I told you we went way back, right?"

Rogers nodded, his gaze steadily on her.

"He was a dick and a crook. That's why Jericho hired him. Then he brought me on to babysit the old guys."

"Josh was a good man," interjected Myers.

"Bullshit."

"How does a crook get a security clearance to work for a defense contractor on classified work?" asked Knox.

Davis said, "Jericho. She pushed it through, I bet. And you know how many ways there are to beat a polygraph? And what, we haven't had spies in the ranks before?"

"You sound like you know about stuff like that," said Puller. "What's your background?"

"I'm just a party girl who learns fast and thinks quick on her feet."

"Right," said a skeptical Puller. "But why kill Ballard?"

Davis was crossing and uncrossing her legs.

"You can go and pee if you need to," Knox said.

Davis jumped up. "Thanks." She hurried off to the bathroom.

When the door closed behind her, Myers said in a low voice, "She's lying."

"About what?" asked Puller.

"About Ballard. He wasn't killed. He's not dead."

"So where is he?"

She pointed to the bed. "Right there. That's Chris Ballard."

"Why should we believe you?" said Rogers.

"She already lied about being adopted." Myers looked around nervously. "And there's something else."

"What?" asked Knox.

"Davis has a gun."

Rogers said, "I've seen her use it. She saved my life."

Myers dropped her voice to a whisper. "That's not what I mean. She has a gun on her *now*. I saw her put it in her robe pocket before we left the house."

Puller and Knox instantly rose and pulled their weapons while Rogers looked on.

They glided over to the bathroom door, one on either side of it.

The bullet hit an inch above Puller's head. He dropped to the floor and rolled as another shot shattered the lamp on the nightstand. Knox cried out as a shard of glass cut her face.

Myers turned and fired again. This shot found its mark as the bullet slammed into the forehead of the old man. He slumped over, dead. Another shot ricocheted off a metal lamppost and burned a tunnel across Puller's left forearm.

Rogers threw a chair at Myers, but it missed. She pointed her gun at his head.

The next instant the bathroom door was thrown open. Davis came out firing. Her first shot hit Myers in the shoulder and Myers's gun fell to the floor. The second shot hit Myers in the neck.

That was the kill shot.

Myers screamed and clutched at the wound in her neck, which was gushing enough blood that she would only have seconds left to live.

She looked at Davis, who still had her pistol aimed at her, then dropped to the floor, convulsively twitched once, and lay still.

Puller, Knox, and Rogers stared at Davis, their guns pointed at her head. Davis slowly lowered her pistol.

"What the hell just happened?" exclaimed Knox. "Why did Myers start shooting?"

"Because she wanted to kill all of you," said Davis.

Puller said, "But why? We offered her a deal."

"She wasn't interested in a deal."

"Why not?" demanded Knox.

"Because she's Claire Jericho's daughter," replied Davis.

69

Knox and Puller had triaged each other using supplies from Puller's duffel. The wound on Puller's arm wasn't deep but had bled profusely. They had finally gotten it under control. Knox's cheek was bandaged where the glass had cut it.

Rogers stood over Myers's body.

Davis sat down in a chair. "Did she tell you I was lying?"

Puller nodded. "And that you had a gun. We thought you'd gone in there to get it out and then ambush us."

"No, I just really had to pee. But I didn't know that Myers was armed. When I heard the shooting I pretty much knew what was happening, though."

Knox looked at the dead man in the bed. "She said this was the real Ballard. Why did she kill him?"

"Because he's not the real Ballard. Like I told you, he's dead."

"How are you so sure?" asked Puller. "Did someone tell you?"

"Josh brought me on to play the part of companion to Ballard. The real Ballard. He knew I—well, he knew I was used to skirting the rules just like him."

"Wait a minute, you were babysitting the *real* Christopher Ballard?" said Knox.

Davis nodded. "Then he just died. Nobody shot him. I lied about that."

She glanced at Rogers, who was staring directly at her. "I tend to lie as my first instinct on things." She smiled and Rogers smiled back at her.

"This was about eighteen months ago. I went into his bedroom one morning to bring him his coffee. And there he was stone cold dead. I called Josh. And he called Jericho. And they came out and had a powwow over what to do."

"And they decided on a replacement?" said Puller.

"Two, actually. A spare, just in case. You see, Ballard had Alzheimer's. Before he died he didn't know his own name. So it wasn't like the replacements would need to carry on a conversation. And nobody came to visit Ballard. He had no family that I knew of."

"But why the need to create the impression that he was still alive?" said Knox.

"I don't know," replied Davis. "I just know that the staff was well paid to keep their silence. If the truth did come out they all would lose their jobs, so they had no incentive to talk. And the guys they got as replacements weren't right in the head, so they weren't going to talk to anyone."

"I threw who I thought was Ballard out the window," said Rogers.

"At first they thought the guy had gone nuts and dove out the window," said Davis.

"And they called in the spare?" said Knox.

"Yes."

Knox sat down next to Davis. "Can you tie Jericho to any of this?"

"It would be my word against hers. And when they check into my background I'm not sure how credible I'll be."

She glanced at Rogers, who was staring at her.

"I'd believe you," he said, garnering a smile from Davis.

Puller's phone buzzed. When he answered it Robert Puller didn't waste a second. He said, "Wherever you are, get the hell out. Now!"

Puller hustled everyone out of the room and into his vehicle. They sped off into the darkness.

"Puller," said Knox nervously.

He held up a hand and then hit a key on his phone.

His brother answered on the first ring. "Are you out?"

"Yes. What's going on?"

"Did you kidnap three people from Ballard's estate?"

"How the hell did you know about that?"

"So it's true."

"I wouldn't say abducted."

"What would you say?"

"Rescued."

"So they were being held against their will?"

"We think so."

"You *think* so? And they're all now safe?"

Puller eyed Knox before drawing a deep breath and saying into the phone, "One is. Two are dead."

"Tell me everything," barked his brother.

Puller did so and then waited for Robert's response. He could hear his brother's elevated breathing, which he did not take as a good sign.

"This is a shitstorm, John."

"Is it?"

"They're going to find Helen Myers and an old man, who may or may not be Chris Ballard, and who they are alleging you kidnapped, shot to death in a motel room rented by you. Does that pretty much cover it?"

"Pretty much."

"And what would you call that?"

"Well, if you put it that way, shitstorm seems appropriate. But how did they find where we'd gone so fast?"

"Did you check anybody for an electronic tracker? Or they could have just traced the chip in one of their cell phones."

Puller sighed. "Damn. Look, Bobby, give it to me straight, does our side want Jericho to go down? If not, we're just spinning our wheels here."

"Unless you can show she's been selling secrets, no."

"And the serial killings?"

"Three decades old and too many holes."

"Great. Then we've got nothing on her. And it looks like I'm going to be arrested for kidnapping and murder."

"I think I found the motive for the subterfuge with Ballard."

"What?"

"As I told you before, Ballard controls the patents."

"And if something happens to him?"

"I had a DoD lawyer check through discreet channels."

"Gee, don't keep me in suspense, Bobby. I'm a little tense right now."

"Ballard set up a charitable foundation. Every last penny and asset goes to it when he dies."

"So a charity gets patents that are being used in DoD work? How exactly does that play out with the project they're doing at Atalanta Group?"

"Atalanta Group would have kept working on them. The underlying licensing contract they have guarantees that."

"Then I'm not getting the motive."

"The contracts with the government only cover *military* applications. Atalanta Group has no control over or rights to the commercial applications. Those revert to the beneficiary under the will, in this case the foundation. Ballard dies, they're going to come in and take over that part of it hook, line, and sinker."

Puller said, "And Jericho's dealings with Charpentier get cratered if that happens? Because what she's selling him *are* the commercial applications. And they might find out what she's been doing?"

"Exactly. So they had to make it seem that Ballard was still alive."

"But we can't get to Jericho with what we have."

"Without Quentin and Myers I don't see how we nail her. And, John, you really need to focus. They're going to come after you for what happened tonight. I don't mean Jericho. I mean the law." He paused. "You could go to prison for this."

"I don't care about that," shouted Puller. "But this means we're not going to find out what happened to Mom."

"We are going to find out what happened to Mom."

"How? We've got nothing."

"No, we have something. Something she wants."

"What?"

"Rogers," said his brother.

Puller shot a glance at Rogers, who just stared back at him blankly.

Into the phone Puller said, "We can't do that. Do you know what this guy has—"

His brother interrupted. "John, will you trust me? I know what I'm doing. Just trust me."

Puller sat there holding the phone and feeling more lost than he ever had in his life.

"Okay, Bobby, okay."

70

ROBERT PULLER WAS in his dress blues. Not out of respect for the person opposite him. He had no respect for her. The dress uniform was about him. Claire Jericho eyed him across her desk. She said, "I think the lecture at the Pentagon was the last time we saw each other. Quite a while."

"I've been busy, so have you."

"And of course you had your little prison sojourn at Leavenworth."

"It was a good time to think and read. No interruptions."

"Your career is back on its accelerated path, I'm told."

"And you're still doing what you've always done."

"You're far more subtle than your father."

"My brother told me you and our father had met. Didn't quite see eye to eye?"

"I was trying to spare your brother's feelings. It was actually more aptly a tank battle."

"My dad led men on the ground. He didn't see the need to be tucked away in armor. He had enough of his own."

"Merely a metaphor."

"And I'm not here to talk about him. I'm here to talk about my mother."

"So I understand."

"You got my email?"

She said, "Cryptic. I appreciate the effort."

"It's why I'm here in person. To conclude the arrangement."

"It's delicate."

"And also straightforward."

"With assurances that this has been signed off on at the highest levels? There will be no blowback?"

"I think I covered that in my *cryptic* email."

She picked up a pen and twirled it between her fingers. "Is it really that important to you?"

"You're a mother, correct?"

"*Was* a mother, since my daughter was murdered."

"And you still don't understand the reason I'm here, then?"

"I understand the sentiment. I'm just wondering if it's worth all this fuss."

Robert Puller gripped the edge of his chair to keep himself from launching across the desk and gripping her neck.

"Well, *I* think it is worth the fuss."

"So Rogers, then, in exchange?"

Robert nodded. "And my brother and his friends will walk away from this unharmed in any way."

"So your cryptic email said. But I'm not so sure about that. They did considerable damage. And I'm giving up a lot as it is."

"I have to insist on that point."

"I'll think about it," she said airily, seeming to enjoy her advantage over him on this part of the negotiations.

"And you want particulars? Location only? You must understand that I had no personal involvement. It was the responsibility of others. And I am powerless to bring back the dead."

Robert Puller again gripped the chair. "I want both particulars and location."

Jericho sat back. "Show me the approvals."

Puller opened the briefcase he'd brought with him, took out an electronic tablet, brought the requisite pages up, and slid it across to her.

She took several minutes looking over them. Finally she nodded and passed the device back to him.

"Rather astonishing," she said. "I would hardly think people at that level would care."

"People at that level have great respect for my father."

She clasped her hands and inclined slightly toward him. "It must be very difficult to live your entire life in the shadow of your father."

"I've always considered it an honor."

She gave him an amused look. "It's not healthy to deceive yourself."

"The particulars and the location?"

She spent five minutes telling him this. He keyed all of it into his tablet.

Jericho said, "So, as you can see, wrong place, wrong time. Just unbelievably unlucky for her. Dimitri, or Rogers rather, had just killed Audrey Moore. He had evidently taken her as she left work at Building Q. He must have been lurking nearby. One of the guards heard something and went to investigate and saw what was going on. He called in reinforcements. As the guards were trying to capture Rogers, your mother came along and saw Rogers, the dead woman, everything. Your mother apparently cried out, and turned to run. One of the guards reacted badly if instinctively. He struck her with his gun. And she died. Again, there was nothing I could do. I wasn't even there."

"So you *already* said."

"Of course I would have liked things to have been handled differently, but back then we required absolute secrecy. It seemed the only way. The burial was a proper one," she added offhandedly.

Puller snapped his briefcase closed and stood, slipping his cap under his arm. "You said you knew my father?"

"Yes."

"Did you know my mother?"

Jericho's eyelids fluttered. "I might have seen her around the installation from time to time."

"She was beautiful. And more kind than she was beautiful. Everyone loved her."

"I'm sure every son sees his mother in that light."

"No they don't. So you knew it was her, then? Walking by?"

"As I said, I wasn't there."

"Rogers says he didn't see my mother, but that you were there."

She chortled. "Oh, well, then by all means, put him on the witness stand. How many people has he murdered thus far?"

Puller continued as though he hadn't heard her. "So your prized creation escapes and is methodically killing women on your staff because he can't get to you."

"Is that what he told you?" she interrupted.

Puller ignored this. "Because he can't get to you," he repeated. "And then he's located right near Building Q killing another woman, and you're not there?"

She spread her hands. "I was busy."

"But you knew after the fact at the very least."

"I think I already answered that question. But so what if I did?"

"I wonder if it pleased you."

She looked at him curiously. "How so?"

"Getting back at my father in that way."

"Why would I want to get back at him?"

"You described your relationship as a tank battle. That hardly seems friendly."

"So what? Many people don't agree on things. That doesn't mean they all run out and try to injure each other."

"Granted, but you strike me as the petty sort who would turn any criticism, no matter how minor, into a vendetta."

"You're being tiresome," replied Jericho, starting to shuffle some papers on her desk.

Puller continued as though she hadn't spoken. "And when my father didn't see eye to eye with someone it was never a minor thing. He probably got right in your face and said things that you found unforgivable. So, considering your vindictive nature, you were probably thrilled to have caused him great personal pain, even if he didn't know its source."

She set aside the papers and gazed steadily at him. "Let me remind you that Rogers was the monster, not me. He was the killer, not me."

Robert said imperturbably, "You created it. But we can agree to disagree on that point. But no communication? Not even anonymously, that would have given her family, *my* family some closure?"

"It never occurred to me," she said bluntly.

"No, I imagine it wouldn't."

"I was simply doing my job."

"So your *job* was stealing secrets from the government and selling them to a foreign agent for your own personal gain?"

She wearily shook her head. "Tiresome again, Robert. Do you have any proof whatsoever?"

"We did. But they're both dead. Josh Quentin, I'm sure, at your hands."

"I will put your unfortunate remarks down to your unstable emotional state. But any more talk like that and I will not agree to let your brother walk away from this unscathed. I hope I make myself clear on that point."

"Actually, I've said all I came here to say."

"Good. And Rogers? When can I expect him?"

"Soon. Very soon."

CHAPTER

71

PULLER LOOKED DOWN at the patch of dirt. His brother was next to him. Knox stood a few feet behind them. And behind her was Paul Rogers.

They were thirty miles from Williamsburg, on a lonely stretch off Interstate 64 on the way to Richmond. A tree stood in front of them. It was massive. Thirty years ago it might have just been a sapling. On the north side of it was a sunken patch of ground.

They had not come alone. There was a forensics team with them.

A man wearing a CID windbreaker came up to Puller.

"You ready for us to proceed, Chief Puller?"

Puller said curtly, "Go ahead."

The team moved forward, staked out the spot with tape, and began to dig.

Six feet later they were done.

Ropes were unraveled into the hole. Men in hazmat suits scrambled into the opening in the dirt. The rope was secured to the object. The order was given for the men above to pull.

They did, and the object soon came into view.

A metal box.

It was heavily stained and one side was partially crumpled, but it was still intact. Whatever was inside was not visible.

For that Puller breathed a silent prayer of thanks.

The box was loaded into the back of a waiting van. It pulled off while the team continued to process the scene.

Puller watched them for a bit and then he turned and looked at his brother.

"You ready to go?" he asked.

"In a bit."

Robert walked around the area for a few minutes, seemingly taking in everything about the patch of ground that might have constituted the resting place of their mother for the last three decades. Puller followed his every move with his eyes.

Rogers finally came over to him, rubbing the back of his head. "I'm . . . I'm sorry, Puller."

"You had nothing to do with this."

"But if she hadn't seen what I was doing."

"I don't blame you. As far as I'm concerned, next to my mother you're the most blameless person in the whole thing."

Rogers turned and walked over and stood next to Knox. She started quietly talking to him.

Robert squatted next to the hole. His brother joined him.

"What are you thinking, Bobby?" asked Puller.

"That it's a peaceful place. That she was resting in peace."

"We still have to confirm that it's her."

Yet Puller knew that it was. The only reason they had been directed here was because this was the payoff. The information about this location, with no strings or prosecutions attached. Jericho was home free.

Puller still felt sick about it. He had never felt so helpless in his life. No skill he had, no weapon he could wield was of any use to him right now.

"It *is* peaceful," said Puller. "A lot of flowers. She always loved flowers." He glanced once more at Knox. Her face was granite. She finally walked away with Rogers behind her. They climbed into a waiting SUV.

They all drove to the morgue. By the time they got there the box had been opened and the remains taken out and placed on a metal autopsy table.

By now it was simply bones with bits of clothing, and small sprouts of hair here and there.

Knox and the Puller brothers looked at it through a window. Puller felt the creep of tears to his eyes

Robert ran his gaze up and down the remains, his eyes alighting on the bits of clothing.

"Do you think it's her?" said Puller in a low, tremulous voice.

Robert nodded. "The pattern on the dress she was wearing. That's it." He pointed to a patch of fabric around the bony feet. He pointed to another remnant. "And the shoes. What's left of them. And that's Mom's hair color."

"You remember her clothes and shoes?"

"I remember everything about that night, John." He put a hand on the wall to steady himself. He suddenly bent over and sucked in several deep breaths while Puller put an arm around his brother's shoulders, supporting him. Finally Robert straightened.

He nodded. "It's Mom. We finally found her, John."

Both brothers continued to look at the remains until the medical examiner came over to the table. The shade on the window was lowered as he began his work.

Knox walked over to Puller and Robert. "They're here," she said tersely.

Waiting in the lobby for them were a dozen MPs in body armor and carrying AR-15 assault rifles, along with a three-star who introduced himself as General Randall Blair.

This was the other payoff. Rogers in return for no prosecutions against Puller and the others for their assorted "crimes."

Knox slid over to Rogers and whispered something in his ear. Rogers nodded and then looked blankly at the group of soldiers.

Blair pointed at Rogers. "Take that man into custody." He quickly said to Rogers, "We will have no compunction in shooting you down if you so much as think about attacking."

Rogers glanced at Knox and slowly put his hands behind his back. Two of the MPs shackled him with extra-thick chains.

Blair said, "I have been instructed to admonish all of you to pursue this matter no further. If you do, you will be subject to the consequences. This is an internal DoD matter and it will be pursued accordingly."

"You mean it will be covered up," retorted Puller.

Blair seemed to be struggling to keep his temper in check. "All I know, Chief Puller, is that this is where the matter ends. You have your mother's remains. And so you have closure."

"Fuck closure," roared Puller, who took a step forward before his brother grabbed his arm as three of the MPs leveled their AR-15s at him.

Puller barked, "So that's what you guys are going to do? Just bury this? Again? Let her keep on going? That's what it means to you to wear the uniform?" He looked straight at the MPs. "Covering up the truth?"

The men stared back at him, completely unmoved by his words.

Blair erupted, "You are one more outburst from a court-martial, soldier." He stuck a thick finger in Puller's face. "I don't care who your old man is!"

"Let it go, John," said his brother quietly as he gripped his arm.

"I'm not letting this go."

Knox came over to him and took his other arm. "Yes you are."

She nodded at Blair. He and the MPs left with the shackled Rogers.

A moment later Puller's phone buzzed.

It was a text.

From Claire Jericho.

I'm so very sorry about your mother.

Puller threw the phone across the room.

CHAPTER

72

THE REMAINS WERE confirmed as Jackie Puller. The medical examiner concluded that she had died from a blunt force trauma to the head, which corroborated what Jericho had told Robert about the guard hitting Jackie with his gun.

Their mother was turned over to the Puller brothers and they undertook the details for her burial. The question was whether they would tell their father and have him attend the funeral, if that was even possible. They decided to visit their dad and see how it went.

The hallway was quiet as they walked down it. Puller Sr.'s outbursts had become less pronounced the longer he was a patient here.

They entered the room and saw that he was in bed, his crown of white hair just visible over the blanket. The brothers glanced at each other before walking over to stand on either side of the bed.

"Dad?" said Robert.

The old man didn't stir.

"Dad, it's about Mom," added Puller.

Now their father blinked his eyes open and slowly turned his head to look first at Robert and then at John.

Robert sat down in a chair and took his father's large, weathered hand and gripped it firmly.

"We found her. We found Mom."

Puller Sr. started blinking rapidly.

"She didn't leave us, Dad," said Puller. "She...she was killed by...someone. Thirty years ago."

Puller Sr. blinked some more as he turned over to stare up at them. Then they could both see tears trickling down his cheeks.

Robert said, "She's going to be buried, Dad. We're going to have a funeral for her at Fort Monroe. We"—he shot his brother a glance—"we wanted to know if you would like to come, if you think you can manage it."

The tears kept sliding down the old man's face.

Robert pulled something from his pocket. It was an old cassette recorder.

"What's that?" whispered Puller.

Robert set it down on the nightstand and turned it on. A moment later they heard a woman's voice singing.

"That's Mom," exclaimed Puller. "Where did you get that?"

"Lucy Bristow. She recorded it years ago when Mom sang in the church choir."

They turned to see their father reach out and touch the recorder, his eyes now full of tears, a smile etched on his face.

He mouthed one word: "Jackie."

* * *

The funeral was two days later. It was a beautiful sunny day at Fort Monroe. The breeze off the water was refreshing. The sky was streaked with the contrails of military jets taking off from the naval station across the channel.

All three Puller men were in their dress uniforms. The senior Puller's trio of stars reflected off the bright sun. The funeral service was at the Catholic church where Jackie had worshipped and been a volunteer. Father Rooney had come out of retirement to perform the funeral Mass.

The Army had offered to send some junior personnel to attend the funeral. The Pullers had turned the offer down.

Puller had actually used some choicer language than that, but that was the gist.

Inside the church, her coffin was placed so that Jackie Puller would be facing the altar, in accordance with Catholic tradition. A priest's funeral would have had him facing the congregation, as he would have done in life.

Rooney spoke openly and deeply personally of Jackie Puller and all that she had done and meant to so many, most of all her sons and husband.

Puller glanced around the church where he had attended Mass as a young boy.

He looked over at one elderly lady who was clutching her rosary.

And then it struck him.

Sunday best.

He said in a low voice, "Sunday best."

His brother, obviously hearing this, turned to him and said, "What?"

"Mom *was* coming here that night. She was coming to pray over things before visiting Bristow after he called her. She was coming to seek God's help on what to do." He added in a hollow tone, "And maybe not just about with Bristow. But with Dad too."

After finishing the service, Rooney slowly made his way down to the three men and gave them each his personal condolences.

Puller Sr. clung to the priest's hand so tightly that Puller thought he saw Rooney wince in pain, but the old priest gamely hung in there until the old soldier relinquished his grip.

The Puller brothers were pallbearers, easily hoisting the coffin with their mother's remains. Tears streamed down their faces as they performed this task, both at the church and at the gravesite.

They were not tough, hardened soldiers now.

They were simply bereaved sons.

Many people who had known the Pullers were there, including Stan Demirjian, who had come up and saluted Lieutenant General John Puller and then spent the rest of the time helping the old warrior get around, with a supportive hand ready whenever it was needed. Also there were Carol Powers and her family, the retired CID agent Vincent DiRenzo, and attorney Shireen Kirk. Lucy Bristow, whose husband Jackie had been going to meet that night, walked over to the Pullers and offered her condolences. Puller Sr. seemed to recognize her and gave her a nod.

It was telling to Puller that none of the military higher-ups were there. They obviously saw their attendance here as detrimental to their careers.

And they had all obeyed that order.

As Puller sat listening to Father Rooney delivering the gravesite service, Knox, who was sitting next to him and wearing a simple black dress, took his hand. When she squeezed it, he squeezed back.

After the service was over the Puller brothers loaded their father into the van they had driven down in.

Stan Demirjian came over to them. In a low voice he said, "I always knew your father was innocent. Always."

"Thanks, Mr. Demirjian," said Robert. "That means a lot."

"And even though I know why she wrote the letter, it was wrong for Lynda to send it to the Army. You can't do that sort of thing to people just based on what you're feeling and without any real facts to back you up."

The men shook hands and Demirjian gave them both sharp salutes and departed.

After he left Puller took something from his pocket. "Speaking of letters."

"What is that?" asked Robert.

"The original letter from Mrs. Demirjian. Ted Hull sent it to me."

"What are you going to do with it?" asked Robert.

Puller took something else from his pocket and held it up. "I brought this." It was a lighter. "You want to do the honors?"

Puller gripped one edge of the letter while Robert ignited another edge with the lighter's flame.

Puller held on to the letter as long as he could. When the flames were about to reach his fingers he let it go. The paper rose into the air, continued to burn, and finally disappeared into blackened curls of ash carried away by the breeze.

"Is there really no way, Bobby?" said Puller.

"Charpentier has disappeared with no leads. Myers and Quentin are dead. The official word is that the body of the old man *is* Chris Ballard. I'm sure they have the forensics to support that, even if it is all bullshit."

"And the secrets they were selling? If people dig into that?"

"No one's going to dig, John. Look at it from DoD's point of view. The truth comes out they all look bad. It could set back defense research for decades. Reputations and silver stars falling like rain. I'm not saying the powers that be are happy about this. I'm just saying no one apparently wants to go down that road. And even if they did, Jericho's had more than enough time to get rid of all the evidence."

"So that's it, then?"

"Yes, that's it."

Puller saw Knox heading over. "Are you riding back with us?" he asked.

She shook her head. "I've got some things I need to attend to."

"Any word on Rogers?"

"No, I don't know what they're going to do with him. Maybe he'll end up at Gitmo, buried forever."

Puller said, "None of this is right. None of this is fair."

Knox glanced at Robert before saying, "All of this is…life."

She kissed him on the cheek, hugged Robert, and then turned and walked off.

"Things good between you two?" Robert asked.

Puller watched Knox disappear from sight before answering. "I don't know."

CHAPTER

73

Paul Rogers looked around at the cell he was in. It resembled the one he had been in for the last ten years. The only difference was he was the only prisoner in this particular facility. They had come in late at night, but he had seen clearly that it was a military building and it was not meant to hold prisoners. But there was a secure area and he was in it.

There were bars all around, allowing the guards who stood watch around the clock a dead-on view of him.

There was a toilet and a hose for a shower. His meals were passed through the door while half a dozen guards aimed automatic weapons at him.

There was a comfortable bunk.

And nothing else.

He lay there day after day. When the pain hit him, forcing him to his knees in agony, the guards stood by and watched. He assumed their orders were not to intervene in any way. And they followed orders.

When he retched, which he often did, they passed towels through the bars for him to clean up his mess.

And on it went day after day.

In his mind he counted them off, just as he had in prison.

Eight days. Nine. Ten. Two weeks.

He wondered what they were planning to do with him. Kill him? Autopsy him? And then cremate him?

Those were his best guesses.

He was sure the guards had been told he was a murderer and also guilty of treason. They would have no sympathy for him.

And he didn't want any.

Once, someone arrived carrying a medical bag.

One of the guards hit him with what he assumed was the same gas that Jericho had deployed against him. He fell senseless to the floor.

Later, when he awoke, he saw the bandages on his arms and legs. When he looked under them he saw the incisions. They had taken pieces of him away. Maybe for analysis.

They are kicking the tires of the freak.

He was just waiting. Biding his time. He ate his food, drank his water, used the toilet, showered with the hose. Slept and woke. Slept and woke.

Yes, just biding his time. His patience, he had proven, was infinite.

Then one day he had a visitor, a middle-aged man who arrived with a briefcase and a polite, professional attitude. He spoke through the bars to Rogers after the guards had backed away to allow them privacy.

Rogers had listened to everything carefully.

The man had ended the meeting by saying, "Good luck."

"It's never really about luck, though, is it?" Rogers had replied.

And finally, after five more days, the time came.

"We're moving you," the head guard said.

"Why?"

The guard didn't bother to answer.

He saw the bottle coming and then he was sprayed in the face with the gas. He fell heavily to the floor.

They lifted him off the floor and carried him to a waiting Army transport truck, where he was put into the back and strapped down to the floor. Six guards climbed in with him, guns resting on their thighs.

They set off. Their route took them along some back roads, and then they reached a highway and the truck sped up. They reached a bridge and drove across it.

One of the guards peeked through the back flap. "Damn, that's a beautiful sight. Nothing like a bridge over water on a fine night."

A second later Rogers ripped the straps off.

"Holy shit!" exclaimed the guard nearest to him.

He reached for his weapon but didn't get there before Rogers threw him against the man next to him. Both went down in a tumble of arms and legs.

One guard got off a burst from his weapon but missed. He did not get a second chance. Rogers grabbed him by the shoulder and, using him as a weapon, smashed him against the other guards, who were knocked off their feet and thrown against the hard wooden sides of the truck.

Rogers flung open the canvas flap and looked out.

It was dark. There were car lights behind him. He looked to his right and saw the side of the bridge. He looked across the water and recognized Naval Station Norfolk, which meant that Fort Monroe was just across the channel.

He bent his legs and jumped to the right.

He cleared the concrete side of the bridge and went into a dive.

He didn't know how far down it was, but it was long enough.

He straightened out, led with his hands, and cleanly broke

the surface of the water. He went under, angled out his descent, and then headed back to the surface.

He stayed there only a few seconds before going back under.

The guards had recovered and were firing at him from the bridge. The bullets pinged into the water, but at this distance and in the dark they would be lucky to hit their target.

And they weren't lucky. Tonight, the luck all seemed to be with Rogers. Yet, like he had told the visitor, it was never about luck. The bottle he'd been sprayed with had held nothing but oxygen. The guard's comment about the bridge had been his signal to act. The rest of it had been up to Rogers.

But a little luck never hurt either.

He struck off for shore with powerful strokes of his arms and kicks of his legs. The channel was not very wide. They would deploy people to cover as much of it as possible.

But Rogers had spent a long time here training, and a great deal of it had been in this body of water. He had discovered landing spots that he suspected few knew about.

He pointed himself toward one of them and in short order arrived there. It was wooded and isolated, and when he came ashore his only companions were woodland creatures that ran away at his approach.

He had one more task to perform.

And then he was done.

CHAPTER

74

Eight stories tall.

And she was perched right on top.

Of course.

Veronica Knox looked at her watch and then walked toward the building. She was dressed in a long black trench coat with the collar turned up. Her features were tight, her gut even tighter.

In the lobby she was searched and her gun and phone taken from her. She was escorted up in the elevator by an armed security guard. The elevator opened directly into the vestibule of Claire Jericho's apartment.

The woman was waiting there for her. She was dressed in a dark pantsuit. She took off her glasses and rubbed away a smudge.

The guard went back down in the elevator, leaving the two women facing one another.

"I was surprised you wanted to meet," said Jericho. She made no indication she was going to invite Knox into the apartment.

"Unfinished business," replied Knox.

"Really? I'm aware of none."

"Rogers has escaped."

"I'm aware of that."

"You could be in danger."

Jericho smiled. "And, what, you came here to warn me because you're concerned about my safety?"

"I've checked. You have a great many friends in high places."

She shrugged. "I've been doing this a long time. You build relationships."

"You're getting away with murder, you know."

Jericho looked disappointed. "If this was the purpose for the visit, I'm afraid you're wasting your time. And I have other things to do."

"Did it hurt to lose your daughter?"

"Oh, you mean Helen?"

"Yes, Helen Myers," Knox said tightly.

"I know what you want me to say. That it did hurt. That I miss her. That I'm grieving. But the truth is we didn't really know each other. She was with her father most of her life, until he died, and then she came to me for help. And I did help. With setting her up in business. I feel like I was a good mentor to her. But that was really the sum total of our relationship. So, am I sorry she's dead? Of course I am. Do I have the same level of grief as, say, your friend John Puller over losing his mother?" She shook her head. "The answer of course is and has to be no." She paused. "And how are John and his brother doing? Are they holding up well?"

"You don't have the right to ask that," Knox said sharply.

"I was just being polite."

"The unfinished business," said Knox.

Jericho sighed resignedly. "You're not going to shoot me. I know your weapon was taken. If you're thinking of attacking me with your hands, please think again." She drew a small pistol from her pocket and aimed it at Knox.

"That's not my style," said Knox. "It's a bit amateurish, actually."

Jericho smiled again. "Yes, of course. You and your group were so thoroughly professional in all that you did. Accomplishing what, exactly?"

"I also have friends in high places."

"Yes, of course you do," Jericho said patronizingly. "And I'm sure they look up from time to time and try to see my friends in *higher* places."

"Do you remember Mack Taubman?"

Jericho pursed her lips. "Well?"

"He was a mentor of mine when I started out. Actually like a father to me. When I got involved in this case I went to him, questioned him about it. It was clear that he had some knowledge of what had happened back then, but he wouldn't talk about it. He was scared. Scared, when he was the bravest man I knew."

"And your point?" asked a clearly bored Jericho.

"He was found dead shortly after I met with him. They think it was suicide, but I know better. I think he contacted you. Maybe he finally wanted the truth to come out. Only you couldn't allow that."

"Oh, so now you have me involved in his death as well?" She laughed lightly. "Are there no horrors of which I'm not capable? And you speak of amateurism? Look in the mirror, Agent Knox." She checked her watch. "Now, if there's nothing else? I do have a country to keep safe."

Knox stared at her for a few moments and then shook her head.

"No, that's it. Thank you for meeting with me."

Jericho gave a mock bow and pushed the button for the elevator. The car came up and Knox got on with the guard. She looked back at Jericho staring at her.

"I trust this will be the last time I will see you, Agent Knox."

"I can guarantee it," said Knox as the doors closed.

Jericho put the gun back in her pocket, turned, and went back into the apartment.

Thus she did not see the pair of hands emerge in the crevice of the elevator's outer doors. The fingers gripped and pushed and the doors came open.

Paul Rogers climbed up into the vestibule. When Knox had gone up to the apartment he had ridden on top of the elevator car after getting into the shaft through an air duct opening. When the car had descended Rogers had already climbed onto one of the metal beams supporting the shaft and waited there.

He slipped across the vestibule and saw Jericho at her desk, her back to him. She was working on her laptop, some complicated bit of science that held her full attention.

She only looked up when the hands closed around her neck.

* * *

Down on the street Knox stood on the pavement looking up at the top floor of the building. The wind was picking up. As it whipped her hair she drew her coat collar up some more and put her hands in her pockets. Though it wasn't possible, Knox thought she heard the snap of a spine eight stories up.

I told you I had friends in high places.

Like your apartment.

Her phone buzzed. She took it out and looked at the text. Then Knox punched in the numbers and made the call.

"It's done," she said quietly.

"John can never know about this," said the voice. "He's not wired that way."

"He will *never* know about this," Knox said. "I *can* keep a secret."

Knox put her phone away, turned, and walked off into the darkness.

On the other end of the finished call Robert Puller put the phone down on his desk.

He thought about the death of Claire Jericho, but only for a few moments.

Then he put it out of his mind and turned to work of importance.

CHAPTER

75

THE PULLER BROTHERS walked down the hall of one of the world's great labyrinths. The Pentagon was a place well known to the brothers. They were both in uniform and marched along confident in where they were going.

They had been summoned, by a four-star no less.

Johnny Coleman, Vice Chairman of the Joint Chiefs of Staff. Though he had no operational command in the position, he was outranked only by the Chairman of the Joint Chiefs. And because the Chairman of the Joint Chiefs was with the Air Force, Coleman outranked all the other Army four-stars. Coleman had been one of Fighting John Puller's junior officers, before going on to carve out a legendary career of his own.

"What do you think he wants?" asked Puller as they walked along.

"It's either going to be really good news or really bad news," replied his older brother.

"You heard what happened to Jericho?" asked Puller.

"I heard," said his brother.

"They never found Rogers."

"Heard that too."

"If it was him, how did he find out where she lived? That was classified."

"No idea," said Robert.

They reached Coleman's offices. The flag of the Vice Chair was the American bald eagle with its wings spread horizontally. Its talons gripped three arrows, and thirteen red and white stripes representing the original colonies on a shield. It was a regal and intimidating image, and Coleman presented the same figure.

He was a big man, six-four and north of two-fifty, with a broad, thick chest and a grip of iron. His gray hair was cut very short and his voice was a bullhorn that had been used to lead men for nearly four decades now.

He was in his dress blues, with shelves of medals and ribbons. As he told the brothers as he led them into his interior office, he had a formal event to attend after their meeting.

They sat down in Coleman's office, the Vice Chair behind his battleship-big desk and the brothers on the other side.

Coleman plunged right in.

"Helluva time for you both and General Puller. Your mother was one of the finest human beings I have ever had the honor to know. It's a tragedy all around." He paused and fiddled with a pencil. "I have been briefed on all this. In fact, I inserted myself into this situation chiefly because it was the Puller family. As you know, I served under your father. He taught me more in the two years I was with his command than in the rest of the time I've been in the Army. In my mind there has been no better pure fighting officer than your father. At least in my experience."

"Thank you, sir," said Robert.

"Now let me get down to it." He looked at Puller. "Your Army failed you, Chief Puller. You served it faithfully and we did not return the favor. I have been informed what happened three decades ago. I mean what *really* happened. And I am appalled. And I don't simply speak for myself. Chairman Halverson has been made aware of this situation and fully supports my position." He paused again. "In a perfect world, the research project undertaken by Chris Ballard and Claire Jericho three decades ago should never have happened. The murders of those women should not have been covered up. And what happened to your mother...?" He broke the pencil in half. "I know that Jericho has been found dead. Officially, she committed suicide. Now, the whole truth of the matter can still come out. The Army will take its lumps and it should. The deaths of the women, your mother, Jericho, everything. You say the word and all of this comes out. I'm not putting any pressure on you one way or another. I mean that. The Army royally fucked up."

He sat back and looked at the pair.

Robert and Puller exchanged a single glance, but a lot was communicated during those few moments.

Puller said, "I think the appropriate parties have been punished adequately, sir. And I think the Army has learned a valuable lesson. So, no, it need not be made public."

Coleman nodded, his face not revealing whether he agreed with this decision or not. He opened his desk drawer and took out a file. He slid on wire-rimmed glasses and looked at the pages.

"As I understand it, your father was not considered a suspect in your mother's disappearance because he was out of the country. Recently, though, this was found to be incorrect. And then he became a suspect thirty years later."

"He came back a day early," noted Puller.

"And this is the reason why." Coleman slid the file across. Both brothers looked stunned. Puller turned the file around and the two began to read down the pages. When they were done they both looked up.

Puller said, "He came back to confront Ballard and Jericho?"

Coleman nodded. "This super-soldier program was highly classified but not entirely a secret. Your father was a one-star stationed at Fort Monroe where this program was operational. Now, he was not the commandant of the fort, but that didn't matter to a man like Fighting John Puller. Wherever he was stationed was his turf and he would defend it with his life if need be."

Puller said, "So he found out about the program? Jericho told me that she knew my father. And they didn't exactly see eye to eye on things."

Coleman said, "Oh they knew each other all right. And eye to eye? Let me put it a little more bluntly. Your father personally thought her work was horseshit, using his term. He told me that war needed to be fought by real men. Real men had to bleed and die. Only then would we not want to fight wars. If we could create robots to do our fighting, he thought, we'd be at war all the time."

"There's a lot of wisdom in that philosophy," noted Robert.

"Your father had seen more combat than just about anyone I knew. He knew how terrible it was. He thought Jericho was a cancer that the Army should just cut out of itself."

"But he didn't win that battle?" said Puller slowly.

Coleman shook his head. "Only battle I know the man to have lost. Ballard and Jericho were too well entrenched. They had too many connections. They managed huge budgets that got many an officer promoted up the ranks. It was wrong. It was cronyism at its worst. And it still happened."

"And our father?"

"He never let it drop. Fought it for years." He eyed them closely. "And it finally cost him. It cost him dearly."

Robert got there faster than Puller.

"It cost him his fourth star."

Coleman nodded. "They couldn't very well deny him the second and third stars. He flat-out earned those. But when you get to four, there's more politics than merit. And the stand your father had taken came home to roost, because he had pissed off a lot of people who would determine if he got the fourth star or not. And he didn't get it. And he was basically forced to retire."

Coleman stopped and tapped the fourth star on his shoulder. "When I got this pinned on, do you know who I was thinking about? Your old man. He deserved the fourth star far more than I ever did. And ever since I got it part of me has been ashamed that I walk around with it while he never had that honor."

Coleman sighed and sat back. "I know his current condition. But I want to propose something to both of you." He paused, seemingly to marshal his thoughts. "We've never done this before and it carries no official weight. But I've run this up the flagpole and got nothing but salutes from both the brass and the civilian side." He paused again. "We want to award an honorary fourth star to your father. I wish it could be the real deal, but that's not possible now. But we want to do this. Out of respect for your father. We want to try to make this, if not right, at least better." He leaned forward. "What do you say?"

"I say it's about time," both Pullers replied simultaneously.

CHAPTER

76

THE CEREMONY WAS carried out in Puller Sr.'s room at the VA. Dignitaries both military and civilian were in attendance, including the Secretary of Defense and the Chairman of the Joint Chiefs. General Coleman presided over the presentation of the honorary fourth star.

Puller Sr. at first did not seem to understand what was going on, but as the ceremony continued and Coleman whispered some words to him and he saw the star, he seemed to grasp the enormity of what was happening.

When it was over and everyone left, though, Puller motioned for his sons to take off his uniform jacket. They helped him out of it and then he tapped the cassette recorder that was on his bedside table.

Robert quickly turned it on and Puller Sr. sat back on his bed, turned to face the recorder, closed his eyes, and smiled as he listened to his wife singing.

They left him there and headed out.

"I don't think the fourth star meant as much to him as hearing her voice does," said Robert.

"Not even close," said Puller. He hesitated.

Robert noticed this and said, "What?"

"Coleman said Dad confronted Jericho. Do you think he

ever thought Jericho was responsible for Mom's disappearance?"

"I think if Dad remotely thought that was what happened he would have gone over and shot Jericho himself."

"You're right."

"So what happens to the stuff they were doing at Building Q?"

"It'll go on. The company is under a government contract."

"Anne Shepard described some of the stuff they're doing there. The liquid armor, the electrical stuff that makes soldiers think faster on the battlefield. Some of it actually sounded good."

"Yeah, but just think if we spent that money on early childhood education and nutrition."

"Right."

"And I can guarantee that somewhere in the military-industrial complex people are working on stuff that will mean one day a million Paul Rogerses will be running around doing the fighting. And then it's lights-out for the human race."

"That's why I like hanging with you, Bobby. You're always so uplifting."

* * *

When Puller got back to his apartment, someone was waiting for him.

Veronica Knox said, "I heard about the fourth star. I think that's great."

"Well, the truth is he preferred hearing my mother's voice to the fourth star."

When she looked puzzled he quickly explained.

"I think that's the most romantic thing I've ever heard."

He looked at her in surprise. "Romantic? I didn't think you thought about stuff like that, Knox."

"There's obviously a lot you still don't know about me."

He let her in to the apartment and took a minute to let his cat, AWOL, out. They sat at his small kitchen table.

Puller said, "They said Jericho killed herself. But Bobby got a look at the postmortem report on her. Her spine was crushed. And there was something else."

"What?"

"A ring was found in her stomach."

"Really? A ring?"

"It was inscribed with a phrase, *For the greater good*. And it had the initials *CJ*. Claire Jericho." He looked at her. "Rogers wore a ring."

"That's right, he did," said Knox. "I remember seeing it."

"What I can't figure out is how Rogers found out where Jericho lived. It was classified. Bobby couldn't figure it out either."

"Well, he was a resourceful guy. I guess he found a way. But what does it matter now?" Before Puller could say anything Knox added, "Now, let's move on to something else."

She pulled an envelope from her pocket.

He looked at it and then glanced at her. "Don't tell me those are two plane tickets to Rome?"

"Okay, I won't, because they're not. They're two tickets to a Nats baseball game. And I'll spring for the hot dogs and beer too."

He smiled. "The theory being start small?"

"Considering who we are, I think it's best." She leaned across the table and kissed him.

"So does this mean no more secrets?"

She eyed him directly. "Can anyone ever promise that, Puller?"

He considered this. "I guess not."

They took a walk around the neighborhood with Knox's hand slipped inside his. When she looked at him he seemed lost in thought.

"What's going on up there?" she asked.

"Just wondering where Rogers is."

She nodded. "Wherever he is, I wish him a better life than the one he's had so far."

* * *

The car pulled up to the shack at the end of the dirt road.

The woman got out and walked up to the door. It opened before she got to it.

Suzanne Davis looked at Paul Rogers. He was pale and thin and rubbing the back of his head.

"You ready?" she asked.

"You sure about this?" he said.

"You ask me that again, I'm going to shoot you in the nuts. And I don't care if you can't feel pain, that's still going to hurt mentally."

They walked out to her car and climbed in.

"Where to?" asked Rogers.

"I just feel like driving until I stop feeling like driving."

"Sounds like a plan to me."

"I'm surprised they let you walk away," she said.

Rogers touched the spot on his head. "They took it out, the implant. It changed me. I'm...better."

He took a prescription bottle out of his pocket, popped some pills, and swallowed them with his spit.

She eyed him. "Where'd you get those?"

"Friends. In high places."

"Are they helping?"

"Yeah. In addition to removing the implant they got hold of the tests that Jericho did, and figured out some of what was going on with me. They think there might be a way to reverse it. For now, this keeps me from getting any worse."

She reached into her purse and held up a plastic baggie.

"What's that?"

"Prime weed."

"Where'd you get that?"

"From friends in *low* places."

Davis navigated them to a highway, where she sped up and put the car on cruise control. She settled back in her seat and looked at him.

"How did it feel?"

"How did what feel?"

"Jericho?"

Rogers stared out the windshield at the night sky.

"I really didn't feel good about it," he said at last, his voice strained. "I wonder what that says about me?"

Davis reached over and took his hand. "I think that's actually a positive thing, Paul."

He glanced at her. "This is going to be a rocky road, Davis. Feel free to eject at any time."

"You remember when I told you my druggie dad died in prison and my mom croaked on crack?"

"Yeah, but you were bullshitting."

"No, I wasn't. I stuck with them to the end. I think I can manage you."

Rogers looked back out the window. "Maybe I can get a job... somewhere."

"Maybe I can too. Maybe we can get an apartment. Have, you know, a life or something."

"Is that what you want?" he asked, shooting her a glance.

"Why the hell not?" She tightened her grip on his hand. "Doesn't everybody deserve a life?"

"It won't be like living at Ballard's," he said.

"That was all smoke and mirrors. I prefer reality, actually."

"I never thanked you for saving my life. Myers had a kill shot on me."

"I let you down before, I won't again."

"What are you talking about?" he said.

"When you were on the gurney all numbed up. I just walked away and left you there."

"What could you do?"

"I could have tried, but I just walked away."

She looked over at him. "I'm sorry."

He shrugged. "You came through in the end. That's what counts."

She held his gaze. "I'll always have your back from now on, Paul. Always."

"And why is that?"

"Because we're a lot alike."

"How so?"

"Damaged goods. But we have potential."

"I'll have your back too."

"I never doubted it. It's just the way you're *wired*."

They exchanged a quick smile and then both looked ahead.

They drove on.

To somewhere other than here.

ACKNOWLEDGMENTS

To Michelle, for always being there for me.

To Michael Pietsch, for always being so supportive.

To Jamie Raab, for always being in my corner.

To Lindsey Rose, Andy Dodds, Karen Torres, Anthony Goff, Bob Castillo, Michele McGonigle, Andrew Duncan, Christopher Murphy, Dave Epstein, Tracy Dowd, Brian McLendon, Matthew Ballast, Lukas Fauset, Deb Futter, Beth deGuzman, Jessica Krueger, Oscar Stern, Michele Karas, Stephanie Sirabian, Brigid Pearson, Flamur Tonuzi, Blanca Aulet, Joseph Benincase, Tiffany Sanchez, Ali Cutrone, and everyone at Grand Central Publishing, for having my back.

To Aaron and Arleen Priest, Lucy Childs Baker, Lisa Erbach Vance, Mitch Hoffman (and thanks for another fine editing job), Frances Jalet-Miller, and John Richmond, for being such great partners.

To Melissa Edwards, thanks for all your hard work. I wish you the best in your new endeavor.

To Anthony Forbes Watson, Jeremy Trevathan, Trisha Jackson, Katie James, Alex Saunders, Sara Lloyd, Amy Lines, Stuart Dwyer, Geoff Duffield, Jonathan Atkins, Anna Bond, Sarah Willcox, Leanne Williams, Sarah McLean,

Charlotte Williams, and Neil Lang at Pan Macmillan, for making me feel so very special.

To Praveen Naidoo and his team at Pan Macmillan in Australia, for all you do.

To Caspian Dennis and Sandy Violette, for being great agents and being especially fun at parties.

To Kyf Brewer and Orlagh Cassidy, for your amazing audio performances.

To Steven Maat and the entire Bruna team, for all you do for me in Holland.

To Bob Schule and Chuck Betack, for yet another eagle-eye reading of a manuscript.

To Jeff Pasquino, U.S. Army caretaker site manager, Fort Monroe, and Glenn Oder and John Hutcheson of the Fort Monroe Authority, for your time, wisdom, and one terrific tour of a scenic and memorable Virginia treasure. I encourage anyone interested in American history to go visit Fort Monroe.

To Lieutenant General David Halverson, USA (Ret.), and Karen Halverson, hope you liked the "promotion," even if I put you in the Air Force! Thank you for your service and best of luck in the future.

To Roland Ottewell, for a great copyediting job.

To auction winners Chris Ballard, Lynda Demirjian, Vincent DiRenzo, Ted Hull, and David Shorr, I hope you enjoyed your characters. Thanks for supporting such wonderful organizations.

To Kristen White and Michelle Butler, for keeping Columbus Rose on course.

And to Natasha Collin, thanks for all the great years at the Wish You Well Foundation. I wish you all the best as you move on to your next career.

Amos Decker will return in David Baldacci's explosive new thriller

To solve a high-profile murder, Decker must plunge headlong into the world of Washington, D.C. politics, and he'll discover that his extraordinary brainpower will only get him so far in a place where money, prestige, and connections—rather than truth—are the name of the game...

Look for *TheFix*

Coming in April 2017

A preview follows.

CHAPTER

I

IT WAS NORMALLY one of the safest places on earth, but not today.

The J. Edgar Hoover Building was the world headquarters of the FBI. It opened in 1975 and had not aged well—a blocks-long chunk of badly dilapidated concrete with honeycomb windows and fire alarms and toilets that didn't work. The Bureau was trying like mad to build a new facility to house eleven thousand employees, but a new location hadn't even been decided on. So the opening of a new facility was about two billion dollars and seven years away.

For now, this was home.

The tall man striding down the street was Walter Dabney. He had taken an Uber Black car to a coffee shop down the street, ordered some breakfast, and was walking the rest of the way. He was in his sixties, with thinning salt-and-pepper hair parted on the side. It looked to have been recently cut, with a bit of elusive cowlick in the back. His dark suit was expensive and fit his portly frame well. A colorful pocket square adorned its front. He wore a lanyard around his neck loaded with IDs sufficient to allow him access into the Hoover Building with an escort along for the ride. His light green eyes were alert. He walked with a determined swagger, his briefcase making pendulum arcs in the air.

A woman was coming from the opposite direction. Anne Berkshire had taken the Metro here. She was in her late fifties, petite, with gray hair cut in parentheses around her long oval face. She was not walking with a swagger; indeed, Berkshire looked nervous and ill at ease. As she approached the Hoover Building she seemed to hesitate. There was no lanyard around her neck. The only ID she possessed was the driver's license in her purse.

It was late morning and the streets were not as crowded as they would have been earlier. Still, Pennsylvania Avenue hummed with activity as cars passed up and down the famous boulevard, some vehicles making their way into an underground garage at the Hoover Building.

Dabney picked up his pace a bit, his Allen Edmonds wingtips striking the stained pavement with purpose. He started to whistle a cheery tune. The man seemed not to have a care in the world.

Berkshire was now walking faster too, as though she might fall over from nerves or sheer inertia if she didn't. Her gaze went to the left and then swung right. She seemed to take in everything with that one sweeping glance. But then her eyes seemed unfocused, as though she wasn't really seeing anything.

About thirty yards behind Dabney, Amos Decker trudged along alone. He was six-five and built like the football player he had once been. He'd been on a diet for several months now and had dropped a chunk of weight, but he could stand to lose quite a bit more. He was dressed in khaki pants stained at the cuff and a long, rumpled Ohio State Buckeyes pullover that concealed the Glock pistol riding in a holster on his waistband. His size fourteen shoes hit the pavement with noisy splats. His hair was, as was typical for Decker, disheveled, to put it kindly. Decker worked at the FBI on a joint task force. He was on his way to a meeting at the Hoover Building.

He was not looking forward to it. He sensed that a change was coming, and Decker did not like change. He'd experienced enough of that in the last two years to last him a lifetime.

He saw Dabney up ahead but didn't focus on him. He didn't see Berkshire because he wasn't looking that far up the street. He passed by the garage entrance and nodded at the uniformed FBI security officer in a small windowed guard shack situated on the sidewalk. The ramrod-straight man nodded back, his eyes covered by sunglasses as his gaze dutifully swept the street. His right hand was perched on top of his holstered service weapon. It was a nine mil chambered with Speer Gold Dot G2 rounds that the FBI used because of their penetration capability. "One shot, one down" could have been the ammo's motto.

A bird zipped across in front of Decker, perched on a lamppost, and looked down at the passersby. The air was chilly, and Decker shivered a bit even in his thick pullover. The sun was hidden behind cloud cover that had materialized on the horizon about an hour ago, passed over the Potomac, and settled upon northwest Washington like an oppressive Godlike hand.

Up ahead, Dabney was nearing the end of the block, where he would turn left and make his way to the visitors' entrance. There he would pass through a security checkpoint where his escort would be waiting. Years ago, public tours were freely given and people could view the famed FBI lab and watch special agents practicing their aim on the shooting range.

In the modern era of terrorism that was no more. After 9/11 the tours were canceled, but they were restarted in 2008. The FBI had even put in an education center for visitors. But a request for a visit had to be filed at least a month ahead of time to allow the FBI to do a thorough background check.

Most federal buildings were now fortresses, hard to get into and maybe even harder to get out of.

Berkshire noted Dabney because they were heading in the same general direction. In a few moments she would hang a right at the corner.

Dabney slowed as he approached the corner.

Berkshire, by contrast, quickened her pace.

Decker continued to lope along, his long strides eating up ground until he was only about ten yards behind Dabney.

Berkshire was about five yards beyond Dabney.

A second later that distance was halved.

Moments after that, they were barely three feet apart.

As they made the turn, their shoulders drew within a foot of each other.

Decker now saw Berkshire because she was so close to Dabney. He was about ten feet behind the pair when he started to make the turn too.

Berkshire looked over at Dabney, seemingly noticing him for the first time. Dabney didn't look back at her, at least not initially.

A few seconds later Dabney glanced over and saw her staring at him. He smiled, and if he'd been wearing a hat, he might have even doffed it to her in a show of courtesy.

Berkshire didn't smile back.

Her hand went to her purse clasp.

Dabney slowed a bit more.

Behind them, Decker spotted a street vendor selling

breakfast burritos and wondered if he had time to buy one before his meeting. When he decided he didn't and his waistline would be worse off for it anyway, he looked back; Berkshire was now right next to Dabney.

Decker didn't think anything of it; he just assumed they knew each other and were rendezvousing here. He looked at his watch to check the time. He didn't want to be late.

When he looked back up, he froze.

Dabney had fallen two steps behind Berkshire. He was aiming a compact Beretta at the back of her head. She didn't seem to realize what was happening.

Decker reached for his weapon, and was about to call out, when Dabney pulled the trigger.

Berkshire jerked forward as the round slammed into the back of her head at an upward angle. It blew out her medulla, pierced her brainpan, banged off her skull, and exited through her nose, leaving a wound three times the size of the entry due to the bullet's built-up wall of kinetic energy.

She fell forward onto the pavement, her face mostly obliterated, the concrete tatted with her blood.

His gun out, Decker ran forward as others on the street screamed and ran away, because Dabney was still wielding his weapon.

His heart pounding, Decker aimed his Glock at Dabney and shouted, "FBI, put your gun down. Now!"

Dabney turned to him.

He did not put down his gun.

Decker could hear the running footsteps behind him. The guard from the shack was sprinting toward them, his own gun out.

Decker glanced quickly over his shoulder, saw this, and held up his creds with his free hand. "I'm with the FBI. He just shot the woman."

Decker let his lanyard go and assumed a two-handed shooting stance, his muzzle aimed at Dabney's chest. The FBI uniform ran up to stand next to him, his gun pointed at Dabney.

The guard said, "Put the gun down, now! Last chance, or we *will* shoot."

Dabney looked first at the guard and then at Decker.

And smiled.

"Don't," shouted Decker.

Walter Dabney pressed the gun's muzzle to the bottom of his chin and pulled the trigger for a second and final time.

CHAPTER

2

D ARKNESS.

It awaited us all, individually, in our final moments.

Amos Decker was thinking that as he sat in the chair and studied the body.

Anne Berkshire lay on a metal table in the FBI's morgue. All her clothes had been taken off and placed in evidence bags. Her naked body was under a sheet, her destroyed face covered as well, though the fabric was stained with her blood and tissue.

A postmortem was legally required, though there was no doubt whatsoever as to what had caused the woman's death.

Walter Dabney, by an extraordinary twist, was not dead. Not *yet*, anyway. The doctors at the hospital where he had been rushed were holding out no hope that he would recover, or even regain consciousness. The bullet had driven right through his brain and it was a miracle he had not died instantly.

Alex Jamison and Special Agent Ross Bogart, two of Decker's colleagues on a joint task force composed of civilian and FBI agents, were with Dabney right now. If he regained consciousness, they would want to capture anything he might utter that would explain why he had murdered

Anne Berkshire on a public street and then attempted to take his own life. Dabney recovering to the point of being questioned was simply not going to happen, the doctors had told them.

So for now, Decker simply sat in the darkness and stared at the covered body.

Although the room was not dark for him.

For Decker it was an ethereally bright blue. A near-fatal hit he'd received on the football field had commingled his sensory pathways, a condition known as synesthesia. For him, death was represented by the color blue. He had seen it on the street when Dabney had killed Berkshire.

And he was seeing it now.

He had given statements to the DC police and the FBI, as had the security guard who joined him at the scene. There hadn't been much to say. Dabney had pulled a gun from his briefcase and shot Berkshire and then himself. That was crystal clear. What wasn't clear was why he had done it.

The overhead lights came on and a woman in a white lab coat walked in. The medical examiner introduced herself as Lynne Wainwright. She was in her forties, with the compressed, slightly haunted features of a person who had seen every sort of violence one human could wreak on another. Decker rose, showed her his ID, and said he was with an FBI task force. And that he had witnessed the murder.

Decker glanced at Todd Milligan, the fourth member of the joint task force, who entered the room just then. A fifth member of the group, Lisa Davenport, a psychologist by training, had not returned to the task force after their case involving Melvin Mars. She had opted to return to private practice in Chicago.

Milligan was in his midthirties, six feet tall, with close-cropped hair and a physique that appeared chiseled out of granite. He and Decker had initially butted heads, but now the two men got along as well as Decker could with anyone.

Decker had trouble relating to people. That had not always been the case, because he was not the same person he had once been.

In addition to the synesthesia, Decker also had hyperthymesia, or perfect recall, after suffering a brain trauma on the same vicious hit in his very short career in the NFL. It had also altered his personality, changing him from gregarious and fun-loving to aloof and lacking the ability to recognize social cues—a skill most people took for granted. People first meeting him would assume he was somewhere on the autism spectrum.

And they might not be far off in that assumption.

"How you doing, Decker?" said Milligan. He was dressed like always, in a dark suit with a spotless crisp white shirt and striped tie. Next to him, the shabbily attired Decker looked borderline homeless.

"Better than she is," said Decker, indicating Berkshire's body. "What do we know about her so far?"

Milligan took out a small electronic notebook from his inner coat pocket and scrolled down the screen. While he was doing that, Decker watched as Wainwright removed the sheet from Berkshire's body and prepared the instruments necessary to perform the autopsy.

"Anne Meredith Berkshire, fifty-nine, unmarried, substitute schoolteacher at a Catholic school in Fairfax County. She has no children. She lives, or lived, rather, in Reston. No relatives have come forward, but we're still checking."

"Why was she down at the Hoover Building?"

"We don't know. She wasn't scheduled to teach today."

"Walter Dabney?"

"Sixty-one, married with four grown daughters. Has a consulting practice. Does work with the Bureau and other agencies. He worked at NSA for ten years. Lives in McLean in a big house. And has a second home in Naples, Florida. He's done very well for himself."

"*Did* very well for himself," corrected Decker. "His wife and kids?"

"We spoke with his wife. She's hysterical. The kids are spread all over the place. One lives in France. They're all coming here."

"Any of them have any idea why he would do this?"

"We haven't spoken to them all, but nothing pops so far. They're all still in shock."

Decker next asked the most obvious question. "Any connection between Berkshire and Dabney?"

"We're just starting out, but nothing as yet. You think he was just looking to shoot someone before he killed himself, and she was the closest?"

"She was definitely the closest," said Decker. "But if you're going to kill yourself, why take an innocent person along? What would be the point?"

"Maybe the guy went nuts. We might find something in his background to explain him going off the deep end."

"He had a briefcase and an ID. He was heading to the Hoover Building. Was he going to a meeting?"

"Yes. We confirmed that he had a meeting to go over a project his firm was handling."

"So he goes off the 'deep end,' but he could still put on a suit and come downtown for a meeting?"

Milligan nodded. "I see the inconsistency. But it's still possible."

"Anything's possible, until it's not," Decker replied.

Decker walked over to stand next to Wainwright. "Murder weapon was a Beretta nine mil. Contact wound at the base of the neck with an upward trajectory. She died on impact."

Wainwright was readying a Stryker saw that she would use to cut open Berkshire's skull. She said, "Definitely jibes with the external injuries."

"If Dabney dies will you be doing the post?"

She nodded. "The Bureau is taking the lead on this since Dabney was a contractor for them and it happened on their doorstep. And they like the same ME to do related posts for consistency. So I'm your girl."

Decker turned away from her and said to Milligan, "Have they assigned a team to the case yet? Or will the locals be leading the charge?"

"They *have* assigned a team, and no, the locals will not be in charge. The Bureau will."

"Who's the team? Do you know them?"

"I know them very well, because they're *us*."

Decker blinked. "Come again?"

"Bogart's team, meaning we, have been assigned to the case."

"But we do cold cases."

"Well, that's what the meeting today was about. They were changing our assignment. Cold to hot cases. And since you were on the scene of this one, it made sense to let us work it. So we're a go."

"Even though I'm a witness to the crime?"

"It's not as though there's going to be any doubt as to what happened, Decker. And there were lots of witnesses to what he did. They don't need you."

Decker nodded and looked down at Berkshire's body.

The pulse of blue assailed him from all corners. He felt slightly sick to his stomach.

Wainwright glanced over and registered the name on Decker's ID. "Wait a minute. Amos Decker. Are you the guy who can't forget anything?"

When Decker didn't say anything, Milligan said quickly, "Yes, he is."

Wainwright said, "You guys have solved quite a few cases over the last several months. Principally the Melvin Mars matter."

"It was a team effort," said Milligan. "But we couldn't have done it without Decker."

Decker stirred and pointed to a purple smudge on the back of Berkshire's hand. "What's that?"

"Let's have a closer look," she said.

Wainwright swung a magnifying glass on a rotating arm around and positioned it over the mark. She turned on a light and aimed it at the dead woman's hand. Peering through the glass, she said, "Appears to be a stamp of some sort."

Decker took a look through the glass. "Dominion Hospice."

He looked at Milligan, who was already tapping keys on his notebook. Milligan read down the screen: "Okay, got it. It's over near Reston Hospital. They handle terminal cases, obviously."

Decker looked down at Berkshire. "If the mark is still on her hand, presumably she went there today. A shower would have taken it off."

"Do you think she went to visit someone?" asked Milligan.

"Well, she didn't look terminal to me, until Dabney blew her brains out."

He walked out without another word.

Wainwright looked at Milligan with raised eyebrows at this abrupt departure.

"He kind of just does that...a lot," said Milligan. "I've sort of gotten used to it."

"Then you're a better person than me," replied Wainwright. She held up the Stryker saw. "I might just clock him with this."

CHAPTER

3

THE CHEST ROSE and fell with the spasmodic twitch of someone not long for this world. It was as though the lungs were the weary rear guard holding out, as the spirit prepared to move onward from the body.

Alex Jamison was in her late twenties, tall, slim, pretty, and brunette. She sat on the right side of the hospital bed in the CCU. Ross Bogart, a senior FBI special agent in his forties, with a bit of gray the only thing marring his perfectly combed dark hair, stood on the left. His fingers clutched the bed's safety rail.

In the bed, hooked up to a complex array of monitoring lines and tubes carrying medications, lay Walter Dabney. His right eye was an empty crater because the bullet he'd fired into his chin had erupted from there after catapulting through parts of his brain. The skin of his face was deathly gray where it wasn't swollen and stained by burst capillaries. His breathing was erratic and the monitor showed his vitals to be fluctuating all over the place. He was in the critical care unit—the place designated for the sickest and most badly injured patients at the hospital.

But he wasn't just injured; Dabney was dying.

The doctors who had been in and out during the day had

all confirmed that it was simply a matter of time before the brain told the heart to stop pumping. And there was nothing they could do about it. The damage was such that no medicine and no surgery could bring the man back. They were just counting down the time until death.

Mrs. Dabney had gotten here thirty minutes after she'd been visited by the FBI and told what had happened. She was a potential witness and they would have to question her, but right now she was simply a grieving widow-to-be.

She was currently in the bathroom throwing up, a nurse assisting her.

Bogart eyed Jamison. She seemed to sense his attention and glanced up.

"Any word from Decker?" he asked.

She checked her phone and shook her head. "He was going to be at the morgue with Berkshire's body." She thumbed in a text to him and sent it off.

"I copied Todd on it," she said.

Bogart nodded. "Good."

They both knew that Decker was not always the best at communicating. In fact, he pretty much sucked at it.

Bogart looked down at Dabney again. "Nothing in the guy's record to indicate something like this happening. And no connection that we can find to Berkshire."

Jamison said, "There must be *something* unless it was completely random. And that doesn't make much sense either."

Bogart nodded in agreement and then glanced at the monitor. The dying man's heart rate and respiration danced around like bare feet on sizzling coals. "Chances are very good he's going to die without saying anything."

"But if he does say something we'll be here."

The bathroom door opened and out came the nurse and

Ellie Dabney. She was tall and broad-shouldered, with long legs and a slender waist. Her features were quite attractive, the jaw elegantly structured, the cheekbones high and firm, the eyes large and a pleasing light blue. Her hair was long and she had let it go naturally silver. She looked like she might have been quite the athlete in her youth. Now in her early sixties, the mother of four grown children with three grandchildren and one mortally wounded husband, the stricken woman appeared about as close to death as one could get without actually being deceased.

Bogart placed a chair next to the bed for her as Jamison rose and helped the nurse guide her over to the chair, into which she fell rather than sat. The nurse checked the monitor, gave Bogart an ominous look, and left, closing the door behind her.

Ellie had reached through the rails and gripped her husband's hand, her forehead resting against the top of the bed rail.

Bogart stepped back and Jamison resumed her seat. They exchanged glances while listening to the woman's quiet sobs.

"Mrs. Dabney, we can arrange to have your children brought here when they get into town," he said after a few moments.

She didn't respond to this at first but finally nodded.

"Do you have that information or is there someone else we can—?"

She lifted her head and without looking at him said, "My daughter Jules, she...she'll know that." She pulled a phone from her pocket, tapped some keys, and handed it to him.

Bogart wrote the phone number down and walked out of the room.

Jamison put a hand on the other woman's shoulder and said, "I'm so very sorry, Mrs. Dabney."

"Did he...did Walter really h-hurt someone? The FBI... they...they said..."

"We don't have to talk about that now."

Ellie turned her tear-stained face to Jamison. "He couldn't have. Are you sure someone didn't shoot him? You see, Walter wouldn't hurt anything. H-he..." Her voice trailed off and she placed her forehead back on the rail.

The monitor started to beep and they both glanced at it, but the device quieted down.

"We are sure, Mrs. Dabney. I wish I could tell you otherwise. There were a lot of witnesses."

Ellie blew her nose on a tissue and said in a firmer voice, "He's not going to recover, is he?"

"The doctors aren't hopeful, no."

"I...I didn't even know he owned a gun."

After studying the woman for a few seconds, Jamison asked, "Did you notice a change in your husband recently?"

"In what way?" Ellie said absently.

"Mood? Concerns at work? Appetite changed? Maybe he drank more than normal? Any signs of depression?"

Ellie sat back in her chair, wadded the tissue up in her hand, and stared down at her lap.

Outside the door footsteps could be heard, along with occasional running feet, the sounds of a monitor alarm, voices over a PA, and equipment and patients being rolled up and down the corridor. The air smelled like hospitals always smelled: antiseptic and close. And there was also an ominous tenseness, as though only a monitor's sudden warning screech separated the living from the dead.

"Walter didn't talk about business at home. He didn't really drink at home either, although I know that he did at business dinners and industry events, that sort of thing. I attended some with him. But he only drank enough to socialize, to get deals done, build contacts, you know, that sort of thing."

"I understand. Were there any financial worries?"

"Not that I knew of. But Walter handled all that. We never had any bill collectors show up at the house, if that's what you mean."

"Did his mood change?"

She dabbed at her eyes and shot a glance at her husband before quickly looking away, as though she was uncomfortable conveying information about him to a stranger.

"He had a variety of moods. He worked very hard, and when business was good he was happy. When it was down, he got depressed, just like anybody would."

"So nothing out of the ordinary?"

Ellie balled up the tissue even more and then tossed it into the trash can. With finality. She turned to Jamison, who waited patiently. If being around Amos Decker had taught her anything, it was patience, for both positive and negative reasons.

"He went on a trip recently."

"Where?"

"That was the unusual thing. He didn't tell me where. He had never done that before."

"How long was he gone?" Jamison asked.

"I think about four days. It could have been longer. He was on another trip in New York and left from there. He called me and said something unexpected had come up and that he had to attend to it and wasn't sure how long he'd be gone."

"Plane, train? Another country?"

"I don't know. He did tell me it had to do with a potential client. He had to smooth over something. The way he described it the matter didn't seem too significant. I suppose his office would have handled the travel arrangements."

"Okay, and he mentioned nothing to you about it when he got home?"

"Nothing. I just assumed it was business. But from that day on, there was something, I don't know, off."

"And when was this?"

"A month ago."

"And your husband has his own consulting firm?"

Ellie nodded. "Walter Dabney and Associates. It's located in Reston. Everything they worked on was pretty much classified. It started out with just my husband, but now about a hundred people work there. He has partners at the firm, but Walter is president and owns a controlling interest." Her eyes widened. "Oh my God, I guess I'll own it now." She looked in alarm at Jamison. "Does that mean I'll have to run it? I don't know anything about his business. I don't even have a security clearance."

Jamison gripped her hand. "I don't think you need to worry about those details right now, Mrs. Dabney."

Ellie relaxed and looked back at her husband. "What was the person's name again? That Walter...? They told me, but I can't remember. Everything is just a blur right now."

"Anne Berkshire. She was a substitute teacher at a high school in Fairfax. Do you know her?"

Ellie shook her head. "I never heard of her. And I don't know why Walter would know her either. A high-school teacher? Walt and I had our children early. Jules, our oldest, is thirty-eight. And our oldest grandkid is only in first grade. And they don't even live in Virginia anyway. And we're not Catholic; we're Presbyterian."

"Right. Well, thank you for the information. You've been very helpful."

"Will I need to get a lawyer?" Ellie blurted out.

Jamison looked uncomfortable. "I'm really not the one to

advise you about that. If you or your husband used a lawyer or know one, I'd check with that person."

Ellie nodded dumbly and then reached through the rails and gripped her husband's hand once more.

A minute later Bogart came back in. "It's all taken care of, Mrs. Dabney. According to your daughter, everyone except Natalie will be in by tonight."

"Natalie lives in Paris. I tried to phone her but no one answered. And it wasn't...it wasn't something I could tell her by email."

"Your daughter Jules reached her and told her the situation. She's trying to get a flight here as soon as possible."

"I really can't believe this is happening," said Ellie. "When Walter left this morning everything was...perfect. And now?" She looked up at them. "It's all gone. Just like that."

Just like that, thought Jamison.